Outcaste

Also By Ellen Renner

Tribute

Castle of Shadows
City of Thieves

Outcaste

Ellen Renner

First published in Great Britain in 2015 by Hot Key Books
Northburgh House, 10 Northburgh Street, London EC1V 0AT

A CIP catalogue record for this book is available from the British Library.

ISBN: 978-1-4714-0065-0

1

This book is typeset in 10.5 Berling LT Std using Atomik ePublisher

Printed and bound by Clays Ltd, St Ives Plc

www.hotkeybooks.com

Hot Key Books is part of the Bonnier Publishing Group
www.bonnierpublishing.com

For William

1

My breath drifts in front of my eyes, starched white by cold. A ghost, I think. It looks like the frailest of remnants. And then I think how odd it is that my head always seems cluttered with nonsense when I am most afraid.

It is nearly sunrise. The world is grey mist, but there is light enough for this fight. My eyes never leave my opponent's face. I will see his attack there, before his body moves. Despite hours of practice, Bruin's sword remains an awkward weight in my hand. *Arms and shoulders loose! Stop strangling the hilt!* I balance on the balls of my feet, legs bent, ready to spring.

His eyelids widen. And I'm leaping backwards, moving my blade to block as he lunges. The stillness of dawn is broken by the ring of metal on metal. His sword bounces off mine, jarring my arm. I dodge sideways, hoping his bulk will slow him as I shorten my stroke and stab at his exposed flank. But the Guardian is as quick as he is large: he whirls effortlessly, scoops my blade away with a downward parry that nearly knocks it from my hand. I'm off balance, stumbling backwards. Easy prey. As I gasp my next breath, my mind white with panic, he ripostes, the point of his sword driving towards my chest.

Metal blade! All my inbred mage fears take over. Instead of trying to block, I hurl myself away. I fall on my back, spread-eagled. My sword flies from my hand. The Guardian steps forward. The point of his blade advances remorselessly, digs into the leather of my jerkin. Otter towers over me, his forehead not even damp from effort.

'First mistake: you lost your balance.

'Second mistake: you panicked.

'Result: you're dead.'

He pushes the point of his sword into the leather over my heart to emphasise each mistake. My face is clammy with sweat. Metal. There is metal a tick and a shove away from my heart. The Guardian knows my fear. He knows he's making my stomach churn.

For a moment, I fantasise. All I need to do is direct a thought of power at the metal stick prodding me in the chest and mix its iron with water.

'One more poke and that sword is rust!'

'She might mean it, Guardian. And we're short of weapons already.' Aidan the Maker slouches forward from where he's been leaning against the trunk of a tree. Otter shrugs, steps back, and the Maker reaches down his hand. I take it, and he pulls me to my feet. 'Otter's right, though. That was clumsy. Footwork! Remember?'

'Oh . . .' I snatch my hand away. I'm too angry to care that his eyes are the blue of a kingfisher's wings. Or that over the months that have passed since the day he clattered into my father's courtyard on horseback, tied to the saddle, a prisoner and hostage, I have grown to love him. An unwise love. I am a mage and Aidan is a non-magic Maker – the sworn enemy of my kind.

He puts his hands up and backs off, grinning. 'Don't blame me! You begged us to teach you to fight with Bruin's sword. Well, do you want to learn or not?'

'I said so, didn't I?'

But he's right. Magic has always come easily to me. I'm not used to failure. Ashamed, I turn to find my sword.

If ever metal made for killing mages could be called beautiful, the sword crafted by Bruin the blacksmith – the sword I inherited, the sword I intend to use to kill my father, Benedict, Archmage of Asphodel – is that weapon.

The sun edges into the sky and the frozen plains become a silver sea. Below the sword's bronze crossguard, the long blade floats dark on the frosted grass. A blade made of thin strips of iron twisted together, worked and reworked, forged and re-forged, to a strength, flexibility and sharpness no blacksmith has achieved before or since. Once now, this weapon has tasted my father's blood.

I grip the leather-wrapped hilt and wipe melting frost off the blade with my sleeve. I *will* learn to use this weapon! Although I can never hope for half Aidan's skill. He grew up fighting with metal. As for Otter . . . a Guardian is trained from childhood in the craft of killing: a slave whose body, mind and soul are dedicated to protecting the archmage who owns them. In a swordfight – any fight – even a Maker like Aidan would stand no chance against him.

I fumble my sword into its leather scabbard and dart a glance at Otter. He is ridiculously tall, with the honed muscles of a warrior. He has wide cheekbones, light brown skin and dark hair tied in a plait at the back of his neck. His face is as familiar to me as my own. I first saw it when I was a small child and he a boy. We grew up together. But I don't know him at all. Until a few weeks ago, he was my father's Guardian . . . and my enemy.

I push the doubts away: I have no choice. None of us do. Otter claims to lead an army of Tribute slaves like himself in rebellion against my father. Before we fled Asphodel, he saved my life, and Aidan's. He and his soldiers attacked the city and rescued the last of the Knowledge Seekers of Asphodel – the survivors of a covert band of non-magic rebels who plotted my father's downfall. Now he and a small detachment of his Tributes guide us towards the Great Wall of the Makers and our dream of a new life in the free cities of the north.

As usual, I can't see what Otter is thinking behind those amber-coloured eyes. I'm an empath, but I have never been able to read this man. I realise I'm staring and pat the hilt of my sword to show I'm ready for another bout.

The Guardian shakes his head. 'Perhaps Aidan should take over your instruction from now on. In any case, further lessons will have to wait. It's dawn. Zara, you're on patrol.'

Did he sense my doubts? I would be sorry, except this means precious time alone with Aidan. I nod and try to ignore the rush of guilty delight.

Otter turns on his heel and strides towards camp and the sounds of preparation: of mules being harnessed and loaded; the hushed voices of the Knowledge Seekers. I hear the hope in their voices. And the fear. We are hunted: my father does not give up easily.

I give Aidan a tentative smile, which he returns just as hesitantly, before loping after Otter. I watch the red leather of his jerkin disappear into the bustle, following the familiar set of his shoulders and the dark straw of his hair until the last moment. Then I close my eyes, prepare my mind and raise my head to find the swift. There she flies: a dark crescent turning lazy circles overhead. She waits for me.

The miracle of this bird, which has followed us from the first day of our flight from Asphodel, is something I dare not even think about too closely. Instead, I ready myself for the first magic of the day. I stand, feet apart, eyes skyward, watching the swift spiral in the grey sky. And I detach a small strand of my consciousness and send it rushing skywards to join her. In the space of time between one breath and another, I am inside the bird's mind, watching through her eyes, feeling the wind beneath our wings, tasting the air through the nostrils in our beak.

The rest of me – part of my mind and all of my body – crunches through leaf-litter beneath the trees. I find my pack and shoulder it for the day's march. I fall into step towards the rear of the convoy. My human senses note the crackle of frosted grass beneath my boots, the stink of men and women unbathed for too long, the patient snorting of the mules. But my heart and soul are with the swift. I'm a mage. This is what I was meant to do.

I see the earth spin below me, hear the wind sing in the bird's hollow bones. I revel in the intoxication of flight. I have slipped the grasp of Time himself. I forget I am on watch and so make my third mistake of the morning. For the space of half-a-dozen heartbeats I fail to recognise what the bird has seen.

They rise out of the long grasses, black leather dripping with melting hoar frost. They are a long time rising, a long time stretching tall, this demon seed sown by my father. Jackals. Predators. Children.

Tribute soldiers – dressed in leather and carrying wooden shields and pikes – emerge from the long grass of the northern plains where they have been waiting in ambush. Unlike Otter's rebels, these teenagers are still enslaved. The warrior mages who lead them stand behind the children, black robes flag-flapping in the wind. Four, no . . . five mages! One lurches up to hover just above the ground: a rare warrior mage who can fly – a little.

I've already left the bird. My split-off strand of consciousness tumbles out of the sky back into my mind. My human lungs suck deep and I scream out the warning: '*Ware! Ware! Ambush!*'

I gather my power, thicken the air beneath my feet. And I'm flying again, climbing high into the air, but this time in my own body. Below me Knowledge Seekers scatter across the frost-bitten ground. Screams of terror join the battle cries. Otter's deep baritone thunders through the chaos. I glimpse our expedition leader moving with astonishing speed in one so large, sword held high as he charges the attackers.

Aidan! I don't dare look for him. But even as I swoop down on the flying warrior mage, watching the man's face twist with shock and fear; even as I suck water from the damp wind and forge it into a blade of ice; even as I hurl the frozen spike towards the mage's throat . . . even as I use magic against one of my own, I think of Aidan: the Maker I have come to love. The boy Benedict is desperate to kill before he can reach his people and tell them of my father's treachery.

The mage flings up a hasty shield of toughened air, but the spike shatters it like a soap bubble and shoots on into the man's throat. Blood, red as last summer's poppies, carpets the ground as the ice blade explodes out the back of his neck and plunges on to bury itself in the mud. The mage follows, his body thudding to earth to lie face upwards, a look of disbelief in his staring eyes. I have killed in battle for the first time. And I feel nothing but self-loathing at my carelessness . . . and fear for my friends and companions. We are sorely outnumbered.

I hear Otter roaring orders somewhere behind me as I alight beside the dead mage. I need all my strength for this fight: I can't afford the drain of flying. It's up to me to deal with my own kind. Typical battle mages, they have sent the Tribute soldiers ahead of them while they skulk behind the main assault, picking off easy prey.

A male mage uses magic to wrest the pike from one of Otter's soldiers, whirls it round in the air and shoots it like a javelin at its owner. It plunges into the girl's chest. I'm running. Cursing as I loose sight of the mage in the maelstrom of bodies and kicking, screaming mules. A woman in the blue robes of a counter sprints past me, eyes wide and unseeing, mouth open in a continuous scream. Blood streams from a gash in her arm. It's Fredda, one of the council leaders. She runs towards the cover of a small copse of aspen trees near the river. A female battle mage darts across frozen grass after the fleeing Knowledge Seeker and I sprint after them both. As I rush down the slope towards the copse, I slow my breathing and focus on my target. I order a strip of grass to break free of the earth, to tangle and twist into a long snaking rope. It's effortless, this. Need seems to have unlocked something inside my brain: it's as though I've found the key to a hidden room where a secret store of magic lies waiting to be woken.

For a moment, I'm terrified by the sense of my own power, then I forget everything in a surge of exhilaration. *This is so easy!* I feel drunk with magic. I make the rope lift one end into the air, snake forward and loop the mage's legs. She falls full-length with a stunned shout, crow-black on the grass-stripped earth. The counter has just reached the trees. She stumbles to a stop, stares in shock.

There isn't time to go to her, to try to stop her bleeding. The mage squirms to her feet, kicking the grass rope to pieces. The other battle mages have spotted me and followed us to the riverside. The woman mage I attacked retreats towards them, leaving Fredda cowering in the aspen grove.

The battle mages watch me. I can sense their confusion. They never thought they would face another magic-user. They're killers, but they're used to easy prey. Battle mages are the weakest of magekind – those whose gifts are too mean to earn them a place of ease and luxury in the city-states. Instead, they live itinerant lives with the Tribute army of their archmage, only returning to their home cities on leave.

They are frightened of me. They've seen enough to know: I'm an adept – or near enough. Their most powerful companion, the one who could fly, who would have lorded over them, secure in his superiority, lies dead already. But there are four left. Four against one.

I'm vaguely aware of my heart pounding in my chest and my breath coming too quickly. Two men, two women. All much older than me: hardened battle mages. They edge towards each other as I walk towards them, begin to retreat towards the safety of the non-magic battle. I hear Otter's voice in the distance. I glance up the slope to where the battle is raging, and see a flash of scarlet. At the moment I glimpse the Maker the mages attack.

Two lumps of earth spring into the air from in front of my feet, transform into rough-hewn hand shapes and fasten themselves around my neck. Fingers of clay grip my throat: cold, wet, inhumanly strong. Squeezing. Crushing. I drop to my knees. As the world glares white and starts to fade, I gather water from the air and push it into the strangling clay. I feel my opponent's resistance, a brief struggle. Then the earthen hands crumble into mud and slop to the ground. I'm shivering. Not shock. The air is growing colder. Someone's sucking heat from the air. That means one thing: a fireball!

The battle mages have joined their magic. As one person, their arms sweep over their heads in a throwing gesture. Fire arcs towards me. I find a new plateau of concentration: I stand motionless, staring into my own mind as I conjure a wall of water, sucking it from the mud beneath my feet. Blue as a bank of forget-me-nots, a cliff of water rises from the ground in front of me, sweeps forward in a mighty wave, extinguishing the fireball.

I hear the strangled shout of the first mage to be caught as he is knocked off his feet, tossed on the crest of the wave like a tree branch in a flood. The wave towers over the remaining mages as they turn to flee. Part of my mind sees the backward glance of the woman who conjured fire, her face distorted with fear.

I release the crushing power of the water. I am killing my own: breaking the first precept. But there is too much at stake: too many lives to protect. Too many deaths to avenge.

I tell the water to sink back into the ground. Black robed bodies lie half-buried in the sodden mud, broken. My legs seem disjointed, my movements clumsy. My body is paying the price for a profligate use of magic. Much more and I will collapse. Even so, I shoot out a thread of consciousness to investigate. Three of my opponents are dead, one dying. I did this. Bitterness rises up my throat. I can't afford to think about it, so I look for Aidan. I see him almost at once. Then I am running, tugging Bruin's sword from its scabbard.

2

The Maker is caught in an eddy, separated from the rest of our people. The main battle has moved away from him, and he fights on alone with the furiosity of the damned. His sword flashes ceaselessly as he fends off three attackers.

The Tributes – two boys and a girl, underfed and clothed in tattered leather – circle Aidan, waiting for an opening. They are armed with wooden pikes, and their faces scowl with hopeless determination and terror. Children who have no choice but to fight and die for the mages who own them. I have to stop them hurting Aidan, but I hate the idea of killing them.

I thicken the air around Aidan until it is as dense and hard as solid wood. Then I push with my mind. The air-wall hits the Tributes and sends them sprawling backwards. I stagger as I release the air: my body can't take much more magic. Aidan glances around, and I'm granted a wolfish grin. And then we are standing side by side, swords held ready, as the Tributes scramble up and attack.

A pike, its wicked black point hardened by fire, lunges at my throat. A twist of my wrist, and my blade beats the pike aside. My body takes over and I lunge forward and counterattack. The point of my sword impales the leather shield of my attacker. I see her eyes widen in fear as I swing my sword up, taking her shield with it. I could bring Bruin's blade down now, split her skull open with one downward stroke. Instead, I leap up and kick her in the stomach, sending her sprawling backwards, the pike flying from her hand.

I tear her shield from my sword and crouch in readiness, heart pounding. Out of the corner of my eye I see Aidan strike. One of the boys stumbles, wounded in the leg. Aidan plunges his sword into the boy's throat, yanks it free in a shower of blood. As the boy crumples, the Maker whirls to confront the other Tribute, but he turns and flees, shamble-limbed. The girl scrambles to her feet and follows, her weapon lying forgotten in the bloodstained grass.

Somewhere to our left, the clash of weapons stutters, the screams of battle-hate fade. I hear Otter's voice in the distance, shouting orders to his soldiers to round up the fleeing Tributes. It's over.

How long since the ambush? Fifteen minutes? Twenty? I stare at the bodies half-hidden in the trampled grass, and feel sick. We've won, but the cost is high: so many dead children. Slaves, like my half-sister. If Benedict hadn't murdered her, would Swift have ended her life like this? Leagues from home, fighting in the Maker War?

Aidan cleans his sword on a handful of grass and shoves it in its scabbard. The Maker turns to me and his eyes are shining. He grabs me and swings me round and round until I forget my bitter thoughts and we're both giddy and laughing.

Can this be happening? Ever since the day when my father mentally invaded Aidan's mind and took over his body, I have almost lost hope that the Maker will ever be able to forget that I am a magic-user – one of those his people fear and hate and call demons.

'Zara! We did it! We beat them. You were amazing. You killed five mages! Five!' The emotions coming off him are making me drunk. His eyes grow dark and he pulls me to him and crushes my mouth with a kiss so fierce and demanding I can't breathe or think.

Too soon – for breathing seems totally unnecessary – Aidan removes his mouth from mine. We stand, foreheads touching. I feel the heat of his skin, the weight of his hands on my shoulders. He takes a deep breath and steps back. 'Nice kiss.' Aidan clears his throat. 'And your footwork was a bit better. Not much, but seeing that we're starting from a pretty low level of swordsmanship . . . hey!' He backs away, eyes sparkling. 'No hitting!'

I stop chasing the Maker and turn away to search the air for the bird that is my sister's namesake. To share the miracle of our survival.

And make my fourth mistake.

Aidan's laugh dies away and is reborn as a war cry.

I whirl around. A pair of bloodstained Tributes stumble from a copse of trees and rush at the Maker. Aidan pulls his sword free with a warning shout and runs to meet them.

I plunge after him. As soon as I move, the Tributes stop their advance and I see that neither of them is carrying a weapon. As one, they turn and flee in the direction they came. Their disjointed, jerky movements are uncanny. The hairs on the back of my head prickle. *Oh gods!*

'Aidan!' I scream. 'No! It's a trap!'

But the Maker is a dozen strides ahead.

'Aidan!' But he doesn't hear me. Or doesn't choose to. I don't dare use magic to stop him: not knowing who and what almost certainly waits for us. If I'm right, our only chance depends on me staying undetected.

I must fight from inside Elsewhere, a state of meditation which causes my body to become invisible. It is the mind-magic of the thieving tribe – only another thief can see someone while they are in Elsewhere. It took me much effort to learn this secret magic of the thieves: the magic that has prevented Benedict from destroying their guild in Asphodel.

I negotiate the mental path into Elsewhere as I sprint after Aidan. Idiot! He of all people should have recognised the signs of a living body inhabited by an adept! Terror burns ice-hot. Fool that I am, I dared to think we had won: that Benedict would be so easily defeated. The ambush was only a diversion. My father's trap is sprung.

Sword held ready, the Maker sprints after the fleeing Tributes, who scramble back up the hill and disappear into scrubby woods.

I'm panting before I'm halfway up the slope. As I crest the hill, enter the fringed shadow of slender birch and pine, I feel him: Aidan. Empaths are rare among magekind, but I am one. Now I sense the moment the Maker's bloodlust shifts to uncertainty. Morphs into fear.

Somewhere ahead. Beyond these trees.

I'm sprinting through the trees, exhaustion forgotten. Leaping over fallen branches, twisting and darting through the tree trunks. Sliding down a steep slope. Falling. Tumbling head over heels to jump up at once, battered and bruised. Running again.

The trees open like a curtain parting and I plunge through. Stumble to a halt. Fifty feet away, in a small meadow encircled by foothills, stand three mages. They are dressed in short black robes, but these are no mere battle mages. The air crackles with magic. These are hunters of a different breed – adepts! My father's crack troops. Adepts sent from Asphodel to hunt us down and make the kill.

Two slight, leather-clad bodies lie motionless a few feet away from the trio. Used and discarded. I haven't time to spare their deaths more than a thought, for Aidan himself is stretched on the ground inside a deadly triangle of magic. My heart clenches cold and hard. He lies face-up, his entire body wrapped in a net of toughened air like a moth in a chrysalis.

The sight glues my feet to the ground: what chance have I got against three adepts? I realise I am afraid. After Aidan, I am the person my father most wants to destroy. I'm going to die now too. Even if I wasn't nearly spent of magic, I stand no chance against a single adept, let alone three. But I can't leave the Maker to die alone. Only, I want to inflict some damage before they kill us. My mind flits to and fro, searching for a way.

'Name, Maker!' shouts the hawk-nosed woman adept. 'Give us your name, and you can have an easy death. Tell us, or I'll strip the skin from you layer by layer. And it will hurt, kine. It will hurt.'

They want to make certain they've got their man. Killing the wrong Maker – leaving Aidan alive to expose the lie of

Benedict's truce with the Makers – is a mistake my father would not forgive lightly.

Lord Time, help me to think!

Aidan is silent. Stubborn to the death. But I sense his terror. It's overwhelming me – stopping my brain from working. I find no inspiration . . . there is nothing but the hope that the invisibility of Elsewhere will allow me to inflict a little damage.

As I ready for my assault, I think: *So strange, that this is the time and place.* I hadn't pictured my death happening like this. Time's one mercy is that we never know our fate. I feel, rather than see, the swift circling overhead. *Sister. Stay with me.*

I feel the blood pounding in my veins; the stones and soil beneath my feet. Hear the wind in the trees behind on the hillside and the faint scrape of my boots as I step forward . . . and deeper into Elsewhere in the same moment.

My magic will be less powerful here in the sanctuary the thieves taught me to visit – but it will give me one good strike. Not enough – not nearly enough. Twiss's face flashes into my head. I have not seen the young thief since last night in camp. I pray the lord Time has kept her safe during the battle.

I creep across the open meadow, step around the dead Tributes. I edge slowly forward until I'm a stone's throw from Aidan and his tormentors. He lies on the ground between them, still tight-wrapped with magic. The Maker gazes skyward, unable to move. I wish I could say goodbye, touch him one last time.

I gather the remnants of my concentration and ease myself down to sit cross-legged, bruising my knee on a large, sharp-edged flint. I pry the stone from the ground with careful fingers: it is axe-shaped, razor-edged. When the gods offer a weapon, it is well to use it.

The youngest adept, the blond man, is laughing. A throaty chuckle. I have heard that laugh so often in my life: the preening bleat of the tormentor. I choose him, then. He is talking to his companions: 'He's a pretty creature, our lad or not. If we had more time I would greatly enjoy some private games with this one.'

'Time is what we haven't got.' The third adept, a middle-aged man, speaks. 'It has to be him. The description fits. Let's kill him and be done. The Guardian is nearby. There's the girl to find still, and I hear she's tricky. Do the job, Pin. Or I will. We haven't time to torture his name from him.'

'We need to be sure!' the woman, Pin, snaps. 'I'll get it from him.' Her lips draw back from her teeth. I feel her preparing.

No time for subtlety. I grab all the energy I can from myself, from the air, from the woman adept herself – quickly, quickly. My mind seizes the flint and sends it hurtling through the air as fast as my thought. Faster than the swift can fly. Before the adepts can do more than stiffen in alarm at the scent of magic, the stone strikes the blond man in the side of the neck and severs his head from his body.

The blood is bright crimson, the very colour of Aidan's jerkin. It spurts from the stump of the dead man's neck, and the headless body folds, arms flopping dismally, and crumples onto its side.

I follow him down. Too much magic. I have drained myself of energy. I fall onto my side in a mirror image of my victim. I lie, shattered, empty. And watch my fate come to me.

Death is tall and dark-haired. She strolls through the frozen meadow towards us without a break in her movement. Steady, graceful. The god comes for me.

The surviving male adept is screaming. Hysterical. Shooting spikes of hardened air at the spot where I was sitting a moment before. They fly over my prone body and crash harmlessly to earth. But that won't save me: Death comes.

The female mage crouches, a hand on Aidan. She keeps him bound with magic as her eyes shoot back and forth, searching. 'Zara!' she calls. 'Come out of your hiding place now, or the Maker dies! I'll kill him, Zara! Surrender, or he dies a horrible death. If you give yourself up, I'll spare his life. Both of you will live. I promise!'

Lies. Lies and lies. Aidan is as good as dead already. As am I. I can't move, even if I wanted to. I'm done. I watch Death approach. She strides more quickly now. My vision is swimming. The god's face melts in and out of view, fuzzy. Yet . . . why does Death seem so familiar? Is it the same for everyone? She reminds me . . .

'Out now, Zara! I give you the count of ten!' The female adept's voice takes on an edge of panic. The man must hear something, sense something. He turns. Sees Death coming. But . . . only *I* should be able to see Death come for me. And Aidan – if he could look – but he is trussed and stares at the sky.

I blink to clear my eyes. Peer at the face of Death. *Oh gods!* Am I mad? I don't understand.

'Archmage!' cries the male adept. 'Why are you here? What –'

The newcomer raises her hand gently without breaking stride, and the adept drops like a stone and lies unmoving, eyes open.

I don't know how she killed him so effortlessly, so casually. I stop trying to make sense from madness and watch the female adept lurch to her feet, stare at her dead companion. A look of horror transfigures her face. But she's tough, this one. A fighter.

The air over the meadow grows even more chill as the adept gathers all the heat she can and melds it into a giant fireball. Glowing red and blue, the huge globe of fire spins in the air above the last of Benedict's adepts. She raises her arm to hurl it at the intruder.

The dark-haired woman comes – at last – to a halt, a few feet in front of Aidan's prone body. She smiles at his captor – as though in greeting – at the very moment the adept shouts with the effort of releasing her fireball. Simultaneously, the stranger raises both her arms into the air. And my father's adept is sucked into the sky, as into a whirlwind. She disappears into the revolving flames above her head. There is a foul smell of burning flesh, like a moth in candlelight. The fireball disintegrates in a shower of sparks and glowing embers. Fragments of charred bone drop like brittle snow onto the ground.

The net of air encircling Aidan disappears the moment the adept dies. He groans and rolls over, pushes himself up to kneeling. Stares at the stranger.

She smiles down at him. Tall, slender as a willow tree. Black-haired and golden-robed.

'Who the hell are you?' Aidan asks.

'Your saviour, Maker,' the woman says. 'Now, if you would be so kind as to find Otter? Tell the Guardian that he is needed to fetch Zara from Elsewhere. Oh, and tell him Falu is here.'

3

Otter harvested me from the ground. My head lolls in the crook of his arm as he carries me towards the remains of our camp. I am cradled inside silence. The bowl of the sky swings above me like an inverted pendulum, and I catch sight of the swift carving arcs of delight. Then a sideways dip of my head reveals bodies sprawled on the ground.

Sound returns to my ears in a rush: the rustling of blood-stained grass; the distant honk of a goose; and through the wall of his chest, the Guardian's voice, rumbling. My nose wakes next. The man who carries me reeks of killing: he is metallic with blood. I manage to turn my head away. Still, I breathe in the stink of battle.

The sounds of aftermath surround us: moans, weeping, angry cries. Otter shouts orders. Aidan does not speak. Does not take hold of my dangling hand in an attempt to comfort us both. Instead, I feel the Maker's fear – his loathing of magic and magic-users – bright and boundless as the sky. I hear his footsteps trailing behind. One set of footsteps.

'Where is she?' I have to search for enough breath to speak the words.

'Gone.' Otter doesn't pretend to misunderstand.

'Why?'

'Questions later, Zara. Now we need to survive.'

'But she knew . . . *Elsewhere!*'

The Guardian says nothing. Only one person can have told Falu, Archmage of Thynis – and my father's most trusted ally – of the existence of Elsewhere. A betrayal so deep that I cannot grasp the beginning or end of Otter's treachery. He has given the thieves' only weapon to their greatest enemy! I think of Twiss and want to weep. Otter is collaborating with Falu. But to what end? And *why*?

The Guardian roars at his soldiers and dazed Knowledge Seekers alike, bullying them to hurry. Mules are reloaded, possessions gathered from where they were dumped, wounds roughly patched and the injured loaded onto makeshift stretchers.

My muscles are coming to life with a sharp prickling of pins and needles. I desperately want to push away the arms holding me and have to force myself to stillness. A mule is led forward and Otter swings me, like a lanky sack of potatoes, onto its back.

'Can you sit unaided?'

'Yes.' I look past him, over his head. I'm too confused, too angry, to trust my face. I am a good horsewoman. I will stay on the mule.

'You're lying.' Otter's voice is chilly. *What right has he – the traitor – to be angry with me?* And then I remember. I was on watch. I didn't see the ambush in time. My head sinks.

'Aidan, she's in your charge.' I feel the Guardian's gaze but don't raise my head. He cannot hate me more than I loathe myself. All those Tributes. I blink to keep the tears back. Weeping won't help them now.

I do not mourn the battle mages. They would have killed me. But today I have broken the code by which all magic-users live. Except for the duel to become archmage – or when rebels such as my mother are put to death for heresy – mages do not kill other mages. I am beyond redemption: an outcaste.

Mentally, I shrug. I made my choice years ago, when my father murdered my beloved Tribute slave – his other daughter and my half-sister, Swift. I'm used to belonging nowhere. What troubles me more is the memory of Falu. Why did she save us? What is Otter's connection with her? What secret has the Guardian been keeping from us all?

'Zara?'

I lift my head to find Aidan standing at the head of the mule, reins in his hand.

'If you can sit on the beast by yourself, I'll lead it.'

I nod. Even with the mess inside my head, I can feel the Maker's emotions plainly, as always. For a moment, I resent the connection. I need space to think about what has just happened – about Otter and Falu, and my father's ambush within an ambush – and Aidan's emotions press on me. That isn't fair. The Maker doesn't know I'm an empath, and he is as disturbed and confused as I am.

The mule only takes half a dozen strides before its shambling gait has me sliding slowly off the blanket, no matter how hard I try to hang onto a fistful of mane. I lean forward, grab the animal's neck with both arms.

'Oy! Have a care, Maker, or she'll be off!'

Twiss's voice. The mule crunches to a halt, blocking the convoy fleeing the battleground. Shouts, curses, as animals and humans swerve to avoid us.

Aidan whirls round; his face goes red with embarrassment when he sees the thief shoving me back onto the animal.

Twiss reaches out her hand. 'Give me the reins, Maker.'

The Maker hesitates, but I feel his desire to be gone.

'Go,' I say.

'Can you even ride, thief?' A world of contempt in Aidan's voice. He and Twiss have never liked each other.

'I can sit on a mule if I have to. I'll take care of Zara!'

She snatches the reins. Aidan stands, uncertain. Then shrugs and turns on his heel. He strides towards the front of the convoy. Doubtless looking for Tabitha the silversmith and her son Thaddeus, his young apprentice. I watch him go, both relieved and sad.

When I glance down I see the thief watching me, her pointed brown face under its cropped black hair far too cynical for a twelve year old. 'Shove up and hold these,' she says, her voice curt. She is angry with me too. I sigh, take the reins and wriggle forward on the mule's haunches. Twiss grabs the back of my jacket and leaps onto the animal's back with the agility of a true thief. She reaches around me to take the reins, clucks to the animal and kicks its sides. The mule snorts but, recognising a being even more stubborn than itself, begins the shambling march towards the Wall of the Makers.

With all the haste and fear of those who have just outwitted Death, we abandon the battlefield, and leave the dead to the crows and jackals.

* * *

'We've lost nine people,' Otter says. 'Four Knowledge Seekers killed, three wounded. And five of my soldiers dead.' His jaw hardens as he says this. It has been a hard day's march to a new camp site, far from the site of the ambush. There has been no sign of scouts or trackers. No sign of any other human beings.

We have made camp on the site of another ruined farmstead. This one still has most of the old house standing, its walls and part of its roof intact. We are gathered in the other remaining building: a small stone barn. It has a roof, but no door.

Otter asked three of us to meet with him here: Philip the artist, leader of the Knowledge Seekers, Aidan and myself. Only half our council. Of course, Mistress Quint, the apothecary, is busy tending the wounded, but Hammeth the blacksmith is missing, as is Mistress Fredda the counter. And Twiss, who is our only representative of the Thieves' Guild. The Guardian wants privacy.

The last light of this awful day strays through the open doorway. It flickers across Otter's face. He looks at me and my stomach tenses.

'Report, Zara: how many battle mages?'

'Five.'

'Did any escape?'

I speak slowly to keep my voice from shaking: 'All dead.'

A nod: no expression on his face. Nothing. Even though he knows I have never killed in battle before.

'You were slow to spot the ambush.' His eyes never leave my face.

'I . . .' My mouth dries. There is nothing I can say so I listen to the silence grow. But I don't flinch from his gaze.

'Your scouts didn't spot them either.'

Aidan's voice makes me jump. I dare a glance at him. I would love to think that the Maker is defending me, but this is about him and Otter.

'Zara had only just gone on duty. They picked a good time for their ambush and we weren't prepared. That's your fault, not hers. You're supposed to be leading this expedition.'

'I *am* leading it.'

Tension curdles the cold air.

'Provoking confrontation is not helpful, Aidan,' Philip intervenes. 'Squabbling amongst ourselves is a sure path to defeat.'

The tall, fair-haired Knowledge Seeker is the only member of our company the Maker respects and admires. Aidan is an engineer, and for years Philip has focused his inventive mind on designing weapons of war. The two spend every moment they can together, studying Philip's designs in daylight hours and talking about them long into the nights.

The Maker frowns at the rebuke, but remains silent.

'Otter is right,' I say. 'I should have spotted the ambush sooner. I can only promise that it won't happen again. But . . .' I see the Guardian's gaze flicker.

'Falu,' I say.

Otter remains silent. But he will have to explain: that is the real reason for this meeting.

'The ambush was a smokescreen,' I continue. 'My father's real aim was to find Aidan and kill him. And it nearly worked.

Aidan and I should have died. Falu saved us. I want you to tell us why, Otter. Why did the Archmage of Thynis betray her closest ally?'

The Guardian's eyes have gone thick and opaque. Anger pushes away the fog of tiredness creeping over me: he's covering up – keeping everything to himself, as always!

'You're in league with her!' I stare into his eyes and wish I could scratch the information from his head with my fingers. 'She asked for you. *For you!* And she knew about Elsewhere!'

Still he says nothing, and my worst suspicions are confirmed. 'You've sold out the thieves! You've given away their secret – their only weapon – to the mages! How could you?'

The Guardian doesn't even flinch at my words. He says: 'Allies barter. I needed something to trade. Do you really think, Zara, that you are the only mage ever to have a conscience?' Otter's voice is suddenly scathing. 'Falu sees that tyranny will lead you mages to death as inevitably as the great river Yaaryn flows into the sea. She knows the survival of magekind depends on defeating your father. She wants to open a dialogue with the Knowledge Seekers, to create a new alliance based on power sharing.'

Impossible! An *archmage* seeking freedom for kine? For the non-magic? The Archmage of Thynis, a heretic like my mother? Like me?

'I don't believe you!'

My mother died for the heresy of believing kine to be fully human. My dear old teacher, Gerontius, killed himself rather than face trial and execution when his alliance with the Knowledge Seekers was discovered. I have good reason to know that I'm not the only mage ever to recognise evil and fight it at any cost – I'm still paying the price of their bravery and self-sacrifice. But Otter isn't telling us the whole truth and that means I *cannot* trust him.

Aidan is silent, his emotions a tumble of confusion. But Philip the artist speaks: 'And do you want magekind to survive, Otter? You, above all? You have better cause than most, Guardian, to know that the power mages hold in their minds must inevitably lead to corruption.'

Inevitably? Is that what Philip thinks? That I am damned too? I stare in shock at the Knowledge Seeker.

'You are one of the exceptions, Zara.' I see Philip's fondness for me in his eyes, but behind that is a wall of implacable hatred for my race. *Gods! Is there never to be peace?*

'No,' Otter says.

'What do you mean, Guardian?' Aidan has recovered his voice.

'That no one is exempt from the seduction of power. Not even Zara.'

'Not even *you*?' I throw the words back at Otter. 'Do you alone remain untainted?'

'Not even me.'

'Are you admitting it?' I attack. 'Are you saying that Falu has bought your loyalty? Do you belong to her?'

When Otter speaks, his voice is a stone dragged over slate: 'I was firstborn and therefore destined to be given to the mages as a slave. When I was five years old they came and took me as Tribute. The last memory I have of my mother is of her screams as a guard tore me from her arms and shoved her to the ground outside our house. I heard her calling my name as they carried me away.

'She was a thief. Her tribe cast her out when she married for love outside her guild. Time gave her little grace: my father was a carter. I never knew him. He died of a fever soon after I was born. When my mother lost me, she lost all. I went back, when I was old enough, to find her, but our house was lived in by others. Neighbours said she disappeared a few days after I was taken. She went back to her own kind. Mistress Floster told me my mother begged to rejoin the Thieves' Guild. She asked to be trained as an assassin and died within months, without ever having killed a single mage. After she told me that, Floster agreed to tutor me herself. I visited the catacombs most nights. She taught me a great deal.'

He looks at me, and his eyes kindle with an old pain. 'I was never your father's slave. You cannot imagine what that freedom cost. But know that the price was too high for me to ever sell myself to anyone. Falu is my ally, Zara. We share a goal: the defeat of your father. She has her reasons; I have mine. We use each other, if you like.'

I don't know what to believe. I think I do have some idea of what the Guardian's freedom must have cost him – the horrifying loneliness of living among those who must never know your thoughts and feelings. I too have lived as a spy. But I had Swift, and Gerontius. He had no one. No one except Floster, in those rare times he managed to escape his duties long enough to visit the catacombs.

I remember the fifteen-year-old boy who joined my father's household as Benedict's new Guardian when I was ten.

Remember how I hated and feared the newcomer, knowing that his mind and very soul belonged to my father. I was wrong then, but . . .

'I believe you, Otter. But I don't trust Falu. She lives for power. She is no lover of kine. I've known her all my life. She may not be as vile as the others, but she's still an archmage. She's using you. What proof have you that she's trustworthy?'

'She could have betrayed me any time these past five years,' Otter says.

Five years! He's been colluding with Falu for five years?

'Oh gods!' I breathe.

'And you don't know her very well, do you, Zara?' the Guardian continues. 'Or you would know that she was your mother's greatest friend.'

Surprise leaves me voiceless. Eleanor and Falu? I hardly remember my mother, so Otter could be right. Or Falu could have lied to him.

'Falu saved the Maker, Zara.' Otter shrugs. 'The one soul your father needs dead. I don't care whether you believe her to be a friend or not, but if you can figure out why she would do that, if she is loyal to Benedict and the alliance, then you tell me.'

I shake my head helplessly. Turn to Philip. The artist is grim-faced.

'I think we must trust Otter, Zara,' he says at last. 'All the evidence is on his side of the balance. I understand your unease. Indeed, I share it. But the facts speak for themselves.'

'I don't like it!' Aidan mutters. He's been pacing restlessly, but now he pauses beside Philip.

'Do you like being alive, Maker?' Otter's voice is cold. 'You were a fool to go after the Tributes. Blood lust is a nasty thing: it unhinges judgement. And for what? The joy of killing those pathetic child-slaves? If you were a soldier of mine, I'd have you whipped.'

'Damn you!' Aidan lunges for the Guardian. Philip grabs his shoulder and tugs him back.

'I fought like a Maker!' Aidan cries. 'We fight to win! You don't know what you're talking about. You weren't there!'

The light is failing. The barn is full of shadows and I can't see Otter's expression, but his voice doesn't alter. 'You have Falu to thank for your skin, Maker. If we didn't need you to convince your people that Benedict's truce is false, I wouldn't much care if you lived or died, but you nearly killed Zara through your stupidity. I don't forgive that so easily.'

'That's not fair,' I interrupt. 'You kill Tributes . . .' My words dry on my tongue. He's right about Aidan; the Maker lost his head. He gave himself over to blood lust. I felt it at the time. But I won't admit it to the Guardian.

'There's been enough death for one day,' Otter says shortly. 'Time for you to make up for missing the ambush, Zara. How much reserves have you got?'

Healing. I have a new-found talent for repairing muscle and bone. I can't stop a fever or cure a wasting sickness, like the one that carried off a baby last week, but I can mend damaged bodies. Sometimes. It's demanding magic and burns energy at a ferocious rate. I'm dangerously tired. But these people are injured because I failed to spot the ambush. I nod, anxious to stop thinking about Aidan, about Falu, to do something positive. 'I'm good.'

'She's not!' Aidan pushes closer, grips my arm. 'Look at her: she can hardly stand. I won't let you risk Zara.'

Otter narrows his eyes. 'It's her decision, not yours, Maker.'

I pull my arm away from Aidan. Shadows obscure the expression on his face. 'I'm fine,' I mutter. 'But thank you.'

I see the shape of Aidan's head move as he glances at Otter. 'That was a good fight we did together, Zara.' His voice warms, grows caressing. 'It felt right, you at my back.'

Why is he doing this? Is it to get back at Otter? Or does he mean it? His emotions are a toxic mixture of longing and anger, remembered exhilaration and fear.

Has he really, finally, forgiven me for being a mage? Can he forget what and who I am? What my father did to him? Or will he reject me again?

I nod, backing away.

'Zara.' Otter stands in the doorway, framed by moonlight. 'This way. A man is dying.'

4

I follow Otter into a star-spangled dusk, towards the ruined farmhouse. I make myself stride out, ignoring the weakness in my legs, aware of hunger sharp as a belly-full of knives. Extreme magic eats you up and you must eat in return or pay a high price. I ignore my body. Enough people have died because of me.

I push aside the horse blanket serving as a door and bend my head to duck through a low doorway. This room would have been the living space and kitchen. The plaster is long gone and the bare stone walls are lit by orange firelight. The earth floor strikes chill and damp, despite the fire roaring in the hearth, belching oily black smoke. Some of it drifts up the remains of the chimney, but the rest thickens the air.

Mistress Quint, the apothecary, bends over a figure lying on a blood-stained blanket. Otter goes to stand beside her, and crosses his arms over his chest in a gesture of willful stillness.

Quint glances up, her plump face frustrated, her round black eyes angry. She hates Death. I sense her fury at losing the fight. And then my eyes turn to the figure on the bed. And my stomach heaves.

It's Hammeth, the blacksmith, a stupid, cruel man who sought my death a few short weeks ago. Hammeth is a large man of thirty, not old, yet the months of forced inactivity in the catacombs have taken their toll: his once powerful arm muscles lie slack. Quint presses a wad of bloodstained cloth against his left side. She glares up at me, shaking her head over and over.

'There is an organ on the left side. Here.' She presses the bandage with a finger and Hammeth grunts in pain. He is gasping, pale, his half-open eyes focused on something over our heads. 'The spleen,' Quint continues, her eyes boring into mine. 'If it is damaged, the patient will often bleed to death. I can do nothing! It is with the gods. Unless you, Zara? Can you heal this? It's a puncture wound. A pike speared his spleen like a chicken on a spit. He's only alive now out of sheer stubbornness!'

I look from Quint to Hammeth. He doesn't even seem to know I'm here. Would he prefer to die, rather than let a hated mage perform magic on his body? I don't know. Only that I don't want to touch this man with my mind. Why should I risk my life for his? I lied to Otter: I'm near to collapse. If a mage performs too much magic, they will use up their store of body energy and slip into a sleep from which they may never wake.

I glance up, catch Otter's eyes. His face is as unreadable as ever. 'Only if you have the will and the strength, Zara,' he says. 'Hammeth is our only blacksmith. But I don't want to lose you. You are of great value to us.'

Value. Well, it is something: to be valuable.

'Time does not favour us, Zara!' Quint snaps. Her round body is almost bouncing with frustration. And, against my instincts, I found I have decided.

I take a deep breath and sink down to sit cross-legged on the cold ground beside the dying blacksmith. I close my eyes, steady my breathing, detach a small strand of my consciousness and force it, hesitant and shrinking, towards the man lying half-conscious on the bed. Four times I have done this now: attempted to heal with my mind and magic. Thrice I have succeeded. But only last week, there was the woman with the pain in her belly. She died screaming, her fear flooding the air around us, seeping into the very stones she lay upon. I still dream about it.

Hammeth does not scream. He's grunting, his breathing harsh, rapid. Growing fainter. Yes, he is dying.

I sit motionless, my body growing chill as the clay. A thin thread of my consciousness enters the wound beneath Quint's impatient hand. It's a brutal puncture: compressing, tearing, ripping, destroying. And suddenly, I have forgotten myself, forgotten that I hate and distrust this man. I hate the wound more. I hate its mindless destructiveness. My mind ventures further into the wound, tracing the tunnel bored through flesh, tearing muscle, piercing layers of fat, shredding blood vessels. I follow the hole to the outer wall of the spleen and meet a wall of blood pushing out from the organ. I wade through it, in and on to the very back of the wound, where the pike's flint-stone tip hit a rib and chipped the bone itself.

This is where I must start: gluing bone, knitting tissue, binding flesh, attaching blood vessels. I lose myself in the puzzle of the work: concentrate on the strands of muscle and tissue that must be encouraged to regrow, to re-attach, to heal themselves. Quickly! Some blood vessels are too torn to mend, so I cauterise them with a sudden blast of heat drawn from the dying body itself. I lose track of time as I re-attach, order growth, reverse damage. The spleen is malleable, quick to mend, and the bleeding slows to a faint weeping as I retrace my journey through the wound, mending muscle and tissue as I go. Finally, I find myself oozing backwards through a layer of fat and emerging into air once more to regrow the skin itself. Nothing remains but a circular scar. The work is done.

It's cold. I'm shivering, ill. What has happened? Why am I sitting in the mud? I open my eyes, close them again at once, and feel my body slump as nausea and giddiness flood through me. I hear Otter's voice in my ears; feel his breath on my frozen face; his strong hands holding, lifting.

'. . . half-kills herself for that turd of a crawler. If Zara dies, I'll flippin' spear his liver myself and feed it to the jackals!'

'Hush, Twiss! There's been enough killing to last me my life and a hundred more. Zara will live. She will, won't she, Aidan?'

The arm that cradles me tightens. Tugs me close. I'm leaning against someone's chest. My legs dangle astride a saddle-less horse – no, it must be one of our mules – which is walking at a steady, lolloping pace. My head lolls sideways onto a sturdy shoulder. Warm breath tickles my ear as the owner of the arm speaks. I feel the words rumbling deep in his chest, harsh and angry: 'She *must* live!'

Aidan? It's Aidan who holds me. I sense his emotions: anger and worry. For me! A tear slips hot-footed down my face, tickling. I try to sit up.

'Keep still, Zara. Or you'll have us both off.' Aidan's arm pulls me close again. I relax, allow myself to lean against him, drawn to his warmth. I'm shivering.

'Zara! You're awake!' A hand grips my ankle. I look down and see Twiss's cat-like face break into a glorious smile.

'Zara? Dear girl, how are you feeling?' Tabitha the silversmith walks on the other side of the mule. Her large grey eyes are dark-ringed with fatigue. She holds her young son – Aidan's apprentice, Thaddeus – by one hand. They both smile shyly up at me.

'You need this. Here.' Twiss digs in her leather waist pouch, then shoves a fistful of something sticky into my hand. 'Eat it!' she orders. 'You've used up too much of yourself. Why are you so stupid sometimes?' Her gift of anger warms me even more. I shift my aching tailbone, try to relax the muscles in my legs and feet that are starting to spasm.

'Eat it!'

Obediently, I raise my hand, examine the contents. She's right: I am ravenous. I've pushed myself to the very limits my body can stand and I know I'm lucky to have woken from that long sleep. I need to eat. But what . . .? I open my fingers to find a gummy mixture of raisins, dried olives, and shreds of dried meat. *Meat!* My mouth falls open and I shoot a dark look at Twiss. She's stolen this. Dried fruit and meat are pure gold.

'Eat!' The thief meets me look for look. I swallow the words of reproach and replace them in my mouth with her gift.

Oh, the marvel of food! I try to chew slowly, to savour the richness of the flavours. It's been so long since I had meat or olives. I can't remember when I last chewed a raisin and felt the sweetness flood my mouth. All is gone too soon, and I lick my hand unashamedly. Oh gods, would that I had more!

'Thank you, Twiss,' I say, when I have breath enough. 'You've saved my life.'

'Yeah. Well, don't be so pissing stupid next time. You got no business using yourself up healing that piece of –'

'Shut up, brat.'

Twiss glares at Aidan, but miraculously, doesn't retort. I can feel what the restraint is costing her. She's doing it for me. I reach down and touch her shoulder. And then she's off, scampering away in her too-large woollen jacket and clumping boots. I watch her slender shape melt towards the front of the marching band of travellers. She will be off to find Otter. Or will roam the edges of the other travellers, solitary, like the swift.

The swift! I yank forward out of Aidan's grasp, crane my neck to look up at the sky. It's not there. The swift has chosen freedom after all. Sadness squeezes my heart. Twiss is right: I'm stupid. It was a bird, no more. It's gone south, as it should.

'How long?' My voice cracks; my mouth and throat are parched. Tabitha takes a stoppered wooden bottle from her girdle, uncorks it and offers it up. I grip the leather cover with both hands as I gulp the water, which will have been gathered fresh from the river this morning. It tastes of the mountains.

'You've slept through a day, a night, and another day,' Aidan says.

He must be right: it's evening. The sun balances just above the horizon. I peer ahead, and with a jolt, I see the first of the foothills lying less than a day's journey ahead of us. The river has dwindled to a stream. It unwinds from the foothills, tumbling down its rocky bed towards the plains. And then I hear myself gasp as I see – clearly and for the first time with human eyes – the Great Wall of the Makers.

The Wall rises, a twenty-foot-high ribbon of golden sandstone undulating across the upper foothills – ageless, as though built by gods rather than women and men. Crenellated towers rise from its snaking body at regular intervals. And there . . . I put a warning hand on Aidan's arm.

In the far distance I see a moving group of figures, threading a careful path along the base of one of the foothills to our right, making their way in our direction. They are too far away for me to see what clothes or uniform they wear. Surely not Makers on this side of the Wall, even if they still believe in my father's ruse of a truce. No one is panicking, so it can't be a Tribute army patrol.

'Otter's people.' Aidan's voice is low in my ear. 'He disappeared most of the night, came back early this morning. He's met with his secret army, arranged for some of them to help us find a place to hide out and guard the Knowledge Seekers – in case of another attack when he and I go to Gengst to meet my people tomorrow.'

Aidan and Otter? Alone and unprotected? Is this Falu's idea? Is it a trap?

I unclasp Aidan's arm, swing my leg over and slide off the mule.

'Zara?'

'Zara, are you strong enough to walk?' Tabitha asks.

Talking uses energy; I need all I have. I nod to Tabitha and set off on unsteady legs through the meandering cluster of people and mules, towards the front of the group. I need to find Otter.

The Maker lets me go. Good! I don't need cosseting, I tell myself, ignoring a small sadness in a corner of my mind.

Most of the Knowledge Seekers nod to me as I pass through them: '*Good to have you with us again, Zara.*' '*Glad to see you well again.*' More often, a shy: '*Hello!*' A few draw back still, in superstition. Fearing to touch even the sleeve of my coat. To them I am still a demon mage: even though I have travelled and fought beside them these long weeks.

I near a crude litter made of sawn sapling trunks and rope, pulled by one of the pack mules. Even before I look at the occupant's face, I know: Hammeth. So, he lived. I meet the gaze of the blacksmith. His eyes are a cloudy hazel. His clothes are bloodstained, his face lined. But he looks healthier than any man has a right to after losing so much blood. He stares back at me, his eyes wide with surprise, hatred, fear, then . . . slow and grudging, a mulish look of gratitude crosses his face. He gives me a curt, brief nod of acknowledgement. Then looks away as I pass.

I push thoughts of the blacksmith from my mind as I spot Otter near the front of our band of foot-sore travellers and trudging mules. He stands half a head taller than anyone else, his heavy dark hair drawn into a plait at the back of his neck, his broad shoulders swaying in easy rhythm as he strides, head constantly moving, scanning the countryside around us for danger.

I order my legs into a trot. Otter turns when I am feet away and waits for me to catch up. When I do, his wide-spaced eyes scan my face. At the sight of his face – so secretive, so calm – at the sense of unconscious power that emanates from both his mind and body, I find myself relaxing for a moment. Smiling. And then I remember Falu.

'Zara.'

It's all he says, but I feel welcomed. And suddenly ashamed of my doubts. Otter nods once and turns to walk on more slowly. Still, I have to stretch my legs to keep up with him.

'Have you eaten?' he asks.

'Twiss brought me food. I fear it was stolen.'

An almost-smile. 'It's good you're awake now. Have you seen?' He raises one bare, muscled arm to gesture towards the band of approaching Tributes, still a mile or more in the distance.

'Your people?' And in answer to his nod, I ask my question: 'Aidan said you and he are going to meet his people after we reach camp tomorrow. Is that right?' I don't try to keep the question from my voice.

'Yes.'

And that is all. No explanation, no discussion. My doubts return, full force.

'You were planning to go without me!'

'We *are* going without you. Tomorrow we reach one of my permanent strongholds hidden in the foothills. It will be safe for you and the Knowledge Seekers to stay there while Aidan and I negotiate with his people. There will be a council meeting then, Zara. You can protest formally if you wish, but you are not coming into Gengst with us.'

'Can we talk about this?'

But he carries on, strolling away from me with absolute, maddening certainty towards his advancing troupe of soldiers.

I trot till I catch him up and walk beside him, matching his stride, silent as he is himself.

I don't argue: it's impossible to argue with Otter. He simply states what will happen. And then makes it happen. I don't know how to win this battle of wills. And this contest will have to wait in any case, because I want to find out what happened after the real battle, the one we so nearly lost because of my carelessness.

Without warning, images of the mages I killed flood through my head, parading in front of my eyes with devastating clarity. I hear their screams, see the blood, the wall of water . . . I am haunted. I must make some sort of noise, for Otter pauses and turns to me, frowning.

'What's wrong, Zara?'

'The Tribute soldiers we captured. Where are they? What happened to them?'

'They are with us. They joined my army. Most do, you know. Not always. Sometimes, when the brainwashing is too severe, when slavery is too engrained and it's clear they'll run back to their masters, then they must die. I won't lie to you. Fortunately, this time, the survivors were more than happy to join us.'

Thank Time!

I nod at Otter. His openness is encouraging, and I am wondering whether to ask him again to explain his plans for getting Aidan into Gengst when it happens again: I'm flying, making a spike of ice, hurling it at the warrior mage. I feel the man's fear in the moment before it plunges into his neck. See life drain from his eyes. I hear the woman mage scream again as the wall of water crushes her. Taste her despair.

I stop walking and swallow convulsively as my stomach ponders whether or not to reject the food it's just been given. I stare at the dried, yellow stalks of grass between my feet for the space of half a dozen shuddering breaths before I remember that I'm not alone. I look up and Otter is still watching me. I glance away at the band of Knowledge Seekers trudging past, most staring at us as they go.

'Zara.'

I make myself look him in the eyes.

'I'm sorry,' he says. 'I do not enjoy killing either. But we will not win our freedom and stop this endless war without bloodshed. You know this.'

He waits, and at last I nod. I do know it. But I hate it too.

'You have killed your own now. In battle. Can you accept that?'

Trust Otter to touch the sore spot. He watches me a moment longer. For that moment, the understanding in his eyes is unbearable. He nods and strides off to greet his people, and I sigh with relief and watch him walk away, my chest knotted tight with emotions I can't even begin to unpick. I trail slowly after him. I'm shivering again, my body feels heavy as clay. I should seek out Aidan, ask for a ride into camp on the mule. But I know I won't.

It's not a steep hill, but my legs are aching by the time I reach the top. I've stolen away from the night's camp, which is hidden at the base of this hill. I need to be alone in order to think. I try to ignore the ever-present ache of hunger and wrap my jacket even more tightly around me as I come to a halt and turn to face the Wall of the Makers. It looks so near now, and magical in the moonlight.

There will be an air-frost in the morning: the sky is clear and still. Countless bright pinpricks of white, blue, red, pink, pale green shimmer overhead, snail trails tracing across the blackness of the night. Starlight, mage light of gods, spears down out of the sky. The moon is waxing full. The land of the north lies transformed in its chill light. Its alchemy has changed the Wall from gold to silver. It stretches from horizon to horizon, drained of colour, cold and fierce.

Tomorrow Aidan and Otter will travel to the other side of that wall. What sort of place is Gengst-on-the-Wall? What sort of people live there? Surely the Makers will help the Knowledge Seekers, give us sanctuary. Welcome us as allies against magekind. I try to imagine what our new lives will be. What will it be like to live in that city crouching on the far side of the wall, its towers shining white-gold in the moonlight?

We're so close. In Gengst we will find the safety, the home we seek.

A worm in my mind reminds me that my father will not have given up. My father will stop at nothing to keep Aidan from reaching Gengst. If the Maker alerts his people to Benedict's treachery, his plan to destroy Gengst and all its inhabitants, it will be a great setback to my father's ambition to be remembered as the Archmage who exterminated the Maker race, who won victory for magekind after generations of war.

I shiver, and wrap my jacket even tighter. I don't know what shape the terror will take, the thing that is hunting us down, but I know it is coming. *Otter is wrong!* Aidan will need me tomorrow. I can't abandon him. Not now. Not having come so far.

An icy cold hand grips the back of my neck.

I cringe from its grip and whirl around, just stopping myself from magicking the hand and its owner down the hillside. '*Twiss!* Don't sneak up on me like that! I could have hurt you.'

The thief stands, hands on hips, glaring at me in disgust. 'I been standing here ages and you never knew! What are you playin' at, sneaking out of camp to lolly-gag in plain sight on a hill top? The moon shows you off clear as anything. If I were a soldier off the Wall, you'd be dead!'

'I was perfectly safe,' I lie. Twiss is right – I've been careless, but I'm not going to admit it: she's bossy enough already. 'You only surprised me because you used Elsewhere to sneak up on me. Makers can't do not-seen-not-heard.'

She grabs my shoulder and tugs me towards a hollow lying just below the brow of the hill. 'Sit down here, outta sight. You'll never make a thief! First rule is don't be seen!'

I settle onto heather, huddle with my arms around my knees, and feel Twiss crouch beside me. I like having her sitting next to me: fierce, vibrantly alive but . . . sadly . . . not silent. Since that night when she saved my life by taking me to the thieves' den in the catacombs beneath Asphodel, Twiss has felt she owns me. Just a little bit.

'You shouldn't be here. Otter told you –'

'Please stop quoting Otter at me, Twiss! I'm not one of his soldiers.'

'He's in charge.'

'Not of me. And since when have you done what you're told? You're not supposed to leave camp either.'

'I followed you! Someone's gotta look after you. That Maker boy of yours don't want to.'

'He isn't "my" Maker boy. And I don't need looking after. Not by Aidan or Otter or even you. I can look after myself! I have done my whole life.'

Twiss just snorts. But a small, bony, cold hand sneaks into mine and holds it tight. And I am so surprised that I lose the words I was about to say. I hold the thief's hand as carefully as if it was a newborn chick. And blink up at the stars until my vision clears.

We sit in silence.

'I'm sorry, Twiss,' I murmur at last. 'I was careless. You're right. I wish you weren't but you are. I came up here to think.'

Just silence.

'Something happened to me, Twiss, that day we fought Benedict. The day you nearly killed him.'

Her hand convulses, pulls away. My heart aches at its going. But Twiss herself sits still. I take a breath and continue.

'You're the only person I can tell. Because you were there; you fought him like she did. But you lived. Swift died.'

Twiss listens.

I tell her the story I have never told anyone: the story of my half-sister, Ita, who my father gave to me to be my slave when we were both five years old. Why I named her Swift, because she reminded me of my favourite bird. Of how we loved each other, and how I taught her to read, even though it was forbidden. And of the night she died. We were nine years old when my father murdered her.

Twiss's hand creeps back into mine. She waits.

'The paperweight, Twiss,' I say. 'The one I tried to kill him with that night when he attacked Swift. I think my father has somehow imprisoned someone inside it. I heard a voice calling me from inside the glass. I felt someone.'

'You heard? Or did you want to hear the voice so much you made it up?'

The question I have asked myself a hundred times. A thousand.

'I don't know. I think the voice was real. Tabitha's son, Thaddeus, told me about being locked away in a place like the catacombs but made of glass. A glass labyrinth. And there was a woman already there who took care of him. He said she looked like me. Swift could almost have been my twin. Before I found out she was my half-sister, I always thought that was why my father chose Swift to be my Tribute child: because, except for her dark hair, she looked like me.'

The silent stars watch.

'If I'm right . . .' I take a deep breath. 'Twiss, I believe my sister is alive. I think Benedict has been keeping her prisoner all these years, trapped in the paperweight. It's decorated with his mage mark. It would be like him, to imprison his half-kine daughter inside his own soul sign.' Memories of the night he found us in his library – the last night I saw my sister alive – assault me; my voice shakes. 'Swift always told me he never could bear to give anything up that belonged to him.' I clench my jaw and let the old emotions sweep through me like a brush fire, but without fire's cleansing. Tarry lumps of hate stick in my heart and throat.

'You're gonna go back.' She's quick, this girl. She's guessed.

'I have to.'

'Then I'll come too. To keep my promise to Bruin.' Her husky voice growls the words and I feel once more the pain of her loss, undimmed over the months. Twiss, the mage-killer. Twiss, aged all of twelve.

I stare up at the stars and wonder what the future holds, and if even the gods know the answer to that question.

5

Our final encampment lies somewhere deep within the foothills. We are too close to the Wall to move in daytime. It is moonrise, and like a snake writhing through a chicken house, we worm through the foothills towards Otter's stronghold, threading a path between enemy camps.

For the last half-hour or so, we have travelled beside a mountain stream. The trees thicken on either bank and we are forced to walk in the stream bed itself. I stumble and slip over mossy stones and fallen branches, wet to my knees. Every few ticks there is a faint splash followed by a muttered curse as someone misses their footing. The mules have had their harnesses and iron shoes wrapped with strips of torn blankets. Their muffled hooves softly splat the shallow water.

The hills either side of us grow closer, become a valley which narrows as we climb. We squeeze our way, single-file, between walls of sheer rock. Suddenly, the sides of the canyon lean together over our heads and join. It's like when I was lost in the catacombs beneath Asphodel. Only this time I can't use mage light. I grit my teeth and stumble on, chasing the comforting noise of the person trudging ahead of me. At least the water is gone: dry pebbles slide and shift beneath my frozen feet.

With a suddenness that takes my breath, the walls fall back and the tunnel opens into a space lit by a faint dawn light. I stagger to a stop and squint around a roofless cavern, a sandstone room as large as my father's entire palazzo, already full to overflowing with a strange people, tents, animals. The new morning is full of movement, of smells. The unmistakable smell of burning wood makes my heart leap: warmth! And then my twitching nostrils catch the scent of food. *Cooked food!* Oh gods, this is heaven!

Knowledge Seekers shuffle like caged bears and look around with wondering eyes. I glimpse Otter, directing groups of Knowledge Seekers to various tents, into the charge of Tribute soldiers. Despite the distraction of the promise of warmth, food and rest, I'm struck by how different these Tributes are to those I grew up with in Asphodel. His rebels move with an aliveness – a will – I've never seen in enslaved Tributes.

Otter sorts the Knowledge Seekers into groups. Philip, Mistress Quint, all the surviving members of the Knowledge Seekers' council are detached and disappear into a tent. The council is preparing to meet.

'Zara, we're wanted.' My head jerks round and I nearly bump noses with Aidan. His eyes are strangely shy. My heart lurches. 'Sorry,' Aidan says. *Is he actually blushing?* 'The council is meeting.' He takes my arm and steers me through the crowd. 'You've been avoiding me,' Aidan says. 'I need to talk to you. About tonight.'

'I want to go with you.' I try to tug my arm away but Aidan won't let go. 'Benedict isn't going to let you just stroll into Gengst, you know!'

Aidan sighs. 'Look, much as I hate to, I agree with Otter this time. It isn't safe for you. You don't understand.'

I can tell that he means it: the Maker is worried.

'What? Tell me.'

'If you were discovered . . .' His voice trails off. 'Mages are hated in Gengst,' he says at last. 'Really, really hated. If it became known that you're a mage I wouldn't be able to protect you. No one would – not me, not my father, not Otter. Do you understand?'

'But . . .' I stare at him as I realise he doesn't just mean tonight. He means forever. Everything: Swift's dream and mine – for a place, a home. Everything is broken all of a sudden. It knocks the breath from me and I just stand and look at him. Finally, I find some silly, stupid words. The words of a lonely child: 'Where am I to go? I thought I was coming with you. To live in Gengst.'

'Otter thinks you should live with his Tribute army. Keep moving. Keep hidden. Keep out of Gengst, where you could be trapped. If anyone betrayed you . . .' He doesn't say Hammeth's name, but I know he's thinking about the blacksmith.

'I'm to be homeless forever? Wandering the plains like an outlaw?' I look at his face, hoping I'll see an answer there, but knowing I won't. There isn't an answer. Aidan is right. I can't go into Gengst. I have nowhere. And I have been blind – a fool – not to realise. Or did I choose not to see?

'I'll visit you! Otter will be back and forth between his camps and Gengst all the time. I'll come with him.' The Maker's voice stumbles in his eagerness to reassure. To comfort. 'I'll be working with him; working with Philip. I need to build the machines, Zara. With Philip's machines, we can win the war. And when we've defeated Benedict, you and I can –'

'What?' My voice sounds dead; I feel dead.

'It'll be different then.'

'I'll still be a mage.'

'But we'll have won the war. There will be peace. We'll make it work.'

I try to believe him.

'Come to the meeting,' Aidan pleads.

And suddenly I know he mostly wants to feel better himself. Going to the council meeting won't make me happier: it would be excruciating.

'We need to make plans,' he says. 'Not just tonight and getting me into Gengst, but the future . . . you, me, Tabitha, Philip . . . we can make this work, Zara!'

I back away. Keep backing. That future doesn't exist for me.

'I can't, Aidan. I need to think. I . . .' I turn and run into the crowd.

I walk with my head up, winding a careful path through those who live here. I see cheerful and worried faces, tired, bored, happy. Strangers' faces. Soon I reach the canyon wall. I stare at the yellow stone rising up thirty feet to the night sky. Lifeless, hard stone. This stony place is to be my new home. Not Gengst. I will never travel past the Wall. I reach out and touch the canyon wall, and feel something springy and soft. A plant. Growing in the stone, but still alive. My fingers grip, start to tear, to rip it out.

'Zara? This isn't the time for gardening: the council is meeting.'

Some part of my mind notices that the Guardian has attempted a joke.

Otter's hand takes mine, detaches my fingers from the plant. He stares down at me. 'We need to talk about tonight. We need to talk about keeping you safe.'

I flinch from his eyes and gaze over his shoulder instead. 'Why do you want me at the meeting? Aidan has explained the situation. I know I can't go into the city.'

'You're part of the council, Zara. We need your advice and support.'

'I'm sorry, you'll have to do without.'

I pull my hand from his grasp. The Guardian doesn't move away. I step forward, hoping he will give way and let me past, but he's as solid and unmoving as the stone wall. I stop, lest I touch him again – I don't want to be touched by anyone right now, especially not Otter, with his certainty, his calm, emotion-free mind. I find I'm staring at his left shoulder – at the oval scar of a continuous, sharp cornered line burnt into his skin. The familiar lines of my father's mage mark shine from his brown skin, glossy white. The sight makes me nauseous. Hidden beneath a thick cosmetic supplied by the apothecary, Mistress Quint, I carry the same mark on the left side of my face. It was put there at my naming ceremony, carved by magic and inlaid with silver. Now it seems to burn my skin. Benedict owns us both. Is our dream of freedom a childish fantasy? Like the life I thought I would have in Gengst – the new life I promised Swift I would find for us both?

'Let me by. Please.'

'Talk to me. It isn't forever. We want you to survive, Zara! You'll still be with us. But living with my people here. We can work this out.'

'I need time.' I'm balancing on the edge of control. I don't want to talk to this man, don't want to look at him. I edge backwards and Otter makes the mistake of reaching out. He lays his hand upon my shoulder. Very, very carefully – because I've had a lifetime to learn caution even when frustration and loss devour me from the inside out – I harden a sheet of air between us until a paper-thin, invisible wall takes shape. I test the strength of it, and then I grab the air-wall with my mind and push. I collect the energy of the wind itself and use it against the Guardian.

Otter staggers backwards. His eyes grow wide in alarm. *At last! A human reaction.*

'Zara! Don't do this. You mustn't . . .'

Yes. I know. I must never use magic against my own – against those I've chosen to belong to. But I am. I have. I've killed my own kind. And the non-magic will not have me. I am outside everything. Everyone. Cast out. Outcaste. There is no place for me.

I push.

He can do nothing. For a tick – an eternity equally terrifying and wondrous – I'm in the grip of a whirlwind of dark, raw ecstasy. Otter cannot control me. No one can control me. No one will hurt me ever again. I will do as I wish.

Slowly, steadily, I use my magic to shove the Guardian away, staring straight into his eyes as I do so. Daring him to try to fight me. Knowing he can't. He doesn't say another word. His face is calm now: no outrage, no anger. Not even disapproval. But he doesn't give way either. He makes me push him back, fighting each reluctant backward step with all his considerable strength, until finally there is a clear space between us and I can turn and walk away into the morning.

The sun slides across the sky above the cavern, from east to west, as I prowl the camp. It slips out of sight altogether and the air grows dim. An hour to sunset, perhaps. Otter and Aidan won't leave before midnight. Hours yet. I should just leave. Just go. But where? I don't know. I don't know anything. I can't decide what to do. I can't think at all.

Twiss follows me all day, clinging like a shadow for an hour or so, then disappearing for short periods. She brings me water to drink and food. No matter how much I drink, my mouth stays dry; the food tastes of nothing. I only eat because Twiss is wearing a scowl that tells me she's holding her tongue only through great effort. She's the only person I can bear to have near me now . . . as long as she doesn't talk.

At last the reflected sunlight disappears in the blink of an eagle's eye: swallowed by the surrounding mountains. Death calls her child back underground. I have to decide what I am going to do. Will I stay with Otter's Tribute army, the boys and girls who will hate me worse than the Knowledge Seekers if ever they find out who and what I am? If I decide not to stay, then I must find the energy to gather a few supplies and make my way back onto the plains, in search of a band of gypsies, or an abandoned farmstead somewhere in a quiet, unvisited hole where I could somehow live. Alone. That's the problem:

Twiss is my jailor – I won't escape her easily. And I can't take her with me. Because I don't really expect to live very long once I leave here.

And what about Swift? a voice in my head asks. *What of the promise you made to her ghost all those years ago: the promise to avenge her death? Your promise to stop the enslavement of Tribute children? And* . . . the voice continues, ignoring my demands that it be silent . . . *what about Aidan? He's still in danger. Or don't you care? Is your love so weak, so easily defeated?* I press my hands over my ears in a vain attempt to shut out the voice. *Coward! Foresworn! What's a little heartache? What's being alone? You should be used to it now. Well?*

'Twiss.' I lift my head at last, defeated. The thief is squatting on her haunches, arms wrapped around knees, watching me. She could sit like that all day without moving, I imagine. 'Where are they now?' My throat is sore, my voice hoarse. 'What's happening?'

'I was waitin' for you to get over feeling sorry for yourself.' She wrinkles her nose in disapproval and I feel her relief at being able to tell me off at last. 'Otter's gone with your Maker boy –' She sees the look in my eye. 'Uh . . . Otter and Aidan have gone off to meet some big-arse in the Maker army. Someone Aidan's brother is pally with. This guy is supposed to take 'em into the city.'

My heart begins to thud, slow and heavy. My sense that something is wrong grows. I can't go with Aidan, but at least I can watch from a distance and make sure he's all right. 'How long ago?'

She shrugs. 'Maybe as long as it takes to heat a forge from cold.'

I sigh. Time is a different god to those who cannot read clocks. I'm none the wiser, but it sounds a long time. Too long? I jump to my feet. 'Did you see the direction they went?'

She nods.

'Good. Show me.'

Can thieves see in the dark? Is it another of their magical abilities? Ironic that the tribe that most hates all magic-users – the Thieves' Guild, sworn enemies of magekind – should also prove to be magic-users. Twiss hasn't guessed. Perhaps her mind won't let her. Mages took Bruin from her, as they took her parents before him. Twiss has long known I was a traitor to my own kind, yet I had to nearly die before she could accept me. I don't think she's ready to face the truth about herself yet.

Her hard thin hand grips mine, pulling me on and on into the dark of the winding canyon. High, narrow cliffs to the right and left shut out most of the moon and starlight. Only a ribbon of white unwinds itself far over our heads, like a sparkling reflection of our path.

Twiss trots relentlessly, dodging boulders and rocks, pulling me behind her. Finally, when I'm gasping like a stranded fish, she freezes without warning and I teeter into her.

'Hsssss!' Disapproval at my clumsiness. 'Elsewhere!' she whispers in my ear.

I obey at once, vaguely wondering why Twiss is the only person I let boss me around, and slip into that place in my mind called Elsewhere, where we are invisible to all eyes but those of other thieves. Twiss is already there. We don't go deeply, just far enough so we can't be seen by those we're stalking.

Twiss grips my hand again and, careful to make no noise, we creep on. Finally my straining eyes see a glimmer of firelight huddled at the base of a black mass which rears up into the night like a massive wave of frozen stone. *The Wall!* I am face to face with Swift's dream.

We edge forward, and the sides of the canyon splay out to reveal people gathered round a dying bonfire. I gasp. Twiss drives her elbow in my stomach in warning. Her elbows are sharp and bony, but I hardly notice. Makers! Nearly a dozen of them. Men, dressed in outlandish costume. Men made of metal! None of the books in my father's library contain an illustration of a Maker soldier. No wonder: they are terrifying.

The tight trousers and over-the-knee boots, the leather tunics – all these are familiar from Aidan's clothes – but these men have metal discs strapped to their shoulders. They carry enormous shields of shiny grey metal embossed with elaborate designs, and wear metal hats sporting curved visors and flowing feathers. Their hands wear metal wrist guards, and they have a sword strapped to one hip and a dagger to the other.

And then my stomach turns over: two of these metallic men hold a struggling Aidan, bending his arms behind his back. Four more stand over Otter's body, which lies sprawled face down in front of the fire.

Is Otter dead? Impossible! The Guardian can't be dead: he's indestructible. Yet I know that Otter's very confidence could lead him into danger. The Guardian doesn't move. *If they've killed him I'll . . .*

I have to force myself to stillness. Concentrate on Aidan, who is still alive, thank the gods! He's raging. My heart pounds in my head, but I manage to keep still, keep in Elsewhere. I need to understand what's going on before I act.

'Traitors! Bastards! I'll kill you! Where's my brother? Where's Donal?' Aidan's shouts leap over the swearing of the Makers trying to restrain him. I look for the leader. Who is in charge? There! It must be that one: the short, square-shaped one with the large helmet. The one standing to one side with his arms crossed, looking smug and arrogant. He's my target.

A thief and a mage, against ten Maker soldiers? I don't like the odds. Except I'm not an ordinary mage: I'm nearly an adept, and Twiss is talented, fearless and lucky. But I don't want to risk her life. I glance at her. The flames of the bonfire dance in her eyes. She's scowling with impatience. Whatever I decide to do, Twiss won't be left out, and, in any case, if Otter is dead none of us have much chance of survival in the long run.

I whisper: 'Take my knife and give it to Otter. If he's alive and conscious.' My mouth goes dry at the words. Despite the cold, I'm sweating.

'If he can fight, help him. If he can't, leave him and help Aidan. But wait for me to take out the leader first! And remember: they mustn't know I'm a mage; I'm going to have to make them think we beat them without magic. Or we'll have to kill all of them. And I really don't want to do that, Twiss.'

She nods. I hand her my fighting knife, then loosen Bruin's sword in its scabbard. I give the thief a quick smile, take a deep breath, and then . . .

Twiss and I slide deeper into Elsewhere and, invisible, we walk out to battle those we came here to befriend: the Makers of Gengst-on-the-Wall.

6

Is Otter dead or just unconscious? Although his blood is only half-thief, he can do Elsewhere better than anyone I've ever met. If he was conscious he wouldn't just lie there. He'd slide into Elsewhere and escape. Unless he has a plan . . . or he's dead. *Gods, don't let Otter be dead!* Whatever my ambivalence about the Guardian and his choice of allies, I know that without him, the Knowledge Seekers have no chance. None of us do.

Twiss slithers over the rock-strewn valley floor like a lizard. She circles the shouting, struggling men trying to subdue Aidan, slipping past them, nearer and nearer to Otter's motionless body.

I focus on my own target, try to copy the thief, and glide almost silently over the ground. Aidan belts out another round of oaths, and under the cover of his outburst I dash around the fire, towards the leader of the Maker soldiers. The leader's whole body shouts smugness. Suddenly, he steps around the fire, towards Otter. I jump out of the way as he strides past me.

He walks straight towards Twiss, who is crouched beside Otter. She glances up at the last moment and rolls sideways, just dodging the boot that slams into Otter's side. Otter grunts and, despite my anger at the brutality of the act, I feel a rush of relief: He's alive!

Twiss springs to her feet, still holding my knife in her hand. I can feel her fury from here. She gazes longingly at a spot between the leader's shoulder blades, then stops herself to look a question at me. I shake my head. *Please Time, let Twiss obey me this once!* If she attacks the leader, the whole group of Makers will know there's a magic-user here. I'll have to kill them all. The idea fills me with cold horror.

Twiss backs away with grudging steps, scowling at the leader.

'Get him on his feet!' The leader nods to the men standing over Otter. 'He's coming round. I want to question him before I kill him.' He turns to smile at Aidan, who stops struggling and stares at his captor. His nose is bleeding, his face white with rage beneath the smears of blood.

The man who kicked Otter speaks: 'You're going to live a little while longer, Aidan, son of Fergal. But you will wish you had died here tonight like your friend.'

Aidan ignores the threat: 'Where's Donal, you bastard? You're in the pay of the mages, aren't you? When Donal finds out he'll cut your privates off and shove them down your throat!

'You lot!' Aidan shouts at the metal-clad Maker soldiers: 'Are you just going to stand there and let Mercer betray our people? You know what the mages will do to the city if they get past the Wall!'

The soldiers stare back at him, stony-faced.

'They're mine.' Mercer smiles. 'I didn't get to be a general by trusting the wrong men.' He gestures at Otter, now dangling between two soldiers who hold him by the arms. He seems unconscious. 'You don't seem to realise that we have entered a new age. We are at peace with the magic-users. The Archmage of Asphodel came crawling to *us*, pleading for peace with Maker-kind!

'I only have to hand you and this rebellious slave over to the Archmage to prove that I'm the man he wants to do business with. I've met his representative and he assures me that Archmage Benedict will prove a valuable ally.'

Aidan's bitter laugh bounces off the Wall and echoes through the darkness. 'If you think you can trust Benedict – trust any mage – then you're a bigger fool than I thought.'

'And you are a trouble-maker. You, little boy, are a family disgrace. No one will miss you. Fergal is well rid of you. He's an old man, mind. Far too old to be running Gengst.' Mercer's voice grows taunting. 'Too old to give that pretty wife of his what she needs.' He makes an obscene gesture.

Aidan lunges forward with a strangled cry. One of the soldiers punches him in the kidneys. Aidan collapses with a grunt of pain and is dragged back to standing.

'You've got the only balls in the family, Aidan the Clock, but you aren't going to get the chance to use them.' Mercer moves forward, grabs Aidan's crotch in a mailed fist. Aidan hisses in pain.

I lunge forward but Twiss darts in front of me and grabs my arm. I take a deep breath and struggle for control. She's right: we need to find out how far my father has infiltrated the Maker defences.

The taunting voice continues: 'I think Fergal will die soon. Then the lovely Naveen will need comforting. With the

Archmage of Asphodel as my ally, Gengst will belong to me, as will your mother. Your big brother isn't a problem: he does what he's told, like a good soldier. But you . . . you've always been a wee pain in the arse. A spoilt little mummy's boy, and clever with it. You, I can do without. You were never meant to show up back here alive in any case. You've been a dead man ever since your father sold you to the mages. You just haven't had the good sense to lie down and rot.'

I'm not watching Mercer now, nor even Aidan. Something – some current in the air, some not-quite-heard sound – has made me turn to stare at the Guardian. Slowly, he lifts his head to half-mast and winks at Twiss, who is crouched nearby. Otter's gaze shifts to Mercer. Then his eyes slide past the Maker general and lock on mine. It's as though a bucket of water – icy and hot at the same time – has been upended over my head. I feel oddly calm. I hold Bruin's sword ready in my hand, its point directed at Mercer's back. Otter nods, the slightest downward movement. He's ready.

I glide silently across the camp until I'm right behind the general, check that no one else is looking in my direction, then step out of Elsewhere, grab Mercer's shoulder and push the point of my sword against the patch of neck bulging below his helmet flange.

'Don't move!' I shout. Two of his men lunge forward and I dig the tip of the sword into Mercer's neck just enough to make blood ooze up and begin to drip down the Maker's neck. Mercer yelps and the men freeze. 'Tell them to back off or you're dead!'

'Do it! Back off! The mad bitch means it!' Mercer's voice is shrill. His shoulder trembles beneath my hand but I feel his body tense in preparation. I read his emotions as clearly as if he speaks them aloud: *Just a woman. I can take the sword off her.*

As he starts to coil his muscles, I stick the soles of his boots to the ground. I tell the leather to grow into the stone of the valley floor, then step aside as Mercer attempts to whirl around.

'What the –?' The general flails his arms like the sails of a windmill. I release his boots as he overbalances and topples onto his back. Before he can move, I stamp a foot onto his chest and shove the tip of Bruin's sword under the Maker's chin. His head strains away from the touch of metal, and his swearing stops as though by magic. The rush of footsteps from behind stops too. Good. I don't want to use more magic if I can help it. I'm hoping even Mercer hasn't realised what happened.

'Clumsy,' I say. 'Lost your balance?'

Before he can answer, I push the sword forward just enough to make him gasp. 'Tell your men to lay down their iron or you're dead, General Mercer.' I retract the sword tip a fraction, never taking my eyes from his. Sweat pimples on his cheeks; his lips are pulled back from his teeth in a grimace of fear and frustration. If he could kill me with a thought, I'd be dead. But I'm the only one here who can do that.

'Obey her!' Mercer gasps. 'Do what she says!'

I give him a chilly smile. I don't like this man. His emotions are slimier than anyone I've met since Aluid. I sense that he hates me for being a woman. I've never encountered these feelings before in anyone. At least, not this intensely: it's like Hammeth at Tabitha's trial, only a hundred times worse. Mercer must be mentally unbalanced. His betrayal of Aidan; his plot to seize power; his liaison with Benedict, which no sane Maker could surely stomach. Yes: the man is mad.

Two of the soldiers standing near Otter must have come to the same conclusion. They suddenly go for their swords. Quickly, I stick the blades to the insides of their scabbards, and as they tug away fruitlessly Otter lurches upright with a hair-raising yell. He flings off the two men holding his arms. One of these pulls his weapon free before I can stop him and advances on Otter, arm raised to take a sideways swipe at the Guardian's neck.

Twiss darts forward and tosses my knife to Otter. The Guardian crouches low in a pirouette, graceful as a dancer. He spins beneath the hacking sword, arms outstretched, and slices open the belly of his attacker. The man collapses with a scream, entrails spilling onto the ground in a foam of blood.

The man's screams dwindle to thick, bewildered moans. The other soldiers back away from their writhing companion, their eyes locked on Otter, who grabs the dying man's sword and crouches in a fighting stance, sword and knife reaching out in deadly welcome. One by one, the soldiers raise their hands in a gesture of surrender. But they continue to back away.

'Stop where you are!' I shout. 'Or your general dies!'

If anything, the soldiers retreat more quickly. Now the men holding Aidan by the arms let him go and back away too, arms raised. Why isn't Otter doing anything? But he merely straightens, lowers his weapons, and watches them go. Doesn't he realise we can't let them get away to tell my father's people where we are?

'Stop!' I shout again. 'Stand still!'

As if at a silent signal, all eight of them turn tail and run into the night, scattering like startled rabbits. *Pestilence!* I'll have to stop them myself. But how? They've scattered in different directions.

'Otter!' I cry. 'What do we do now? Otter!' I whirl around. *What is wrong with the man? Is his brain hurt after all?* Otter meets my outraged face with a slow smile. Then he puts two fingers in his mouth and shrills forth a whistle that shrieks through the night and bounces off the Wall of the Makers.

At the sound, Mercer writhes sideways, batting at my sword with a clenched fist. I kick his hand away from the blade and stamp my foot so hard into his stomach that I drive the wind from his lungs. As he lies gasping for air, I push Bruin's blade against the underside of his chin. Blood wells up and begins to trickle down his neck. The Maker general's eyes grow wide. I can almost see him try to melt into the ground, to get away from the sharp metal nicking the skin of his neck.

'Please . . . please, don't kill me!' he gasps. 'Let me go. I'm rich. I'll give everything to you! You'll be wealthy beyond your wildest dreams. You can have anything. *Anything!* Just . . .'

'Shut up!' I hiss. The sight of his sweating, gasping face makes me feel sick. I look up and Mercer gasps in pain as my arm jerks in surprise. Groups of Tribute soldiers – Otter's soldiers – are stalking through the darkness towards us. In the fading light of the dying bonfire, I can see that they herd the escaped Maker soldiers before them like straying sheep. All eight have been captured. Relief makes my shoulders sag, and once more Mercer whimpers.

I ignore him. Twiss catches my eye: grins. She's no longer in Elsewhere. She sits on a boulder in plain sight, watching the action as if we were strolling players at a fair.

I throw an accusing look at Otter. 'You had a trap set all along? Why didn't you tell me? I risked . . . Twiss and I . . . Oh, *pestilence*, Otter!'

He shrugs, but the faintest shadow of a grin remains on his face. 'You don't think I trusted the general, do you? I keep my ears open. Mercer has a bit of a reputation –'

But before he can say another word, a figure barrels forward, pushing past Otter.

'Aidan! No!'

Aidan doesn't answer. He doesn't even look at me. He just lunges for my sword hand. I leap backwards and hide the sword behind my back. My eyes meet the Maker's furious glare. We don't speak. Aidan stops advancing. Stands, panting, furious. The look in his eyes is bruising. He doesn't ask for the sword: he knows I won't give it to him. Instead he turns to Otter, who is standing, arms folded across his chest, watching us.

'Give me your knife, Otter.' Aidan's face is white and strained, but his voice is oddly calm. 'I'm going to kill this filthy traitor.'

Mercer squeals, rolls onto his belly and tries to wriggle away in the dirt. Aidan turns and swiftly kicks the general in the side so that the man curls up like a slug that's been poked with a stick.

'You're mistaken, Aidan,' Otter says. 'You want the general alive and well. He's your seal of safe passage into Gengst.'

'What?' Aidan puts the heel of his boot on Mercer's head, slowly pushes the man's face into the dirt. Just as I'm about to intervene, Aidan stops pushing. He speaks without moving his eyes from the general: 'What rubbish are you talking, Guardian? The man is mine. His life is forfeit.'

Mercer manages a muffled groan of protest.

'Kill him and your best chance of getting home in one piece dies with him. Your choice, of course.' Otter's tone is faintly ironic. He stands, arms crossed, as though nothing that has just happened is of any interest to him. Infuriating, arrogant man!

'Please explain what you mean,' I snap. 'Mercer works for the Archmage. He's not going to suddenly help us get inside Gengst.'

'Oh, I think he will.' Otter motions to two of his Tribute soldiers. 'Secure this one, and take great care of him. I need him alive and in one piece.'

The Tributes hurry forward and, after a moment's hesitation, Aidan steps back and frowns at Otter. 'Go on then, if you have a plan. I'm willing to wait to kill the bastard. For a little while anyway.'

The Tributes yank Mercer to his feet and tie his arms behind his back. The Maker general doesn't struggle as they lead him away. His face is ashen and his nose bloody. I sense utter defeat, laced with bitter hatred. He's still dangerous, this man. Perhaps Aidan is right and the general is safer dead.

'Go on then,' Aidan says, once the Tributes are out of earshot. 'How exactly is Mercer going to provide us with safe passage? He'd die first.'

'You're wrong. That's just what he wouldn't do,' Otter says. 'You make the mistake of imagining other men think and feel as you do. It's you who are going to have to die, Aidan of Gengst.'

7

The Wall of the Makers. All the lonely years of my childhood I imagined it. Each night Sorrow rescued me. Her great wings beat to the rhythm of my heart as she carried me over the desolate plains to the Wall and the snow-shining cities of the Makers . . . where Swift waited.

Now – even though the cold breeze scours my face – I can't quite believe that the cliff of stone rearing up out of the land is not the stuff of my dreams.

We have been winding upwards through the foothills for nearly an hour, our path angling ever closer to the Wall. We trudge through light-speckled groves of birch and alder. If I was flying in a bird, I would look down from the wind-tossed sky to see the sun glint on the armour of a dozen Maker soldiers, their progress slowed by a stretcher which is carried by four of their company. The stretcher is cobbled together out of a blanket tied to a frame of birch saplings stripped of twigs and leaves and bound with rope. It bears the blood-stained body of Aidan, youngest son of Fergal, Lord Mayor of Gengst-on-the-Wall.

But I am not flying. I am earthbound, and I march with the rest. My hand rests on the side of the litter and I gaze from time to time at its contents. But unlike the others, I walk invisibly in Elsewhere. My eyes scan, my ears strain, searching for any hint of threat.

The trees thin to a fringe of leafless trunks, then stop altogether. The grass and scrub becomes blackened earth. The Makers fire the land to leave no hiding place for besiegers. Yet, even though this earth has been scorched for generations, I can see a few clumps of grass breaking through the hard crust, evidence of Benedict's false truce.

Our stately progress brings us to the top of a long shallow hill. As one, the whole procession halts. Taken unawares, I almost barge into the soldier in front of me. Swearing silently, I regain my balance and peer over the nearest shoulder.

The Wall is a massive cliff of tightly mortared blocks of golden sandstone, peppered with hard bluestone dug from the mountains. It clings to the sharp dragon spines of the Northern Mountains, falling and twisting from horizon to horizon. Its snaking length is punctuated by fortified towers. I glimpse the rooftops of Gengst-on-the-Wall, and my heartbeat stutters at the bittersweet sight of Aidan's home, which gave him as hostage to the enemy.

An enormous gatehouse marks the only way into the city by foot. The gatehouse is overhung by a defensive platform jutting out on stone corbels and windowed with arrow-slits. As our procession begins to climb down the hill, a bell starts to toll in warning. Still we march in slow, measured steps towards the gate. I retreat more firmly into Elsewhere, trying to ignore my heart pounding against my ribs. I glance once more at Aidan's body lying unmoving on the litter, his bloodstained clothes, his pale face. I must not make a single mistake, or the violence perpetrated on him – on all of us – will never be avenged.

Human voices join the warning bell, shouting down from the platform over the gatehouse. I look up and see bristling iron-tipped shafts pointed at us from every arrow-slit. The wooden heads of catapults crouch like giants beside each crenellation, ready to fling stone, broken glass and metal shards. Or worst of all: demon's breath – molten fire that clings to whatever it touches and cannot be extinguished by water. The thought of it makes my skin crawl.

Our procession halts on a bit of level ground a double arrow's flight from the gate. The soldier beside Mercer raises a pole and a standard flutters in cracks and flaps in the cold wind: a blue banner showing a trowel overlaid with an arrow. Overhead, the bronze mouth of the bell bellows note after note until I think the distant glaciers that stab like shark's teeth against the ice-blue sky will crack and slide into avalanche. My ears ring with the sound.

In between the peels I hear the sound of horses' iron shoes clattering on the causeway above us . . . trumpets . . . the shouting of male voices. And through the grilled front of a massive portcullis I see the ancient iron straps and black oak of the legendary Gate of Destiny, which guards the only road to pierce the whole of the Wall. A gate which, before my father's truce, legend claims had never been opened. Now, slowly and with a great groaning of wood and screeching of iron, the portcullis begins to rise. I hold my breath as it inches upwards. The city of Gengst is opening its mouth to welcome home the traitor, General Mercer.

The portcullis clunks up out of sight, lifted by machinery I cannot even begin to imagine, but which Philip, leader of the Knowledge Seekers, would probably kill to examine. Beyond the gate I see twin doors of oak, wide enough to let six horses ride abreast, studded and strapped with heavy black iron. They begin to swing inward, to the creaking of enormous hinges.

The doors open onto the stone throat of a leviathan. Torchlight glimmers on dozens of metal men, on spikes and arrow tips, metal swords and shields. The soldiers shout and gesture at us, and our party shuffles forward, the litter bearers taking fresh grip. We pace, one behind the other, into the mouth of Gengst, until all dozen of us are inside the gatehouse. Iron men surround us, hands on sword hilts.

The chamber is round, close-roofed with stone supported by a circle of great stone ribs rising from all sides to meet over our heads. The weight of the fortress presses down and I clearly see the holes in the ceiling where boiling water, burning ash and fiery demon's breath could pour down on us at any moment. I can almost see the soldiers overhead, waiting for the order to be given.

I feel panic well up and press numb fingers on Aidan's hands where they lie crossed upon his breast. The huge doors swing inward behind us with the screech of a giant in its death throes. And clang shut.

It's a moment I never thought would come. *I* – Zara of Asphodel, mage and adept, spy and traitor – I am inside a Maker city! I barely recognise how extraordinary the moment is before it's gone. On the opposite side of the room, a second iron portcullis slowly rises. We face a pair of iron-bound doors twin to the ones we have just passed through. A miniature door – a wicket – is set into the right-hand door. The wicket is barely as wide as a man's shoulders, and so short that most adults would have to bend to pass through.

A quartet from the iron soldiers separate from the rest to position themselves either side of this wicket, which opens to reveal an elderly grey-haired man in what I recognise as courtly Maker garb: high boots, tight woollen trousers and a long elaborate tunic over a green shirt which has full sleeves slashed in a diagonal pattern to show the yellow fabric beneath.

The newcomer persuades his barrel chest and belly through the opening. His bright blue eyes fasten on our party. I see a look of recognition as he spies Mercer, but his gaze dismisses the general and slides past to fasten onto the stretcher and its contents. The old man's face pales. His eyes shoot back to pierce Mercer. And the hawk-like fierceness in them sends a shock through my entire body.

I step carefully away from the litter. I know who the grandee is. He has come to meet the man who promised to bring his son safely home. He is Fergal, head of the Council of Gengst. Aidan's father.

The chamber seems to grow dimmer. Total silence as Fergal the Clock stands, white-faced, staring at the litter. Then he groans, and slowly walks forward until he is standing beside Aidan. He stares down at his son's still face, then closes his eyes. Without opening his eyes or moving a muscle, the old man speaks: '*Mercer!*'

'Father, hear me.' One of the iron soldiers springs forward. He wears a coquette of ribbons on his helmet. It must be

Donal, Aidan's older brother. Donal bends his head to his father. 'We must take Aidan home. To Mother. That first of all. Then, when the rites have been said and my brother's soul sent on its journey . . . then we can question the general and find out how my brother died.'

Donal pulls off his helmet and gazes over his father's head at the litter. He's taller than Aidan, much taller than their father. Nearly as tall as Otter. He has a long, oval face with pale ivory skin in striking contrast to his black hair, dark arched brows and neat beard. He's an extraordinarily beautiful man, I realise. He looks nothing like Aidan.

'Naveen can wait to cry over her son's body,' his father replies. 'I want answers. *Mercer!*' Fergal has recovered already. The old man turns to confront the Maker general, who stands – as he has since Fergal's arrival – head bowed and hands clasped in front of him.

Mercer raises a white and sweaty face. His eyes are wide and staring. They look anywhere, everywhere, but at Fergal. Or the litter.

The tall soldier who stands close behind him speaks: 'The general cannot answer your questions. My fault, I fear. I told him that if he spoke so much as a single word until I gave him permission, I would kill him.' The man's sword hand is resting on his weapon's hilt; the other now reaches up to grip Mercer's shoulder. 'But now that we are safely in your city, I'm sure the general would welcome a long discussion with you, Fergal the Clockmaker.'

With each word the soldier speaks, I feel confusion and alarm well up in the Maker soldiers who surround us.

'You might find it interesting to ask General Mercer about his recent past,' the calm voice continues. 'In particular, his dealings with the Archmage Benedict and how he plotted to betray your son, to overthrow yourself and deliver your city to certain destruction by mageki—'

The stunned silence breaks and the stone chamber erupts in a confusion of shouts and swearing.

'*Silence!* Be silent, I tell you!' As the hubbub reluctantly dies, the old man stares at the speaker. His eyes narrow and he says, in a soft, threatening voice, '*Overthrow me? Deliver my city?*' The old man raises his head contemptuously, reminding me of Aidan. 'Who are you? What is this plot you speak of?'

'You must ask your general.'

Fergal's eyes dart to the cowering general. 'Mercer! What does your man mean?'

Mercer pants, his eyes look wildly for escape. He raises his hands to block his face, revealing leather strips binding his wrists. He shouts: 'They are outlaws! Mage-lovers. They have killed my men and taken me hostage. It's a plot to breach the Wall. Kill them! Kill them quick!'

I hold my breath. In this moment the Fates will decide all our futures.

Donal's right hand darts towards his sword hilt. I curse as I prepare to bind the blade to its scabbard. Any whiff of magic will be disastrous. If my identity is discovered, my life will be worth less than a flea's. But Donal seems to think better of his action, and crosses his arms instead. *Thank the gods!*

'Who are you, soldier?' Aidan's brother addresses Mercer's captor. 'Identify yourself. I don't recognise your voice.'

'I'm not Mercer's man.' Without releasing his hold on the general, the man reaches up his free hand and removes his helmet. A broad face with wide-set amber-coloured eyes surveys Fergal and his son. 'My name is Otter. I'm the leader of the rebel Tribute army. We're here to offer our alliance in the fight against the mages. And these aren't Mercer's soldiers; they're mine.'

'He's the Archmage's own Guardian!' shouts Mercer, who is wriggling, trying to free himself from Otter's restraining grip. 'Kill him. Kill them all!'

'Take them!' shouts Donal, his hand flying to his sword hilt. I've no choice: I order the metal of the blade to stick to its wooden scabbard and gather my concentration for the battle that must now be waged, my eyes seeking out Otter, looking for his signal.

'Hold on, big brother!'

The body on the litter lurches upright.

Donal's hand drops from his sword belt. Fergal swings round with an oath.

'Please don't attack my friends,' Aidan says as he swings two blood-stained legs over the side of his death bier, and jumps lightly to the ground. He grins at the expressions on the faces of his father and brother. 'They've saved my life more than once, so it would seem rather ungrateful, don't you think?'

The white paste on Aidan's face glows ghoulishly; rust-coloured blood stains drip from chest to thigh.

'A-Aidan?' Fergal the Clockmaker's jaw drops. He stares at his son and his red face turns as white as Aidan's. 'Are you alive, son . . . or the walking dead? Your face . . .'

'Just paint, Father.' Aidan grins and wipes away a smear of white with a sleeve. 'If I hadn't played dead until I was safely inside the Wall, I would be dead in truth. I have some news that Benedict of Asphodel doesn't want you to hear and, given the stakes, he's bound to have more than one traitor lying in wait for me.'

Aidan wipes the rest of his face clean, then steps forward, until he stands face to face with his father. The old man shakes his head. 'It can't be!'

Aidan reaches out and grips Fergal's right hand. 'Living flesh, Father, not a ghost.'

Fergal reaches a trembling finger to touch Aidan's cheek. 'Living flesh indeed.'

Suddenly, Aidan drops his father's hand and steps back, gazing round the room. His voice cuts through the murmur of confusion: 'The truce is a sham!' he shouts. 'The Archmage wanted one of Fergal's sons as a hostage for the foulest of reasons: Benedict planned to send my body home without my soul in it.'

Aidan's voice is bitter. I know he's remembering Benedict invading his mind and taking control of his body – an assault that damanged his love for me almost past mending. Now he addresses his father: 'He would have walked in here inside the shell of your son. He planned to murder you and every member of the council. With the leaders of Gengst dead, his next deed would have been to destroy the Gate and thus surrender the city to its enemies. The armies of all magekind are gathered in the plains. We passed them on our journey here. Do you believe me now?'

Fergal's face turns muddy grey. He stares open-mouthed at his youngest son: 'I can't believe . . . Surely . . .' The old man retreats one uncertain step from Aidan. Then, slowly, he turns his head. Looks at Mercer. The general is shaking so hard only Otter's grip keeps him upright.

'N-no! He lies!' Mercer stutters. 'Benedict promised . . .' And he breaks off, his eyes wide with terror. The general's feet give way and he collapses onto his knees. Otter releases him, steps back.

A muttered oath. Donal lunges towards the prisoner, his face a mask of pure hatred. Aidan grabs his shoulder. 'No, Brother. He's mine. Bring the bastard here, Otter, if you will.' Aidan's voice is deadly. 'I want to see his face when he confesses.'

The look in Aidan's eyes makes me shudder. I try to close down his emotions: hatred stops my mind thinking clearly and I need all my wits about me.

Otter tugs Mercer to his feet and pushes the cringing general towards us. As soon as the Guardian moves, half a dozen of the Maker soldiers draw their swords. Their eyes are trained on Otter, and I can see they remember Mercer's accusation. Guardians are hated and feared by the non-magic nearly as much as the archmages they serve.

My body tenses in preparation. I take a firmer grip on Elsewhere in case I have to intervene.

'Put your weapons away! *Now!* These people are my friends!' Aidan roars.

'Do as he says!' Fergal orders, and the soldiers lower their arms.

Mercer seems to shrink inside his own skin. His eyes flick from face to face, glazed with hopeless terror. I pray that Aidan will let his father deal with the traitor.

'Perhaps it would be better for this interview to take place in private, Aidan,' Otter says, tugging the general upright as his legs seem to fail him again. 'Before witnesses, other councillors, perhaps?'

'Oh, he'll have a trial all right, Guardian. Don't worry!' Aidan's eyes narrow as he looks at the cringing prisoner. 'Before the entire council. Before the very men who trussed me up and gave me to Benedict of Asphodel! And he can tell them first-hand of Benedict's treachery and of their own gullible stupidity!' Aidan throws a contemptuous glance at his father, who winces.

'You'll spill your guts before you die, won't you, my friend?' Aidan reaches out and tugs the general's head up by the hair. The man's eyes veer wildly from side to side. He wails: a bubbling, hissing sound that makes my skin crawl. Then, with a superhuman effort, Mercer tugs free of Aidan.

Both Aidan and Otter lunge for their prisoner, but the general veers with the intuition of the hunted animal and dodges past Donal.

Aidan's brother draws his sword and plunges the blade deep into the general's back. The sword penetrates clothing and flesh with a soft sucking noise. I hear a bone snap and the point of Donal's blade explodes out of the Mercer's chest. The general lurches to a sudden stop as a giant hand has grabbed him out of life. Mercer is transfixed, spitted like a kitchen fowl. For a second, even Time does not breathe. Then:

'Donal! What have you done?' roars Fergal.

Aidan lunges forward and tugs his brother away from the dying man. Mercer staggers from side to side, miraculously still on his feet. His hands clutch at the point of the blade as though trying to push it back into his body. His mouth opens as if to scream. I hear a wet gurgle. A fountain of blood spouts from Mercer's open mouth. His eyes glaze and finally relinquish their look of horror. The flow of blood from his mouth slows to a trickle. With a sigh, the general collapses onto his face.

A puddle of blood wells from beneath the body and slowly spreads, crimson and sticky, across the stones. I am attacked by an onslaught of emotions from all sides.

'You didn't need to kill him, Donal!' shouts Fergal. 'There was nowhere for him to run!'

Aidan raises a shocked face to stare at his brother. His eyes flare blue hot with rage. He clenches his left fist, marches forward, and lands a haymaker punch on Donal that knocks the bigger man onto his back. 'Mercer told me you were a fool!' Aidan hisses.

His brother scrambles to his feet, rubbing a bruised jaw. 'I'm sorry.' Donal's voice is thick with emotion. His pale cheeks are flushed red as he turns to his father. 'My shame, Father.' He bows his head. 'The bastard betrayed you . . . betrayed us all! He tried to kill my brother! I lost my head.' The words choke off, and Donal squares his shoulders and stands to attention. 'I gladly accept whatever discipline you order.'

I look from Donal to Aidan, who is still shaking with rage. Then catch Otter's eye. The Guardian's shoulders rise in an almost imperceptible shrug. But his face is grim.

Fergal shakes his head. Sighs. 'What is done cannot be undone, Donal. Your hastiness may have lost us invaluable intelligence. Enough! Have your men clear that thing away.'

He gestures at Mercer's body. 'I will take your brother to see his mother. Come, my son. You must clean yourself up before Naveen has sight of you.'

'Otter and his soldiers.' Aidan frowns at his father as he gestures to the rest of his party. His anger is fading and I sense his eagerness to see his mother. 'Otter leads the rebel forces. He is to be treated with the utmost respect.'

'It is so ordered,' Fergal says. 'Sir.' The clockmaker studies Otter with curiosity. 'I hope you will join us in Council once Aidan has seen his mother. I will call a special meeting to discuss the disturbing news you bring.'

'Donal!' Fergal turns to frown at his elder son, who has been listening, pale-faced and silent. 'You and I will talk later tonight. For now, take General Otter's men and quarter them in the garrison. Decent quarters, mind. And see they're fed.' The old man turns to stiffly incline his head at the Guardian. 'Gentle sir, I trust you will come with us now and accept the hospitality of my house. It is little enough thanks for the gift of my son, alive and safely home.'

'Thank you.' Otter glances sideways at me, and a quick jerk of his head tells me I am to follow him. I dodge through the men striding to and fro. As I follow the others, I wonder how long I'll have to remain invisible and undetected in Elsewhere. The danger may be over for Aidan and Otter; it has just begun for me.

As Fergal leads us towards the wicket door, Aidan quickly glances around and I know that he's wondering where I am – if I'm safe. The Maker turns back around with a frown of frustration and follows his father out the gate. Otter ducks low and disappears after them. I squeeze after Otter, pressing close behind him before the gate is closed. And then, for the first time since the Maker Wars – since all magic-users were exterminated in the North Lands three generations ago – a mage enters the city of Gengst-on-the-Wall.

8

The golden city of Gengst is soot-tarnished. Smoke from countless chimneys is chased through the streets by the north wind. Everywhere I look, I see tall narrow houses lining cobbled streets. Every wall is black-crusted and scabby from the gritty smoke. The city stinks of firerock. As if conjured by magic, a crowd gathers as we step foot onto the streets of Gengst. Strangers everywhere. Staring. Pointing and muttering. Pale faced. Dressed in Maker wool and leather.

It's easy to see who is poor, who rich: the puffy hats they wear are made either of drab-coloured wool or brightly dyed silk and feathers. Poor or not, the women wear long robes corseted at the waist rather than leggings. The men are dressed like Aidan: boots over the knee, tight leggings, woollen jackets. From all sides, the sharp vowels of northern voices buffet us: 'Out-folk! Who are they? Is it true, they are southern rebels? Is that the boy returned? He looks like a ghoul! Is he a dead soul or living?'

My heart thuds with the knowledge that every one of these strangers hates and fears mages. My invisibility seems far too thin and fragile. I strengthen my grip on Elsewhere and squeeze as close to Aidan as I dare. The journey to his father's house seems endless, but I know it's only a few minutes before we enter an avenue of grand houses, wide and tall, each separated from its neighbours by high walls. It's a proud, preening street, and the crowd seems to know that they are not welcome: they remain in the plaza.

Fergal leads us towards the largest house, which sits in solitary grandeur at the end of the avenue. We climb the broad sweeping steps to stand on a porticoed porch before a tall black door. The door is opened at once by a unsmiling old man in a sober suit of green broadcloth. When he sees Aidan his eyes grow white circles of surprise.

'M-master Aidan!' he stammers.

'Don't stand there catching flies, Frip!' says Fergal. 'Let us in, man!'

Frip snaps his mouth shut and manages to bow, swing the door wide and usher us in all at once. I slip through the door hard on Otter's heels but the doorman still manages to graze my elbow in his eagerness to shut out the world.

I sidle to a safe place against a wall, rubbing the bruise and staring around me. Never have I seen a house like this! The hall is as large as that in my father's palazzo, but there are no open archways, no large windows to let in light and air. Every door leading off this hall is shut. It is a gloomy cave of a place, lit by an extravagance of candles in glass mantles. These hang on iron chains from a ceiling the like of which I have never seen. I forget to be careful as I stare up at it, open-mouthed. The ceiling is made of white plaster moulded and decorated with long garlands of fruit and foliage.

Narrow panels of carved wood cover the walls, alternating with mirrors of silvered glass in gilt frames, which seem to catch and hoard the candlelight in their depths rather than reflect it back into the room. And on every side, against each wall, on every piece of furniture, clocks tick. Tall narrow clocks line the walls, the glass in their wooden bellies displaying swaying pendulums. Smaller clocks with jewel-like mechanisms beneath glass domes crouch on every surface, ticking with mindless persistence.

Time's grace! The entire house is a shrine to the god. Frip takes a round mallet and bangs it onto a huge bronze disc that hangs in a wooden frame. The resulting noise – like a huge bell in a clock tower – wakes me to my danger. I leap out of the way as a trio of servants bustles into the hall from a door hidden in the panelling behind me. They wear dark green broadcloth like the doorman and, once in the room, line up to gaze with respectful enquiry at Fergal. I see the two men each give a startled glance at Aidan and his bloodstained clothes before their faces go masklike. The third servant, a young woman, plump and blond, gasps as she spots him. Her round red mouth falls open and her pink face grows even pinker.

'Well, Boots, your young master is home,' Fergal says jovially to the oldest man. The grey-haired servant nods and bestows a brief, serious smile on Aidan.

'Yes, Master. The mistress will be overjoyed.'

'Indeed, but she mustn't see him looking like this: the boy would frighten Death herself. Take him away to his room and have a bath drawn. Come to my office first, son, once you're dressed. I'll have food brought to her drawing room; I assume you're half-famished.'

Aidan gives another quick glance around the hall, a faint frown of frustration between his brows. I wish I could touch his hand to tell him I'm here, safe in his house. Instead, I watch him follow the servant down the hall and out of sight up the wide oak stairs.

'Worm, this is Sir Otter.' Fergal addresses the remaining male servant, a thin stooped man with white-blond hair and colourless skin. 'I put him in your special charge. He is an honoured guest. Put him in the blue room, and see that he has everything he needs.'

'Sir!' Worm bows to the clockmaker; turns and bows to Otter. 'If you would follow me, sir?' Without waiting for an answer, Worm heads for the stairs.

Otter nods his thanks to Fergal, shoots an imperative glance at me. He doesn't need to worry: there's no way I'm staying here in this strange house on my own. Clinging to Elsewhere, I dart between the Makers after Otter.

Worm floats up the stairs, through doors and down corridors so quickly that Otter and I have to trot to keep up. In my anxiety not to be left behind, I'm almost treading on the Guardian's heels. When the servant comes to an abrupt stop outside one of the countless panelled wooden doors on the second floor, Otter is forced to stop so suddenly that I bump into him. It's like running face-first into a leather wall. I grab his shoulders to keep from falling as Worm pushes open the door and turns back to the Guardian with a smile at once superior and servile.

'Your room, sir. I shall order hot water, clean clothes and a suitable luncheon to be brought at once. Is there anything else your honour requires?' His eyes are glazed with humble-seeming propriety but I sense it hides a sharp curiosity.

'Only that you bring plenty of food,' Otter replies. 'We've been marching long and hard through the night.'

'Certainly, sir.' Worm steps back beside the open door and stands, staring straight ahead. Oh no! Worm is waiting to shut the door after the Guardian. Quickly, I edge round Otter, gingerly step over the threshold and enter the room first. As I put weight on my right foot, the floorboard creaks. *Pestilence!*

'Old houses talk in their sleep.' Otter's voice is casual as he steps forward. He shoves me further into the room. *Damn the Guardian!* I half-fall, half-leap to the safety of a thick rug, and hear Worm's bland: 'Indeed, sir.'

The door shuts, the latch clicks.

I sink down where I stand and cradle my head on my knees. 'Thank heavens!' I moan.

And am rewarded with a swift kick to my backside. I look around, outraged, to see Otter glaring at me. He jerks his head towards the door. Then, in a passable imitation of my voice, only a tone lower, he mutters rather loudly: 'Thank heavens for some rest at last. But ye gods, I would murder for food, a hot bath and a pretty woman!'

I stare at him. And then I hear it: the soft pattering of footsteps heading back down the corridor. Worm indeed!

'The sneaking little spy!' I hiss. But only after quickly sending a strand of consciousness to check that the corridor is indeed empty.

'Impatience will kill you, Zara, if you don't take care.'

'A pretty woman?' I ask archly. I have no desire to be lectured by the Guardian about my carelessness. He's far too aware of his own perfection as it is. 'You would do murder, would you?'

Otter crosses his arms, looks at me and sighs. He doesn't answer my question. 'You'd best come out of Elsewhere while you can.'

I do as he suggests, and lie back and stretch out on the rug. 'Bliss!' I sigh, as I feel my muscles begin to relax at last. 'I've never had to do that so long before. I'm shattered.'

'Hmm,' he grunts as he settles down on the floor beside me, cross-legged. I look up to see him studying me, his light brown eyes thoughtful.

'Well?'

'Worm. Interesting name.'

'It suits him. Wriggling, sneaky creature,' I say unfairly, for my impression of Worm is that he has a talent for stillness. 'But that's not what you mean . . .' I lurch upright, heart pounding. 'Do you think he's a spy? *For my father?*'

'I still wonder if you wouldn't be safer with my people in the plains. But as it proved, we did need your magic to keep hot tempers from hasty actions until Fergal and his people could be brought to accept the truth of Mercer's treachery. But don't ever forget that you're only safe as long as you stay in Elsewhere! Mercer won't be Benedict's only spy in Gengst. We need a long talk with Aidan about his city as soon as possible.'

'Donal was a fool to kill Mercer.' Bloody images flicker in front of my eyes. I shudder and push them back into the dark.

'Possibly.' Otter shrugs. 'The man would have died soon enough. And suffered torture as a surety that he told all he knew. I doubt that Mercer would have disclosed much more. Benedict would never be foolish enough to allow his creatures to know of each other's existence.'

I lie back down. 'Hmm.' I let the worries float away and wonder instead where Aidan is, what he's doing, if he's asleep. The long march here, the long time in Elsewhere, the stress of the past few hours drag me quickly towards sleep. As I drift away, I'm aware of Otter sitting silently beside me, lost in thought.

I wake to softness and warmth. I'm in a bed! A proper *bed*. I haven't slept in a bed for months; nearly a year. Glorious! I feel a soft mattress, pillows cradling my head, clean warm wool against my skin. I don't want this amazing dream – if it is a dream – to end, but my stomach is grinding my belly into shreds with hunger, and I smell . . . I smell . . .

'Food!' I lurch upright and stare about me. And grab the blanket that's wrapped around me like a cocoon and pull it up to my neck, hunger forgotten.

'Otter! What th—'

'Shush! Whisper if you must talk. But it would be better if you could just keep quiet, Zara.'

He turns from where he's sitting, at an ornately carved and painted table that looks like an overgrown toy fit for a doll's house. He's clean and dressed in the Maker style: glossy black boots over the knee, mouse-coloured woollen trousers and a white linen shirt.

'I'm not wearing any clothes!' I hiss in a furious whisper.

'I know.' He takes a bite of bread. I watch his jaw slowly chewing and my belly shrieks with jealousy. Water leaks from my mouth and dribbles down my chin. I swipe at it quickly, but too late: he's seen.

Otter snorts, begins to cough. Sips from a beer mug.

'I hope it chokes you!'

He grins. And I see a person I don't recognise. It's disconcerting and I find I'm too hungry to stay angry.

'Why am I naked?'

'I wasn't putting you in my clean sheets in your dirty clothes. And you were as filthy as your clothes so I wrapped you up in a blanket. I have to sleep in that bed too, you know.' He takes another bite. Calm. Infuriating.

'Well, never mind that, I'm starving.'

'You can eat when you've bathed, Zara. Elsewhere won't stop you stinking. The servants will come back soon to clear away the bath and it'll be too late. And people might start to wonder why I'm followed around by an invisible niff.' He smiles. Again. I want to hit him.

'I did try to wake you when they brought the hot water, so you could clean up. It would have made things rather easier as I've had to shove you under the bed twice now. You do sleep soundly. Go on, the bath's over there. Water's a bit cold now, but it's still clean: I washed in the basin.'

He glances to a copper hip bath sitting in front of a roaring fire, surrounded by a clutter of water cans and towels, and a pile of discarded clothes, neatly folded. 'We'll have to hide your clothes, of course. Aidan brought some old ones of his. They're there, behind the screen. Go bathe and get dressed and then you can eat. I've saved you a bit, but I'm still hungry and if you don't hurry I can't make any promises.'

My gaze shifts from his face to the panelled screen beside the bathtub, then to the small table with the remains of a joint of ham and a loaf of bread. I lick my lips and look back at Otter. He wouldn't . . .

I secure the blanket around me, jump off the bed, scurry across the cold floor, and pull the screen in front of the bath. In a moment, the blanket is hanging over the screen and I'm easing an unwilling foot into the water.

'It's freezing!' I whisper loudly.

'It can't be colder than room temperature. Don't be a coward, Zara. This ham tastes even better than it smells. It won't last much longer.'

I groan and quickly squat down in the chilly water until I'm sitting up to my waist. I begin shivering at once. I grab the chunk of brownish soap from the dish and quickly lather up, washing my hair first. Then I stand, grab a water can and awkwardly rinse myself off. I'm shaking so badly that half the water splashes onto the floor.

'Need a hand?'

'*Piss off!*' I hiss between chattering teeth as I lurch out of the bath and stand dripping.

Another snort from the other side of the screen.

At least I remembered to whisper: Twiss would be proud of me. I hope she's behaving herself in the canyon safehold. And I wonder when I'll see her again.

I grab a towel and rub myself dry. Better. And despite nearly dying of cold, it is gorgeous to feel clean again. Hanging over a small chair, I find soft, woollen underbreeches, with dark worsted breeches to go over them. Neatly folded on the floor are long black socks, along with garters and soft leather shoes a size too big. There's a woollen undershirt just my size, a linen shirt, and a beautiful blue leather tunic to wear over it, complete with silver buttons. I dress myself more quickly than I have ever dressed, and whip out from behind the screen, tugging my damp hair back out of my face. It will frizz as it dries unless I plait it, but I don't care. I plonk down opposite Otter, carve off a chunk of ham and shove it into my mouth. And I chew. And as I chew, I smile. Bliss.

Otter laughs.

9

Two dozen voices erupt in mutters and shouts. Male voices. I press even harder into the wall behind me, until my shoulder blades complain. I am fiercely aware – as I have been ever since I set foot in this chamber – that I am the only woman in a room of men. *Why are there no women here? Surely there are female councillors, as well as male?*

Hidden in Elsewhere, I stand at the back of the large downstairs room which Fergal commandeered to serve as the emergency council chamber. It has a high plaster ceiling and walls of panelled wood, mellow with wax. I have taken refuge at the back of the room, standing between the two windows facing onto the street so their light will not cast my shadow. They stretch from ceiling to floor and let in a flood of morning sunshine which illuminates the speakers on the other side of the room as though they were on a stage.

Aidan stands on the other side of the room, across a sea of hastily arranged rows of chairs full of irate and frightened men. He has dressed carefully for his speech. His gleaming boots, spotless white shirt and black leather jerkin studded with silver look new and costly. He seems a stranger. This is his world, his home.

Aidan has just finished speaking, and the councillors don't seem to like what he had to say. Too many emotions – too much hatred and fear. I retreat further into Elsewhere and the oppression lifts.

'You have heard my son's evidence. Do you dare doubt it?' Fergal leaps to his feet from his chair in the front row. 'Mercer as much as admitted his guilt before he died.'

Aidan frowns at his father and the clockmaker sits down again.

One of the councillors stands up. 'These are serious charges. Are we to believe our newfound peace is a lie on your say-so only, young man? Our entire future is at stake here. We have an opportunity to build a new world where our sons don't have to live and die as soldiers; where our engineers can build machines of creation, not destruction; where our womenfolk no longer fear that their sons will die before they do; where girls will not go without husbands. Mercer is dead by your brother's hand! Did you kill him so he couldn't defend himself? Did you betray your bond as hostage, break the truce, and run home here to lie to us about your own cowardice? Are you, Aidan, son of Fergal the Clockmaker, the real traitor?'

The chamber erupts. Half the councillors are on their feet, shaking fists at Aidan, at each other, shouting. Aidan glares at the speaker, his blue eyes blazing contempt.

Otter warned me. He told me Aidan might not be believed. But even so, I'm aghast at such stupidity. Anything, it seems, can be believed if people wish to be blind.

The Guardian stands up, somehow managing to look even taller than he is. He walks with measured steps to the front of the room and stands beside Aidan. The sunlight throws the two men's shadows behind them onto the floor and up the panelled wall behind. The Guardian's eyes travel from face to face. He waits.

Silence seeps from the edges of the room inward until the only sound is that of breathing and the occasional nervous cough. I feel it too, pressed against the wall, my heart hammering with anxiety. This is another Otter still. One perhaps only his rebel Tribute soldiers have seen. I cannot take my eyes from his face.

'Councillors of Gengst!' The Guardian's voice rumbles through the silence. So confident. Where does he find it, this belief in himself? I shake my head, wondering again at the miracle that is my father's former Guardian, a man who survived childhood tortures and obscenities of thought and deed that would have sent most people screaming into madness.

'If you choose not to believe a child of your own city perhaps you would prefer to hear the evidence of one of the Archmage's children. Oh no,' he raises his voice to quell the shocked outcries. 'Not a child of his loins. A child created by the evil he represents. I am Otter. I was taken at the age of five from my mother and given as Tribute. All of you know of that dread tax: the child tax the mages enact on all non-magic commoners. The firstborn of every non-magic person living in the mage lands is given first into slavery and then to Death as the Tribute soldiers who fight and die on your Wall. You know about Tributes. Your business is killing them. Killing children.'

Councillors jump to their feet in protest. The outcry stutters as Otter strips off his tunic and shirt and stands, bare chested.

Silver Guardian bands encircle each muscular bicep. He turns and exhibits the round shiny white scar on his right shoulder: my father's mage mark branded into his flesh. At the sight of the silver bands and white brand, the room falls silent.

'I am Otter!' His voice rings through the room. 'I was the Guardian of Benedict, Archmage of Asphodel. He thought my mind cleansed. He believed that I was his creature. The Archmage tried to steal my mind, my soul, my identity. He failed!' It is a triumphant cry. It rings with remembered suffering which bruises my heart and twists my stomach with pain. And suddenly I realise I'm reading Otter! The man whose emotions are always hidden. Shock runs through me like cold water. Then, in a flash, the emotions are gone again.

The Guardian's voice lowers, turns rich and rhythmic: 'I am Otter. I have beaten the Archmage in battle. I and my rebel soldiers laid waste to Asphodel and left it in flames. That city is not destroyed. Nor is Benedict yet dead. But I will see the destruction of that place and all cities built upon the bones of Tribute children.

'I brought your son home to you, Fergal the Clockmaker. I and my soldiers risked our lives to bring him here, not for his good or yours, but so we could join forces to fight a common enemy.

'I was there when Mercer took Aidan prisoner. I heard the general confess his alliance with Benedict, his ambition to rule Gengst, his plot against the life of your chief councillor. Councillors, you doubt my word?

'If you are so foolish that you cannot believe one of your own children, then believe a child of Death. Or you too will die. And so will your children and your womenfolk, and every living being in this and every other Maker city.'

I feel the emotions around me swirl into a whirlwind of growing horror. He's getting through. They begin to believe.

Otter's gaze travels the room, capturing each councillor in turn. 'Choose, men of Gengst. Will it be life . . . or death?'

Otter scoops his shirt and tunic from the floor and unhurriedly pulls them on, to a stunned silence. Once dressed, he steps backwards, until he stands shoulder to shoulder with Aidan. The Guardian crosses his arms and waits, his broad face serene once more. Aidan's face has gone white. The room is so full of emotion I can't sense what he's feeling. I hold my breath and wait. All depends on this moment.

One councillor stands, begins to clap. Another follows. And another. And then the entire council is on its feet. Otter has won another battle. And power has shifted. But, I notice, Aidan's face remains a mask.

'And how are we going to get them into the city?' Aidan glares at Otter. Hostility laces the air: prickly, uneasy. I sigh. Why can't Aidan and Otter do anything together without arguing first? I pull my knees to my chest and rest my aching head on them. It's good to be out of Elsewhere. The emotional turmoil of the council meeting was exhausting. We are in Otter's room. I maintain a thread of consciousness in the corridor to check we are not overheard, but that is small, almost restful magic.

'Your spies and our own tell us that every mile of the Wall is now guarded by phalanxes of Tributes,' Aidan continues. 'Benedict knows I'm alive: that the city of Gengst knows the truth. The false truce is over. He won't just let the Knowledge Seekers walk in through the front door!'

Aidan paces – up and down, up and down – as he argues. Otter lounges on a chair which looks ready to break beneath his weight; booted legs stretched full length, ankles crossed. He leans back, his hands clasped behind his head.

Aidan keeps glancing at me as he paces. I think he does it to reassure himself that I am really here. I try not to notice when he looks at me from under frowning brows and his eyes suddenly go soft and dark. It does very strange things to my stomach.

'The Wall is too heavily guarded now for the Knowledge Seekers to come into the city through the gate,' Otter replies. 'They will have to climb over the Wall under cover of darkness. I assume your soldiers use ladders for access?'

'Ladders?' I interrupt. 'Philip will have a fit! How will he get his precious papers over the Wall by ladder? What about the mules?'

'Most of the mules will have been eaten by now, Zara.' Otter raises his eyebrows at my shocked expression. 'Would you rather your friends starved? And we'll manage something for Philip's papers. If we must. Aidan can invent a machine. Or . . . would that be too difficult?'

'A machine already exists,' Aidan retorts stiffly. 'It is called a hoist. Surely, even you . . .' He breaks off and rolls his eyes. 'Ho ho.'

'Come along, Aidan,' Otter says peaceably. 'We've been through too much together to be at outs over trivial matters. Do you really care that the council believed me and not you?

Surely you know human nature well enough to understand that most of us will believe a stranger before our own neighbour?'

'And as to that . . .' I lean forward, staring hard at Aidan. It's time to ask the question that's been haunting me from the moment I entered the council chamber of Gengst-on-the-Wall: 'Why are there no women in your council?'

Aidan had just opened his mouth to reply to Otter. Now he turns to me, mouth still gaping. He sees the look in my eyes and closes his mouth, quickly. 'Because there never have been, Zara. Our customs are different.'

'But women must be half the adult population of Gengst. If they don't share in decision-making, then . . .' Cold disbelief creeps over me. 'Then they're nothing more than servants and slaves!' I stare at him, struggling to comprehend. 'Why should your women be treated differently to your men? Do they have no say in the city's governance? Why would you not use the skills and talents of half your people? And why on earth do your women put up with it?'

'You just don't understand, Zara.' Aidan crosses his arms and sighs. 'It's different here. And we have important business to deal with.'

'I think you might want to rephrase that, Maker,' Otter says, quietly.

I hardly hear the Guardian. My head feels like it will explode.

'How can you think this isn't *important*? Do you think women are . . .' The inevitable logic hits me: women here are treated like kine. 'That women are somehow less fully human than men?'

'Of course it's important!' Aidan stutters. 'Of course women are fully human! But they aren't as strong as men. That's why it's different for you. You're a mage. But Maker men have to protect their women. That's how it works here. Women have their jobs: to raise children and look after their families. But politics and war are men's work. For Makers, I mean.' His eyes plead with me. 'I'm not saying our way is always right. I mean . . . until I met you, until I met women like Tabitha and Mistress Quint, I just never thought about any of this.'

I think of Swift; of her dreams for a land where she could become who she was meant to be, and feel sick to my stomach.

'The Maker world may not turn out to be just as you imagined, Zara.' Otter's voice has taken on the quietly insistent tone I've come to recognise. He's trying to get me to do what he wants. *Damn him!* I don't want to listen, but Otter won't shut up:

'Injustice is never something to be forgotten or taken lightly. But Aidan is right about timing. If we don't defeat your father, soon neither women nor men will exist in this city. Or in any other city in the northlands. And I doubt you or I will live too long either. And I have things I want to do before I die. So . . . let us concentrate and work out a plan.'

'You already have a plan,' I mutter. 'You always have a plan. You are a very annoying man, Otter. Sometimes.'

'Thank you. And you can be annoying too. But not often.'

Through tear-smudge, I see him smile at me. I don't care: I hurt too much. I've just lost something. Something I won't find again because now I know it doesn't exist. I've lost Swift's dream – of a country, a city, one place in this world – where people live together in harmony; where all can learn and where the only limits are their own abilities. A place without enslavement of mind, spirit or body. I look at Otter, and his eyes tell me he's lived his whole life knowing what I've just found out. And he's survived. His smile wills me to be brave. But I'm not Otter. I'm not that strong.

'Zara, I want you to meet my mother. She's the best person I've ever met. And I'm not saying that just because she's my mother.' The rush of words stumbles to a stop. Aidan gives me an embarrassed grin. 'I think you would like each other.' His face grows serious. 'And you'd find out that things aren't so bad for women here.'

I look away. I need space. What does he want from me? Permission to carry on thinking the ways of his people are good and fine? They aren't. Justice is a simple thing, really. That's what I learned when I was nine: justice is simple. It's just nearly impossible to find.

'Not bad for women?' I stare at him in disbelief. 'You told me they drugged your mother when they took you to give as hostage to Benedict. You didn't even get to say goodbye to her. I didn't understand but it all makes sense now. She had no say in you going, did she? No power to stop it. Yet you are her child as much as your father's.' I turn away again. I won't look in his blue eyes and drown there. I need to think. To decide what to do . . .

'Zara!' His left hand captures mine and holds it tight. His free hand cups the side of my face, gently turns my head until our eyes meet. A few weeks ago, I would have given thanks to all the gods that Aidan of Gengst-on-the-Wall wanted to touch me. 'I agree with you! What they did to Mother was unspeakable. I hated Father for it. It was unjust and demeaning and they did it because she is a woman. I'm on your side! But . . . I was brought up differently, and I need time to think all this through. Please be patient with me. I'm not responsible for the good or the bad things about Maker society. I don't want the credit *or* the blame. All right?'

Am I blaming him for the sins of his ancestors? Expecting too much? If time is all it takes . . . I nod.

Aidan leans forward. My heart begins to pound in my ears. His eyelids droop and his nose touches mine with a playful little bump. He smiles. Leans forward again and presses his ever-so-slightly open lips to mine.

I don't ever want him to stop kissing me. But he does. He pulls me into his arms and holds me there. Gently, sweetly. I rest in his arms. Our heads lean against each other, cheek to cheek. I breathe in the particular smell that belongs to him: spicy, warm. His beard stubble prickles my skin, his breath tickling my right earlobe.

'Meet my mother. Get to know her. She's the only one who matters to me. I don't care what the others think. But I want her to like you.' He whispers the words into my ear. Pleading. This boy does not often plead, I think to myself, part of my mind still working despite the dizziness singing through my body.

'Why?' I ask. 'Why does it matter to you if she likes me?'

'You know why.' Words puff into my ear, soft, beguiling. But they can't make me forget what I am – or what it's cost me. I can't believe in fables and myth-tales.

'She won't, Aidan. I'm a mage. How can she possibly *like* me?'

'You saved my life, Zara.' He pulls back to look into my eyes. 'She would love anyone who did that.'

'Even a demon?'

His lips press together. I've made him angry. I'm sorry, but I'm not going to play pretend. Not about this.

'I have to stay invisible in Elsewhere in this city lest someone see me and kill me for being a mage! I can't live here, Aidan. I'm not stupid. Nor are you. How do you think it could ever work out between us? I-I'm not even sure you . . .'

'I what?' His voice is hard and flat.

The look in his eyes frightens me, but I have to say this: 'When we left Asphodel to come here you couldn't even bear to look at me, let alone touch me. I'm still not sure you can ever forgive me for being a mage. For being Benedict's daughter.'

For a moment his face doesn't change. He looks into my eyes for a long time, and I sense frustration, determination. Then, to my surprise, his anger fades. He nods. 'You're right, Zara. I had to wait until I was sure too. That I could see you for who you are – not *what* you are. I am sure now. I love you, Zara of Asphodel. I don't even think I wish you weren't a mage. I think . . . I may love you because you are.' He frowns, and I sense his desire to convince me, to understand himself.

'It was good,' he says slowly, his eyes remembering, 'having you fighting beside me on the journey here. It made me feel special, that you love me. I've never met another girl like you. I can't imagine wanting another girl now. They're just . . . so *ordinary*.' He starts to say something else. Shakes his head. His eyes are intent, pleading. 'I'm making a mess of this. Sorry. But that's why I want you to meet my mother. Do you understand now? Because, the two of you – you're the only people I love in the world. I need you. Both of you.'

He's telling the truth. And I know it's not easy for him to think about these things, let alone talk about them. But I can't help worrying about the gap between what he and I want and what may be possible in this world. We're trapped in Time. Sometime in the future . . . perhaps. If he and I and Otter succeed. If the leaves drift to the left and not the right. If the fish leaps and falls back into the water on its right side. If . . . if.

'I'm a mage, Aidan. That's not ever going to change. I can't live here.'

'I'll make people understand that you're different,' he says. 'When the war is over and we've won.' His eyes burn with determination. 'We'll make it all right. You and me, Zara. We can do anything, together.' And he looks at me with such love in his eyes I can't tell him I don't believe him. That there are some wounds so ancient, so bloody, they take lifetimes to heal.

10

The city of Gengst-on-the-Wall is buzzing with the news that the truce is over. I weave a wary path between workers going home at the end of day and sensation seekers hurrying to the ramparts to gaze out at the campfires of their enemies. Smoke from enemy campfires blots out the southern horizon. Tribute soldiers and warrior mages mass on the scorched earth outside the city: a human wall confronting that made of stone. No one – other than a thief in Elsewhere – can enter or leave the city in daylight. Gengst is once more under seige.

The streets I pass through are as crowded with emotions as people: excitement, fear, worry, determination. I share all these emotions, but for a different reason: the Knowledge Seekers enter Gengst tonight. The foothills are swarming with enemy troops, and Otter fears even his stronghold isn't safe now. He has gone to order his army to retreat to a safer position and oversee tonight's rescue. We have to get the last Knowledge Seekers of Asphodel inside Gengst before they are discovered.

Soon I will see Twiss again! And it will be a relief to know that the others are safe at last.

Aidan has been with the Maker army all morning, preparing the site on the Wall where the crossing will take place, setting up defences and organising a wooden hoist for Philip's papers – the plans for the war machines he hopes to build with the engineers of Gengst.

I dodge past some stragglers meandering towards the city centre and climb two flights of stone steps to a gatehouse where a soldier waits to check the passes of all those wishing to go onto the ramparts of the city walls. I slip past him through the gate and onto a stone pavement wide as a road. Up here I finally understand just how massive the Wall is: I peer through the crenellated openings of the outer wall. In the dim light of dusk I can just make out the ground falling away far below. This pavement, stretching between the outer and inner walls, is wide enough for six horses to travel abreast. A generation of adepts would struggle to construct such an endless dragon of a wall. It feels as if it was put here by the gods.

The Wall's fortified towers loom over my head; giant catapults make strange shapes against the blue-black sky. Suddenly, I understand my father's fear. These Makers and their machines, they will overcome us, given Time's grace. The least powerful will finally conquer those born with gifts the non-magic cannot imagine.

At the thought, I feel a pang deep in my soul. I don't want my own kind to disappear forever! *Surely . . . to lose magic? To lose the power to fly with a bird? Is all that to be gone forever?* All that . . . and the power to kill with a thought. I push away the question, stop looking for an answer that doesn't exist, and walk on.

I look out towards the southern horizon. I can't see the smoke from the enemy camps any longer, only a faint glow, as if dawn approaches from the south rather than the east. I must hurry. This is the darkness we've been waiting for: the time between sunset and moonrise. We have a few hours only, to get our friends safely over the Wall.

I look out into the dark night. Otter is out there somewhere. And Twiss. And the others. Time keep them safe.

Surely I must be near the chosen crossing place now. A light comes into sight, glimmering far ahead of me. *Thank the gods!* The faint white flicker hesitates, wavers back and forth on the path. But even as I watch it fades and disappears. A late sightseer? One of Aidan's men? I feel my way around a curve in the wall and heave a sigh of relief as I see the lights of the work party: half a dozen shaded oil lamps cleverly placed at foot level and spaced well apart, so as to be all but invisible beyond the Wall. Mystery solved.

Cautiously, I move closer. Otter and Aidan think I have stayed behind at the house, but I haven't seen Twiss in days. I'm not going to leave her, Philip and the others to make this attempt without me – just in case things don't go as Otter intends.

I edge a bit nearer the lamps, and the shadowy figures toiling in their dim light. Aidan and his soldiers can't see me in Elsewhere, and Otter is safely below somewhere. The rubbing thud of wood on wood, the soft clink of metal tools, grunts, muttered curses – every sound seems twice as loud as normal. Aidan barks orders in a husky low voice. Tension: I can taste it.

The dark shape of something massive looming above the outer wall. I hear the clunk of iron on stone, the snaking whisper of hemp. This must be the hoist which will haul Philip's papers to safety. It's grown too dark to see the ladders the Knowledge Seekers will climb.

Poor Twiss, she'll have to climb the Wall in the dark and, even though she's nimble as a cat, she hates heights. Will all the Knowledge Seekers be able to climb the ladder? Tabitha and her young son? Plump Mistress Quint? And what about the injured ones like Hammeth, the blacksmith? I don't like him, but I don't want him to fall either. I wonder if Otter has thought . . . of course he has. I squat down out of the wind to wait, straining for any sound of people gathering down below the Wall.

The cold of the Maker autumn seeps past my clothes and my flesh and into my bones. I blow on my fingers, stuff my hands in my armpits and dance silently on frozen feet. Why is it taking so long?

And then: a whistle, from below. It must be Otter! Thank the gods! The darkness near me boils with sudden movement. Half-seen bodies lunge to the outer wall, gather something up and begin to chuck it over the side of the wall. I hear wood clattering on stone, and the scrape and hiss of rope. Of course! Rope ladders with wooden rungs.

There's a sense of urgency, hushed but frantic voices. Suddenly, a shining white light, like a shooting star, rises from somewhere behind me in the city and arcs gracefully into the sky. It explodes directly overhead, illuminating Aidan and his soldiers in a harsh white glare. A flare! But . . . it was set off from this side of the Wall! My stomach clenches. That was a signal to the enemy. We are betrayed!

I twist my head from side to side, straining to see through the dark, to spot a figure, movement, anything to locate the source of the flare. I send out a thread of my consciousness, seeking for any emotion of hatred, fear of discovery, seeking some sign of the saboteur. But it's hopeless. All of us are frightened. All of us fear discovery. And all of us hate.

I turn back to face the dark beyond the Wall and see a bounding, ragged fringe of flames dancing towards the Wall. Enemy torches! The signal was seen; the trap is sprung! Like the moan of the sea as it breaks itself on a shingle beach, I hear the battle cry of my father's Tribute soldiers. *Twiss! Philip!* My friends are out there. The Knowledge Seekers are trapped between an approaching Tribute army and a Wall they don't have time to climb.

Light flares around me on the Wall as the Makers realise the game is up. The ramparts are illuminated by a blaze of torchlight. I see a furious Aidan a few paces to my left, roaring orders while he grabs up a crossbow in one hand and lunges for the nearest ladder. Gods! He's going down himself to help defend the Knowledge Seekers. He'll be frantic about Thaddeus. *Time keep him and the boy safe!*

A dozen Maker soldiers frantically lower more rope ladders and swing over the Wall after Aidan, weapons on their backs. The line of enemy torchlight advances like tide rolling up a flat beach. Too quickly! The moan of Tribute battle cries is now a roar. Who will reach the Knowledge Seekers first?

Other Maker soldiers grab crossbows and longbows from weapon stations and take up positions on the Wall, hoping to pick off the enemy despite the dark. I hear a heavy trundling and see a small catapult loom into sight, pushed by soldiers in half-armour, running. My heart jumps – I hear Otter shouting, somewhere below. Soldiers reach down, lug the first refugee to safety over the Wall. I can't tell who it is. I don't try to see: I'm already airborne.

I thicken the air beneath my feet into a solid column and use it to push myself up. I glide over the top of the Wall and lower myself as quickly as is safe towards the glare of torches being lit below. Otter needs light to get the refugees to safety as quickly as possible. But the light draws my father's Tributes like moths.

As I lower myself towards the ground, I can see them coming: there's enough light from the Wall now to make out a dark stream of leather-clad young men and women pouring up the hill towards the Wall, sprinting towards the refugees. There must be hundreds of Tributes! *Oh Time!* We haven't got a chance.

I can't. I can't. Please gods, don't make me do this!

But as I hover, torn in two with indecision, I see Otter standing with a thin, frail line of those Knowledge Seekers able to fight: a few dozen, no more. They stand side by side with a dozen of Aidan's soldiers, while he and a handful of others help the less able refugees up the ladder. Among the defenders I see Philip, looking ridiculous with a sword, rather than a pen, in his hand. Hammeth, sword held high, looks more the part. And there are Tabitha and Mistress Quint, awkwardly grasping improvised pikes. Preparing to die, for there is no other outcome possible. It's impossible that they should survive. And . . . at last I see her.

Twiss. My thief child, standing with a knife in both hands. She waits, feet apart, head up. She hasn't run away; hasn't disappeared into Elsewhere, although I imagine she'll choose to fight from there when the Tributes reach her. She, alone, has a chance of escape. But knowing Twiss, she won't run.

I won't let her die! I can't. Even though it means . . . *Swift, forgive me!* I have never killed a Tribute soldier. I prayed I would never have to. I push my horror away, lock it into a corner of my mind, waiting to be let out again when all this is over. If I live.

I rise higher in the air and swoop towards the advancing Tributes. They're scrambling on the flat open ground, into the burnt-off area in front of the Wall. I find a small outcrop of rock and alight on it. This is going to take every bit of concentration and energy I possess. I've never done anything so big. I can't afford Elsewhere so I shift out and become visible. The front rows of Tributes must suddenly see me, caught in the shadow land between their enemies' torches and their own. They scream with the blood-rage and terror of those who must fight or die and rush towards me even faster.

I don't dare look at their faces. I pull all my mind and force into one thought. I lose myself. I stand outside Time. Outside the physical world. I become dirt. I become water vapour in the air above us. I mix them. Pull the water from the air more quickly than I imagined possible. And I mix it with the ground a few feet in front of the young people running towards me, pikes held high, ready to strike. I send the water deep into the dirt, deeper than the roots. I turn the rocks themselves into slurry. Seven feet of wet muck replaces solid ground.

Part of me realises my body is shaking with the effort. Sweat pours down my face and into my unseeing eyes. I am mud; I am water; I am the dryness of the air that gives its moisture. I do not have ears. I do not hear the screams of the Tributes as they stumble into the mire, and are trampled underfoot by those that follow.

I've built the bog wide. Wider than the width of an arrow's flight. The forerunners stood no chance. Those that follow scream, push backwards, but continue to fall as the weight of those charging behind pushes them, in their turn, into the mire. How many bodies? How many before it stops?

My magic is done. To save those I love I have murdered. But I have to believe. Surely. I fight also for the very children who are dying now. For the ones that will follow in their footsteps, if we fail. Surely . . . *Swift, forgive me!*

I let go with my mind. And fall to my knees. I can barely lift my head. I have just done magic beyond anything I thought possible. And have used myself up almost to the point of collapse. I won't be able to fly back over the Wall. I don't think I can even go to Elsewhere now. I slump forward, my ears full of the screams of those I've killed, though their mouths are clogged with mud.

Footsteps rush towards me from the wall, race past. Aidan's men, it must be. Their steps ring with iron. Metal men. And then the sounds of battle. The death cries. It begins. And I shut my eyes and welcome the darkness.

'Zara? Wake up, Zara. You're not so far gone you can't walk.' Otter bends over me, pulls me to my feet. He'll be angry I'm here. But he must know this is my fight as much as his. There's something sticky and warm beneath my fingers, where I hold onto his shoulder.

'Otter? Are you hurt?'

'I'm fine.'

My heart skips, thuds with relief as I look up into his calm eyes in the flickering torchlight. *Thank you, Lord Time. Thank you, Lady Death, for not taking this man from us.*

'We need to go. Now. They're regrouping and will find a way across the mire soon. You are a stubborn young woman, Zara. Thank the gods!' He closes his eyes briefly. Frowns.

My heart begins to race. 'You're hurt!'

'Shut up.' He smiles. 'And go. Here, Twiss, take her. I can't carry you, Zara. You'll have to climb the ladder. Can you do that for me?'

'Have you stopped the bleeding at least?' I try to keep my voice as calm as his.

'Go!' His voice isn't calm any more. His eyes blaze at me with an anger I haven't seen since the day he caught me spying in my father's palazzo. I stumble backwards and feel hands take my arm, tug me away.

'Come on, Zara! We gotta get out of here! Otter'll be all right.' Twiss is panting, her eyes wide. Twiss never looks scared! But I forgot: we have to climb, and Twiss hates heights.

As we stagger towards the Wall, Twiss supports half my weight. As I walk I feel my strength slowly returning. It had better hurry up, because that is one tall wall. We're almost the last waiting at the ladders to go up. Hammeth the blacksmith is lurching slowly up the one remaining ladder, holding on with one hand. The other hangs, useless, dark stains spreading from the elbow. Another wounded. How many dead? My heart redoubles its efforts at the thought. Philip? I can't see him; he must be already above.

Twiss starts up, after Hammeth. She's shaking badly. 'Take it steady, Twiss,' I call. 'I'm right behind you. I'll keep you safe.' I try to sound confident. I put one hand on the first rung and, while I wait for the thief's feet to move clear, I turn to look behind me.

Otter isn't alone after all. He's backing slowly towards us, sword in his good hand. Two Tributes stalk him as he retreats, each with a sharp pike pointing at his chest. He's the last of us. The last to seek safety. He stumbles over one of the bundles strewn over the ground. Leaps backwards as one of the Tributes takes the chance to lunge at him. Otter retreats. Staggering now. Papers flutter in the wind. Scatter. Part of me thinks: *Poor Philip. His life's work.*

But all the rest of me is screaming: *Otter cannot die!*

I can't help him: I have no magic left! I glance up at Twiss. She climbs, stops, climbs again. I don't know what to do. I take another step up the ladder. My legs quiver. *Shut up!* I hiss at them. And I watch Otter and his stalkers. My throat is swollen so tight it feels like it will burst.

The Guardian can't die. It simply isn't possible.

The Tribute on the left of Otter lunges forward again. But this time I am waiting. I hold onto the ladder, knuckles white, and manage to find the thought, tear it out of my mind and send it to the pike the Tribute holds. The wood crumbles to dust. Otter stumbles in mid-riposte. Backs away.

'DAMN YOU, ZARA!' he roars. 'GET UP THE LADDER! NOW!'

In all the years I've known him, I've never heard the Guardian swear. His fury shocks me so much I hardly notice the cold seeping quickly through my body. *Too much magic!* screams my brain. *Any more and you'll die!*

Otter is surely safe now. I climb as quickly as I can after Twiss, who's nearly at the top. She going slower than ever. Trembling. Don't fall, child: I don't have the strength to catch you.

I climb after her, pulling myself up rung after rung. After every step I lean against the ropes, holding on, shaking. *I can't make it. I can't. I've used everything.* I take another step. And then hands are pulling me up to safety. Aidan's voice shouts in my ear. I'm in his arms. He is swearing and laughing all at once. Holding me tight.

'Otter!' Somehow I push away from restraining arms, lean over the Wall. The bodies of two Tributes lie small and tiny and broken on the ground far below. And I can just make out, in the last of the guttering torchlight, Otter's head, still far away, climbing the ladder one-handed. Like Hammeth. I find a last surge of strength, quickly scan the darkness beyond him. More Tributes are coming, climbing over a rough bridge of hacked tree branches and saplings laid across the bog. But they're too far away. They won't make it in time.

Otter is safe.

A fireball explodes out of nowhere. Out of the air itself.

Mage-made!

It shoots straight at Otter, who climbs still. Not knowing Death comes for him.

Desperately, I search for my magic and find . . . nothing. I have nothing left for the Guardian. Not enough strength to scream a warning. I watch, helpless, as a second fireball bursts into view, flying at us with astonishing speed.

The two fireballs, one large and glowing white, one small and golden, collide and explode in a huge conflagration. I wince, blinded. When I blink the dazzle from my eyes, I realise I can't see Otter or the ladder. He's gone. Otter is gone!

The Guardian is dead.

It doesn't feel real.

It was Falu out there: that second golden fireball. It carried her signature colour – and the cedar-like scent of her magic. Even the Archmage of Thynis couldn't save Otter. What hope did I have?

I feel hands pulling me back from the Wall.

'Zara! Come away! Come with me.'

Aidan guides me away from the Wall. Leads me through the dancing torchlight, steering me away from bands of shouting men and metal-clanking soldiers. Twiss and Philip help to hustle me along through crowded streets ringing with the questions of frightened men and women. I know my friends are trying to get me safely away, terrified that someone might realise . . . someone might guess that I am a magic-user. But only I know that there is not one, but two mages at large in Gengst.

11

'There were two adepts. Falu, and . . . one of my father's people.'

I'm staring straight ahead, sitting up in the bed I was made to lie upon an hour ago. I avoid looking at Philip or Aidan or even Mistress Quint fussing around me like a broody hen.

'No, thank you!' I push the cup of hot soup away for a second time. It was a struggle to get the first cupful down without being sick.

The apothecary huffs, and bustles off to find something else to annoy me with. The remnants of the Knowledge Seeker council have been given a set of rooms in Aidan's house. I have been smuggled in as one of them, supposedly a Knowledge Seeker who was injured in the attack. I am out in the open now: no longer hiding in Elsewhere. If any of my companions decide to betray my identity, I won't last an hour. I don't think I care now. Otter is missing, perhaps dead. And our best chance of victory has died with him. I need to be out of here: I must hunt down my father's spy and kill them . . . if I can.

'The first fireball was too powerful, too concentrated, to be the work of a mere battle mage. My father does have a spy in the city, and that person is an adept!' I meet Philip's eyes.

'Yes,' he says after a moment. He looks disconcerted. 'I see.' His sandy eyebrows lower in a frown. 'If you're right – and of course you are, Zara – then the obvious conclusion is that your father guessed that Aidan would make it safely home and his truce would be exposed as the treacherous plot it was.' Philip's eyes narrow in concentration. 'Which means that Benedict knew of the plan to get us into the city. The Tributes were lying in wait to ambush us when we crossed. It's obvious, because of the geography, which stretch of the Wall we were likely to attempt, but how would they know when?'

'So the adept set up the flare that betrayed us,' Aidan says gruffly. 'But how could they know our plans? A clever guess, or is there another Maker traitor in Gengst feeding them information: someone who sold out to Benedict, like Mercer.'

'I think I saw the adept,' I mutter. 'It must have been the spy I was following on the Wall.' *Curse my stupidity! Why didn't I realise?* 'I thought the light was one of your people. But it went out as soon as we got near the hoist.' I sigh. And ask the question at last: 'Is there any news . . .?'

Philip grips my hand and gives it a consoling squeeze.

'My men found the remains of the ladder in pieces on the ground,' Aidan says. 'What wasn't charred was broken into bits by the fall. Otter can't have survived. He was wounded, in any case. The man is dead, Zara. It's unfortunate, but we can carry on fighting without your Guardian. Makers have been fighting mages for generations without his help – or anyone's!'

'You never liked him.' I look up and meet Aidan's eyes. He flinches.

'I – Does it matter?' Aidan jumps to his feet, begins pacing.

'You don't get it,' I say. 'Otter was targeted. The attack on the Wall was about him. You're not important any more, Aidan.'

He gives a humourless laugh: 'Thanks!'

'Don't be silly: I mean to Benedict. And will you please stop pacing? You're making me giddy. Think about it: you were only a danger while the truce was believed. Now you're just another Maker. He wants you dead, but he wants *all* of your people dead. No, it was Otter he was after. Otter knows . . . knew him better than anyone and that made him dangerous. Better than me, even. I only had to see my father a few times a year. Otter spent every day of his life with Benedict, from the age of fifteen.'

The last connection with my old life has been taken away. We grew up together, Otter and I. And always, always, I thought he was the enemy. And he wasn't! If only he had told me . . . I close my eyes and loss hits me like a hammer blow.

Philip grips my shoulders and I realise I've nearly fallen off the bed. 'Zara, you need to rest.'

'I'm perfectly well.' My voice sounds feeble, even to me. 'I've used up too much energy, but I'm not going to die.'

The thought gives me no pleasure. My father has stolen someone else from me. Until this moment I didn't know that I cared about Otter, as a person. How could I? I spent my childhood fearing him. But now I have a hole inside nearly as big as the one hollowed out by Swift's murder.

'One of my father's adepts is hiding in Gengst,' I say. 'I didn't recognise their style but they're powerful. I'm scared, if you really want to know. Or I will be when I'm less tired. They know I'm in here. That I'm alive. My father knows.

Now that Otter is dead, I'm Benedict's target. He will try to kill me next.'

If I'm lucky. But I have one comfort: Twiss and the thieves – they've given me Elsewhere. *If I'm captured I will go into Elsewhere so deeply I'll never come out alive. It's not a bad way to die.*

'Here. Drink this at once! Your face is like chalk.' Quint is back, glaring at me. She's angry. And, with a shock, I realise that the apothecary is fond of me as an actual person – not just a subject of medical study! I'm so surprised I take the steaming mug of watery soup and drink it down. A few minutes later, the room starts to sway and blur. My eyelids close.

'You'll sleep now, silly girl.'

The apothecary's smug voice is the last thing I hear.

My father reaches out his hand – narrow-palmed, long fingered, with oddly opaque fingernails – and lifts his high adept between forefinger and thumb. It's a beautiful chess set: the pieces are carved from rosewood and ebony. Contemptuously, deliberately, Benedict slides his adept onto the square of my last remaining dragon. My father lifts his eyes to mine. Smiles at the horror in my face. He scoops up the dragon and holds it out to me on his open palm, but when I grab for it, Benedict dissolves the wood to dust. He scatters the sawdust over his shoulder, pulls a linen handkerchief from his pocket and wipes its starched whiteness over his palm.

'Well, Zara?' His smile fades. Panic rises in my chest. I cannot breathe. 'Well?' repeats my father. 'Haven't you learned? I will always win, Daughter. I will always

destroy those you love. Give up: why suffer needlessly? Accept your fate. You belong to me: you are my blood, my bone, my future. Come home, Zara. Come home and love only me. Obey me, and I will forgive you.' His reptile's eyes are flat and cold. Their yellow discs grow into swirling suns, filling my vision, dragging me into their depths. My body grows heavy, useless, and I fall fall fall fall fall . . .

Lurch upright, heart pounding. Gasping. Face damp with sweat.

'Zara?' A hand grips mine, warm, strong. 'It's all right. I'm here!'

Aidan gathers me into his arms. As always, when we touch, his emotions flood through me. The warmth of his love stills my mind. My body shudders as the nightmare loosens its grip; I press my face into his shoulder.

'Your father?'

There is a world of understanding in his tone. I nod into his shoulder, not lifting my head, not opening my eyes. I need the reality of his solid flesh, his smell, his touch. It keeps me here. Sane. Safe, for this moment.

Aidan's arms tighten around me as the memory that haunts him comes like a sour stink. I feel him push it away. I feel the effort it takes. The warmth cocooning me doesn't falter. I lift my face and look at him in wonderment.

'What?' He grins at me crookedly. 'Have I grown horns?'

'Something like that.'

'You better now?'

I nod. 'Why are you here, in my room?'

'Old Quint gave you something that knocked you out for ages. I got worried, but she just told me to go away and play! But I thought I'd stick around until you woke up.' He raises an eyebrow, half-irritated still. 'But I have to admit, you don't look like a ghost any more.' He frowns. 'Would your magic really kill you, Zara? If you do too much?'

'Yes.' I shrug.

I don't want to think about the fight on the Wall. About Otter. But I have to ask: 'Is there any news . . .' My question peters out as I see the emotions flicker over his face; feel them flow through his brain: anxiety, impatience, dislike of Otter and guilt about those feelings. But no doubt about Otter's fate.

'He's dead, Zara. You need to come to terms with that. We all do. And move on.'

I press my hands together, palm to palm. Study them, reassured by the sight of my broad palms, my oval pink nails, so unlike Benedict's. I try not to give in to the fear that has been standing over my shoulder, just out of sight, since Otter . . . disappeared. For weeks – since we fled Asphodel – I have believed that Otter was the one destined to defeat my father and end the enslavement of the kine. If Otter is dead, then I must have been wrong. I won't let Benedict win! But I am still reluctant to accept the Guardian's death.

I don't want to argue with Aidan about Otter so I nod solemnly.

The Maker smiles in relief, leans in and bumps his nose gently on mine. Dark copper lashes flirt, droop over blue eyes that tease me with a look of invitation. My stomach goes tense with desire, and my own eyes close as I lean forward and our lips touch.

Kissing no longer seems something new and awkward. I draw back and gaze into his eyes, which look blurred and hot. I lay the palm of my hand against the side of his face, feel the texture of his shaven beard, rough as a cat's tongue against my palm. Lean in again for a second kiss.

Aidan groans and pulls away.

'Enough, Zara! A man can only stand so much!'

I smile at him. I know what I want now. I have never joined physically with man, boy, woman or girl. I have kept myself separate, alone. I was a spy in my father's house since the age of nine, and a spy can never be too careful. In any case, I never met any person in Asphodel I desired enough to want to be intimate with in that way. Aidan is different. Now that I know he really loves me, despite my magic.

I reach out for him again.

'No! Zara.' His smile fades and he pulls away. Jumps off the bed, frowning at me. 'It isn't seemly! We are not yet betrothed.'

His words take my breath away.

'B-betrothed?' I can only stare at him.

'Of course.' As he sees my shock and confusion, a slow smile drives the sternness from his face. 'I love you. I want to marry you, Zara.'

12

It is a scene from a comedy by a troupe of players – ones with a strange sense of humour – this dinner where Makers and Seekers break the first bread together, as a sign of our alliance.

All of us are here: all the remaining members of the Council of the Knowledge Seekers of Asphodel. Plus Tabitha and her son, Thaddeus. And Twiss, at my special request, because I want her near me both for comfort and to keep an eye on her.

We sit in a room full of long tables made of finest walnut wood. As leader of the Knowledge Seekers, Philip sits at the top table, beside Fergal and his wife. The rest of us are sprinkled around the room amongst the grandees. Aidan has arranged for me to sit beside him. We refugees from Asphodel wear the hastily cleaned and patched clothes of our journey, our hair washed and untangled, fingernails pared and cleaned, the men's beards trimmed. But despite our efforts, we look like beggars asked to dine by nobility. Which is precisely what we are: beggars.

Worm and his fellow servants herded us downstairs from our rooms through halls into the great hall lined with clocks and mirrors, shimmering with gilt and the reflected light of hundreds of beeswax candles. And now we stare across at each other and our new companions in the silvery white light cast by massive silver candelabra burning dozens more candles of purest beeswax. The expense! Is this vainglory? Are the Makers so rich?

My brain is still fuzzy with the familiar weariness of over-magicking. The glittering light; the lilting accent of the Makers; trying to smile politely through my tiredness and fear; looking for Twiss; pressing Aidan's hand beneath the table for comfort. I'm battered by emotions on all sides – fear and nervousness from Seekers, curiosity spiced with mistrust from the Makers – it makes my head swim. I close my eyes for a moment, then jump as a servant slides a bowl of broth in front of me.

The hum of voices rises above the clatter of dishes, and my head begins to pound. I sip my soup, and smile at the man on my left, who is leaning towards me.

But it isn't me he wants to talk to. His eyes slide past me as though I'm not here, and he mutters something to the man, an older, square-set Maker in a severe black woollen doublet and plain white linen collar and cuffs, who sits across from Aidan.

I feel myself blushing at the snub, and concentrate on the soup, which tastes of pea and turnip, with a strange spicing I can't identify. It's good though. And I'm ravenous.

As I eat, I look around the table. Philip is in deep conversation with Fergal and his much younger wife, who is tall, dark-haired and beautiful, like her elder son. Donal himself sits at the opposite end of the table, second host. He stares at Tabitha with the look of one bewitched. Even the travel-worn garments the silversmith wears can't disguise her silver-gilt beauty, and I grin to myself at Donal's obvious infatuation. Tabitha seems oblivious to the effect she's having on Aidan's brother. She's murmuring to Thaddeus, who looks upset. His years of imprisonment by my father have left their mark: it is likely that the boy will always be fearful and timid.

'Rum looking bunch.' It's the man on my left. 'Don't know what Fergal is thinking of, letting them stay in Gengst now the Guardian's dead. That man might have been of use, with his army. This lot of scarecrows will only cause problems. More mouths to feed. Best throw them out. Or put them in service. Looks like all they're fit for.'

I nearly spit my soup out. Turn my head and glare at the man. He looks through me. Have I suddenly gone into Elsewhere? Am I invisible? Aidan nudges my knee with his, catches my eye; he's giving me a look. Not invisible then. I take a breath and hold it. Count five ticks and let go.

'Do not be hasty, Connor,' the Maker dressed in black pronounces in a low rumble. 'These people have fortitude or they would not have survived to reach us. They have information of demon-spawn which may prove invaluable. And their leader is Philip the Artist. Even you must acknowledge he is a man worth having among us. A genius, in truth. As for the Guardian: we should thank the gods for their intervention. I cannot believe he was not polluted by his intimacy with the great demon, Benedict. All such are safer dead.'

He's a handsome man of late middle years: broad shouldered, upright, his beard white as the snow lying on the mountain tops. His dark brown eyes are intelligent. His voice rings with the confidence of the powerful, and his tone pronounces his belief that he speaks unquestionable truth. He welcomes Otter's death with a callousness that chills my heart.

'Well, perhaps you know best, Matthiu. But for gods' sakes, the females are scandalously dressed!'

'Surely you're not such a country bumpkin as all that, Connor? We cannot expect other nations to live as we do.' As Aidan speaks, he treads on my foot, making me gasp back the words about to flood from my mouth. Aidan's tone is joking, but there's an edge beneath.

The man called Connor throws him a look of dislike. I feel him swallow his aggression in what must be an acknowledgement of Fergal's power.

'As you say, boy. Different customs.' And now the Maker does allow himself to notice me. And assaults me with a look of combined dislike and lust that makes my stomach squirm. What a filthy man!

For a moment I fantasise about making his bowl of steaming soup tip gently backwards and pour its contents into his lap. It would take the merest thought. But Aidan is right: I can't afford to draw attention to myself. If any Maker at this table knew who and what I am, I would not live long. Nor would my friends: no Knowledge Seeker would be forgiven for taking a mage, let alone Benedict's daughter, in companionship and trust. That probably guarantees that I won't be betrayed by any in my own party. But . . . and it is a fact never far from my mind: the flare that betrayed the Knowledge Seekers' crossing of the Wall proves that my father has a spy in this city. I am sure that it is the same adept who killed Otter.

I did enough magic that night for the spy to guess that I'm here in the city. They can try to kill me themselves, or they can betray me to the Makers, which would be the safer course. If I don't root out the adept and kill them, it's only a matter of time until my identity is discovered.

I've been staring into space, forgetting to eat. Aidan nudges me under the table, gives me another of his warning looks. Then grins so disarmingly my head goes fuzzy again. I finish my soup, hoping food will clear my brain, and jump again as the empty bowl is whisked away and a plate of fish slides into its place.

The smell of honey, vinegar and onions fills my nose and my stomach grinds with insistent sharpness. It seems years since I tasted fish. I take a quivering fork and spoon and scoop white flesh and sweet-sour sauce into my mouth. *Praise be to the gods!* Either hunger sauces this fish better than seems possible, or Fergal's cook is a genius.

Snatches of conversation waft in and out of my attention as I scoop in mouthful after mouthful.

Mistress Quint is seated opposite me. She has been directing her attention to her food, between smiling and nodding at her companions. She alone of us seems oblivious to the tension in the room. But I nearly choke on my fish as her voice rises, outrage in every tone: 'I beg your pardon, sir? Surely you cannot mean any such thing!'

Like every other soul at the table, I stop eating to watch with rising alarm as Mistress Quint drops her fork onto her plate of fish and stares with round black eyes of outrage at the magpie-clad Matthiu. 'Why on earth should women not use the talents which the gods gave them?'

Oh gods! What has the Maker said to her?

'A woman's only useful talent is to serve her menfolk.' Matthiu's rumble rises to a growl of dislike. He makes a dismissive gesture with one hand and looks down his nose at Quint. 'And if I had my ways, we would return to the old customs, where females were seated at separate tables so as not to lessen the quality of discussion.'

'You are a fool, sir.' Quint gives an angry laugh, smiling and nodding. I've never seen her so furious. 'I'm sorry to have to say it, but you are *plainly* an idiot. Aidan, why is such a person invited here to insult us?' Quint bounces forward to lean past the magpie man and stare accusingly at Aidan.

I catch her eye. 'Ignore such insults, I beg you, Mistress Quint. For tonight at least.'

'Mistress!' It is Philip. The whole table has fallen silent; is listening. Ghoulish attention, surprise, shock, outrage muddy the air of the room. 'This is not the time or place for such a discussion.'

'I did not start it, Philip!' protests the apothecary. 'This *gentleman* did. And do not take that tone with me. I am Mistress of my Guild and you have no authority to reprimand me!'

'Guildleader?' Matthiu's pompous expression crumples into horror. 'I cannot believe this, even of southern slaves.'

'Slaves?' Now it is Hammeth who lumbers to his feet. All six feet of muscular blacksmith scowls at the older man. 'Who are you who call us so? Whoever you are, I doubt you would survive a month in Asphodel. Don't pretend to know what you don't know, old man. And watch your tongue, or I may have to watch it for you!' He glares truculently at Philip, who has jumped to his feet as well.

'Benedict would be delighted at this display!' Philip's voice rings out and the hubbub dies down. Makers and Seekers glare at each other. 'Allies with all to gain and everything to lose, quarrelling like children. Knowledge Seeker or Maker, we are the same: we are non-magic people who seek the defeat of magekind.'

As ever, when magekind is discussed by those without magic, I feel a frisson of unease. These people, all of them, even those I think of as my friends and companions, they all want to wipe my race from the earth. And I am helping them to destroy my own kind. I shudder. Aidan presses my hand. I realise he's been holding it under the table for many ticks now. I turn and look at him. I want to hold him, to be comforted. His face is white. His lips thin with stress. It hangs on a thread: this alliance.

'Ah, Matthiu,' sings out a voice I don't recognise. 'Charming as always.' Aidan's hand tightens painfully. I follow the direction of his gaze and see – half-obscured behind a wide, morose-looking gentleman in wine-coloured velvet – a young Maker woman.

At the exact moment I spot her, her gaze shifts from the magpie Matthiu to my face, and I am confronted by two sapphire-bright eyes. She has a mane of tawny hair and a pointed fox face. Shock floods through me – Aidan's eyes, his sharp chin and cheekbones. *Why did he never tell me he had a sister?*

Her hair springs from the V of a widow's peak on her forehead, curly to the point of frizz, the same colour as his: a strawy mingling of yellow, black, bronze and brown. A dimple dances beside her mouth as her glance skips past me and fixes on her brother. As hard as I tune my empathic senses, this young woman gives off a strong wariness at odds with her amused expression. It's as though she looks out from a citadel inside her mind.

'Try not to let the grumpy old bear worry you, Mistress,' the young woman calls down the table to Quint, who blinks with astonishment. 'His bark is not worse than his bite, alas, but my father can draw his teeth, and he knows it. So fear not: we of Fergal the Clock's house will protect you. Although it is no joke being female in this country, as you will doubtless find.'

'Tut-tut! Shut your mouth, shameless hussy.' Fergal glares down the table at his daughter, but he smiles as he says it. And I sense a release of tension in every Maker in the room bar Matthiu.

'Well, Father. If you *will* invite the witchfinder to dine, when you know our guests have different ways and they will not understand. For shame, you never consult me, your wisest and most loyal advisor.'

Witchfinder? Unease trickles up my spine. I stop, just in time, my instinctive urge to turn and look at Matthiu.

Fergal roars with laughter, as though the idea of his daughter advising him is a plum bit of foolery. And that makes me shiver too, for I see in the young woman's eyes the sardonic knowledge that she speaks the truth. And knows she will not be believed.

Ye gods! What is this place?

The fish begins to swim uneasily in my stomach.

Fergal leans across the table and says to Philip in a voice both proud and puzzled: 'She plays the fool for us all, you know. I need no jester in my household when Hazel is here.'

The large gentleman dressed in wine velvet takes hold of Hazel's hand. 'Best set out your advert for one then, Fergal,' he rumbles. 'I press the lady to name the day.' She smiles sweetly at him, slides her hand from his and taps him on the nose with an arch finger.

'And I shall be pressed indeed, dear Grammos, before that day comes. Squashed flat on dear old Matthiu's truthing press like a book. But with my pages left unread.' And she winks so bawdily at the stout man that he gulps himself into a coughing fit.

I hear Matthiu mutter: 'May that day come soon, lady.'

The chill in my stomach thickens.

'You never told me you had a sister!' I lean sideways towards Aidan and hiss at him.

'I wish to the gods most days that I didn't!' he whispers back. 'Damn the girl! Some day she'll go too far, and even our father won't be able to save her. She's a fool!'

'Is she?' I watch the mournful Grammos attempt to attract Hazel's full attention. She feeds him attention like an over-eager puppy, tossing the scrap of the odd glance and word. But her eyes roam the table, watching, never resting. Coming time and again to my face. And in them I see an interest and speculation which are the mirror of my own.

13

I have fought warrior mages and adepts, been nearly killed by my own father. Why should visiting Aidan's mother make me so ridiculously nervous? I wipe my sweaty hands on my trousers, and the familiar feel of the leather comforts me. I'm wearing my old clothes, the clothes of our long journey from Asphodel. They have been cleaned and mended, but I know they look plain and worn next to the rich wools and linens of the Makers. The servants offered me a dress, like those the women wear here, but the long skirts were heavy and hard to walk in. We have a tailor in our company; she is busy sewing new clothes for all of us. Until they are ready, I wear my old ones. I am Zara. Twiss and Aidan, Philip, Tabitha and Quint are my friends and family now. I am not alone.

I have brushed and plaited my hair, trying to tame its coppery wildness. I tied a scarf over it – remembering my father's spy – but Aidan teased it from my head as soon as I opened the door and stepped into the corridor.

'Your hair is too beautiful to hide away,' he said as he tucked the scarf into his pocket and gave me a quick kiss. His eyes danced with excitement and nervousness. Perhaps I caught the anxious feeling in the pit of my stomach from him. He cares so much – too much – that this meeting goes well.

Aidan has walked beside me, not touching me, only gesturing left or right as we climb stairs and turn from landing to corridor. Now his pace slows as we walk down a corridor laid with soft, patterned rugs and lined with tall doors of white-limed wood. Even here, clocks in long cases stand against the walls like ticking sentinels. Aidan pauses before one of the whitened doors, grabs both my hands and squeezes them so hard I nearly yelp.

He looks nearly breathless with anticipation. 'She's got to love you as much as I do! Just be yourself. But remember: no one must guess who you are, so be careful. Mother may seem quiet, but she's sharp.'

I nod, but my heart speeds up as I catch a whiff of his anxiety: he's worried despite his bold words. So am I, and not just about slipping up and giving away my identity. Why should Naveen welcome a stranger into her family, a girl from the world of her enemies?

Aidan gives me a last, imploring look, turns and knocks on the door.

A woman's voice replies, low and soft. I can't make out her words. Aidan twists the doorknob and pushes the door open. He gestures me to go before him and I step into a bright room full of light colours and soft fabrics.

The ornate gilt and richly carved woodwork of the rest of the house is swept away here. The walls are papered a pale green. Cream and gold curtains dress the tall windows. A lute, its wooden, pear-shaped body mellow with age, its long neck decorated with inlaid mother-of-pearl, lies on a round table made of walnut wood. Next to it lies a wooden hoop containing a cloth half-embroidered. Vases on the window sills overflow with autumn herbs and flowers.

Two women sit beside a marble fireplace. The grate is heaped with firerock and the flames flicker orange-blue. Naveen stares into the fire. Hazel is reading a book, her face hidden by a waterfall of tawny hair. The long skirts of her costume puddle on the floor: yellow, blue, red. Emerald-green shoes peep from underneath. She seems unaware of our entrance, lost in an inward world.

Beside the bright colours and vivid hair of her daughter, Aidan's mother ought to fade into obscurity, but her quiet presence dominates the room. Unquestionably the mother of Aidan's older brother, Naveen sits tall and straight-backed. Her dark hair is drawn back from her oval face and contained in a starched white cap. She turns her head at the sound of our approach. Her eyes are the colour of lake water, and her skin the pale cream of the far north. She wears long robes of a rich amethyst silk, gathered tight at waist and bust, and an under-kirtle of white linen revealed in the slit bell-sleeves of her over-robe and at the low-cut neck of her costume.

Aidan's mother must be forty, but looks slender and youthful still. Naveen is one of those whose feelings don't scream for my attention, which is a relief. I don't want to know what Aidan's mother thinks of me. It's obvious what she thinks of her younger son: she worships him. Even though her expression does not change, her entire face begins to glow with emotion.

It's too intimate and too painful: I can't even remember my mother's face. I shift my glance to Hazel, who still seems lost in her book.

'Welcome, Zara.' Naveen is watching me. She smiles. 'Let us introduce ourselves properly. It is clear you and I must get to know each other.

'Please, come and sit here.' She gestures to the empty chair drawn next to hers and I dutifully sit, glad of the warmth of the firerock burning in the grate. I wear my woollen jacket indoors, yet to my southern blood the house still feels cold.

Aidan goes to stand beside the fireplace. He leans on the mantle and glances from his mother to me and back again. Hazel has put aside her book and watches all three of us.

'You have had a difficult journey.' The words are kind but Naveen's tone is neutral. 'You have lost everything, you Knowledge Seekers. Tell me, why do you call yourselves that?'

While I reach for my carefully prepared answer, I see Hazel's bright blue eyes fasten on me.

'Because we believe the search for knowledge to be the true calling of every person,' I say.

'Even the women?' Hazel's voice is sharp, swift as an arrow in flight.

A day ago her question would have puzzled me. I pretend not to understand. 'Of course. Why would it not?'

But she answers with yet another question: 'Women are allowed to seek knowledge in your land? To learn?'

'Only those who are magic-users. Mages do not allow any without magic to learn to read, to learn more than they need to do to perform their job, to be a member of their guild. It is a crime punishable by death for a kine – whether male or female – to learn to read. But we are rebels. That is why we have fled Asphodel and seek your help and a place of refuge amongst you.'

'Can *you* read?'

'Yes . . .' I have decided it would be too complicated to pretend illiteracy. 'A few of us have taught ourselves –'

'Even though you are a woman?' Hazel interrupts.

'Enough of your awkwardness, Sister! I don't –'

'Please, Aidan!' I throw him a glance sharp enough to stop his tongue. He subsides and leans back against the mantle, but his lips are pressed thin with irritation. What is it he doesn't want me to know? He's seething with anxiety. I look at Hazel. 'I don't understand your question.'

'Is there no distinction between men and women in your country then?' This from Naveen. She glances, almost unwillingly, towards her daughter.

'Of course not. Women carry children in their bodies until birth, but that is the only difference.'

'But men are stronger!' Hazel raises an arch eyebrow.

'Not in mind or magic.' I shrug. 'An ox is stronger than a human. Does that make them superior?'

Her gleeful smile is like lightning: gone so quickly I wonder if I have imagined it.

'Those who hold sway through power, magical or physical, are tyrants. That is why we Knowledge Seekers have fled our mage overlords. Why we seek to join forces with you Makers and defeat the tyrants once and for all.' The speech sounds dry and rehearsed even to my ears.

'So, you will fight with tyrants against tyrants? How curious.' Hazel begins to laugh – a joyless sound, like a stream chuckling over a stony bed.

'Hazel! Enough!' Naveen's face is suddenly thunderous.

'Pay her no mind,' Aidan mutters. 'My sister has odd notions.'

Hazel glances at me from beneath bronze eyelashes, a dimple forming beside her pursed, disapproving mouth. 'So unsuitable a daughter I am,' she sighs. 'Such a trial to my poor parents. Aidan didn't tell you he had a sister, did he? But then, I'm only a woman.' She picks up her book and begins once more to read.

'Do you have family, Zara?'

I'm a fraction of a tick too slow. Naveen has noticed. But I hope she will put my distraction down to her daughter's behaviour. Aidan, though, frowns at me even though he's more in danger of giving away my secret than I am. I'm used to lying, to pretending, to acting a lie every moment of my life. Aidan is as easy to read as Hazel's book.

'My parents are dead,' I say. And feel that it is the truth: my father died for me the day he invaded my mind; the moment he murdered my sister.

'No brothers or sisters?'

I shake my head.

'I'm very sorry,' Naveen says. 'Family is all that matters, all that lasts.' She glances at Aidan. 'And how did they die, your parents?'

'The mages killed them.' I look straight into her eyes and hear my voice speak with absolute certainty. 'For heresy. They were scribes, but they taught themselves to read.'

'I don't understand,' Naveen says. 'How can a scribe be illiterate?'

'Only mages are allowed to be educated in reading and writing. Non-magic users must not learn to read, on pain of death. Most guilds can manage without reading and writing; they have developed ways of coping with the work the mages demand. But my parents were scribes. It sometimes happens that scribes learn to read through the copying of texts and examining the illuminations and illustrations in the books and scrolls. So it was with my parents. They taught themselves to read, and then they taught me. They were betrayed. Someone informed.

'When the mages came for them, I was away from the house, shopping for the evening meal. One of our people, one of the Knowledge Seekers, heard what had happened and searched for me in the city. They took me away and hid me. I never saw my parents again.'

'How old were you?'

'Thirteen.'

'So, you have lived for three years without a mother. Very sad.'

'I will turn seventeen in three weeks,' I say, realising it is true: I've nearly reached the age of adulthood. 'It's been nearly four years.'

'How did you survive?'

'I worked for the Knowledge Seekers. There is a hidden community of illegals: we are itinerant, never staying with one family of Seekers too long, selling our talents on the black market to pay for our keep. I taught other Knowledge Seekers to read. People like Philip the Artist.'

'Ah, yes!' Naveen leans forward, eyes bright with excitement. 'Philip! It is an honour to have the Nonpareil as a guest in my house. So you were the great man's teacher? How funny.'

'Why so?'

'My mother means, it seems odd to her that a young woman should teach a male, especially one so much older and so famous.' Hazel's voice is gently mocking. 'Women here are not thought to be capable of learning, let alone teaching. Even my own mother believes so. She does not trust the evidence of her own brain, which shows her every day that she is ten times more intelligent than my father.'

Naveen keeps her eyes on my face – ignoring Hazel's outburst – but her lips tighten. Aidan groans. Hazel watches us all beneath lazy eyelids, a half-smile never gone from her lips.

'But you were taught to read,' I protest. Since the Gengst council room I have begun to suspect much of what Hazel says, but I can't believe it is so bleak as Aidan's sister paints it here. Or, surely, Aidan wouldn't be so confident that I will fit in here.

Hazel shrugs. 'Only because some learning in womenfolk of my class is considered a social accomplishment. I have no opportunity to *use* my knowledge.' She leans forward, her face vivid with curiosity: 'Your women will not thrive here, you know. The men of Gengst will not let them work. It would be far too dangerous, too subversive. How will you cope, I wonder, you female Knowledge Seekers?'

Not work? It is unthinkable! 'Half our guild members are women,' I protest. 'Of course we will work. What else would we do?'

I stare at the three faces in turn and it is clear, even without an empath's magic, to see that they don't understand. I almost feel Aidan wince at my words. Did he forget to tell me this vital bit of information? Do any of the Knowledge Seeker women realise their situation? This is disaster. I think of what Tabitha will say, and Mistress Quint, and feel sick. I want to get away by myself. To think what best to do. To plan.

But I am trapped for long minutes, making polite conversation, avoiding Aidan's eye. Finally, as soon as I judge it possible, I murmur about a sudden headache and beg to be excused. I stand and curtsy my respect to his mother; to his sister, who looks oddly sad now, then turn and leave the room.

14

I press my back against the door of that charming prison of a room and take a deep breath to clear my head. When I look up, it's just in time to catch the startled stare of the female servant I noticed when I first arrived here with Aidan and Otter. Then I was invisible in Elsewhere, but it's clear she can see me now – and equally clear she regrets being seen herself. I get a blast of guilt: she's been eavesdropping, or trying to. And she doesn't like me at all.

'Do you want to go inside?' I step away from the door. My head is spinning and I can hardly take in, let alone analyse, the emotions flaring out of this girl at the sight of me. So much antagonism! I feel a momentary flare of alarm, but then the servant shakes her head, blushes, turns and hurries down the corridor and out of sight. Odd. Worrying? She can't know who I am. And her emotions seem too personal, too strong, to be those of a spy. A mystery, but one which will have to wait.

Back in the small, chilly room where I sleep, I climb into the bed and sit, staring at the opposite wall and the room's only decoration: a painting of a bowl of fruit. The apples and pears are so impossibly glossy they look like they would break your teeth. I pull the feather quilt and woollen blankets up to my nose. It's a detestable painting. And this is a foul little room. The walls are a scabby green and the fire has gone out. What am I going to do? Why am I even here? Otter is dead. The revolution is over before it began. My father has won. And the Makers . . .

A tear rolls down my nose. Oh . . . *pestilence*!

I turn over, ignore the rumbling in my stomach complaining at the absence of lunch. I want . . . I need quiet. I need it to *stop*: all this noise in my head. All the questions I can't answer. I'm skirting the edge of a deep lake of fear and loneliness, which is almost as terrifying as my father. I will decide what to do in a few hours. Now I need to rest. I need peace. There's only one place in this life where that exists. I let myself slip into Elsewhere. I go far enough to dull the nagging voices in my head, far enough to drift into sleep.

Wake up, Zara! Wake up or you will stop breathing. Wake up or you will die! Zara! Listen to me! You must wake up! It's an irritating buzz, like the droning of a bluebottle against a window pane. I push the voice away, settle deeper into Elsewhere. Soft, comfortable, kind Elsewhere.

Zara! Can you hear me? Wake up, Zara! Pounding now, screaming, shouting. And someone coughing. A rasping, hoarse, tearing cough. Pour soul! The sound of it makes my chest hurt in sympathy. My ribs stretch, my lungs strain for air.

I see dragons dancing: blue, green, golden beasts with glittering scales. Am I a dragon? I'm breathing smoke.

Zara! Wake up! Now! Swift's voice. She *is* alive! My sister pulls me out of Elsewhere like a fish on a line, scooped into the net of wakefulness. And into hell. The room is black with heavy, oily smoke. And I am dying.

Darkness. Suffocation. The nightmare horrors of my childhood have returned to destroy me. The smoke: it's the smoke that is killing me. I must get away from it. But my body is wracked to spasms with coughing. I can't draw air into my lungs. To concentrate, to think my magic, I must breathe!

More voices outside my door, crying my name. Pounding. The door shakes in its frame, but it holds. This is a strong house. A dark house. A house that wishes my death.

No. It is my father who wishes my death. Benedict has done this. If he cannot have me, he will kill me. He fears his child now. He knows I want to destroy him. And I will, dear Father.

But not if I die. I gather the shreds of concentration I can find and begin to urge the smoke to climb higher, away from the bed. Smoke is not difficult to direct. I push it to the top of the room, herd it towards the chimney. There is a layer of clean air around me now, but my lungs are too sick to stop coughing. I drive the smoke further up into the chimney.

It resists, flowing back out into the room. There's something blocking the chimney! My consciousness goes seeking. And finds . . . an oily black lump of cloth and burnt feathers. My quilt! Someone has shoved my feather quilt up the chimney and lit a huge fire. Firerock spills out of the grate, heaped high on the hearth and spilling out onto the charred floorboards. The hearthrug is smoking. A few more ticks, a minute or two, and the entire room will be in flames. Someone is trying to kill me.

I hear Hazel's voice, and now Twiss, shouting my name. Where is Swift? She was here. She woke me. A hysterical Mistress Quint wails in the background.

Pick the lock, Twiss, I whisper inside my head. And then I'm back in the fight. I'm battling a dizziness, a heaviness, that tells me I won't be conscious much longer. So . . . I gather all my will, and drill a hole in the cloth of the quilt. One by one, slowly at first, and then in a flock – a streaming non-bird of smothering softness – I send the feathers flying on the hot air of the fire. Up up up. Through the twisting, creosoted tunnel of the chimney and out into the winter sky. Freedom: I give them freedom. And the smoke follows.

Vomiting smoke is not a happy thing. When my body forgives me enough to stop the punishment, I sit in a heap on the corridor floor, leaning forward, my head resting on shaky knees, and wait for my throat to stop burning. *Where's Swift? She was here. I heard her!*

Quint hands me a flagon and I sip it without even asking what's inside: it's honey and lemon, and mead, which I usually detest. But I drink thirstily, and hand the flagon back to her for more. The honey soothes my throat and the mead calms my brain and slows my heart, which is thumping fit to burst.

'Why did you do it, Zara?' Hazel sits cross-legged opposite me, watching, her face unreadable. A sharp fox of a woman. What does she mean?

'Do what?' I croak. And immediately wish I hadn't tried to speak: my throat is stripped and raw.

'Try to kill yourself. Is it because of what I said about your women not being allowed to work here?' She sounds more curious than sad, but it takes me a moment to take in what she's just said.

'Our women? Not allowed to work?' Quint hands me the refilled flagon then turns to stare at Hazel. What do you mean?'

Hazel smiles at her but says nothing – thank Time! She returns her foxy gaze to my face.

My mouth opens but no words come out. I hadn't thought to be accused of self-murder! And I can't explain the truth.

'What the hell are you talking about?' Twiss emerges from the remains of my room in time to hear the Maker's question. Her face, thundery before, darkens to full cloudburst. 'Zara never tried to do herself. Don't be a donkey. Someone wanted to murder her.'

'The room was locked from the inside, child.' Hazel looks at the thief, eyebrows raised in wary amusement. 'Her quilt was shoved up the chimney and a week's worth of firerock heaped in the fireplace and set alight. I applaud your loyalty but surely it's more help to Zara to find out what is troubling her so sore?'

'You don't know her. I do.' Twiss glares. 'An' you don't know nothing about any of us or what we done. We got enemies you ain't got a clue about.'

'Twiss!' My voice comes out a cracked and hoarse hiss. The thief's lips tighten but she stops arguing and comes to squat beside me. I shoot Quint a warning look and she huffs and bustles away down the corridor.

'Neat job,' Twiss whispers, eyes still glaring at Hazel. 'Picked the lock and in and out while you was sleeping. Any longer and you'd be dead.' She wrinkles her nose. 'How come you slept so sound then, Zara?' The glint in her eye tells me she's guessed.

I look away. And she growls in anger as her suspicions are confirmed. 'Bloody fool!' she hisses. 'If I can't trust you I'll have to sleep with you; and I got stuff to do, Zara.'

Stuff? What does the thief mean?

'Later!' I manage to whisper back. I don't dare look at Hazel, but I feel the sharpness of her interest.

Twiss just grunts. Then groans as boots clatter up the corridor at a gallop. 'Oh piss!' she mutters. 'Here comes Mr What-We-Don't-Need.'

Aidan lurches to a stop in front of me, face white. 'What the hell happened, Zara?'

I shake my head. I can't tell him: not in front of his sister. And I can't let it become known that I've been the target of an assassination attempt. People would ask why: why I alone was targeted, out of all the Knowledge Seekers? What makes the red-headed girl so special? I'm trapped.

'It was a moment of hysteria.' My voice is a hoarse croak. I hate having to live this lie. But what can I do? I swallow hard, try to find some spit to moisten the words I must speak: 'I lost . . . balance. Did something stupid. It won't happen again.'

'She tried to kill herself, Brother. I expect it's all been too much: losing her family and home, then the dreadful journey here. And now the prospect of marrying you, no doubt. But she's safe there, at least. Our mother won't let her darling marry a failed suicide, no matter how beautiful. The girls of Gengst can celebrate the return of the receptacle of all their maidenly dreams and lustful yearnings.'

Aidan whirls around, outraged. And Hazel backs away, laughing. Turns and runs. But not before she gives me a last, speculative look.

'I assume you did not, in fact, try to kill yourself?' Philip strides restlessly up and down in front of the fireplace of my new bedchamber. I sit on the edge of a chair and watch him. So much energy: the artist is never still except when he is drawing. He runs his hands impatiently through his blond hair, making it stand straight up from his head. He looks tired. Strained. He misses Otter nearly as much as I do.

'Of course she didn't,' Aidan snaps. He leaps up from where he's been lounging on the bed, begins to pace too. 'But she's got to pretend she did.'

'I fear so.' Philip sighs. 'That was well done, Zara. I know letting the Makers think you have attempted suicide will not have been easy.'

I shrug, even though Philip's praise is a rare thing.

'I told you Benedict would come for me next,' I croak. And resolve not to speak again today. My throat hurts foully.

Aidan tenses. 'He won't touch you!' the Maker mutters. But I can feel his fear. 'You won't be left alone again,' he says. 'The bastard won't get a second chance!'

'I agree,' Philip says. 'Until the spy is caught you will need to be kept under watch, Zara.'

And what good will that do? I don't say it out loud. They both know: they're playing pretend. No one here is a match for a high adept. Not even me. Sitting here, waiting, would be to wait for Death. I'm not prepared to do that. I will make a plan. I won't be defeated by Benedict or his spy. But until I have my plan, I won't waste time arguing with my friends. They're frightened. So am I!

'Where's Twiss?' I whisper. *Trying not to think: Where's Swift? Was it my sister's voice? A hallucination?* Swift is dead! I have to let go of her. Twiss is very much alive though, and it hurts that the thief isn't here. I try not to mind, but I do. She disappeared almost as soon as Aidan arrived. Does she hate him so much?

'Forget the brat!' Aidan plops back onto the bed, making the springs groan. 'She's the least of our worries. I'd be glad if she disappeared for good.' He sees the look on my face. 'I didn't mean that, Zara. It's just . . . Hazel's right. It's going to be really hard now to get my parents to agree to our betrothal.'

'Just as well, Aidan.' Philip's voice is lemon-sour. 'You and I have work to do. The city is in no immediate danger, despite the seige. The Wall has stood against the Tribute armies of generations of mages. But we are meant to be building the machines that will defeat the mages for once and all, and now we have a dangerous spy on the loose. I don't need you to be playing a lovelorn suitor. We're all of us safer if Zara stays as quietly out of notice as possible. If you had thought to consult me –'

'Consult you about who I intend to marry? Who the hell do you think you are?' Aidan shouts. Then groans, leaps off the bed and holds out his hand in apology. 'Sorry, Philip. But you just don't understand. You've never been in love. And you're old.'

Despite my sore throat, I nearly splutter at the look of outrage on Philip's face. The artist has his vanities, as we all do. And he's probably not much past forty, after all.

'Well thank you for that, Aidan of Gengst.' The Nonpareil

gives his most elegant and chilly court bow. 'As my love life is something of which you have no knowledge, I would thank you to keep your opinions to yourself.'

I do splutter. And both turn around wearing identical expressions of outrage. I dissolve in giggles. Gods' mercy! That hurts! But worth it!

'The point is,' Philip says in a stiff voice, 'that we have to find Benedict's agent – adept or not – before they kill Zara.'

A chill runs down my back as I face my situation again. How do I fight a hidden enemy? The last time I battled an adept I nearly died and that was an open battle. The spy won't fight fair; won't give me a chance to fight back. I was lucky this time, that's all. I'm an easy target.

Suddenly, my plan comes to me! This could work. I know it. I feel a surge of excitement. There's only one way to stop myself being killed, but . . . Philip and Aidan will never agree. I fear I have no choice: I can't tell them.

A knock, and the door opens.

'May I come in?' Hazel sweeps in without waiting for an answer. She carries several books in her arms. When she sees Aidan, she rolls her eyes. But when she catches sight of Philip, standing beside the fireplace, her face glows red. 'Oh. I am sorry; I hope I don't intrude . . . Sir Philip.'

He inclines his head in answer. I'm amused to see that Hazel's obvious awe has puffed him up nicely after Aidan's slight. But I'm even more amazed at Hazel's reaction to the Knowledge Seeker: where is the acidic jokester now?

She seems totally caught off guard, a look in her eyes that I cannot read. The expression is only there for a tick, then the

Maker girl produces her public smile. She turns to me and says, with disarming lightness, 'I brought these for you, Zara.'

Hazel hands me one of two leather-clad volumes. 'Poems. They aren't too bad, and they're short at least, for when your head aches. And mostly cheerful.' She gives me a look.

'I'm not about to kill myself,' I whisper in my ragged voice.

'Good. Please don't.' Her tone is breezy, and I almost warm to her. 'And this . . .' She offers me the second book. '. . . is a northern saga written by a religious hermit. Quite entertaining in places. And it might help you start to understand this strange place you've come to. The North isn't all bad, you know. There are some compensations. The fish are quite tasty.' She smiles, sharing the joke. I feel I've passed some sort of threshold with Hazel. Why? I'm more puzzled than ever by Aidan's sister.

'May I come visit you tomorrow? I would like to get to know you better.' Is this more of her strange humour? I wish I could read her emotions better, but she is one of those who remain opaque. Should I put her off? I open my mouth like one of her northern fish, gasping for an answer, but she presses my hand and whirls around to confront Philip, like a soldier plunging headlong into battle.

'I have a favour to beg of you, sir.'

Her voice trembles, ever so slightly. What can be bothering the woman? Despite my worries, I'm intrigued.

So, it seems, is Philip. He is not a man who seems to notice women sexually. I have often wondered if he prefers his own gender. Or simply has no interest in physical relations with either. I would have said the latter. But there is something about Hazel which has attracted his attention.

She is a woman who would attract the attention of many men, but it would take a brave or – I think of the broad, mauve gentleman at dinner – a very foolish man to attempt a wooing in the face of her barbed wit. In our country, she is the sort of person who would do the wooing, or have none at all. But the rules, as I am only too aware, are not the same in the land of the Makers.

'I'm sure you've no need to beg, Madam.' Philip inclines his head, warily. 'How can I be of assistance?'

Hazel squares her shoulders, dips a hand into an embroidered pocket worn on a ribbon around her waist, and pulls out a leather-bound notebook. She steps forward and proffers it to the Seeker. 'Would you take this book away with you, sir? And glance through the contents when you have a few moments you do not value highly? I would welcome . . . I wish you to tell me if I waste my time in this endeavour.' She thrusts the book out at him, her whole arm trembling.

Philip looks taken aback. He takes the book and holds it, glancing down at the cover, but making no move to open it. 'If I am correct about what this volume contains,' he says, raising his eyes at last to hers, 'then I shall be pleased to examine it. But I *will* tell you the truth, mistress.'

'I know,' she says. 'I thank you for that.'

'I hope you may.'

Hazel nods. She steps backwards, turns without a word and walks from the room. And I have no idea what has just happened.

15

'Where have you been?'

Twiss ignores my question.

'I'm sleeping here tonight,' she says. 'You ain't safe on your own. Not if you're set on being a blame fool!' It's the only reprimand she's given me for fleeing into Elsewhere too deeply.

She sighs and says, 'Right pissin' mess, this place. We shouldn't have come.' Her face is glum. No, it's worse than that – she's worried, and Twiss isn't one of life's worriers.

'About Otter . . .' I begin cautiously. Comforting Twiss can be a dangerous business, but like all the young thieves of Asphodel, she idolised the Guardian.

'Isn't about that!' she growls. Hands off it is.

'All right.' I take a breath. 'So what exactly is wrong? Other than the fact that Benedict has set a rogue adept loose in Gengst, of course. Anything else bothering you?'

Twiss rolls her eyes.

'All right.' Try again. And then I have it. 'Is this about the job Mistress Floster gave you to do here? Making contact with the guild of thieves in the city?' Her scowl tells me I'm right.

'Is there a problem?'

'The problem is that there ain't no thieves!' She stares at me. Behind the mulish expression I see real fear. 'I been everywhere: markets, never-never shops, back streets, doss houses, even down the sewers. And I ain't seen no thieves. Nary a one.'

'But that's . . .' I stare at her. 'Do you mean no one steals here?'

'Course there's stealin'. But it ain't proper. Amateurs.' Her voice drips scorn. 'Just poor folks or chancers. And they're crap at it in any case. There's easy pickin's –'

'Twiss!'

She rolls her eyes. 'Don't fash yourself! I ain't so stupid. Floster give me a job to do and I've done my best . . . only I don't know what to make of this place, Zara.' She frowns. 'I'll keep huntin' but I know I won't find nothin'. There ain't a Thieves' Guild in this cursed place. It ain't human!'

She collapses cross-legged next to the fireplace, grabs up the poker in a grubby fist and jabs at the coals. Anxiety rises from her like steam. I go over and kneel down beside her.

'What will you do?' I ask, after a time listening to the coals sizzle. They smell of mineral, of rock – the smoke is strange and bitter. 'Go back to Floster to report? You can't make that journey by yourself, Twiss. Maybe I should come with you.' Part of me leaps at the idea of escaping this city that feels like a deathtrap.

'You can't go back. He'll kill you.' She doesn't need to say who.

'He's already tried. His agent won't give up. I'm not safe here.'

'Safer than out there.' She jerks her head in the direction of the Wall, and the foothills beyond that lead to the plains we've just spent weeks crossing. Death waits there too.

'I can't just sit here in the open like a target!' I leap to my feet, rubbing my arms to try to warm up. Reminding myself of my plan, and that I'm not dead yet.

'I need you, Twiss. You're the only one who can help me. I have a plan but it means I'll have to disappear. Hide in Elsewhere and hunt them down. Elsewhere is the one weapon I've got. And you. Together we can find them and stop them.'

'I won't help you.'

I stop moving and just stare at her, all the words knocked out of me. I know that Twiss would die to save my life. As I would for her.

'You have to stay right here, in this room, where it's safe.'

It's like she's reciting a lesson.

'Where me and Philip and that Maker of yours can keep guard. We won't let that bastard get you. We're bound to catch the spy soon. But if you go wandering around you'll end up dead before moonrise.'

So that's it! Philip and Aidan have got to her already.

'If I stay here I'm a perfect target.' I force myself to speak calmly.

'And if you lose yourself in the city?' she asks. 'The spy knows the city, they know you, and they'll be expecting just this sorta thing and you won't last a day. The last thing they'll expect is for you to stay put. Just trust us, Zara. Besides, you can't live in Elsewhere all the time: it's too tiring. Your only chance is to stay put and keep your nerve.'

I had counted on Twiss. Now I'll have to lie to her too, and I hate that. But if I'm sticking to my plan, the pretence has to begin now, so I mutter: 'Like that's easy!'

'Nothing's easy!' Twiss turns her back on me and pokes the fire viciously. 'We need to trap this bastard and kill 'em quick. Then I got a job to do.'

'What job?' Something in her voice drags me away from contemplating my own worries. 'I thought you'd finished. You said there isn't a guild.'

'I'm going to find out why they ain't here. There'll be a reason. There's *always* a reason.' And she lifts her head and stares into the stinking blue flames.

'We can't stay in Gengst if half of us are denied . . .' Fredda the Counter's voice dies to a whisper at the hugeness of what she's trying to define, '. . . everything!' she says at last. The rest of the Knowledge Seeker council watch her, silent and grim faced. We are crowded into the small parlour attached to Philip's bedchamber, talking in hushed voices, fearful of those we hoped would befriend us.

'Our women would not be allowed to exist as who and what we are. We would lose ourselves. It is impossible! We can't stay here.'

Quint is nodding furiously.

'So where do we go, then? To live on in the clouds?' Hammeth growls. 'Back to Asphodel and death? Because that's the only thing left.'

'And this is a living death!' Quint snaps. 'My life *is* my work!'

'Hammeth is right,' I say. 'We have nowhere else to go. And surely, the Makers can be made to understand that our ways are different from theirs. Their whole society was born out of a battle for freedom; they can't deny it to half their people forever. Surely . . .' Quint is staring at me as though I'm mad. Which ought to be amusing coming from her, but isn't.

'May I speak?' It's Tabitha, here on sufferance. The silversmith is one of our greatest craftworkers, but she is not a member of the council. Worse, she is a traitor who betrayed the Knowledge Seekers to Benedict when my father held her son hostage. Many died because she could not sacrifice her child to torture and death. There are some in this room who still think she should have paid for her betrayal with her life.

'Of course,' Philip says. He is always exceedingly polite to Tabitha.

'Thank you.' She bows her silver-gold head for a moment. Since her trial and reprieve, Tabitha is humble and hesitant before her former peers. The silversmith will be the last of all to forgive herself. When she raises her head again, her fine-boned face is drawn. 'I am sorry, Zara. I can't agree with you on one count.' She looks ill as she says it. 'I do not think the Makers will change their views on women. Not for a very long time, if ever. I have had discussions these past days with Aidan's brother, Donal.'

'And we know why!' snorts Hammeth.

She ignores him, but her colour heightens. 'Whatever the reason for Donal's interest, Hammeth, the fact remains that I have learned much from our discussions. I have learned that Makers are brought up, men and women alike, to believe that the female is lesser than and inferior to the male. It is just as we were taught about ourselves in Asphodel: we were trained to think of ourselves as somehow less human than mages because we are unable to do magic. Both these ideologies are built on the same principle: power. Most Makers will not accept women as equals to men. Not for generations, if ever.'

'That can't be true!' I cry.

'Zara, I'm sorry. We need to face our situation as it exists. I learned years ago not to trust false hopes.'

'And your opinion on our course of action, Tabitha?' Philip asks. I feel his approval. Tabitha is leading us where Philip himself wants to go. But I don't!

'Compromise,' Tabitha says. 'We, the women of Asphodel, we will have to give up our integrity so the group may survive. It will not be lightly done. Or easily. But the only other option is death. And I want my son to live.'

Quint shakes her head, her lower lip mulish. 'I will not stop healing people. I would rather die. What you speak of is a life not worth living.'

I've never seen her like this. The bounce and joy are gone. What remains is a small, round, angry woman.

I don't know what to think. Who is right? Quint, or Tabitha?

'Maybe . . .' Hammeth's voice is unusually hesitant. 'Maybe, Philip, you could negotiate a deal with the Makers. Ask them to allow our women to work inside the group. Only for us. So Mistress Quint doctors us, and Fredda does whatever it is counters'll do here. And Tabitha, she makes her silver. We can still trade that to the Makers; they don't need to know who made it, and Tabitha's the best silversmith I ever knew of. It would be a crime for her not to work.' He clears his throat, blushes. Hammeth was the lead hound baying for the silversmith's blood at her trial. 'We live separate and that way they don't have to see what they don't like. It ain't perfect,'

Hammeth says quickly, as Quint opens her mouth to protest. 'But it means we all stay as we are where it matters: here, in this group. And then when this filthy war is over, we can go back to Asphodel. Once the mages are dead and gone.' His eyes shift to me, shift away. I don't totally belong, then.

'I don't like it,' Quint says, sullen, angry. 'It's dissembling. It's lying!'

'It's survival, mistress,' Tabitha says quietly. 'Perhaps it is the answer.'

'I think it makes a great deal of sense,' says Philip. 'If the council agrees, I will open negotiations with the Makers. After all, we have skills to sell them. We do not come to the bargaining table completely empty handed.' The Seeker sounds like he's trying to convince himself. And remembering the man Connor's words at dinner, I wonder how much bargaining power the last Knowledge Seekers of Asphodel actually have.

16

We file out of Philip's rooms. The council drifts apart in quiet clusters of two or three as they head back to their own chambers and enforced inactivity. I'm about to do the same when Mistress Quint scurries up beside me.

'Zara, I would like to talk to you about all this, please. If you can spare the time, of course.'

In anyone else I would think they were being sarcastic. But the Mistress is bobbing up and down anxiously, her black button eyes wide and pleading. I feel her upset and I owe this woman my life, several times over. 'Of course. Where . . .?'

'My room please. I have some potions simmering that I must get back to.' She smiles faintly in relief and patters on ahead, motioning to me to follow. As we reach the door to her chamber, I hear footsteps behind us.

'Zara! Wait!'

Aidan. *Oh, pestilence!* I pretend I haven't heard him and walk faster.

'Zara! Please! Talk to us.'

Hazel's voice this time. I don't want to see her any more than her brother. 'Mistress Quint, quickly. Open the door.'

But the apothecary has turned around and is staring at the footrace behind us in amazement.

The clump-jangle of spurred boots announces Aidan's arrival. I turn to confront him.

'Not now, Aidan. I'm busy.'

Hazel sprints down the corridor towards us, rainbow skirts lifted above darting green shoes, a look of intense enjoyment on her face.

'Yes, now.'

'Young man, I wish to examine my patient – without your help!'

Aidan glares past my ear at Quint. 'And I want to talk to the woman I intend to marry!'

A hand reaches up, grabs Aidan's shoulder and tugs him to one side. And I'm staring into Hazel's pointed face, blue eyes vivid with excitement.

'Oy!' Aidan tries to shove his sister out of the way, but she's wedged herself in the door frame and hangs on, knuckles white.

'Do what Zara says and shut up for just a tick or five, brother dear!' she hisses. Aidan looks surprised, but subsides.

'Zara, listen to us. We want to help. Talk to us, please. We're on your side. *Both* of us.' And she gives me a look so imploring – so desperate – that I can't do anything other than stand aside and let them enter the room. I shut the door after the Makers, and stand with my back to it, wondering what to do.

By the seven gods, this is awkward! I won't be able to talk openly with Quint. And Hazel mustn't know I'm a mage. Can I trust Quint to remember that?

'Oh well . . .' The apothecary still looks taken aback. She shrugs and begins tugging forward chairs. She pushes one towards Hazel. 'Do sit, young lady.'

Hazel collapses into the chair, eyebrows raised in amusement. Soon all four of us sit in a circle in the chilly bedroom, looking helplessly at each other. All except Hazel, who's struggling to suppress a smile. A small fire glows like a red eye in the tiny iron grate of the fireplace. Occasionally, a grudging blue flame licks up from the firerocks. I notice Quint has improvised a sort of hob. Potions in clay pots heat on top of what looks like a bit of metal grating held over the fire on brick legs. It looks precarious.

'What is it you want to say?' I ask Aidan.

'I saw the council coming out of Philip's rooms. You've had a meeting, obviously.'

I shrug. It's none of Aidan's business. Nor his sister's.

'Oh, come on, Zara! It's about Knowledge Seeker women and the alliance between our people, isn't it?'

Quint sheds haphazardness as I watch. Her eyes narrow in calculation. 'Zara, should we discuss this before . . . outsiders?'

'I'm not an outsider!' barks Aidan. 'As it happens, I'm the closest thing Zara has to family!'

'A bit possessive there, Brother?' Hazel's voice is sharp. 'Zara might have her own thoughts on the matter. You don't own her yet, and besides, the rather scruffy little girl might argue with you.'

'Twiss?' Aidan splutters. 'She's just a child and besides that she's a . . .' He remembers in time and clamps his mouth shut, looking horrified. Why? He was about to call Twiss a thief. So why look so horrified? She *is* a thief.

'Jealous, Aidan?' Hazel's sharp eyes fix on me.

'Wasp!' Aidan hisses, but his face flushes.

'We digress!' Mistress Quint looks at me, wobbling her whole chair in anxiety. 'Do we discuss council business? Aidan, I know, is an exception. But . . .' The apothecary frowns uncertainly at Hazel. Receives a smile that would melt a lesser woman, and coughs in confusion.

'I would be interested in Hazel's views on the matter,' I say, after a moment of hard thinking. 'She is better placed than Aidan to understand what it is to be a woman in this place.'

'I thought so!' Hazel pounces. 'Your meeting was about how Maker women live. And your fears for yourselves. Please,' she pleads directly at Quint. 'I'm on your side. I want to know what you discussed. What you intend to do. Believe me, I am not a disinterested party.'

Quint nods at last. 'Very well. Zara, you start. I find I can hardly speak on the subject for upset.'

'As Makers, you know how the non-magic are treated by magekind,' I say. 'They are denied full humanity and enslaved. We come here in search of freedom, and find that women are treated little better than those the mages call kine.'

'You are correct,' Hazel replies. 'Females are not thought to be fully human by the men of my country.' She sounds amused, but I see the glint of something darker in her eyes.

Aidan shifts uneasily in his chair. He's frowning. But he stays silent.

Hazel continues. 'Women cannot own property here: they *are* property. Our mother was sold at fifteen to my father. No money exchanged hands, but she was sold, in truth, to strengthen a political alliance between the two families. Married to an old man of forty-five for his sexual pleasures and to bear his children. It has killed something in her soul.'

Aidan jumps up from his chair. 'How dare you say that? Mother would never say so!'

'No. She wouldn't dare think it: it would destroy her. But deep inside, she knows. Believe me.' Hazel slowly stands and turns to face her brother. 'And what you mean, Aidan, is how dare I *think* such a thing? Well, I do think it. I live it every day of my life. Try, for once, to imagine what your life would have been like had you been born a girl. Put yourself in my place, Brother! It's taken all my wits to keep what little freedom I possess.'

'By scaring off your suitors . . .' He says it slowly. 'I thought you were just . . .'

'What? A fool? Someone who delights in mischief? You've never thought about me at all. Not properly.'

They look at each other for long ticks. So alike: the same height, same hair. A muscle in Aidan's jaw clenches. I sense anger, but also confusion. And guilt? He slowly lowers himself into his chair again.

'The life here damages the women of this land.' Hazel's voice is hesitant. I think she must be speaking words she's long thought but never dared say out loud. 'Maker women have no political or financial power. Even our minds are enslaved. Most women aren't educated and those that are don't dare think as I do. My mother, for instance. She knows, but she won't let herself think about it. She'd go mad. And she has too much to lose. She lives through us. Through her sons, anyway. Oh gods!'

She sighs. 'Intriguing that women in the mage city-states are free. I wonder why . . .'

She looks at me. 'Do you know why?'

I shake my head. Her words have stunned me, as they have Aidan. It's so much worse than I imagined.

'It has to be about power,' Hazel muses. 'Everything is about power . . . Ah!' Her eyes widen. 'Of course! Because of their magic, mage women are as powerful as the men. Male mages cannot control you with the strength of their bodies, cannot pretend they are stronger and therefore somehow superior. And the society of their non-magic slaves copies that of its masters. Intriguing that good can come out of the evil of magic.' She shudders. 'But the point that concerns you Knowledge Seekers is that none of your women will be able to work at your trades here.'

'We will!' Quint says. 'I am a healer. Leader of the guild of apothecaries of Asphodel. That is who I am. I work.'

Hazel's eyes widen. 'You have my respect, Mistress. But please, take care. This is not your world. Not your city. Is doing your work worth dying for?'

I stare at Aidan's sister. 'Are you serious? Aidan?'

He's been staring at the floor. Now he lifts his eyes. 'If Mistress Quint or Tabitha were to set up shop and work at their trades in the city . . . if they were to try . . . I don't know what would happen. It's not a situation that's ever arisen.'

My mouth goes dry.

'Why didn't you tell me any of this? All the time, on the journey here. You let Tabitha think . . .' I stop myself. He looks miserable enough. And recriminations won't help anything.

I take a deep breath. 'Perhaps we can find a solution. Philip is going to negotiate a deal so that our women can work within our group if nowhere else.'

Hazel blushes at the mention of Philip's name. 'Perhaps . . .' she says. 'Perhaps that might be allowed. But be very careful, all of you. And pray that we win the war soon so you can return to your cities. And if you do so, I will come with you!'

The apothecary rises to her feet, knees wobbling. Her face is pale. She stands looking from Hazel to me, suddenly resembling a small plump child, lost and alone. She wrings her hands and gazes at me imploringly. 'It will be all right. Won't it?'

17

As I lay my hand on the doorknob of the bedroom I've been assigned, I hear a noise inside the room. I snatch my hand away and stand, staring at the door, heart pounding. Is it the adept? If I use magic to find out, they'll spot me at once. How simple, how elegant, to just sit inside, waiting. And kill me as soon as I cross the threshold.

Do I go in and hope by some miracle to win a magic duel? Retreat? Or just stand here until they hear my heart thudding louder and louder? Then I remember the gift given to me by the thieves of Asphodel. If the gods are with me I can strike before my father's assassin realises I'm here. I might have a slim chance, and that is enough. No more waiting, letting them chose the time and place. Let's finish this. The bastard killed Otter. I desire nothing more than to return the favour.

I slip gently and deeply into the safety of Elsewhere. I am now invisible to all eyes except those of a trained member of Twiss's guild. I'm not-seen, and now I must use all the skill I've learned, and be not-heard as well. I grip the doorknob, concentrate on being wholly present in every movement. I ease the door open, praying to the great god Time that the hinges don't squeak. The god heeds my plea, and the door swings inward without a noise. I ease myself onto the balls of my feet and the soft leather soles of my boots allow me to stalk, cat-like and soundless, into the room. I gather my magic. Look for my prey . . . and lurch out of Elsewhere.

'What are you doing in my room?'

The maid leaps to her feet and jerks around, a guilty flush turning her pink face even pinker.

She's been searching my meager possessions: rummaging through the pack that contains a few precious letters; a single book saved from my father's ruined library. A comb. And: importantly, the thick cosmetic that covers the silver mage marks inscribed on my cheeks and forehead. The maid holds the jar in her hand. Has she just opened, or just closed it?

A fine sweat beads on my forehead as I think what it would mean if she – or any Maker – knew what that jar contained, and what it concealed.

'Ah!' She squeals a breathless scream. 'Where did you come from? I never heard the door.'

'That's no answer!' I hold her gaze. And see, as though I'm looking through a window into her mind, jealousy, fear and dislike of me verging on hatred. But she doesn't even know me! Why hate? Why jealousy? A reason occurs to me, but I don't want to believe it.

'Why are you searching my room?' I step forward, trying to intimidate. 'Answer me!'

'I'm not . . . I'm just tidying.' She stuffs the jar back into my pack. Straightens, lifts her chin. 'And you can't prove otherwise. No one would listen to you, anyway. Dirty mage slave! Look at you: dressed like that. In trousers! What man would look at you?'

It's true. My heart feels scraped raw.

'I think Aidan will believe me. Don't you?'

Her full-lipped mouth convulses. Confirmation. My throat is intolerably dry. 'I think you should leave,' I manage to say. 'And I don't want to find you in my room ever again. Is that clear?'

She stands, clenching her fists convulsively. 'He won't marry you!' she spits at last. Desperate to inflict hurt. If only she knew. 'Your kind are slave fodder! He's destined for better than you! He will make a grand alliance!'

'He won't marry you either, then.' I watch her mouth open and close. See the pain in her eyes. The defeat. And then she looks past me as though I don't exist and marches towards the door.

'Wait!' I call. Without turning around, I ask: 'What's your name?'

'Alissa,' she says. 'Not that it's your business.'

'And how old were you when he first took you to his bed, Alissa?'

I hear a gasp. 'How d-dare . . . I'm not a slut like you!'

The door slams. Footsteps run away down the hall.

Slut. Is that what they call women who sleep with those whom they desire? And do they label men the same? What sort of insane place is this? What twisted gods do they worship? Where have you led me, Swift, with your childish dreams?

Aidan has brought a chess board. He's setting out the pieces. The air of my bedroom is thick with unspoken words.

'Twiss is supposed to be here with me. I thought you had to work. Where is she?'

Aidan's fingers root amongst the wooden figures. As I watch his face, I can't stop thinking of his mouth on Alissa's. His muscled brown skin pressing on her soft pink flesh.

'The thief has disappeared again,' he replies at last. 'So you're stuck with me.'

'Where has she gone?'

Aidan shrugs to indicate both ignorance and lack of concern, and places a warrior mage on the board.

Twiss, what are you up to? But I can guess: she's trying to solve the mystery of the lack of thieves in Gengst. Time keep the girl safe!

'You're supposed to be working with Philip on weapons,' I say, several moments later. Aidan sets a black dragon in its place, brows furrowed in concentration.

'We start tomorrow. Thaddeus is very excited.'

'You'll take him?'

'He's my apprentice.' His eyebrows raise in a question.

'And Tabitha is happy with that?'

'Yes,' he says quietly. 'Very happy. She wants him to have a future. And he needs to keep busy. Or he starts . . . remembering.'

'I see.' Poor lad. I'm glad Aidan cares for him. He has two people who love him. Perhaps, someday, the nightmares will fade.

But Aidan's words mean that the silversmith doesn't believe we will return to Asphodel. And Tabitha is making sure her son will survive. I can't blame her, but I hope she's wrong. The idea of being trapped here in Gengst forever . . .

'Are you sure you don't have any idea where Twiss is?' I ask again. 'Did she tell anyone where she was going?'

He grimaces. 'You know her better than that. Of course not.'

'I'm worried about her. Keep an eye out for her, Aidan. Please. For me.'

The Maker stops rearranging the already neat chessboard; looks me in the eye. 'Is the brat up to something?'

I shake my head. Then, because I have to know how much he knows, how much he hasn't told me about his city: 'Has she asked you about a thieving community in Gengst? What do you know about a guild here, Aidan?'

'There isn't one.' He shrugs. 'I never heard of such a thing before I went to Asphodel and met Twiss and the rest of them. Thank the gods, we don't have such a thing here.'

'Why do you say that? The thieves saved your life! And mine!'

'Calm down. I didn't mean . . . of course I'm grateful to Mistress Floster and Marcus and the rest of them.'

'And Twiss!'

'And Twiss.' He rolls his eyes. 'But the thieves of Asphodel are different. Their enemy is the same as ours. They're not *real* thieves.'

My laugh is short. 'If you were a crawler in Asphodel, I think you'd find they were.'

'Crawler?'

'Non-thieves. Their victims, in other words.'

'All right.' Exasperation. 'I only mean there's no guild here. Never was, as far as I know. Things are different here.'

'I'm beginning to see just how much.' My voice trails away.

His eyes jump to my face.

I reach out and make the first move. Archmage's Tribute pawn to dragon three.

'What do you Makers do with the Tribute soldiers you capture in war, Aidan?'

He drops his own Tribute pawn. Fumbles as he scoops it up. 'Why . . .'

I can almost feel him considering whether or not to lie to me. He makes the right decision.

'They're sold. As slaves. But they aren't killed!' he adds quickly. 'We give them a chance at a life!'

'As slaves.'

'Yes. But if they work for twenty years, they earn their freedom. At least, the men do . . .' His voice trails off.

'And the women?'

'Mostly, they're sold to the comfort houses.' His voice is uneasy.

'What is that?'

His gaze drops to the board. His face is red. 'Men pay to . . .'

'I see.' My heart is hammering in my head. But the muscles of my face feel frozen. 'And they don't ever earn their freedom?'

'Most don't live that long.' His lips grow thin. 'Disease. Or childbirth. Or abortions that go wrong. I don't know what happens to the ones that survive twenty years.' He looks defeated. Angry. 'You can't pretend the same things don't happen in your cities!'

'Rape and prostitution happen, of course.' I look at him. 'All kine are at risk: both men and women. I just hoped . . .'

'Makers are human, Zara!'

'So are mages,' I reply. 'It seems. I thought magic was the problem, you see. I was wrong.'

We play on in silence. The battle is close fought. Neither of us gains the advantage.

'Are there any slaves in this house?' I ask, as the thought occurs to me. Is *she* one? Surely not: the loathing in her voice when she called us 'mage-slaves'.

'Worm. He's the only one.'

I look up, startled. *Worm!* The servant Otter and I caught spying on us. Is it possible . . .? Could my father have planned so far in advance? Put a spy in place in Gengst years ago?

'How long has he been here?'

'Nineteen years. Next year he will be granted his freedom.'

'What will he do then?'

'Find a job, I guess. My father would keep him on, I imagine. He's an efficient enough servant. But most want to go into business. They apprentice themselves: they seem keen to learn and usually have no trouble finding a place. A few, those who live long enough, even join guilds in time. Become proper Makers.'

Aidan's voice carries on, a background sound to the image in my head: Worm, sliding along the corridors. Worm, unlocking the door to my room with magic. Worm, stuffing my feather quilt up the fireplace. I have no proof. Only suspicion.

'Oh, demons take this!' Aidan sends the pieces clattering to the floor with one sweep of his hand.

'Are you always such a bad loser?' I try to joke. But the air is full of tension, like Asphodel when a summer thunderstorm is brewing. For a moment, I smell the pine resin, the tang of rosemary and thyme of my homeland, and am nearly undone with a sadness so deep it seems bottomless. Tears press hot against my eyelids. Begin to trickle down my face.

In a moment, Aidan is up and around the table. He grabs

my shoulders and lifts me up until I'm standing, facing him. His face is inches from my own. I search his eyes.

'I love you, Zara!' His voice, his eyes, plead. He's trembling. So am I. He's so sad. And so am I. Sadness like a deep, drowning well.

I lean forward. Our lips touch, our bodies find each other. We're holding each other so closely, it's like we want to melt together. Become one. Nothing else matters. Oblivion. Sweeter than Elsewhere. I want it. I want him. I don't care what the cost will be.

We are lost to Time.

The room explodes with the crashing of crockery.

What?

Aidan twists around with an oath. He pushes me behind him and I am both touched and amused by his idiotic but sweet desire to protect me. He jerks the blade from his knife belt and scans the room. The ewer of water on the small dresser under the window is lying shattered on the floor in an explosion of broken shards. Water puddles languidly on the polished floorboards.

We're alone. There's no one else in the room. So how . . .?

And then I catch it: a flicker. The shadow of movement. I peek into Elsewhere. Just enough to confirm.

'Zara?' Aidan is looking for me.

'It's nothing. There's no one here.'

'You went invisible for a moment.' He frowns.

The room is silent. Too silent.

In a moment he'll guess. I step forward, touch his shoulder. Look at him in a way that makes him blink and stare at me like a sleeper woken untimely from a dream.

'Put the knife away,' I say in a throaty voice and lean in for a second kiss. It isn't like the first: I'm too distracted – too angry. But it is very nice nonetheless, and it is deserved punishment!

I pull back to find Aidan's look of disorientation has increased.

'For the sake of all the gods!' His voice is hoarse. 'It isn't seemly that you should kiss me like that! Look at me like . . .'

He pushes me away. Time's grace! What is wrong with him? Face red, Aidan turns away and shoves the knife back in its scabbard. I don't need my empath abilities to know that he's angry. With me!

'What is it, Aidan? How have I upset you?'

'We shouldn't be doing this!'

'Doing what?' I stare at his red, embarrassed face, and suddenly I understand. And the reason is ridiculous . . . and devastating.

'You know . . .' He drops his gaze. Turns away to stare at the broken urn. 'What did that?' His voice is petulant. 'Was it you?'

I stand, hands on hips, looking at his back. Something wet dribbles down my nose and drops off the end, leaving an annoying itch. *Damn Aidan! Damn Otter!* Why Otter? I give up trying to figure that one out and swipe my nose with the back of my arm.

'I didn't break the urn,' I manage to say without sniffing. 'Why? Did it cost a lot? Is that why you're angry with me? Because I can't think of any other reason.'

He lifts his head, shoulders tense, and turns around. Our eyes meet. At least he has the decency to blush.

'What just happened here?' I demand.

'I'm sorry, Zara,' he mumbles. 'It isn't your fault. Not totally.'

'Oh well, that's gracious of you!'

'Sarcasm isn't going to help!'

'Neither is hypocrisy!'

We glare at each other.

'I've told you before,' he begins again. 'We need to be careful. It's easy to get carried away and . . .'

'Sleep together? Is that a bad thing?'

'Maker women don't sleep with their betrothed before marriage.'

'Don't they?' I ask. I stare at him. And think of Alissa. 'And what about Maker men? Do they have sex before marriage?'

'Not with their betrothed! That's what I'm trying to explain.'

'But with other women?'

Aidan opens his mouth. Closes it. 'You don't understand!' He is trying to keep his temper and nearly managing.

'Don't I?' I say softly. 'Men can have sex: that's fine. But women are . . . now, what is the term . . . women are "sluts" if they do. Is that correct?'

He just stares at me.

'Doesn't that strike you as just a little bit unfair?'

'It's how I was raised,' he says at last. 'It's what I believe.'

'I see.' I nod my head. 'Well, I was brought up to think the sexual act was the natural outcome of desire between two people. Nothing more sinister – or more important.'

'But you could get pregnant!' he says, outraged.

My laugh is hard. 'Ma—' I swallow the word as I remember, just in time, Worm, and Alissa, and secret listeners at doors. 'My people,' I say, 'don't have a lot of luck making babies. Anyway, say you decided to have sex with someone here. Not me. One of your maids, for instance.'

Aidan goes very still.

I could stop now. Relent. Be kind. But I don't feel kind. I try to be as honest as I can with Aidan and he has lied to me. Lied by not telling the truth. Perhaps he can't help it; perhaps he doesn't even know what he's doing. But I'm not going to let him get away with it any more.

'That girl. Alissa, for instance,' I say and watch his face grow wooden. 'If you had slept with her, would that make her a slut?'

'Yes.' His eyes stare at me, trapped and angry. But he doesn't duck the question.

'Even if you started it?'

'A woman has a duty to guard her virtue.'

'And would you be a slut as well?'

'A man can't be a slut!'

'I don't see why.'

He's pale now. Biting his lip. Guilt stains the room.

'And if she fell pregnant?'

'She'd be turned out without a reference.'

'And what would happen to her?'

'I don't know!'

'Do you care?'

'I . . .'

'And why not just raise the child? What harm is it to anyone?'

'The servant wouldn't be able to do her job properly.'

'Only for a few months. Is that so terrible when you get a child in return?'

He looks at me like I'm mad. 'But I wouldn't want it! The child would be illegitimate. A bastard.'

'So?'

A blink of disbelief. 'No one could be sure who its father was. A woman who sleeps with one man might sleep with a dozen. The child wouldn't have a proper place in society!'

'Would that matter?'

'Use your head, Zara! You can't have women having babies and no one knowing who the father is!'

'Why not?'

'Because . . . well . . . who would inherit? There would be chaos. How could a man control his property? A father wants his sons to –'

'Yes,' I say. 'It's about power. Hazel was right. It's always about power.'

'Did Alissa tell you . . .?'

'She didn't have to.'

'All that was before I met you.'

'I don't mind about that, Aidan. Well, I do. But not that way. You can sleep with who you want. But don't treat them like a slut afterwards. Not unless you call yourself one as well. Your city is evil. You keep your women in cages. And I'm not going to let you close the prison door on me.'

I take a deep breath. 'I'm not going to marry you.'

'So.' His jaw is clenched. Guilt is swinging towards anger. As it always does. 'How many of "your people" have you slept with then?'

I sense his jealous frustration, but I don't care. I shake my head. 'I'm not going to tell you, Aidan. Maybe twenty. Maybe five. Maybe none. But I'm *not* going to tell you because it's none of your business. I think you should go away now.'

18

'Come out of Elsewhere, Twiss, before I come in and fetch you.'

I'm sitting on the only chair in the room, staring at the window. I don't want to look at the bed, at anything. Except somewhere that isn't here. And the closest I can come to that is the window. It faces the city Wall.

Twiss slides into view, on the opposite side of the room from the broken pitcher. I don't look at her directly.

Silence.

'Ain't you gonna row at me?' The husky voice is sullen.

'I just want to know . . .' I glance up at her at last. All my anger is spent. I feel tired. And sad. 'Why?'

'He's no good for you. He just proved it.'

I look at her. My heart feels stone-heavy. 'Don't you think that's my decision?'

Her mouth grows mulish.

'You're jealous of him.' I sigh, defeated. 'Gods know why, but you are. Just . . . go away now, Twiss. Just get out.'

'I can't! I'm on guard duty! To protect you!'

'Get out. Please.'

'This is my room too!' Plaintive.

I close my eyes and wait. At last I hear Twiss slowly turn and leave the room. For a while I sit and listen to a silence that is only the absence of voices: the hissing of the firerock in the grate and the small creaks and sighs of an old house, the noise of the chair as I draw my jacket around me. The fire has no heat in it. When I can bear it, I open my eyes and sit watching the fire. Do I allow myself hope? I still love Aidan. I don't love how he thinks about women, but he is trying to understand and change. His tenderness towards Thaddeus, his care for Tabitha, his bravery, his ambition to become a great engineer, even his stubbornness: I love all of that in him as much as ever. But I can't marry him. I don't need marriage, but it seems he does. And . . . I can't live here in this place that hates me twice over: for being both mage and female. And he can't live anywhere else. Unless there is a miracle, I must lose him.

I hug myself hard, and wait for the pain the thought brings to fade. If there is to be any hope at all, I have to defeat my father's assassin. And then Benedict himself. Besides, I will go mad if I sit here brooding. Time to act.

Two options offer themselves: to openly carry out my plan to trap the assassin, ignoring the wishes of Philip and the rest of the council, or to trick them. I am reluctant to hurt Philip or Quint, by ignoring their advice. Or to have Twiss growling at me each step of the way, interfering. Being awkward as only she can be. I sigh. Twiss: what can I possibly do about Twiss?

But in the end I don't have to do anything about the thief. Twiss does not return that night to the room we are supposed to share.

I sleep badly. If I survive to escape Gengst, it will be years before I can hope to see Aidan again. The thought is so painful I prefer to lie awake listening for Twiss. And I find myself listening instead for an assassin: for a killer who comes like a lover in the night, bringing Death's kiss. But no one visits the room where I lie, remembering my childhood fear of the dark, and Swift. Swift – my beloved sister, Ita – who lay next to me in my bed and held me close when I shivered from sheer terror of what might be there, in the unseen places. Who sang to me. And told me stories until I could sleep. Out of love. Only love. *Oh Swift! Gods, I miss you.*

The nightmares come, even though I wake. Once more I am in my father's library with my sister. Once more see her fall. Once more throw the glass paperweight at my father's head, aiming with all the skill of my nine-year-old magic. Which is pathetically inadequate.

I stare at the invisible ceiling. 'Benedict. Father of mine,' I whisper to the dark. 'You and I have unfinished business. I won't let your creature do the job for you. That's far too easy. I *will* live. I will live to return to Asphodel, to your house, to the place where you murdered my sister, your own daughter. And I will finish what you started eight years ago. You have my solemn word.'

At last, I sleep.

Aidan and I avoid each other. I glimpse him occasionally, and each time my heart is new-bruised until the pain becomes a constant ache. Twiss remains absent, and each day my anxiety for her increases. Philip is distracted by his machines. He and

Aidan go every day to the warehouses on the northern side of the city where the machines of war are made. Tributes with siege ladders attempt to climb the Wall each night. Each night the Makers' engines and arrows defeat them. Each night children die. Gengst settles into the old, familiar pattern of war.

My daytime guard is now Mistress Quint, who pokes her head into my room several times in an hour to make sure I'm still alive.

For three nights, I wait until she is snoring happily next door, then search the house from the safety of Elsewhere, seeking my enemy. But I see no trace of the assassin, hear only the nighttime noises of humans at sleep, at sex, rising to piss.

The slave, Worm, does not go near my room, or the wing given over to the Knowledge Seekers at all. Perhaps I am wrong about him.

If the house contains no clues, then I must get out into the city. My father's agent must be lurking somewhere close by in Gengst. Watching. Waiting for another chance.

The next morning Mistress Quint disappears after breakfast. She said nothing when she gave me a new pot of cosmetic the night before, just wished me a good night's sleep and rolled off to her own bed. She'll be treating one of the Knowledge Seekers, no doubt. Fredda was sneezing at breakfast. I say a small thank you to the god of bodily humours. Today is my chance, and I'm going to make the most of it.

Quickly, I pull on my outdoor jacket over the indoor one. As I do so, I see Bruin's sword, lying on the floor next to my bed.

I bend down and lift up the leather scabbard of this sword that Bruin's mourning lover, Tabitha, gave to me, the only metal that has tasted my father's flesh. I hold the sword by the hilt, feeling its perfect balance. The metal of this blade is unique: Bruin the blacksmith perfected a new method of forging before he died and this is the only example. Philip has been trying to winkle it off me, but I've resisted. Until the spy is caught I want the sword beside me. It's been my companion since I left Asphodel.

Today though, I must leave the sword behind, tempting as it is to bring it. I mustn't use magic out in the city until I find my enemy – it would alert the high adept to my location. Elsewhere is safe from detection, but moving soundlessly with a heavy sword dangling from my waist will be difficult. One slip and I could have a hysterical Maker crying ghost . . . or demon. Regretfully, I put the sword back beside my bed. I don't like the idea of going into the city on my own without a metal weapon of some sort, though. I pick up the slim leather scabbard of my fighting knife, strap it on.

It's been days since I spent any time in Elsewhere and it shows. Twiss would clip me on the ear in disgust at the noise I make as I creep invisibly down the upper levels towards the grand stair which descends to the hall with its mirrors and ticking long-case clocks.

By the time I reach the wide wooden stair, with its iron and marble bannister, my body has remembered some skill. I am once more as silent as a proper thief. When I reach the hall I pause at the bottom of the stairs for a moment, getting my bearings. How to get out of the house?

Dare I risk magic to unlock a door? If the adept is lying in wait I'll be offering myself as a sacrifice. The walls of clocks in the hall below mutter to themselves. The sound sends an unwelcome shiver up my spine.

'Please, Lord Time, prosper my endeavours and defeat my enemies.' I offer a silent prayer in case I've offended the god by finding his shrines uncanny.

And the god rewards me at once. One of the doors in the hall below opens and Worm backs out, bowing to the room's inhabitant as he shuts the door. He straightens, tugs at his somber green jerkin, smooths his close-lying hair with the palm of his hand, and glides out of sight towards the back of the house and the servants' stairs.

For a moment, I hesitate. Is Worm spying for my father's adept? Or is he merely a slave looking forward to his hard-worked-for freedom? This might be my chance to find out. I race down the last few steps to the hall and catch a glimpse of his narrow green back just before he turns left and disappears.

I slip down the corridor after him, trotting to catch up. I'm grinning to myself. I am filled with a strange sort of happiness. It doesn't matter so much if I die . . . I have always expected to die at my father's hands. But if I must die, better to end like this: fighting back.

I edge down the slick stone steps into the cellar where the servants work. My foot slips and I grab the handrail to keep myself from tumbling all the way down. The stairwell is windowless and dark, and I consider kindling mage light. I feel my way down more slowly, and am pleased when the leather soles of my boots find the cold stone of the basement floor. By the light from a row of narrow windows lining the back wall of the large basement which serves as kitchen, servants' dining hall and offices, I catch sight of Worm. He's hesitating outside the door of a room my nighttime wanderings have told me is the steward, Frip's office, ignoring the bustle of other servants coming and going from the various rooms. Worm takes a folded paper from a pocket in the inside of his jacket, smooths it carefully between thin fingers, then knocks on the steward's door.

I slide forward to catch the last of a muttered conversation, half-obscured by the clattering and clankings and cleanings of a dozen green-garbed servants. I dodge this way and that in my attempt to get closer to Worm. And am nearly skewered by a mop-wielding skivvy. The cleaner remembers the something left behind and whirls around and I duck a mop-blow to the head. All is seeming chaos. Frip's voice is a quiet contrast.

'. . . master chooses to use you as his messenger, but never mind all that, Worm. Be off with you, but be quick. I have need of you within a two-hour to help set out the dinner table.'

'Yes, sir.' Worm bows, slides backwards and is away. Smooth, unhurried and astonishingly quick on his feet. I dart and twist between the rush of workers. Worm is already at the door! I'm going to be too late to squeeze out behind him!

I dart forward just as a bucket-carrying woman swerves out of the way of a boy running through the hall with a brace of birds dangling and dripping feathers, on his way to the kitchen. She swears and drops her bucket, which rolls across my path. I fall headlong and land on hands and knees in a puddle of filthy water. The woman, cursing at the jeering boy, hoists her mop and approaches me with a deadly look in her eye.

If I move, I'll make a dripping trail of wet footprints. If I don't: I'll be mopped. As the angry woman raises her mop to assault the puddle of soapy water and potato peelings, I levitate, tell the stinking wetness to slide from me into the puddle on the floor and – now dry – float myself out of the mop's reach with a tick to spare as the woman attacks the puddle with mop, grunts and swears.

No one has noticed. I dodge after Worm, hands and knees stinging.

My heart is thumping wildly. It wasn't difficult magic, but the shifting of elements will have told any adept within two or three bowshots exactly where I am. No help for it.

Worm has been held up at the door by a stream of servants entering with bundles all carrying in foodstuffs, like the boy. One of the travelling merchants that visit the large townhouses must be in the yard. My prey holds the door wide, and I take the chance to slip through between two of the food laden servants. A blast of cold air frosts my lungs as I dash out into the cobbled yard.

A steaming piebald cart horse, all hairy legs and tangled mane, a quilted blanket warming its middle, snuffles and snorts in the yard. He pulls a covered cart laden with goods. The merchant, muffled like the horse against the frost, is clambering awkwardly back into the driver's seat. He swings himself up at last and picks up his whip just as Worm manoeuvres out the door.

The servant ignores a warning shout from the cart's driver, who hauls on his reins as Worm dashes beneath the horse's nose, out the gateway and into the narrow street running along the backs of the houses. I follow, the merchant's curses racing after me.

19

Worm moves swiftly, like a man late for an appointment. I dodge through the narrow street, over slippery cobbles, past men, women and children trudging, heads covered against the icy north wind gusting through the gaps between the houses. I struggle to keep Worm in view and not bump into anyone.

The grey city, seen in the sharp light of a frosty morning, isn't grey at all: the golden sandstone walls glow gently beneath the soot. Silver granite, used for quoins, lintels and arches, sparkles where the sunlight strikes it. The thick stone slabs of the roofs recede in mellow layers, outlining the city against the distant snow-clad mountains. Gengst is beautiful, seen in this clear light: austere but elegant. So different from the pink, blue, green stucco and red tiles of the southern cities, of Asphodel.

I am pierced by an arrow of homesickness. I shiver inside my southern clothes and run even faster, skittering over a patch of black ice, regaining my balance, and racing after Worm.

Carts and horse-drawn wagons clop past, ignoring the townspeople who dart back and forth across the road, muffled to the eyes against the cold.

Worm's green back disappears behind the bulk of three men

in identical black felt bonnets who straddle the pavement, heads bent in discussion, like a trio of portly crows. I edge past, but Worm has disappeared.

Pestilence!

I pant to a stop, eyes searching. Nothing. *Time's eyes!* And then I see it: an alley on the left. At once, I'm off, lungs aching from dragging in cold air. I hesitate at the entrance of the passage. It's dank, narrow and twisting. The bit I can see seems empty. Worm *must* have come this way.

I edge into the alley, nerves tingling. No one can see me . . . It should be a comforting thought, but my blood is boiling with tension. I make myself walk faster. Look behind me and glimpse . . . Was there movement? A half-seen shadow? No. My imagination. It smells damp here. Moss covers the stone walls of the buildings which rise around me like the walls of a narrow canyon, shutting out the rest of the city. A cloud passes high overhead, its shadow darkens the alley, then glides on. I'm frightened of shadows. *What's wrong with me?*

I break into a trot, running almost silently.

The alley takes a sharp right hand turn, and I swing round it and see Worm – to be exact, the tail of his jacket – disappearing into a small door in the side of a building on the right of the alley. I lurch to a stop at the sight, and grab at the nearest wall to keep from falling over. My hand presses into a patch of wet moss. I jerk it away at once, but I've left the impress of a splayed handprint in the moss. The air shifts. Instinctively, I drop to my knees. And hear an air spike hit the wall above my head and shatter. Shards fly, one pierces the skin of my cheek. The pain is bitter.

And I am rolling, rolling. First one way, then twisting to roll in another. Trying to escape the hail of icy spikes of frozen air spewing out of the dim, narrow alley behind me like a flock of maddened starlings. I look for my father's assassin, and glimpse a short dark figure stalking towards me. Then something punches into my left thigh so hard I think for a moment the bone is broken and I gasp in agony. Shock and pain slow my mind. It takes too long before I notice – as I scrape and crawl for my life – that I'm bleeding heavily from the wound. I'm leaving a trail of blood for my killer to see.

I feel magic build.

And, despite the pain, I'm up and hobbling as I heal the hole in my leg with a single, frantic thought. It's a botched job, a mere scabbing-over. Self-magic is the most difficult, and I have no time.

Lord Time!

Botched or not, the wound is closed and the scent-trail of blood stopped. I slide to a halt, fearful of making noise, another mistake like the moss. I turn to face my enemy. Nothing. The assassin must be hidden beyond the corner of a building that bulges into the alley, narrowing the passageway to shoulder-width. If I try magic the adept will locate me at once, and in my weakened state . . . All I can do is hide in Elsewhere. And get out of this alley! Was all this planned? Is Worm in league with my father's agent?

I'm trying not to pant, trying not to breathe. Fear is a blinding white snow in my head. I've never been so terrified. I want to shout: *Who are you? Come out and face me!*

I have to calm down.

Think!

But no clever thoughts come: only more fear. I ease backward. I'm limping heavily. My leg is weaker every minute. The spike must have damaged a muscle. There will be internal bleeding, but I can't do anything about it now. I'm more worried about the small but persistent trickle of blood dribbling from my right cheek. If I use magic to heal it, the assassin will find me at once. I can only hope that the blood continues to soak into my collar, and the bleeding stops soon.

'Zara!'

A man's voice. Familiar, but . . .

'Zara.'

The voice is quiet, calm, pleasant. And so vilely confident. *Bastard!*

'You know you can't win, Zara. Your father doesn't want you dead: he loves you. Come out now. Give up, and I'll take you back to him. There will be no more danger. No more fear. No more loneliness. You'll be back with your own kind. With those who understand you and can take care of you. Come out, child. Give yourself up: step out into the open. Leave these filthy thieving tricks behind and be the mage you are. Nothing bad will happen, I promise.'

My heart is thudding. It's obscenely loud. It hurts my head. Can't he hear it? *Who is it? I know the voice. I know . . . but don't know. Who?*

I only know one thing: if I step out of Elsewhere, I'm dead. I can hear the lies, even if I can't see the liar, standing just out of sight behind the building narrowing the alley. Bastard! He's so plausible. So believeab—

And in that fraction of a tick, I see his face in my mind. *Oh gods. Oh Lord Time! It's Pyramus!*

Realisation knocks the breath from my body. I'm as good as dead.

Pyramus: my father's spymaster. The most powerful adept in Asphodel after Benedict himself. So anonymous that I can't even remember his face – only the slight, round-shouldered, deadly shape of him.

Shock drops me to my knees.

'You're wounded, Zara.' Smug, smooth, plausible. But is there a note of asperity creeping into his voice?

'I'm so sorry I had to do that. Just come out now, into the open where I can see you. All will be well. You're the daughter of the Archmage, Zara. No one would dare hurt you.'

Except my father or one of his creatures, Pyramus. Except you!

I'm shaking so hard I can't stand up again. I have to move, to get out of here. And I can't use magic. I have to fight a high adept without magic; like a commoner. What fear they must feel: I understand it now fully. Only now. And I have one weapon a commoner would not: the gift Twiss gave me. I breathe, try to remember her lessons. Merge deeper into Elsewhere. And the calmness I need is waiting for me there.

I'm breathing again. The shivering shock lessens. Even the pain in my thigh is numbed. Somehow I find the physical strength to lever myself back onto my feet. Using every muscle, every control Twiss taught, to make no sound. One sound. One mistake. I hear Otter's voice: 'Result: you're dead.'

I should get out of here. But Pyramus will be expecting me to retreat. Will have laid traps. So I'll do something mad.

I ease slowly, stiffly and painfully forward. Creep back up the alley towards the corner of the building narrowing the alley to a bottleneck. I go so very slowly, slipping on the damp, mossy cobbles. And all the time, he's talking. His voice sounds nearer with every step. Calling to me. Persuading. Reasonable.

I unsheathe my knife. Hold it out, creep towards the droning, pleasant, seductive voice. Every particle of stone, fragment of mud vibrates in front of my eyes in a super reality. I sniff for my enemy, like a wolf, but smell only damp, old stone and firerock smoke. So I feel for the disturbance of the elements which is magic building, preparing to strike.

I reach the concealing corner. Ease round. So slowly. Even Pyramus won't expect . . . will he? Every nerve in my body is at full vibration, and I sense, rather than see, the shimmer of magic stretched thin and waiting like the strand of a spider's web. Just in time, I jerk my hand back in the fraction of a tick before the knife point pierces his air ward.

Bastard! May all the demons and serpents of the underworld take him!

I back up quickly, fearful even in Elsewhere. And feel it. The second ward. Only I've already passed through it.

The net comes. Woven of air and stronger than metal. Wraps around me, tightens, squashing the blade from my fingers and wrapping me up and up. I fall to the ground, compress, squashed into a human ball, feel the knife long ways against my left knee where it was captured by the net as it fell. Point out, the gods decreed. Point in and I would have another hole in me. I lie waiting, wrapped like a fly, curled tight on the ground.

He doesn't even laugh.

No gloating. Pyramus is far too professional. A job accomplished. Now to finish it. I hear the footsteps. See, from one eyelid squashed to half-mast, the dark muffled shape of a slight, round-shouldered figure.

'You should have believed me, Zara.'

I leave Elsewhere. I'm caught. And outside I'll have more energy for the fight. Which is useless. We both know that he's won. But still, I will fight. I gather my magic. And he feels it, of course. The web tightens around my throat. I can't breathe.

'Don't be childish. I thought better of you. Don't disappoint me, Zara.'

Now there *is* arrogance. Smugness. The strangling strands around my throat loosen . . . slightly.

I can't speak. Can't move. Can barely breathe. But I can still die. Pyramus: you don't know everything. You won't win! I can go so far into Elsewhere I will never come back.

But what is the point, if he is going to kill me anyway? Curiosity conquers, even now. I wait to find out what my father has decreed.

'I didn't lie to you, Zara. Benedict wants you back more than he wants you dead. Against my advice – but he is the Archmage, not I. I hoped to kill you in my first attack; but as you have survived, I must therefore honour your father's decree that you live, if possible. I will smuggle you out of this accursed place and take you back to Asphodel and to the Archmage. He can deal with you. I imagine, before he's done, that you will wish I *had* killed you.'

I must act now: while I still have consciousness, and strength enough to call Death. I must travel deep into Elsewhere – so deep there's no turning back. I will. I must. It's not fearful. Elsewhere is a gentle, bewitching place. I've nearly gone too far before: seduced by its peace. I must . . . go . . . now.

I journey to the threshold, a slow floating, a giving up, a letting go. Almost. I look into the depths of Elsewhere, past the point of no return. Into a tunnel made of particles of light in every rainbow colour, spinning so rapidly their colours melt together. Elsewhere sings of warmth, of quiet immensity, of peace everlasting. Death waits.

Defeat. An unpleasant word. Swift . . . what should I do?

Wings. I hear the sound of wings. She's coming for me. The clapping, clattering noise grows louder, closer. Not wings. Feet. Shouting. Voices.

And quickly as it formed, the air web collapses. I sprawl unbound on the cold stones of the alley, arms and legs spread-eagled. Eyes open, staring up at the sky. Too exhausted, too ill and shocked to move. To understand. Until he bends over me. Puts fingertips to my throat to feel for a pulse. And when he finds one, hisses as if my skin burns him.

'Are you alive? Or am I dead?' I mouth the words; breathless.

'Time take you! Damn you, Zara! Damn you to perdition!'

Swearing is becoming a habit with Otter.

20

It is a slow, agonising journey back to the house of Fergal the Clock. Several times during that endless hour, I wish I had died in the alley.

All the time his Tribute soldiers are making a litter from the very door Worm disappeared through – hefting me onto it, wrapping me in blankets and strapping me down, carrying me crunching through the snow-clad streets of Gengst – I am desperate to ask Otter so many questions.

But he's gone again. Off to seek for Mistress Quint, who is missing. It seems the spike that tore a hole in my leg may have torn through a blood vessel. My leg throbs in time to the beat of my heart: racing, racing. I'm too weak to try to heal myself now. My mind floats between now and past, lost in the labyrinth of time and memory. What is real? What have I imagined? Did my mind invent Otter?

No. His grip on my hand was too crushing. The look in his eyes too . . . what was the look in his eyes? And where is Quint? I feel a minnow of fear swimming frantically round and round in the watery looseness of my head. Has Mistress Quint done something stupid?

'Where did Otter go? Where has he been?' The teenage soldiers who carry me back to Aidan's father's house ignore my questions. 'Where is Worm? What is that house? Where is the assassin? Is he dead? Did you kill him?'

So many questions. Each met with silence. If my swollen tongue spoke the words; if I did not dream the asking. Tilting, sliding, walls looming, winter sun glaring. Bright bright blue sky of the north. A raging thirst. And the brighter blue of Aidan's eyes, staring down at me when I open my own again.

'Zara.' The sound of his voice is bittersweet.

He doesn't leave my side again, until Otter returns. How much later, I don't know. I'm not wholly in this place now. I have travelled halfway to the land where Death lives. Only Aidan holds my hand so tightly. Calls my name so angrily. So forlornly.

I open my eyes again to see Quint bending over me. Weeping. Ah, some poor soul is ill unto death, then. Quint hates losing. She gives me something thick and bitter to drink. And I tilt, head over heels, into oblivion.

I open my eyes, and do not know where I am. *When* am I? Alas, I know who I am. But . . . I try to grab hold of shifting memories. Half thoughts. I drift in and out, in and out. Why can't I wake?

And as I fight the waves of blackness, as my body slowly returns to me, I feel more ill than any time since Swift's death. But why? What has happened to me? Where am I? And *when*? I stare at a chilly white ceiling. Cold, clean, distant. I lie in a narrow bed clad in white linen. My face hurts; and my leg, my left thigh and my right cheek.

Like a spike of frozen air, memory comes.

Pyramus!

I must have made a sound, for suddenly Quint is there, holding my head as I vomit into a bowl. When I've retched up all I have, she lowers me back onto the pillows with a clucking noise. A damp cloth cools my forehead, cleans my mouth. And when I am strong enough, I open my eyes again, and see the apothecary watching, gauging.

At last, she smiles. Only a little. 'You will live,' she says. Quint places the bowl of puke on the floor. Rinses her hands in a basin of fresh water. Returns to stand, rocking gently back and forth on her heels in the way I always like to think of her: like a child's wobble doll.

'You are a . . . bloody . . . little . . . fool.'

Did *Quint* just say that?

'Who gave you permission to leave this house? You nearly killed yourself!' She breaks off her tirade. Her face is flushed. Her round black eyes indignant. She clears her throat. 'Never mind. That outburst was not professional. I apologise. But really, Zara! You frightened me!' The tip of her nose is bright red. The apothecary turns and bustles out of sight. Returns a moment later with a mug.

'Drink this. Drink it! It's only boiled water with a pinch of dried tree bark to keep your fever down. You've lost a great deal of blood. Your humours are out of balance.'

The mug is shoved against my mouth. Warm and bitter, the water stings my cracked lips. I gulp greedily. Quint takes the mug away when it's empty. I lift a stupidly weak hand and wipe dribble from the corner of my mouth. Then I find enough spit and courage to speak. 'Otter. Where?'

'Hunting.' Her round face grows grim. 'The city's in an uproar. They know a mage is loose in Gengst. You have never seen anything like the panic. The terror. I was nearly . . .' She pauses. Looks thoughtful and averts her eyes.

'Nearly what?' The minnow is a full-sized trout now. 'Where did you go, Mistress? You weren't in this house.'

Now her face is bright red. 'Just a bit of sightseeing. No harm!'

She's a dreadful liar, but pushing the point will only make her more stubborn. She's safe now, which is the point.

'Twiss . . .' I wince. My leg is throbbing in time to my heartbeat. That and the hot, heavy pain in my head tell me I'm feverish.

'The child isn't here.' Quint tries to sound unconcerned and singularly fails. My heart speeds up. 'But Otter says she's fine so she will be.'

It will have to do. I'm not going anywhere for a while. Not until I get strong enough to heal the hole in my leg.

A knock on the door. Before the apothecary can answer, it opens and Aidan edges inside. Hesitant. The moment he sees me, awake, his eyes light up.

'Can I talk to her?' His eyes don't leave me. But he doesn't insist. Doesn't bolt inside. He's asking permission. This is amazing, on the level of small miracles. Quint sniffs, but graciously nods her head.

'A few minutes only. She needs rest.'

'Of course.' And the Maker walks carefully, as if he's on a narrow, high cliff, across the bare wooden floor to my bed. I listen to his boots squeak with an oiled murmur as he nears.

Watch his face and try to read what is written there. My head is so hot with fever I can't feel his emotions. I'm grateful for that. Aidan is tiring, even when he's happy.

Quint shoves forward a chair. 'I'll leave the two of you alone. Ten minutes only, young man.'

'Thank you.'

So formal. So polite. He sets the chair carefully beside my bed. The same precise, careful movements. And sits down on the very edge of its seat. Sits and looks at me. Smiles. Carefully. Gingerly. It's almost like we're meeting for the first time ever.

'Zara? How are you feeling?'

'S'all right.'

'The truth?' Again: a request. Not a demand. I sigh, disarmed.

'Not great,' I say. 'Would you mind?' I nod at the cup Quint has just placed on the bedside table. 'I can't lift it without spilling.'

'Thirsty?'

I nod. He smiles, gently. Lifts the cup and holds it out for me, as tenderly as Quint herself. Drinking comes easier this time. The warm wetness rinses some of the fog from my head. Perhaps . . . perhaps I will feel better soon.

I pull my head away. Nod my thanks, and Aidan returns the mug to the table. Turns his vivid eyes back to me.

'We almost lost you.' His voice is quiet, but his eyes burn blue fire. Oddly, I think of my mage light. And am filled with a childish desire to do that simple, first magic again.

'I almost lost you, Zara,' he repeats. 'It hurt. It hurt more than anything ever. Please be all right.'

'I am,' I say. 'I'll be on my feet soon.' I frown at him. My nearly getting killed doesn't change our situation. Has he forgotten? Or is Aidan pretending to himself yet again that the world is how he wants it to be, rather than how it is?

'Not that soon.' He glances at my leg. 'It'll be a couple of weeks, Quint says. At least you'll have to stay put and out of trouble!'

I sigh. Deserved, I suppose. 'I'm sorry. I was going mad, trapped inside. Do you know what I mean?'

He nods. 'Oh yeah. In your place, I expect I'd have done the same. Or worse.' He grins. 'But, I don't want to lose you. So try . . . *please* try to be sensible?' It's a request.

'I will try, Aidan. But it won't take me two weeks to heal. I should feel strong enough tomorrow to mend my leg myself.'

His face goes solemn. Very solemn. And the back of my neck prickles. What's wrong now?

'You can't do that, Zara.'

'Of course I can. I know mag— I know working on myself is harder than healing someone else, but I can do it. I know I can. I just need a clear head, to concentrate.'

'No.' This time it *is* an order.

'You don't tell me –'

'But I do.'

We both jerk our heads around, Aidan and I. Otter is standing in the doorway.

'And just . . .' I struggle for words; struggle to contain the jumble of emotions racing around my head: joy that he's alive, anger at his trickery. 'Just where in all of perdition have you been?' My voice is as squeaking as a fledgling boy's. It's embarrassing.

'And where's Twiss?' I add, for good measure, lowering my voice by several tones.

The Guardian has changed. He's grown thin. He's tired, worn. I see it in his eyes: in the dark skin beneath his lower lids, in the fine lines around his mouth. My eyes go to his shoulder. The one with the sword wound. But even Otter wears a winter jacket now.

'Well?' I ask.

'I know where Twiss is, and she's fine. You, however . . .'

'Yes?' All my old antagonism at his bossiness, at his presumption – his air of superiority – is rising faster than my temperature. 'I'm what?'

'You are a disobedient, awkward, stubborn liability.' His eyes are cold as the glaciers on the Maker mountains. 'And you will not use your . . . *skills* . . . to heal your leg. You will let it heal by itself. Under the care of Mistress Quint.'

'Why?'

'Why do you think?' His voice is cutting. 'I had to get permission from Aidan's father and the head of the army for my Tributes to enter the city to look for you. Only the truth – that a mage is loose in Gengst – was sufficient to grant me that permission. It wasn't possible to get you back here unobserved. The whole city knows there's a mage on the loose and that a young woman was attacked. It's panic and paranoia out there. Do you have any idea of the trouble you've caused?'

He glares.

My mouth goes drier than ever. My heartbeat speeds as the probabilities begin to present themselves. 'Umm . . .' I say, weakly.

Aidan takes my hand. Presses it firmly, and I glance at him and catch a look of . . . *pity*? Suddenly, I'm very frightened.

Otter walks to the bed and glares down at me. 'These people think magekind are next door to demons. You know that.'

Aidan squeezes harder.

'When people are that frightened, thinking stops. They're looking for someone to blame. A scapegoat. And they've chosen us.'

'W-what do you mean?' I fear I know, and desperately hope I'm wrong.

'The Knowledge Seekers. Rumours are hatching faster than blowflies in a corpse. One of the most popular is that we have a witch amongst us. Someone who called the demons forth, allowed them magical access to the city. Even those who know better – those who know mages are human and don't apparate out of mist and brimstone – have convinced themselves we brought a mage to Gengst. The citizens of Gengst are baying for blood: our blood!'

I'm shaking now. Otter is right. I can't do magic. That's the least of it. My companions, the people who've befriended me despite who I am . . . the very people who trusted me when they didn't have to . . . my friends are in danger because of me. Again.

'I'm sorry.'

'You should be.'

No forgiveness. Not like Aidan.

'It's known that the young woman who was attacked is a Knowledge Seeker. That alone has persuaded the mob not to lynch the whole lot of you. That and my soldiers. But if that victim should suddenly get well . . . the finger of suspicion is going to then find a victim to point at very easily, don't you think?'

Desolation. And guilt. Such guilt. Which is useless. Feeling guilty won't solve the problem I've created.

'What can I do?'

'Nothing, Zara. That is the point. You've done far too much already. Just . . . for once. Do. As. You're. Told.'

'Out!'

Quint barrels across the room. I can barely see her because my eyes are blurred with tears.

'Get out, both of you. I won't have you upsetting my patient, Otter. And Aidan, time is up. Both of you. OUT!'

I don't notice very much for a while. Then I feel Quint's hands on my shoulders, pressing me gently back down on the pillow.

'Sleep,' she says. 'Everything will be all right, Zara. Sleep now, child.'

21

'Where did you go, Mistress? What were you really doing in the city?'

'Nothing to do with you, Zara. Now, deep breath. This is going to hurt.'

I close my eyes. Childish, but . . .

Fingertips brush my thigh, grip the folded linen pad pressed onto the hole in my leg. Peel it back. I gasp as the oozing bits that have crusted onto the cloth pull and pucker the edges of the wound. That was the easy bit. I hear Quint step away, slosh the jar of potion to mix it: the stuff she daubs into open wounds to keep them clean and maggot-free. I dig my fingernails into my palms. She moves back to my bedside. It's so difficult to keep your muscles relaxed and soft when you know that any moment . . .

'Ahh!'

Each time I try not to make a sound. Each time I fail. My leg goes rigid as liquid fire melts into the hole Pyramus's air spike dug in my leg.

'There was a bit of leather from your leggings deep inside,' Quint muses. 'I didn't find it at first. That is, I believe, the cause of this inflammation. But I got it out and your blood was not poisoned. If the blood is poisoned, I can do nothing. But it is well: each time I rinse the wound, the inflammation decreases. We shan't have to do this many more times, Zara. Tomorrow, I can stitch it closed. That will be good.'

'Oh,' I say. Swallowing hard to keep my breakfast down where it should live. 'I'm looking forward to that.'

Quint rolls forward and places a soothing hand on my head. 'Sorry. But it has to be done.'

'Thank you.' I mean it. The Mistress has saved my life. She's happy. Her round black eyes are snapping with glee at having defeated her enemy again.

'Now,' she says, 'I'll change the dressing on your face.'

My face. Suddenly, it hits me: my face. Quint has stuck a cloth over my right cheek, bound it about my head with fine line strips. It doesn't hurt much. Not compared to my leg. But . . . I can't help wondering: what will I look like? There will be a scar. Even my healing magic couldn't have stopped that. But how big? The wound seems to be in the centre of my father's mage mark, the one that was ingrained in my skin when I was a toddler.

Images float in front of my eyes: the whole right side of my face puckered, drawn. The silver lines of the mage mark warped into something foul, hideous. Stupid: it's a small wound. I'm ashamed: I never thought I was vain about my appearance.

'This won't hurt, child.' Quint has noticed.

I can't nod or say anything so I keep still as her deft fingers unwind the binding, pull away the pad of cloth from the wound. She dabs a fresh cloth in her mixture, presses it onto my cheek. A sting. No more. She cleans the area more thoroughly, peering, humming happily.

'Excellent!' She nearly sings the word. 'This is healing beautifully. I have made a special salve to keep the scarring to a minimum. It's on the hob, but it should be ready now. I'll just pop next door and bottle it up. You wait here.'

As if I can do anything else! Suddenly tired, I watch Quint tidy away the soiled cloths and bandages before rolling merrily out the door. I stare at the closed door for a few moments, my mind as blank as its wooden surface.

And blink in surprise as the door opens, slowly. That was quick. And I am slow . . . deathly slow. Fear flares too late: it isn't Quint.

Pyramus?

I bolt up in bed, reach for my magic . . . and slump in relief as a tawny head pokes round the door. Bright blue eyes catch mine. Hazel smiles a question. 'Can I come in, Zara? Just for a moment?'

She slips inside and closes the door silently, before I've had a chance to say yes or no. Leans with her back against the door, studying me. 'I've startled you. Sorry. I should have thought . . .' And her voice trails away as her eyes fasten on my right cheek.

Oh gods! My mage mark! My mother's mark on my unwounded right cheek, and my own mark, on my forehead, are still concealed with cosmetic, but my father's mark is plain to see! Too late, I clamp a hand over the symbol of magehood: threads of silver inlaid in the skin of my cheek in an intricate pattern of swirling lines.

Hazel's eyes move slowly from the mark back to my own, terrified eyes. If she hasn't guessed, she'll know from my face. But I can't do anything. It's too late.

When the apothecary returns, I say nothing. Just lie stone still as Quint daubs ointment on the wound in my cheek. And remember the look in Hazel's eyes: the same shock, the same disgust and loathing that I saw in her brother's eyes the first time we met. How long? How long have I got before she tells someone?

Quint bustles away. The skin on my face tingles, unused to the touch of air. The gaze of human beings. Quint returns, holds out a small round mirror. 'Here. Do look, Zara. Otherwise you'll fret. It isn't nearly as bad as it might have been.'

I feel a compelling fascination. I reach out and take the mirror. Bring it slowly closer until, in its distorted, silvered surface I see myself. The eyes, the nose, the hair, still familiar. At last I make myself look at my right cheek. At the wound my father's assassin made in my face, right in the centre of his master's mage mark.

The irony hits me. My wound will form a shiny white scar just like the one Benedict bears: the only damage I ever managed to inflict upon him. The only mar in his self-image of absolute power. But the symbol of his power that was carved into his child is ruined. The path no longer flows from beginning to end in a timeless cycle: the endless spiral now has a full stop.

I stare, fascinated. Then hand the mirror back.

'None of it matters,' I say softly. I lift my eyes to see Quint's startled expression. I smile, in an attempt to reassure. 'I need to speak to Aidan. Urgently. And . . .' I say his name reluctantly, 'Otter. You had best fetch him too.'

'You can't kill my sister!' Aidan stares at the Guardian, appalled.

'No. I suppose not. I'd have to kill you too, and things start to get rather complicated.' Otter isn't joking. My stomach turns over as I stare at him, as shocked as the Maker.

'Would you kill anyone?' The words blurt out. I regret them: this is my fault. But . . . would he? Does my father's former Guardian have no limits?

'To make the world afresh?' He returns my look, and his mouth slowly curves in the merest hint of a smile. 'If that were possible, Lady, I believe I'd kill even the one I love most to accomplish it. But –' he shrugs – 'I'm not fool enough to believe in perfection. People are people. Human nature doesn't alter. There's no place, no city on earth that will ever be perfect. But things can be better. Much better. All I want is for most people to be able to live a half-decent life. That should be enough for anyone.'

It's almost exactly what Marcus, the thief, said to me so many months ago. A lifetime ago: and we are no closer to that dream.

'You didn't answer the question,' I say.

'Because I don't have the answer.' The Guardian shrugs again. 'I don't know what I would do until the moment comes. But if you're asking would I kill an innocent person if by doing so I'd save a hundred more? Yes.'

I look away.

'I'll find Hazel. Talk to her,' Aidan offers.

'You'll have to. I just hope you can work magic as well as your lady-love.' Otter's voice is dry. 'Because if your sister tells anyone before I can get Zara out of Gengst . . .' He looks at me. 'You will die. I won't be able to save you. Most of my army is still on the plains. The troops I have in the city are not sufficient to defeat the Gengst army, even if it were a good idea. Which it isn't. We're supposed to be working with the Makers to defeat Benedict's forces, not doing his job for him!'

'I'll go into Elsewhere!' I blurt.

'Maybe.' Otter's eyes narrow as he studies me. 'You're not strong yet. But you could. And then, what do you think would happen to the Knowledge Seekers? With the witch-hunt going on in the city?'

His words pound in my head. I stare at him. I know what he's asking me. But do I have the courage?

'That's not going to happen!' Aidan is on his feet, halfway to the door. 'I'll find Hazel. I'll stop her mouth.'

'Aidan!' I cry.

'Don't worry!' His voice is vicious. 'I won't kill her. By the gods, she's my sister! But I'll find a way. I promise! I'll make her understand.' And he's gone at a run.

I look back at Otter. His face is as bleak as my own. Then something, a thought, leaves a passing trail over his face.

'What?'

'There's one other. Someone Hazel will listen to. I'm pretty certain . . .'

'Wait!'

But Otter is gone already. Two of his soldiers enter. Stand either side of the door. Silent. Armed. Watching me. And saying nothing. My protectors? Or my prison guards? I press my fingers against the fresh bandage covering the right side of my face, hiding the fatal mark from their view. Do they know what I am? Would they kill me outright if they did?

* * *

At some point in that endless morning that stretches into the aftermid, I fall asleep beneath the stony gazes of the two Tributes guarding my door. It's a heavy sleep, riddled with half-glimpsed dreams that chase me to the threshold of consciousness where I surface for a gasping moment, like a dolphin sounding, before sinking again.

At last I'm dragged up from the darkness by the sound of a voice repeating my name. The aftermid sun slants low across the wooden floor, catches the foot of my bed, a solid slice of light. Heavy as the knowledge that this is a bad place to be now. It's bad to be me.

'Good afternoon, Zara.' The room is crowded with people and emotions. Quint puts a cool, smooth palm against my forehead. Looks at my eyes for signs of fever. 'Stick out your tongue.'

Aidan stops pacing and looks at me. As do the others: Otter, and beside him . . . Philip. Philip? Then I see Hazel herself. She stands beside Philip, not Aidan. And she is staring at me with a half-fearful, half-disgusted expression I know so well from my weeks and months living in the catacombs with the thieves and Knowledge Seekers. When all feared and mistrusted the mage in their midst.

I do as Quint orders and stick out my tongue, feeling a fool.

'You'll do. Here, let me help you sit up.' Her surprisingly strong arms lift me, arrange my pillows. Then she turns to confront the others. 'She is not yet completely well. If you tire her, I'll have you out of my sick room at once.' She nods twice for emphasis, bobs across the room and plumps down in a small narrow chair beside the window. The sun cuts her shadow out of black paper and lays it on the floor.

'I am sorry to be the cause of so much trouble,' I say. It seems a feeble statement in the circumstances. 'I would leave the city,' I continue in the face of a vast silence stretching between me and the four people standing at the foot of my bed. 'But Otter has said that could be dangerous for the rest of you.' I look at Philip.

The Knowledge Seeker frowns. 'You shouldn't have gone into the city, Zara. Otter was lying in wait for the assassin, and the attempt on your life was meant to take place here, in the house, where we could have had a chance of trapping the villain.'

I stare at him. Otter was using me as bait? *And no one told me?* My gaze shifts to the Guardian. How dare he play with my life and not even tell me? Not even tell me that he was alive?

'If you had treated me as an equal, a grown-up, and told me your plans, this wouldn't have happened,' I say to Otter. 'And you as well.'

I look at Philip, who has the decency – that the Guardian does not – to blush. 'You knew. You might have told me, but you got too caught up in your machines. I'll bet you haven't even remembered to talk to the Gengst council about the women.' I glance at Mistress Quint, who's suddenly looking flustered. 'Have you?'

'This isn't about that, Zara,' Otter says. 'And I make no apologies –'

'No, you never do!'

'She's right,' Aidan says. 'You should have told her she was bait in your trap. You set her up. You set us both up. You should have told us!'

'You're not a good actor, Aidan. And Zara couldn't be trusted not to tell you. Besides, she didn't need to know.'

Arrogant bastard!

'Haven't you talked to my father and the others about your women and their work?' Hazel speaks for the first time. She's frowning in confusion at Philip. 'You promised me.'

Philip draws breath. He turns to Hazel and there's a look in his eye I have never seen before. *I don't believe it! It's happened at last. The Nonpareil is smitten!*

Shamelessly, I tune in my empath senses. Yes, Philip is head over heels. And Hazel? Her emotions are as cloudy as ever: still that wariness, the sense of enclosure. Privacy.

She feels my gaze somehow and at last looks at me directly. We hold each other's eyes for a long time. My heart is hammering. Everything depends on this young woman. Can she accept me as human? Can she put aside everything she's been taught?

'Well,' she says at last. 'You may be a demon, but I still find myself inclined to like you. Especially after everything Philip has told me about how you saved Aidan's life. I think, really, I have to trust you. The next question is, can you trust me?'

Her eyes move from my face to Otter's. No fool, this woman.

'We have no choice, Lady Hazel,' Otter says with his habitual formality. 'If Philip vouches for you, I am happy enough.'

'Not happy, I think,' Hazel corrects. 'But you might let me live?'

'There's no question of that!' I say. 'This is – partly – my fault. If anyone –'

'Could we just drop the death stuff, please?' Aidan snaps. He comes across and sits on the edge of my bed. Takes hold of my hand and squeezes it. Looks up at his sister. 'No one's going to die. Thank you, Sis. I love Zara.'

I want to snatch my hand away: it's too painful. But perhaps I'm wrong not to hope. Maybe . . . after the war . . .

'I begin to believe you, Brother.' Acid amusement in Hazel's voice. But warmth as well as she says: 'You and I, Zara, need to get better acquainted. When you're feeling better. I want to know everything about your people, about what it's like for women there.' Her eyes narrow hungrily, and for a moment, I think I get a glimpse of the real Hazel: the hidden person. Hungry for knowledge. Like Swift. Like Philip. My eyes turn to him, questioningly.

The Knowledge Seeker clears his throat. Is he blushing? 'Hazel is my apprentice,' he says stiffly.

'Apprentice?' Aidan swings around, blank astonishment in his voice. 'Women can't be apprentices here. And what sort of apprentice? I'm your apprentice, if anyone is! Hazel isn't an engineer!'

His sister smiles sardonically, but says nothing.

'No,' Philip says. He steps forward, takes Hazel's hand. She lets him, I notice. But passively. Does she welcome it? 'But Hazel is a very talented artist. Did you not know? I'm training her to become a painter.'

'Artist?' Aidan stares at his sister as though at a stranger. 'She's always sketched. But lots of ladies do that. I didn't think . . . you never said, Hazel.'

'You wouldn't have believed me if I had. Women can't be real artists, Aidan, can they? All we can do is make pretty little drawings.' The bitterness in her voice is undisguised. Aidan blinks. Shakes his head. But before he can reply, there's a knock on the door and one of Otter's Tributes appears, a worried look on his face.

'Yes?' Otter has suddenly tensed.

'There's an official here who demands –'

Two metal men, Maker soldiers in full armour, push past the Tribute into the room.

Otter steps forward, his hand going to his sword hilt. Aidan leaps off the bed and Hazel steps forward to hold him back.

'Don't be a fool, Brother! Wait and see.'

'What are you doing here?' Otter demands. His voice icy.

'These men are my guard, General Otter. They accompany me on official Ministry business.' Matthiu, the man Hazel called the Witchfinder, strides into the room. Tall, upright, severe in a heavy, dark grey woollen coat and white collar with long sharp points. His cap remains on his head. He hasn't taken it off as a sign of respect for the house. It is black and stiff crowned, with a soft felt rim pinned back in the centre of his high forehead with a badge of office: a roundel embroidered in scarlet with the image of flames. Amid the flames, I can just distinguish a crudely worked figure with a screaming white face, propped atop of a pyre of wood. I shiver.

'And what business does your . . . ministry . . .' Otter pronounces the word in a carefully neutral tone, '. . . have here? These people are in my care and under my jurisdiction, as leader of the rebel Tribute army. This was agreed with the Gengst council and the leaders of your military.'

'With respect, General.' Matthiu inclines his head gravely, but the tone of his voice sets my teeth on edge. 'The Ministry is above mere military treaties. You are all under my jurisdiction, as is every inhabitant of this city. And I am here to question the young person who was so unfortunate as to be injured in the atrocity in the city.'

'Atrocity?' I say. 'It's kind of you to take my injury so to heart, sir.' I smile my best false-charming smile. I dislike this man. He feels very very wrong. Every empath sense is screaming. He's one of those: like the dead Aluid. He enjoys, this man, making others suffer.

Unsmiling. Unamused. His obsession has killed any sense of humour the man might have possessed. The lack makes him stupid. He thought I was being serious. 'The atrocity I refer to has nothing to do with you. You are of little import in yourself. The violation was the violation of our great city. The vile fact of one of the demonkind having the . . . the . . .'

Steam is almost rising from the man's nostrils. He is mad. Quite mad. I glance at Aidan. And see a tight-lipped fear. The lunatic has power then.

'. . . having the temerity, the obsceneness of mind, to pollute our city with its presence. It will be destroyed, never fear. We are tracking it down with dogs.'

Dogs. Now that *is* clever. My heart is pounding in my chest. Of course, a posse of men and a few bloodhounds is no match for Pyramus, or any adept. But it's clever. It will keep him moving. Or distract him, at least, with the tedious magic of controlling his scent.

'And how can I help you in this noble aim?' Even to me, my words sound flippant; sarcastic. Funny, as I share his desire to see Pyramus dead.

Aidan sits beside me again, squeezes my hand hard and gives me a warning glance. 'She's not feeling well yet,

Matthiu,' he says quickly. 'Feverish still. She nearly died. I don't think –'

'Not up to you, Aidan. Nor even your father. As you know. If I desire to question someone, question them I will. Nothing is more important than the rooting out of any scent of magic in this city. It will not be tolerated! In anyone.' His eyes travel from Aidan and rest on me, coldly. The threat in them is so strong I can taste as well as see it: bitter bile. He wants a victim, this man. Someone to punish.

'But I want to help,' I say. My heart is flapping about in my chest like a crane taking flight. It feels like it will burst out at any moment. Strange no one has noticed. 'That creature nearly killed me. It was terrifying. So I want to help you but I don't see how I can.' I peer at him, trying to look weak and helpless. Not a far stretch in the circumstances.

His eyes narrow. He advances on the bed, his soldiers keeping pace just behind him. 'What is your name again?'

I swallow. My throat is suddenly dry. What if the name of Benedict's only living child has filtered somehow across the Wall? But it's a common enough name in the south. Too late now. 'Zara,' I say, weakly.

'And how old are you?'

He hasn't heard my name before then. A pulse of relief sends my heart flapping heavy wings.

'Seventeen in a two-week,' I mutter, distracted by the antics going on inside my rib cage. The air seems to have grown thick. Hard to breathe.

'And are you in league with the demons that infest your city of Asphodel, Zara? Do you offer worship to them, above the gods? Promote their evil works?'

He leans forward, mouth open, eyes rapt.

I stare at him. 'Why on earth would I want to help those who murdered my parents?' I ask. I'm angry now. Really angry. 'If I was somehow supporting the mages,' I say, not even trying to disguise my contempt now, 'why on earth would one of them try to kill me?'

'That is exactly what confuses me, young woman. And why I'm here. You're a female of no value, of no connections. Why were you targeted? Can you tell me that?'

I stare at him. I haven't got an explanation.

'And why were you in the city at all? You have no business running around unchaperoned, unless you went to an assignation with the demon! Do you . . .' he bends closer still, his breath sour in my face, '. . . have intimate relations with the creature?'

'I . . . I . . .' My heart is flapping and flopping painfully. Catching. And then it stops beating, and I choke and cough as darkness piles into my head. I can't breathe. I'm dying.

Then with a kick like a miniature stallion, my heart begins beating again. I collapse onto the pillows, feeling nauseous. Suddenly, I hear Quint's voice, raised in protest. Shrill, angry. And she's beside me, her fingers feeling for the life note in my wrist.

'You're killing her!' Quint shrills. 'Her heartbeat is uneven. You will leave at once. All of you!'

'Who the hell are you?' Matthiu's voice is cold as he addresses the Mistress. Although he recognises her, I know, from the dinner.

'I'm her apothecary, as you well know, sir. She is my patient and I will not have her life put at risk so you can indulge in your sadistic pleasures. Out, you sad, sad man. AT ONCE!'

I lie on the bed, close my eyes, and hope I will die quickly. Just to stop all this.

Voices shout, roar. Then:

'Oh, don't be so tiresome, Sir Witchfinder.' Hazel's clear voice rises above the din. She laughs. It's a beautiful laugh, clear like a bell, like a cool stream. Contemptuous, but teasing. 'Really, Matthiu, act your age. Zara is Aidan's bethrothed. Didn't you know? They are to be married next month. And I was meeting her in the town to choose fabric for her bridal clothes. Only, she did not arrive at the shop where I waited. And now, the poor girl lies near to death and you, silly old man, you accuse her of witchcraft? My father will not be pleased. Nor my mother, and you know how she dotes on you. So, let us forget this and let the goodwife get on with her tending. Or my brother will be widowed before he is wed.'

I hardly notice my heart flitting like a frightened bird inside my ribs. I stare at Hazel in awe. It is a consummate performance. And, like all great performers, she knows her audience.

Matthiu turns red. Blusters. But retreats.

'Well, if that is the case – if she had an appointment with you in the town – if the attack was a random act of evil – or an attack on one of our leading families – of course, things begin to look different.'

He frowns, not at all happy to lose a victim just when he was about to set his teeth in them. 'But the demon mage most surely has an ally amongst your tribe!' Matthiu whirls on Philip. 'Its coming so soon after yours cannot be a coincidence!'

'I assure you that is not the case.' Philip's expression, his voice, are fastidious. 'Superstition, man!'

'Don't lecture me, artist, on things you know nothing about!'

The room falls silent but for the chink of china and stone, as Quint grinds something in a pestle. The tension in the air is explosive.

'You, woman!'

Quint is too busy amongst her medicines to bother with a glance in his direction, let alone a response.

'For now, Mistress Quint,' pronounces Matthiu, his voice thick with ill-controlled temper, 'I leave you to your womanly duty of tending the ill. But take care to confine your activities to looking after your own. I smell the stink of witchcraft; and I am watching.'

She continues pounding and stirring.

The Witchfinder turns and leaves.

Otter, who has been silent this whole time, follows Matthiu out of the room without a word to us. Philip, pale and visibly shaking with what could be fear or anger or both, closes the door then stands motionless with his back to us, staring at it.

Quint bustles to my bedside, shoves a phial to my lips and, as I drink its sour contents, I hear Philip mutter at the door: 'You are an amazing creature, Hazel. I stand your slave and admirer. Ye gods. Ye gods!'

Aidan is breathing heavily. Ragged. I turn towards him and, through the white gauze that flicks past and past my eyes, see that he is crying. His sister puts her arms around him and holds him tight. My heartbeat quietens. My eyelids flicker and close. Twice, today, I have nearly died. Time to rest.

22

I have been moved into the family quarters of Fergal the Clock's house. My new room is next to Hazel's. I am officially betrothed: Hazel's clever invention of a betrothal keeps the Witchfinder from my door, but I know it is all pretence. Does Aidan? Do I want him to acknowledge the hopelessness of a future for us? Do I want to give up all hope? Because a miracle has happened: Hazel accepts me. Perhaps, once Pyramus is caught, once things are less dangerous, perhaps all things are possible, even that I can find a new life here with Aidan.

Aidan's brother, Donal, has posted guards outside the Knowledge Seekers' quarters, replacing Otter's Tributes. Maker soldiers prowl the house, armed and clad in metal, carrying wicked looking crossbows of Philip's new design. Tabitha and I join the family at dinner. Donal gazes at her with open adoration. Aidan grins at the sight and winks at me. He is delighted. He's fond of Tabitha, loves her son, Thaddeus, who sits quietly beside his mother, proud to be Aidan's apprentice. Aidan's parents seem shell-shocked by the romantic attachments of their children. Philip is an occasional guest at Fergal's table, but he and Hazel give no sign of their professional relationship. Nor their personal one, if such one exists.

The silversmith and I exchange glances over the table. Tabitha and I: we are surviving, each in our own way.

'Tell me about the Ministry.' I sit beside the fire, watching Aidan and Hazel play fox and geese. Hazel frowns over her red-stained peg, placing it in another hole. She is the fox. Aidan groans. 'Never play this game with my sister,' he says in a mournful voice. 'She always wins.'

'You haven't answered my question.' I raise my eyebrows. 'The Ministry?'

'Which one is that?' Aidan bends his blond head over the pegboard, fingers playing with the grey heads of his last few geese. He's stalling.

'The Ministry of Control, of course. Don't condescend to the woman you intend to marry, Brother.' Hazel is gazing at me, the solemn look in her eyes at odds with her flippant words.

'Control of what?' I ask her.

'Magic.' She shrugs. 'It is the thing we fear most. You must realise.'

'But,' I thought my brain was working again but maybe I'm wrong, 'there isn't any magic here. On this side of the Wall. You killed off all the mages generations ago.'

'Exactly.' Her eyes don't leave mine. Their gaze becomes insistent. *What is she trying to tell me?*

'The Ministry's job is to control witchcraft,' Aidan mutters. 'I don't know exactly what it does. How it goes about controlling . . . I mean . . .' His jaw tightens and I know he's lying. But why? 'The Ministry tests people for magic abilities. And they hunt down witches.'

'Witches?' I ask. 'That's a very peculiar word.'

'Anyone who might be in league with dem— with magekind,' Hazel explains.

'But,' I stare at her, 'that's absurd! Mages don't associate with the non-magic. Other than heretics like me. It simply doesn't happen.'

'It does in some people's imaginations.' Hazel tilts her head in enquiry. 'You, especially, must understand the lure of power.'

She pauses, her eyes so knowing that I shiver: it's as though she has seen my past and my future.

'Power is a drug,' she says. 'It inspires obsessive need, both from those who have power and those with none. I promise you, there are people in our cities who believe they are in league with magekind – the demons we both hate and envy because of their power. These self-proclaimed witches believe some of that power is given to them in exchange for their allegiance. The ability to curse or heal. To bestow luck or mischance.'

'Superstition,' I say, contemptuously.

'Of course. But superstition can be deadly. People die because of it.'

Our eyes meet.

'Testing?' I look at Aidan. 'What did you mean?'

'If someone is suspected of being in league with magekind, they'll be tested. To see if they have been given any magical abilities. That's all.'

But there *is* more. I know it.

'Magic doesn't work like that!' I protest. 'It's a gift you're born with or not. It's passed down to children from parents. That's why mages don't . . . well. Mages don't allow children to be born of mixed parentage.'

'But that must happen, surely.' Hazel's voice is unbelieving. 'Or is there no rape in your cities?'

'There is rape. Mage on kine – what we call the non-magic. Sometimes there are children. If they're known about by the authorities, they are . . . killed.' My throat is dry. 'My sister.'

'Sister?'

'Half-sister. She was murdered.'

'It's always the children,' Hazel mutters. 'I'm sorry, Zara. Very sorry.'

'Diplomacy,' Philip says. The entire Knowledge Seeker council, even me, look to him in hope. He sounds so confident. We are gathered in the parlour joined to the artist's bedchamber. The small, well-lit room has become our council chamber here in Gengst. Our chairs are crowded together to fit, and we talk in hushed tones. Aliens, outsiders in an unwelcoming city.

'The furore in the city is dying down,' Philip continues. 'The immediate danger to us is over, as long as the mage doesn't act again.'

His eyes glance at me, then away, but he may as well have said it aloud. Everyone in this room knows why Pyramus is in Gengst. Knows who he's trying to kill. The Knowledge Seekers know they are in danger because of me.

'We need something of value to offer the Makers in order to be tolerated,' Philip says. 'Fortunately, we have much to offer.'

'*You* may, Philip!' Quint interrupts. 'Not the rest of us, I wager!'

'The Mistress speaks the truth.' Hammeth talks for the first time, his voice slow and troubled. 'My skills are common here. My visits to the foundries have told me I have little to teach the Maker smiths.' His shoulders slump. 'And I still don't like this thing about the women,' he grumbles. 'If they are kept from working for some made-up reason, then which of us will be next? Too much like the demon mages for my taste!'

'We all have talents and knowledge which will be of benefit to the Makers – even you, Hammeth,' Philip says. 'Our metal work is at least as good, arguably better. The Makers excel at producing large numbers of things. But your skills are undoubted. And Tabitha knows the secret of Bruin's new form of iron. The sword Zara inherited.'

'Where is it?' I suddenly realise I haven't seen Bruin's sword since the day of the attack. It's not in the room where I sleep any more.

'Safe,' Philip says tersely.

I take a breath to calm down, and firmly shut my mouth. This isn't the time. I shift on the chair, ease my aching leg. It bears my weight with the aid of a stick. My face is free of bandages, the scarred mage mark hidden by Quint's cosmetic.

'What of Matthiu the Witchfinder?' I ask abruptly. 'Is he still prowling around like a fox outside a chicken coop?'

'Otter can answer that question, not I,' Philip says shortly.

'Yes. But *will* he?'

The Nonpareil frowns.

'All very well for you men,' Quint says suddenly. She is uneasy and angry these days. Trudging and stomping instead of rolling. 'What are we women meant to do without our work?'

'In Time's good grace, Mistress,' soothes Philip. 'Diplomacy, as I said. For now: do your work inside our group only. And do it quietly please, without ostentation. Our survival here is tenuous. Anything could tip the balance against us.'

'It is easy for you to plead patience, Philip!' Quint snaps. 'Off to the factories each day to make your new-fangled killing machines so that even more children die on the Wall of Gengst!' She frowns, mutinously, but falls silent. Philip looks shocked at the attack, but compresses his mouth and does not respond.

I study the apothecary, more worried than ever. My eyes meet those of Tabitha. And I see a concern there which echoes my own.

I sleep badly: this part of the house has unfamiliar sounds. Strange smells. My leg aches. I dream of Aidan. And Pyramus. And my father. Long before the winter sun reaches the eastern mountains, I lie awake, listening to the strange sounds of this old house. To the endless ticking of a dozen clocks in the corridor outside.

A crashing downstairs and I am bolt upright in bed. The clocks tick on as men shout and an army of boots races heavy-footed up Fergal's great stair. I'm out of my bed. I hear again the crashing, splintering of a wooden door forced open. I pull on my clothes with frantic fingers. Shouting. A woman screams. Memory sends me back to my father's house, back to Asphodel, when terror stalked the night.

I grab my knife belt. No point wishing for Bruin's sword: it's gone, and neither Philip nor Otter will tell me where it is. I lean on the bed, pull my boots on sockless. Curse at the stick I have to use. Tear open the door and clump down the hall.

I hear Hazel's sleepy voice call a fretful question.

And then Aidan is beside me, tugging at my arm. I whirl to face him.

'Let go! Don't you hear?'

'I'll go. You go back to your room and stay out of this. I want you safe.'

'We go together, Aidan.'

'Dammit, Zara!' He groans. 'All right. But remember, no –'

'I know!' I hiss. And turn and hobble towards the uproar as quickly as I can. It's coming from the Knowledge Seekers' wing.

By the time we reach the Maker soldiers stationed outside the family wing, Donal has caught us up. The two brothers trot ahead of me, spurs jangling, voices low in argument.

I hear: '. . . send her back to her room!' 'Don't you think I tried?' '. . . who's master . . .?' '. . . piss off and mind your . . .' 'different rules . . .'

The soldiers draw aside at a nod from Donal, and fall in behind us.

Aidan and Donal break into a sprint as we near the source of the upheaval. Torch light flickers on the corridor walls. I catch glimpses over the backs of the men in front of me. Philip, stork-legged in his nightdress, shouting, waving his arms. Pushed aside by a metal soldier. Hammeth, leaning against a wall, hand clapped to his forehead, blood oozing between his fingers. Fredda screaming and shouting, cowering in a doorway. And

Mistress Quint, being dragged along between two massive men clad in metal and leather, her bare feet not even touching the floor. She wears her nightdress, her black hair is not in a bun, as I've always seen it, but streaming long down her shoulders and back. Her face is pale. Her mouth is bleeding. Someone has hit her.

I feel something click inside my head. White hot fire swims into and through me as I spot the Witchfinder General, Matthiu, trudging in front of his victim, a smug smile pursing his lips. He is dressed in all his finery. His polished boots flash in the torch light.

Before I can do anything, Aidan lunges for me, grabs me by the shoulders and tugs me away. He holds my face to his chest, so I can't look, can't see. And he shouts my name, over and over.

I gather my magic. Not even Aidan. Not even for him . . .

He must feel me tensing, preparing. Aidan holds me away from him so we are eye to eye, nose to nose. I'm weeping with rage.

'Zara.' I see his mouth make the words. In between Fredda's screams, Philip's shouts, Hammeth's groans, I hear snatches of Aidan's voice: 'If . . . do any . . . will . . . die. All . . . them!'

I stare at him, defeated, then let him draw me to him and cover my eyes so I can't see. Cover my ears, so I can't hear, as Matthiu the Witchfinder takes away Mistress Quint.

'There will be a trial.'

I stare at my hands. I don't bother to answer Fergal the Clock. When I glance up I see he looks affronted. I don't care. But Aidan does. So I try: 'It won't be a fair one.'

'No,' Hazel says. 'You know that, Father. Please, can't you use your influence?'

'I have no influence with Matthiu.' He sighs. An old man's sigh. And Naveen, who sits beside him, bows her head. We sit at the family breakfast table. Its polished oak-wood and creamy china do not make me feel warmer. I'm shivering.

'And even if I did,' Fergal says, crumpling his napkin and placing it beside his plate, 'I would not intervene. The whole city is crying for your female apothecary's blood. I cannot afford to be seen to interfere with the Ministry over this. Bad enough that the woman was living in my house!' He thumps the table in front of him in frustrated anger. The china plate before him jumps. 'I've washed my hands of her. Guilty of witchcraft or not, the woman was a fool. She will face trial. Her fate is in the hands of the gods.'

I stare at the uneaten breakfast before me: sausage, a poached egg, a fat-speckled slice of blood pudding, and feel sick.

Fergal gets stiffly to his feet. His wife, son and daughter rise in deference. Aidan tugs me to my feet.

'I must to work,' the old man says. He accepts his wife's dutiful kiss on his cheek, and grumbles from the room. He avoids my eye, and I know that Aidan's father is far from pleased with his son's choice of betrothed.

As the others sit, I sink back into my chair and stare at the fire.

'I am sorry for your friend, Zara,' Naveen says after a moment. 'But Mistress Quint knew the risk she was taking. I told her so myself. And yet she continued.'

'Risk? What was she doing?' Only . . . I think I know.

'She was going to the bad parts of town each day. To the slums.' Naveen's face grows sad. She sighs. 'She was treating the ill people there.'

My fears are confirmed. *Why didn't I do something? Find out for certain . . . ask more questions, demand answers. Stop her?*

'But that's a good thing.' My voice is faint. I know what the reply will be. 'She's a brilliant apothecary. She saved many lives in our city and on our journey here. She saved my life.'

'Women are not allowed to be healers,' Hazel says, quietly. 'As far as Matthiu is concerned, she is a witch. He suspects her of being in league with the mage who attacked you.'

'That's madness! Why then would she save my life?' I stare at them all, at Aidan and his women. And see pain, confusion, regret. But no hope.

When Otter stalks into the Knowledge Seeker wing that afternoon, I am waiting. I detached Aidan at last by pretending I wanted to sleep.

The Guardian registers me at once. I'm sitting in front of the broken door of Quint's bedroom, on her own chair, waiting. When he sees me, his expression grows wary.

'You're a bit late.' I clench my fists. Manage to keep my voice calm. 'All the fun is over.'

'I was out of the city,' he says quietly. 'Matthiu knew that. That's why he came this morning. I've only just got back.'

'Where were you?' No good: my voice cracks. I'm losing control.

'I have an army to lead, Zara. A war to fight. You seem to have forgotten.'

'I haven't forgotten that Mistress Quint saved my life! As she saved Hammeth's, and Marcus's.'

'You saved Marcus.'

'Oh . . . shut up!' I leap out of Quint's chair and begin to hobble back and forth.

'Should you be walking on that?'

I stop and look at him. If anger was magic, he'd be fried on the spot.

'What are you going to do?'

He draws in a slow breath. 'Nothing.'

I just stare at him. I can't believe what I just heard.

He doesn't look away. Otter has never been a coward.

'I'm sorry, Zara. But I warned her. Aidan's mother warned her. She knew the risks, and she chose to take them. It was a matter of principle with her. Mistress Quint has chosen her path – she's chosen martyrdom. And I can't help her now.'

'You could . . . you could . . .' The words dry. He's speaking the truth. He hasn't got the power to stop Matthiu.

Do I?

His eyes flicker as he looks at me. Did he see my thought, in my face? *By all the gods!* Good, little, round Quint must not die because she wanted others to live. I can't let it happen . . .

I have to distract him, so I attack:

'Where is Twiss? Is she all right?' I redouble my attack to distract him, in case he is near to guessing my intentions: 'Twiss was in league with you all along, wasn't she? Setting me up to be bait for Pyramus!'

'Keep your voice down, Zara!' he hisses.

'If you mean Worm, he's not here any more. He was turned out. Last week. Just in case he was involved.'

'Nevertheless . . .' His face is stony. He's right, and I chose my words with care.

'That was your plan. And Twiss was in on it.'

He doesn't reply.

'Where is she?'

'I can't tell you that. She's not in danger. You are.'

'Not as much danger as Quint.'

'Leave it, Zara. There is nothing that can be done.'

Parry, riposte. This man is so very dangerous. I take a different tack.

'Where's my sword? Bruin's sword? Does Philip have it? Did you give it to him?'

'No, I didn't, but he does have it. He's analysing the metal and forging process. He and Hammeth are trying to duplicate it. With, I might add, Tabitha's advice and permission.'

I frown in frustration. The sword is Tabitha's to give and take away. I have to accept that. But . . . not Quint. I need to be alone. To think. And as far away from Otter as possible.

'You were supposed to protect them, Guardian,' I say at last. Just that. No more.

And at last, I've scored a hit. The wince is almost imperceptible. The blow to his almighty self-assurance is slight. But hit him I did, and I regret my spiteful words at once.

'I'm sorry, Otter. I didn't mean that. You've done your best.'

I turn away. Grab the cursed stick, and thump back to my new quarters.

23

'I want to visit her.'

'You're shivering.' Aidan tucks my woollen scarf into my coat.

'I know. I'm sorry.'

'Thin southern blood.' He tries a joke. His smile can't erase the worry in his eyes.

We're walking round and round the frozen courtyard garden of his father's house. I need to strengthen my leg, but none of the Knowledge Seekers are safe to walk the streets of Gengst. Only Philip braves the city, escorted to the factory each day by armed guard.

'I want to visit Mistress Quint,' I say again. 'Can't your father call in some political favours?'

Aidan sighs. 'I know how important this is to you, Zara, but it isn't possible. You heard my father: it would be political suicide if the rumour began to circulate that he was befriending Mistress Quint. Besides, it isn't safe for you to be seen to be collaborating with a suspected witch. Matthiu would love to clap you in prison as well, the more so because of your relationship to my family.'

Chill seeps deeper into my bones. Why should I expect Fergal or his family to risk so much for a stranger? Still, I can't help feeling disappointed by his response. 'I feel like I've abandoned her!'

I can't think of any way to save the apothecary. If I do anything that tastes of magic, the remaining Knowledge Seekers will be blamed. They might face the same fate as Quint. I can't risk that.

'You promise not to do anything stupid?' Aidan asks.

'I promise.' I'm worn out with saying it, with reassuring Aidan and Otter and Philip and Tabitha and Hazel. 'I just want to say goodbye. In case . . .' But we both know, there is no question of 'in case'. The outcome of the trial is a foregone conclusion. Quint will die.

After a stilted, awkward dinner with Aidan's family I escape to my room and sit staring at the glowing firerock Aidan has ordered to be heaped in my fireplace. I know I mustn't do magic to help Quint. But I can at least use Elsewhere to visit her one last time. Tomorrow, in the brief hours of daylight, so that I can see my way without need for a lantern.

Aidan was right: like sewage overflowing the gutters, the streets of Gengst are awash with hatred and fear. The stony-faced men and women trudging through the streets – carrying shopping baskets, tending stalls, scurrying out of the wind into taverns or dining houses – watch their neighbours with suspicious, fearful eyes. The tension in the air makes the back of my neck prickle as I hobble slowly and carefully along the less busy streets, invisible in Elsewhere.

I pretended a headache at breakfast and am supposed to be sleeping in my room. I piled cushions in my bed in case anyone ignores my plea that I be left alone until lunch, but it's a poor effort. Nothing like the corpse I created to fool my father when I fled his palazzo. *Gods! I miss magic!*

I take the greatest care as I thread a path through the frozen, fearful streets of the Maker city. No whiff of magic to stir the hatred. But Elsewhere is safe – even Pyramus can't detect me in Elsewhere. I will visit Quint quickly and say goodbye. I owe her that much: the Mistress must not face Death alone and abandoned.

The Ministry for the Control of Witchcraft is built of sparkling golden sandstone. Matthiu must order it to be scrubbed every four-week at least. It is three floors tall and twice as broad. A plain, undecorated building with tall windows and a heavy roof of dark bluestone cut into roofing slates. A wide flight of steps lead to a porticoed porch supported by plain columns of bluestone. The sandstone steps have deep hollows worn into them by the passage of countless feet.

There is a queue of people huddled on the Ministry steps. All are young couples carrying wicker baskets or shoving them along with their feet as the queue shuffles forward. A dismal squalling comes from many of the baskets: the sound of crying babies. Almost none of the parents attempt to comfort their child. The adults stare into space. Totally silent. Avoiding the gaze of their partners, of passers-by. Why are they here, these people? What are they waiting for? And why bring their babies? The sense of misery coming from the men and women waiting in the queue is choking.

I hate this city more and more every day. I'll ask Aidan or Hazel when I get back. But now I have to act. I need to see Quint and get back. Quickly!

I step further into Elsewhere, join the queue, drift carefully past. The people stand so still, so stolidly, that it's easy to slip to the front and dart through the gate in front of the couple the Ministry official gestures forward. I shudder with relief once I leave the pall of fear and distress behind.

I know where Quint will be. Aidan told me that the Ministry's prison lies behind the main building. I see it at once: a single-storeyed, squat building that forms the rear of a quadrangle built around a cobbled courtyard. The courtyard is barren, cheerless. The prison has a single floor of administrative offices. The prison cells must lie below ground.

Two guards stand either side of the entrance, but the door is propped open. Bureaucrats trail in and out. I follow one inside and ease down the stairs, avoiding the few duty guards: hard-faced men who sit, smoking and chatting. Complacency rises into the air . . . along with darker emotions. I retreat further into Elsewhere as the rawness of fear and the stink of sadism twist my stomach. I must try not to feel anything, must get past these dark rooms where people are being tortured, or cling to life, waiting execution or trial.

Quint is kept far from the other prisoners, in a cell at the very end of the dank corridor. Are the Ministry guards afraid of a witch from the other side of the Wall? Perhaps, for they don't come near this end of the prison all the time I'm there.

So in the end, it is as easy – and as hard – as waiting outside her cell until I am brave enough to peer through the barred window of the oak door.

I can just make out a dark shape huddled motionless on the ground. There is no window in her cell. The only light comes from the spyhole I'm looking through. My head obstructs the light, and she looks up at once.

I move my head to one side so a beam of light can enter the spyhole, and I see Quint properly. She's filthy: this woman who always kept herself scrubbed clean. She sits on a pallet of straw. Her clothes are torn and draggled, her plump face sagging under a layer of dirt. But the black button eyes are the same. As is the determination shining from them.

'What do you want?' she demands. 'I'm not going to confess to witchcraft today either, you silly man, so go away.'

My throat clenches tight. I can't drag a single word through it. Quint turns her head away; then, when I don't answer, looks again. And this time she stands up, shoving herself to her feet with difficulty.

'Are they starving you?' I manage to say at last. My voice is a hoarse whisper. My heart thuds and leaps and I realise I'm terrified. Of what it would mean for the other Knowledge Seekers if I am discovered. But even more, I'm afraid of Mistress Quint. Of her pain. Of *her* fear.

Only . . . as I make myself feel her emotions, I find little of those things. I feel her surprise. Delight, as she recognises my voice. Then: 'What do you think you are doing here, young lady? Go away at once! You can do no good here, and you put yourself at great risk!' But she scuttles up to the window. She raises herself onto her toes so her eyes can meet mine. We gaze through the bars at each other.

'Mistress . . .'

'Go back to Aidan's house. Now!' But her eyes cling to me.

'Are they feeding you? Are they mistreating you?'

'They give me food, if you can call it that. But I have little appetite. The filthiness is the worst. Fleas! Can you imagine?' She shudders. 'But they do not beat me. They have not tortured me. I don't think that evil old man feels he needs a confession. The trial is a mockery. I will die; I know that Zara. I only pray it is quick.' And now I do feel fear. But only for a moment. And then her eyes bore into mine.

'Why have you come, Zara? You cannot and *must not* try to get me free. The cost to the others would be unthinkable. I forbid it!'

'I . . .' My eyes are dripping tears; my nose joins in. I ignore them. 'I know, Mistress Quint. I know. I can't do anything to help you. I'm so sorry.'

She stands for a moment. We look at each other. And she nods her head. At last. And I feel a tiny well of hope die. But she is a strong person.

'I've come to say goodbye,' I say. 'And to thank you for saving my life. And to promise. To promise that I will stop this evil if I can.'

'Thank you, dear.' Four dirty fingers, nails broken and black with grime, press out through the bars. I grasp them. Squeeze. 'I'm very fond of you, Zara. And I am touched beyond words that you have come to say goodbye. Fight on, child. But remember your fight is with your father first – not these misguided fools. Now go! Quickly and safely. You should not have come but . . . bless you for it. I am comforted. Do not worry. Otter visits me each day. And Philip comes when he can. I am not alone. But . . . bless you!' Her voice quivers. 'It has done me good to see you. Goodbye, Zara. Keep yourself alive! I insist on that, or all my good work will have been in vain.'

Quint pulls her fingers from mine, turns away and shuffles back to her mattress. She plomps down upon it, and looks across her cell at me. At the shape of my head blocking the mean light they give her.

'Go!' she says.

And I obey.

I remember almost nothing of the journey out of the Ministry. I only notice that the queue of parents and babies is shorter, and that it's harder to move carefully when your eyes are streaming.

Cold air soon dries them. Beautiful, sooty air. I breathe deep to cleanse the prison's poisonous atmosphere from my lungs. I trudge back towards Fergal's house and think of the apothecary who must wait now all the tedious hours and days until the moment of her death. Time is merciless. Do I even believe in the gods any more? I see only the good and evil of humans, magic and non-magic alike. And there is little to choose between them. I find one small comfort to offset the sorrow of that knowledge: I was right: magic is not evil in itself. The Makers are wrong.

I lift my head to make sure I haven't lost myself in twisting streets, and spot a familiar back a dozen paces ahead. *Worm!* Is the man Matthiu's spy? Or my father's? He slinks ahead of me. Furtive. Head turning, oh so casually, to check that he's not being observed before darting down a narrow street. And before I even think to do so, I follow.

What am I doing? I don't know what I can hope to achieve, but Worm is going to meet someone, I'm sure of it. And I want to find out who that is. I won't do anything. I'll keep clear out of it. Stay in Elsewhere. *Like last time?* A voice in my head asks. I begin to shiver. I'm being a fool. It's not worth the risk. To me. To the Knowledge Seekers. I stop walking. I'm going back.

But at that moment, a tall, slender man in a thick woollen cloak, his plain hat worn low, steps from a hidden doorway. My heart skitters, but it's not Pyramus: too tall, too thin. Worm hurries to the man. They begin to talk, heads bent, voices low. I don't know what to do. I don't recognise the tall stranger. This seems to have nothing to do with me or my father's assassin. I turn to retrace my steps and wince as a wave of pure power races up the alley towards me. I stagger as it nearly knocks me down with its force as it rages past. Magic! Adept magic!

I whirl around to see Worm bending over his companion. The tall stranger is kneeling on the wet cobbles, and Worm's hands are clenched around his throat. The air stinks of magic. Worm looks wrong: awkward, disjointed. He's a golum! Like the Tributes who attacked Aidan and me. Worm's mind has been invaded by an adept who is using his body to attack the stranger. Pyramus! It must be.

I turn again and lunge up the alley in the direction of the magic blast. My father's assassin is here, and Pyramus will never be weaker. Most of his concentration will be controlling those hands strangling the life from the cloaked and hatted stranger. I will never have a better chance to kill my father's spy.

I round the corner and spot Pyramus standing in the narrow

street ahead. The adept's plump, round-shouldered body wears the hairy tweed cloak and shabby hat of the merchant who was at Fergal's house the day I was attacked, selling goods from the cart drawn by a piebald horse. Pyramus is staring, straining, a look of unholy glee on his face. He's winning. His victim must be nearly dead.

I slow to a walk and concentrate my will. I draw energy from the air, from the ground, from . . . I'm vaguely aware . . . Pyramus himself. I fashion, quick as a single sharp thought, a thin dagger of pure ice created from the moisture in the damp air of Gengst. Too late, he feels my magic. Too late, he turns his head. I hurl the spike at him with all my strength and skill.

Pyramus squeals with outrage and disbelief. I glimpse fear on his face as he magically cobbles a thin air shield and my ice dagger glances off its shimmering surface and hurtles on to shatter on the wall behind the adept. Before Pyramus can strike back, I'm a dozen paces away, deep still in Elsewhere.

I race towards his victims. If my father's assassin wants the tall stranger dead, then I almost certainly want him alive. But the stranger doesn't need my help. Pyramus's mind has left Worm and the servant lies moaning on the ground. The cloaked stranger struggles to his feet and, as I watch, he raises his arms in a familiar gesture. I feel magic gathering. Magic so powerful the hairs on the back of my neck raise.

A thick curtain of fog seeps like black oil from the ground and obliterates the street behind us, the spot where Pyramus was standing a moment ago. I leap back and press flat against the nearest wall as the cloaked man sends a hail of ice spikes whining through the air into the fog. I hear them shatter on brick and stone. There is no sound of ice smashing into flesh, no scream of pain. The stranger strides forward, inside a pearly air shield. I sense fury and frustration as the stranger walks into the drifts of fog slowly winding away. The last one lifts, and I see that Pyramus has gone.

I creep as far as I dare into Elsewhere. *Gods! What have I done?* Perhaps she won't know. Perhaps she won't realise. I recognised her once she had unleashed her magic and sent the spikes hurling down the alley towards me, and my father's assassin. But perhaps she didn't notice my earlier attack on Pyramus. Perhaps I can get out . . . but I should know better than to underestimate Falu.

The Archmage of Thynis whirls around, her face a white blaze of fury. 'Zara!' she says, her voice low and precise. 'You will come with me. I have a few choice words to say to Otter. And don't even think of trying to escape.'

I don't. Falu terrifies me. But not as much as Pyramus.

I'm in shock. Not only have I just prevented Pyramus from killing Falu, but I have seen an archmage help a kine to his feet and express concern for his welfare! I would never have believed it if I had not seen it with my own eyes.

Worm still looked ill as he nodded to the archmage and staggered off alone down the alley. Knowing the horror of having your mind invaded against your will, I can only respect his strength of purpose. Falu watched him for a moment before turning towards me once more.

'Come here and take my hand, Zara. It isn't safe for you

to be seen in the city, so you will continue in Elsewhere. But don't try to escape. I'm not amused by any of this.'

'I saved your life.'

But I obey. I move nearer and put my hand into her outstretched one. My heart hammers as her fingers close tightly on mine. Her disguise is excellent. With her height and strong chin, she could easily be a man.

'Don't presume,' she snaps. 'Do you imagine me without resources?'

She says no more, but I'm not sure I believe that she was in control. I think Pyramus came very close to killing her.

'Where are we going?' I struggle to keep pace with her strides. My leg is much stronger, but I still limp. The archmage must notice, for she slows her pace.

'No talking,' she says, pausing to peer out into the main street before tugging me after her.

Her head moves constantly. She's looking for any sign of Pyramus. As am I. But it seems my father's spy doesn't favour the odds: the streets are full of Makers hurrying about their business, but there is no sign of a short, round-shouldered merchant, muffled and hatted against the cold.

Falu marches me through narrow streets. I have to dodge to avoid collision several times. Each time, her hand bites into my wrist. The Wall draws near. This is the southwest side, by the sun. And I recognise the place when Falu slows. We near to where the Knowledge Seekers entered Gengst. Where Otter nearly died.

Then I see a pair of Tribute soldiers standing on guard, either side of a door built into the base of the Wall itself. The Maker army has offices and quarters throughout the length of the

Wall. This must be the quarters Fergal assigned to Otter as a garrison for the Tributes that accompanied the Knowledge Seekers into the city.

Falu marches up to the Tributes guarding the entrance. They watch her approach without surprise. So, Falu is known here – at least in disguise.

She nods at the guards. 'I need to see Otter. Urgently.'

'Yes, sir. I'll let him know you're here.' One of the Tributes salutes, and disappears inside. The other studies Falu, then turns her attention to a trio of townspeople who stand a bowshot away, watching and muttering. I feel their hostility and suspicion from here.

My heart begins to thud unpleasantly. I don't want to see Otter. I don't want to be here at all. Unfortunately, the Guardian appears in the doorway almost at once. He registers Falu with mild surprise. His eyes narrow. The next moment he is staring right at me. The Guardian has shifted enough into Elsewhere to see me. His body goes still as his eyes meet mine. Otter takes a deep breath.

'Inside. My office. Now.'

The guard steps aside. And Falu pulls me into the garrison after the Guardian.

'You promised!'

The door has barely closed behind us. Otter's office is a small, bare room full of papers, books and maps. It's surprisingly messy.

'I kept my promise.'

He laughs, not sounding at all amused. 'How do you figure that?'

'I didn't *do* anything. I just said goodbye to her. No one

saw me.'

'The apothecary?' Falu asks. 'You are such a child, Zara.'

'Well, this *child* saved your life, in case you've forgotten!'

'What?' Otter's eyes narrow. His attention shifts to Falu. 'I think you had better explain.'

The Guardian has just given an order to an archmage! I stare at them both, waiting for her to strike him dead, to rebuke him, to . . . something!

Instead, Falu reaches up a languid hand and slides the hat from her head. Her dark hair tumbles down. She shrugs off the woollen cape and drops into the chair facing Otter's desk, crossing her long legs. Like Otter, she is wearing the tight trousers and long boots of a Maker gentleman, but on Falu the effect is rather different.

Otter notices. His eyes journey from the archmage's face to her legs, and back again. And there is an almost-smile – an unspoken acknowledgement. A remembrance of intimacy shared.

It can't be true! I must have misread the emotions in the room. Otter would never . . . I gawp at him, but for the moment, the Guardian seems to have forgotten me. Why don't I feel more pleased?

'I'm waiting.' Otter's voice is dangerously soft.

'Tsk.' A sigh from Falu. She shrugs. 'I made an arrangement to meet one of my agents in the city. Pyramus was obviously following him. He inhabited the man, and tried to strangle me. I think.' She smiles. 'It probably indicates that my cover is blown. I will have to leave the city. But only after I kill Pyramus. Tidily, Guardian, don't worry.'

'You didn't manage to kill him today.' Otter's voice is

carefully noncommittal.

'Unfortunately, Zara intervened and spoilt my trap. She meant the best, but . . . I want her out of the city, Otter. Today. She isn't safe. I don't want that fat little bastard getting near her again.'

'And you just stumbled on this little scene of attempted assassination, did you?' The Guardian's brown eyes have shifted to me. I very much wish they hadn't. I'm still struggling to comprehend the fact that Falu was only pretending to die. If she's not lying.

'No.' I look bleakly at Otter. 'I saw Worm after I left the Ministry. I . . . I followed him. Just for a little while. Then I realised I was being stupid and turned back. But that's when . . .' I shudder. I can still remember the clumsy disjointed movements of Worm's body while he was inhabited.

'Stupid. Yes.' Otter nods. 'You could have cost the lives of your friends. Did visiting Quint make you feel better?'

'It wasn't about that!'

'Wasn't it? Well, Falu is right. You are not going to have the chance to make another mistake. I'll take you out of the city tonight.'

'Out of Gengst?' I stare at the Guardian. 'As soon as Pyramus knows I've left he'll be on my trail, tracking me down before I can reach Asphodel.'

'Then he mustn't know you've gone,' Otter says. 'And you aren't going to Asphodel.'

I don't argue: Otter may have his plans, but I have my own. 'The news will get out – that I'm not living in Fergal's house any more. There are too many servants, too many mouths . . .

I'd have a few days at best.'

'I have said, you can leave Pyramus to me,' Falu interrupts gently.

I glance at her. As I meet her cool gaze, my protest dies on my lips. It is seldom wise to argue with an archmage. Yet less than an hour ago, Pyramus seemed more than a match for Falu. I'll never know what would have happened if I had not intervened.

I frown at Otter. 'Where would I go?'

'To join Twiss.'

My heart leaps at the idea of seeing the thief again. But . . . it hits me. I may never see Aidan again. If things go badly . . . The idea hurts; it hurts badly. I must have allowed myself to hope, despite everything.

'I-I need to tell the others. To say goodbye . . . Aidan –'

'Will just have to miss you.' Otter glances at Falu. 'And you, Lady. If you go after Pyramus, be tidy. This city is a powder keg. One more sniff of magic, and it'll blow sky high. And my alliance with the Makers – our best chance of defeating Benedict – will blow up with it.'

So much at stake. Reluctantly, I push down my annoyance at the Guardian's high-handed treatment. He's right: goodbyes are a luxury we can't afford. Aidan will understand – I hope.

'Of course, dearheart.' Falu's voice is gently taunting.

Dearheart?!

Otter ignores her. 'As long as I make myself clear.'

'But of course; you always do.' Falu smiles sweetly at the Guardian. 'That's one of the reasons we work so well together. Neither of us are frightened of saying what we think. But don't pretend to yourself that you are the elder in this partnership, Otter dear. Or I might have to remind you of the realities of our relationship.'

The archmage waits, her smile cold. A muscle in Otter's jaw tightens, and she nods in acknowledgement of unspoken words. 'Excellent.' Falu rises to her feet, draws on her cloak, twists her hair into a knot on top of her head and dons the man's hat. Then she turns to me.

'Take care of yourself, Zara. Stay alive. It would please me greatly.'

The Archmage of Thynis steps forward, takes my chin in a cool hand and places a gentle kiss on my cheek. My right cheek. The one that bears my mother's mage mark. Still holding my face, she turns her head to glance at Otter. Watching the Guardian as his face stiffens and his eyes grow unaccountably cold.

What was that about?

I resist the impulse to retreat from her touch, but it is a relief when her hand drops from my face. Falu gives me a final, unreadable smile, turns and leaves.

24

The air is different here. The light is different. I am somewhere. Somewhere new. Somewhere . . .

I don't want to fight through the fog in my head. I have no friends out there, wherever 'there' is. I keep my eyes shut and my mind unthinking. I am an unwound clock. I don't want the ticking of Time to start up again.

'Will you just open your eyes and stop pretending? I'm fed up with waiting.'

Twiss!

My eyes pop wide.

I see a small room with walls of wooden boards. A fire burning on a stone hearth; a window covered with shutters that let in cracks of bright light. And Twiss, sitting on the foot of my bed.

She looks just the same: brown pointed cat face, cropped black hair, dark brown eyes beneath thick, frowning black brows. I can't help smiling.

'Where have you been?' I ask.

I don't say: *I've been worried to death!* or *I've missed you so much!* She would just roll her eyes and shrug.

'Here, 'course. I hear you've been making a mess of things, as usual. Always happens when I'm not around to tell you what to do.'

Otter drugged me! The bastard! Even though I'd agreed to come away. He gave me a warm drink, before we set off . . .

I lurch up in the bed.

'Don't even try to get out of bed.' Twiss's eyes harden. 'Otter's got soldiers outside the door,' she says, calmly. 'With Philip's new-fangled crossbows, and they'll shoot you on sight if I give the word.'

She can't mean it. Not Twiss. Her eyes are obsidian stones: no warmth.

'Thought that'd get your attention. This ain't a game, Zara.'

'Do you think you have to tell *me* that?'

Her mouth goes hard. 'Get over yourself. You don't know what's been going on in the Maker cities. I don't want you doing anything stupid. We need you to fight with us when the time comes. So be sensible or I'll call them killers in here. They don't care, but it'd just about break my heart. Don't make me do it, Zara.'

'I need to pee,' I say at last.

She watches, thinking, and her face slowly breaks into a grin. 'Well, that's gonna happen. When you gotta go . . .' She hops off the bed. 'Piss pot's under the bed, Zara. But don't be stupid.'

'I'm not going to try anything,' I grump, as I swing my legs over the side of the bed. I immediately stop moving. I feel nauseous: whatever drug Otter gave me, it's got a nasty sting. 'What do you think I'm going to do?'

'Try to escape and go back to Gengst and save Quint. That's what.'

'I can't save Quint: it might kill the others. I wouldn't do that!'

'And what about running after your Maker boy?'

'I can't live in Gengst. I know that, even if Aidan doesn't. Besides, my father's assassin is still in the city. I can't go back while he's there.'

'Benedict?' Just the one word. She stares at me hard.

'I won't try anything on my own.' *At least, not yet,* I think. I need to rest, to plan. It would be foolish not to work with Otter, to consult with Falu.

'Well, glad to see you've got the use of some brains back. Swear that you won't try nothin'.'

'I swear! Time's teeth! Can I now piss in peace?'

'Sure enough.'

'Tell me.'

I'm sitting on the edge of the bed, sipping water from a wooden cup, waiting for the nausea to fade.

'Where are we? Why are you here? Why is Otter here?'

Twiss has always been able to read me. She knows I wasn't lying to her when I say I'm not going back to Gengst. She also knows that I'd rather die than hurt her. Otter has chosen my jailor well.

'Come have a look round, then. Put that coat on!' I'm glad to be bossed. I keep looking at Twiss, each time getting a thrill of joy that she's alive. I'm so happy to see her I almost forgive Otter for drugging me.

The coat is sheepskin, the curly fleece inward for warmth. Twiss hands me a woollen cap, which I shove on my head. She goes to the door and calls out. And the door swings open to reveal a second, larger room, and Otter's soldiers.

Three crossbows take aim, bolts pointing at my chest, metal heads glinting. My mouth dries to cotton.

'Put 'em away. She won't do nothin' stupid.'

The soldiers look at me, look at Twiss, look at each other, then slowly tip the crossbows up so the bolts point to the low wooden ceiling. But they don't disarm the bows, I notice. And they watch me like I'm a rock adder.

I ignore them, or try to, as I take in my surroundings. We're not in the city any more, that is clear from the glimpses I catch from the window beside the crude planked door. We're standing in what seems to be a kitchen and living area of a tiny house. Two rooms: the bedroom where I woke and this living area, with a big stone hearth taking up the whole of a wall, and a cheerful fire putting out welcome warmth. A stew-pot rests to one side on a hob. I sniff, but there's no welcoming smell of food.

Twiss grabs my arm and pulls me towards the door.

'Now. Don't talk to nobody and don't do nothing I don't tell you. If you do, I can't answer for what'll happen.' Her eyes narrow. I nod. My stomach tightens. She means it.

Twiss pulls open the door and thrusts me out into a new world.

I stand, blinking small brittle snowflakes from my eyelashes. They drift, thin and irritable, from a bright grey sky. The ground is frosted with a layer of white. Footpaths smurch muddy trails between the buildings. Most are little more than huts with bases of field stone and walls of roughly shaped logs plastered with mud. Smoke trails skywards from a dozen chimneys, white-grey columns rising gently to the tops of the canyon walls encircling what seems to be a hidden valley. Bluestone cliffs rise on every side. The lower flanks of the hills are covered with a forest of trees, in such neat rows they must have been planted. The trees are all different ages, from saplings to groaning giants. Needle leaf and broad. In between is the valley floor, and this hidden village.

Twiss tugs me forward and I stumble along, hardly noticing where I'm putting my feet. Women, men and children dig in distant fields, work at building, mending, tending, carrying. I see a young boy sitting at a small table-loom, weaving. I slip on slushy mud and nearly fall. The paths between the huts are covered in tree bark, but muddy patches are worn through in places.

I hear axes chopping, people calling to each other. The distant baaing of sheep from a sheep fold on the hillside. A girl in leather moccasins and a leather coat like mine leads a milk cow through the settlement. She sees Twiss, then me, and her mouth drops open as she carries on slowly walking past. Other people notice, turn, stop working and stare. Watchful eyes travel from me to Otter's guards, who are following a few paces behind. The villagers shrug and go back to their activities. No fuss, no hatred. Do they know what I am?

Most here are dressed like the cowherd. But among them are a fair few of Otter's Tributes. And some others: a few shivering people dressed like Maker townspeople. Young couples. Standing together, each with a small child or baby in their arms. Like the families outside the Ministry. *What is this place?*

'Those families!' I hiss to the thief. 'I saw a queue of people outside the Minstery for the Control of Magic – a queue of young families with babies. Why are the Makers here, Twiss? What do you know about all this? Tell me!'

'I can't tell you nothin' about them.' She looks at the Maker children in the parents' arms and her eyes darken. 'But I'm taking you to talk to Benj and Ash. They'll tell you what they can. And give us some food if we're lucky!' Her voice grows considerably more cheerful at the prospect.

'Where's Otter?'

'Don't know.'

I know that stubborn tone. I'll get nothing more from Twiss.

I should be angry with Otter for drugging me. For leaving his soldiers with instructions to kill me on Twiss's say-so. I'm surprised to find I'm not. Overall, my soul and body are both simply relieved to be free: to be out of Gengst. Away from all that. Away from the hatred. The fear. Away from Pyramus.

And Aidan? a voice asks. Aidan. I think . . . I am beginning to think that I'm even glad to be away from Aidan. Our betrothal was his dream, not mine. His people's contempt for women doesn't mean he can't learn to think differently, can't change. After all, I was born a mage and have long fought my tribe's persecution of the non-magic. But I cannot live in his world and he cannot live in mine. Not yet, if ever. Right now, I don't know what I want, except never to set foot in Gengst again.

The thought of food has galvanised Twiss. She's nearly trotting as she guides me across the clearing to a larger building set beneath the shelter of an ancient apple tree. It is one of the old stone farmhouses of the plains – just like all those ruins we passed by on our journey north. But this one is not a ruin. It is lived in and cared for.

Twiss raps on the heavy oak door, its surface silvered and furrowed with weathering. It opens almost at once to reveal a middle-aged man with the reddened complexion of a northerner who lives his life in the wind and sun. He smiles gently at Twiss, his shrewd eyes rest on me briefly, then he steps back and welcomes us inside.

'Come in. You are welcome. And just in time to share the midday food. My stew is ready to serve up.'

The large room is dim, a floor made of enormous stone flags. A central hearth with a chimney built like a tree stump in the middle of the room, warming all around. And bending over a pot, a slender woman of middle years with short cropped hair wound in a leather scarf beaded with dyed pine needles. As she stands to welcome us, I notice that her skin is nearly the same warm deep brown as Twiss's. A southerner?

Her hair though, is the flax-pale of the true north. Brown eyes watch me.

'They're hungry girls, Benj,' she says. 'Fetch some bowls and let's feed them up.' She smiles at us as the man moves with the slow sure movements that seem a part of him to fetch a pair of deep wooden bowls like the two steaming with stew on a broad board of a table against one wall. She dishes the mixture into the bowls, and the man takes them to join those on the table.

'Come,' says the woman. 'I am Ash. This is Benj. This valley is ours. But we share it with many. You are welcome.'

She points to the long bench where Benj already sits, in front of his bowl of stew. Twiss doesn't need urging. She gives a whoop of anticipation and dives for a seat beside Benj.

'Come on, Zara! I'm hungry.' And pats the bench.

I try to take my seat without any unseemly rush, but in truth, my mouth is watering. The stew smells very good.

'Eat up,' Ash says as she slips into her place. 'Thanks to the gods of Chance,' she mutters as Twiss begins slurping. 'And may Peace live in the valley for all of Time.'

'Time's grace,' I add, her prayer startling the words from me.

'Ah, Time.' Ash smiles at me, then politely lowers her face to her bowl so I can begin to eat.

Venison. Stewed with root vegetables. I taste onion and wild garlic. A barley-like grain, plus other things I can't quite guess. But the whole is very good indeed. And there is flat bread to soak up the juices. Twiss and I are busy for some time.

'The harshest god, don't you think?' She continues her conversation as though there has been no break.

'Time?' I frown in thought and swab up the last of the rich gravy. 'Harsher than Death?'

'Death is only the other side of Birth. You cannot have one without the other.'

'The price we all pay,' Benj says with a smile. 'More mead?'

'Um, no thank you.'

He fills Twiss's mug. I'm not a fan of honey wine, but Twiss obviously is.

'Time is merciless,' Ash continues. 'The river only flows one way, and the past is forever lost to us, and yet we pay the price of it forevermore.'

'Price?'

'The mistakes of our forebears. Their crimes.'

'And their achievements,' says Benj. 'And their love. It's not all dark or all light, Ash dear. As you know.' It's a reprimand, if a gentle one.

Ash shrugs. 'Seems mostly dark to me. But yes, Benj is right: acts of kindness are like fireflies in a moonless night.'

'Who are you? All the people here?'

'Ah,' Benj sighs. 'Who indeed. We're not quite sure, you know.' He smiles.

'I don't understand.'

'There is a tale, passed down through the generations,' he explains. 'A tale of two people who fled the Great Walled City.'

'Gengst?'

A nod from Ash. 'I believe that is its name. I have not been there.' There is disapproval in her voice.

'One was a man whose name is lost to us, the other, a woman called Ash.'

'Your name!'

Ash nods proudly. 'My great-great-great-many times great grandmother,' she says. 'So I'm told. When a baby is born with brown skin, if it's a girl, she's given the name. It is good luck to have an Ash living here. Sometimes there isn't one for generations.'

'Why did they come here?' I ask. Twiss must have heard the story before, she drinks her mead and watches. Occasionally, she looks longingly at the pot of stew sitting beside the hob.

'Ash was a Tribute soldier,' Benj explains. 'The man whose name is lost was a soldier in the Maker army. They found each other, the only two to survive a great battle. Enemies. And they decided to leave the dead to look after the dead. They chose life.

'All sense says they should have died, but the man was one of the last of the plains dwellers. One of those whose family fled the first great war of the Wall, abandoning their farms and smallholdings. They wandered for days, nearly dying many times. But finally they found this place. His old home. And they settled here and had children. And they found others, and brought them here to safety. From the city, from the armies. And since the first days of the Wall, and the war, we have lived here. Hidden. At peace. All of us: Tribute and Maker. But . . .' He stops; looks at me with the same, probing look that greeted me at the door. 'Never before a mage, young woman.'

My mouth dries.

'All are welcome here, Benj.' Ash's voice is short. 'All who come in peace, that is. Those who come to kill do not leave again.'

And her eyes, too, become watchful.

'Will you have more stew?' Benj asks.

25

I walk back through the settlement with Twiss. The soldiers with their crossbows follow at an unvarying ten paces, like mourners in a death procession. The snow has stopped, but the sky has a heaviness to it. The day is dying, giving way to the long northern night.

'The thieves of Gengst, Twiss. What did you find out?'

The damp air muffles my voice. As it thickens the sounds of work, people talking, an axe chopping wood; the noises of a community busy at the never-ending work of self-sufficient survival: food, shelter, warmth.

'They're here,' she says shortly. 'What's left of 'em.'

'What do you mean?' There's something in her voice, in the set of her shoulders . . .

'I promised Otter I'd leave the telling till he got back. There's stuff you need to know.' She looks away in the distance, body stiff. 'I don't know all of it myself.'

Footsteps approach through the slushy dusk; the sound pulls my gaze and I see Otter.

'Zara.' It is both statement and question.

I look up into the Guardian's so-familiar broad face, and

wonder who he is, really, this man I have grown up with. This man I don't know at all.

'Is there news of Quint?'

'The trial is tomorrow,' he says. 'She will be found guilty and executed. Philip and Aidan are petitioning for a more humane death.'

I drag in a breath. 'More humane? Than what?'

'Being burnt alive.'

I remember the badge on Matthiu's bonnet of office. Try to stop the hammering in my chest, the giddiness. Try not to feel my outrage leap into flames, sear the blood in my veins – I can't do this. I can't do anything. But breathe. Control.

I look straight ahead. Walk through the slush. He falls into step beside me.

'And the rest?' I ask, some heartbeats later. 'This place? What's going on, Otter? Twiss won't tell me why there are no thieves in Gengst. And the Maker families, the children and babies. Why are they here?'

'Some things are best discussed indoors. Twiss, you need to be part of this. We'll go to my quarters. It's as private as there is, here.

'You lot. Off duty now, go and get some grub and sleep.' This to the Tributes, who nod obedience and dissolve into four individuals, joshing each other as they stride off towards the outskirts of the settlement.

'Is this where the rest of your army hides?' I ask, as we follow Otter towards a small hut on the edge of the settlement.

'Some of it. Sometimes. There isn't room here for many. But I have an arrangement with Ash.'

'Is this her valley?'

'If there's an Ash born in the generation, they are automatically put in charge of running the community. The bad years happen when there isn't one. This Ash is good. I've known her a while now. She's saved my life more than once.'

'This is where you came! After Pyramus attacked you on the Wall and Falu saved you. You came here to heal.'

He doesn't bother to confirm the obvious. Just waits for my next question. Like an opponent in a sword fight. Or a chess match. It's my move.

'How far away is the Wall?'

'A day's hard march.'

'Did Falu bring you here? To heal?'

'I didn't walk.' A grim smile in his voice.

'Why is Twiss here?'

Otter walks on, silently. I follow him to the edge of the settlement, to a small hut indistinguishable from a dozen others. He opens the door and waits. I won't get an answer except on his terms and in his time, so I push past into the unlit room.

Twiss holds the door open for light, and I watch the Guardian as he kneels and fumbles among the banked-up fire in the hearth. When he stands up, he is holding a smoking and spluttering rush light, which he uses to light two others and set them on a small table in front of the hearth. Then he bends again to feed the coals in the fireplace with dry wood. Twiss shuts the door. In the dim, stinking light of the rush lights and a newborn flame flickering hungrily in the hearth, Twiss and I sit awkwardly facing each other across a square table.

'Will you have something to drink? It's mead.' Otter takes a jug from the small cupboard carved into the wall, uncorks it and pours a portion into a wooden cup. He looks at us.

'Thanks,' says Twiss.

Otter glances at me.

'Last time I accepted a drink from you I ended up unconscious,' I say. 'I'll pass.'

He shrugs and puts the cup in front of Twiss. Brings the jug and another cup and sits at the table. No apology. I was merely a problem to solve. The idea makes me irritable. I'm obviously more tired than I realised. I shut off the unhelpful thoughts as Otter finishes his drink and heaves a tired sigh.

'It's a filthy story, Zara,' he says at last. 'And I need to be able to trust you not to . . .'

'What?'

'Let your emotions rule your occasional good sense, and do something you and all of us will regret.'

'I didn't survive in my father's palazzo for seven and a half years as a spy for the Knowledge Seekers by doing stupid things.'

'True.' He almost smiles. 'But you're damaged. Oh, we all are,' he adds quickly, as I open my mouth to protest. 'But you, Zara . . . you have power I and Twiss don't. If we get angry, if we lose control, there are limits on what we can do. You're a mage. A powerful one, I think. If you got angry enough, you could do a lot of harm to others and to yourself.

'Pyramus is still in Gengst, by the way. Falu hasn't solved that problem for us quite yet, despite her promises.' His voice is neutral, and I wonder once more what their relationship was and is. And why I care.

'He's still looking for you,' Otter says. 'And for me again, since I broke my cover to save you.' His face grows dark. 'I missed my chance to kill him. I may not get another. And if I do, I'm going to need you alive to fight with me.'

'Nice to be wanted,' I say. I try to keep the bitterness out of my voice. And fail utterly.

Otter laughs. A laugh at once harsh and gentle. Like a cat's tongue. 'Oh, I've wanted you for a long time. Might as well want the moon.'

'Well, that's nice,' Twiss snaps scornfully. 'You made a right mess of that, boy. Are you trying to chase her back to that stuck-up Maker?'

'What did you just say?' I stare across the stinking smoke at my father's Guardian, not at all sure I've heard correctly.

'He told you,' Twiss says. 'He's in love with you, stupid! I've known for months. You need to pay attention, Zara.' The thief is intolerably smug.

'Don't worry,' Otter says above the cracking of the fire. He turns and throws another log on it, feeding the hunger. 'I don't intend to do anything about it. And I don't expect you to feel the same way. I'm not such a fool. But I have an interest, Zara. Just to make it plain: I don't hold your life or welfare lightly. But if you get in the way of what I have to do to win this gods-awful war, I will do whatever it takes to get you out of my way. Do you understand?'

'So . . .' I'm numb. 'You love me. But you'll kill me if you have to. Is that what you're saying?'

'Yeah. That about sums it up. Now that's clear, I'll tell you what I learned about Gengst. But first, Twiss can tell you her part.'

The glee on Twiss's face dies at once. She looks at me and I see a deep hurt glowing at the back of her eyes. 'I found out why there ain't a Thieves' Guild in Gengst.' She draws a deep breath. 'They kill 'em. That ministry place. They kill any born thieves off. Like rats. Like vermin. Like the mages did!' Twiss drops her eyes and stares into the wooden cup in front of her. In the flickering rush light, her face shifts in and out of definition.

Madness. Is this Gengst she's talking about, or Asphodel?

'But . . . why?'

'They call us magic-users.' Her voice is scornful. 'Lies! Just because we can do Elsewhere don't mean we're magic-users! Mages can't go to Elsewhere.'

I don't say anything. Twiss herself taught me to go to Elsewhere. But the idea she herself might be a magic-user – be somehow like her enemies, the mages – is too much for her, as I feared it would be.

'No catacombs in Gengst,' she mutters. 'No place to hide, except Elsewhere, and you can't stay there forever. Some never got caught, but they was hunted hard. Miserable lives, living like rats in the sewers. A long time ago a group decided to flee Gengst. Made it over the Wall. Ended up here. And their kids have been here ever since. They go back for the others.'

'What do you mean?'

But Twiss has grabbed the jug of mead and is pouring herself another drink. She doesn't look at either of us. I feel her upset: she is traumatised. Nearly as badly as when her beloved Bruin died.

'Ferrying out those at risk,' Otter explains. 'When possible. A network of people in the city help: thieves who have escaped detection, right-thinking Makers. Oh yes, they exist – of course they do. Hazel is one, didn't you know?' He smiles wearily at the expression on my face. 'An escape route was built years ago – that first group of thieves took years to build a tunnel beneath the Wall. It's about a day's march from here. That's how I mostly get in and out of the City. The most recent refugees from Gengst are those families you've seen here.'

'The ones with small children?'

'Yes.'

'But, they're Makers. Are they thieves too?'

'No. They are not thieves.'

'I don't understand.' Again, I think of the Ministry. Of the parents standing in the winding queue. Of the crying babies left uncomforted in the baskets. 'There was a queue of families like that outside the Ministry. Why were they there? Why have the Maker families I saw today fled Gengst?'

Twiss sighs. Takes a deep drink.

Otter doesn't speak for long ticks.

Then: 'The same reason your sister died – the fear of those who are different.'

The fire chuckles in the hearth, devouring the wood, snapping and shooting sparks onto the floor as pockets of resin explode.

I try to make sense of Otter's words. Did my father kill Swift because he was afraid of her? Of course he did. Not just her: all kine. Why else would literacy be illegal? He feared her hunger for knowledge. Her desire to be free. I don't look at either of them. I feel that the entire world is balanced on a dangerous knife edge and if I move at all, it will slide off and crash.

Otter takes a deep, preparatory breath. 'What do Makers most fear?'

'Mages,' I say.

'No – they fear magic. Any hint of it. Any taste of it.'

'But there aren't any mages left in the Maker world.'

'Magic is born in people,' Otter says. 'You know that better than anyone. It's born in you, or it isn't. But it isn't just as simple as who your parents are. I'm a full thief by talent, but my father kept a market stall. My mother was the thief. In Asphodel, mages mostly mate with mages; commoners with commoners, thieves with thieves. But not always. And the magic had to be there, in some, from the very beginning. It probably never leaves.'

'I don't understand.'

'Ash. She has dark skin, like Twiss.'

'Yes.'

'The first Ash was a Tribute slave from the far south. Dark-skinned, no doubt. And from time to time a new Ash comes along. Magic is like that.'

My heart is starting to beat far too quickly. I see again the queue of miserable parents and crying babies outside the Ministry of Control. *Oh gods! Oh Time, please let it not be so. Please . . . it's too horrible!*

'Those children . . .' I'm shivering uncontrollably.

'The Ministry tests all babies,' Otter says. He reaches out and places his large, warm, calloused hand over mine, and holds it tight. I feel all the warmth of his love, and it makes me want to weep. But I am so frightened, still. So very frightened.

'All children are tested to see if they have magic, from their first months until the age of seven,' Otter says. His voice is full of pity. For me, I know, as much as for the hundreds . . . the thousands . . . the untold generations of innocents . . .

'If there is any sign of magic ability, the children are taken away.'

I wait. The fire steams and hisses.

'The children are killed.'

A long time later, I ask: 'Was Aidan tested?'

'Everyone is tested, Zara. There are no exceptions.'

26

I rise from the bed in the darkest hours. Twiss sleeps on as though drugged. She emptied the bottle of mead in the end. I tug on the sheepskin coat then go to stand at her bedside. I can't see her clearly, just a dark shape curled on the bed. Snores snuffle into the darkness of the wooden room. I wish I could see her face, one last time.

'Goodbye, Twiss. I love you, little sister.'

The softest of whispers, but I needed to say it aloud. Even if I survive . . . even if she does . . . this is the end. She won't forgive me. None of them will. I console myself with the thought that I will almost certainly die.

The Tribute soldiers stationed outside the door of the hut are a slight irritant. I'm in Elsewhere, so they can't see me. But they will see the door open and close. There are two more guards outside the window. Otter isn't taking any chances. But then, he's a careful man. That's why he made me drink a cup of beer before he left us alone in our hut.

I didn't need to pretend anger: 'You don't trust me!' I shouted.

He agreed.

But I was expecting it, prepared: Otter is a thief, but he's no mage. He can't feel magic. And it's not hard to magic a liquid while it's in the cup. In the time it took to lift the beer to my lips, I dispersed its watery particles into the air and stuck the sludgy residue – and the drug it contained – to the bottom of the cup.

The hardest thing came later, once Twiss was snoring next to me, and the Guardian came and stood beside our bed. I felt him looking down at me. Thinking me unconscious, he had no reason to block his emotions. I felt his love, deep mingled with pain and sadness. And when he leant down and kissed me on the forehead with such gentleness, it took every bit of my will to keep still and silent in order to trick him. I had to think, with all my strength, of the children outside the Ministry. To remember Swift and her face, glowing with excitement as she told me of the world where she could be free: the world of the Makers.

Swift sacrificed everything for me: even her life in the end. And I promised her . . .

Time for more magic. A subtle, difficult magic. I slide down to sit on the floor beside the door, rest my back against the wall. I can hear my guards shuffle from foot to foot. A soft murmur as they talk to keep each other awake. Boring work for them.

Not for me: I've made my decision. It's a sort of release, saying goodbye to everyone you love. Now there is only the task ahead of me. Sad as I am, I find a sort of joy in the doing. Magic is my work, as healing is Quint's. I've been kept from it too long.

Slowly, gradually, I build an invisible shell of hardened air around the two guards. Crystallise it until nothing can pass through, not even air itself. And I wait. Slowly, slowly, the Tribute guards breathe up all the air. So slowly, they hardly notice the increasing sleepiness. Tired already. A long watch, after a long day. The graveyard shift. The one on the right is the first to go. Slumping down where she stands. The man lasts a few moments longer, tries to call out, but the shell is soundproof. No one can hear him. And he, too, collapses at last.

I wait a few moments more. To make sure they remain unconscious. Too long and they'll die. I have to guess, and pray I get it right. At the count of thirty ticks, I break the shell. Ease open the door. Stop for a moment to check with my mind, not my hands. Yes: alive.

Close the door, my hand shaking with relief. Fear. Excitement. Fear. Which is more? Banish all such distracting thoughts from my mind and go deep into Elsewhere. Otter is somewhere here, and he's deadly. The time for magic is over. Now I must be a consummate thief.

The patches of snow from yesterday are gone; soaked into the still-warm ground. At least that's one less thing to worry about, although Otter won't need a trail to know where I'm headed. It's Time that is my enemy. I navigate the dangers of the settlement, grateful for the faint light of the quarter moon, dipping in and out from behind patches of thin cloud. Slow careful steps, breaking the rhythm so any sound becomes a random night noise.

All the huts are dark; light and fuel too precious to waste in the hours when work is impossible. It's cold. Damp rises from the ground. Owls hoot in the middle distance. A fox screams – a shivery sound – just as I make it to the northernmost edge of the settlement – the place where I noticed a few people disappear from sight and not return, some of Otter's soldiers among them. The way in and out of the valley must be somewhere ahead.

I leave the settlement behind with a sense of relief, of danger lessened, but also sadness. Had things been different . . . I would have liked to stay in this valley. Stay with Otter? I shake my head and quicken my step. No point in thinking about the impossible. The what-might-have-beens.

I slow my breathing to calm my thoughts and stay deep – deep in Elsewhere. So deep I startle the fox winding its way, liquid-sleek, between the trees. So deep the hunting owls skim within an arm's length of my face. So deep I lose my fear, my sadness, and become movement itself.

The valley stretches higher, the trees thin, and I lose the moon's soft light and am plunged into near-darkness as the valley narrows into a canyon. I stop, lost. A dilemma. I can't see to go on, but do I dare use magic? I don't have a choice. I must either use a touch of mage light or stumble forward by feel, which is too slow and risky. I'll walk into things, make noise. Possibly fall and injure myself. Walking blind into the night isn't something I've stomach for in any case. My old fear of the dark is waiting to pounce.

I conjure a finger-sized flame of blue to dance ahead of me. The sight of it lifts my heart, even though it's so faint, so small. The blue flame lights the path just enough to see as I begin to climb. And it is a proper path now: steps hacked out of the bluestone of the valley walls. The steps grow steeper, become stairs which climb up and up. Before long, I'm panting. Just as it seems the stone stairway will go on to the moon itself, the path stops and I face solid stone.

It takes me several long ticks – far too many – and a stronger light, before I see the sideways twist, the sharp bend in the canyon wall and heave a sigh of relief that this is not a dead end after all. Thank the gods! I edge round the kink.

Hands grab me. Unkind. Ungentle. The knife at my throat is not gentle. The words are not gentle:

'I should kill you now!'

But he doesn't. He hesitates for a fraction of a thought. A tick of regret. And that is his mistake. For shame, Otter! You said you wouldn't let your love stop you. You lied.

One thought: and the knife is rust. Another: and he's squashed against the wall. I turn, and look at him, in the blue of my mage light.

'Too late,' I say. 'Goodbye, Otter.'

'Don't do this, Zara! It's wrong.'

'Since when have you worried about what's right and wrong?' I shake my head. 'You want to win, and you think you need me to do that. You want to control me.'

'That's not true!'

I look at him and sadness fills me brimful. 'I'm sorry, Otter. If things were different . . . but they aren't. I'm not certain of anything, except that what I'm doing is right.'

'Using your power against me, against your friends? Is that right?'

'I don't have friends,' I say, knowing it to be true. 'I'm a mage.'

We look at each other.

'I love you,' he says.

'So did Swift. And who loves her now? She hasn't got anyone else except me. She never did. All those babies. Who loves them? It has to stop, Otter.'

'What are you going to do?'

'You know.'

'You can't change the way people think by magicking them, Zara! They have to do it themselves.'

'I can stop the murderer. This one. This man. Him, I can stop.'

'Kill, you mean.'

'Yes.'

I do want to kill Matthiu. I want him dead: not just to stop him, but because I hate him for what he has done to Quint, to the children, to so many. The man is evil and I intend – I want – to kill him. I'm not going to lie about it. Does that make me evil too? I don't know.

'Pyramus will be waiting. It's a trap, Zara. He'll use the situation, lie in wait like a jackal, hoping you're going to do just this.'

'I don't care. Don't you understand?' I stare at him through a blur of tears. 'There's nothing left. I don't have anywhere now.'

'You have here. And Twiss. And . . . me.'

'It isn't enough.' I shake my head, helpless. 'I'm sorry. I can't live here, hidden away, safe, while they're . . . I can't do it, Otter. Swift died. It has to stop. I'm going to stop a bit of it, anyway.'

'You'll have to kill me.'

'Of course I won't.' I smile at him. 'I don't think I could do that. And I don't have to. That's where I'm luckier than you. I can stop you like this.'

I come out of Elsewhere to gather all my concentration. I tell the stones of the valley to grow, to shift, to rise in a wall around Otter. I see the look of desperation on his face as the valley itself cages him. And then the rising wall of stone blots out his face. I shan't see him again, either. It's a bitter thought.

I leave him inside a shaft of stone, fifteen feet tall, and hear his voice calling to me as I turn and walk away, my blue mage light flickering ahead. It's long cold walk to Gengst. And time is short.

27

It's midday before I catch sight of the Wall of the Makers and the towers and chimneys of the great city of Gengst-on-the-Wall. I remember how magical I thought it was, the first time I saw it.

I've taken longer than I hoped to reach this far: treading a careful way past the camps of my father's Tribute soldiers besieging the city. Past the stinking, smouldering funeral pyres of the dead. The Tributes rest in the daytime, waiting for the cover of darkness to attack the Wall with seige ladders.

I leave Benedict's Tribute army behind and enter the scorched earth of no-man's land. I need to be quick. There isn't time to worry about Pyramus. Otter is doubtless right. The adept is lying in wait. So, it's all up to the Lord Time . . . if the god exists. Will I be granted enough of his grace to finish my job before my father's assassin finds me? Elsewhere will help. But for that, I wouldn't stand a chance. I only hope Otter is slow in climbing his way out of his stone prison, and that Twiss is still sleeping soundly. Time's grace keep them both safe!

I smile at the irony of praying to a god whose existence I doubt as I trot closer and closer to the Wall. Finally, I'm standing in the exact spot where the Knowledge Seekers climbed into

Gengst only a few weeks ago. Only weeks! It seems an age: that time of hope and innocence.

Flying has never been a struggle for me. I can even do it inside Elsewhere. I concentrate, order the air beneath my feet to thicken into columns firm enough to walk upon. And I'm clambering up the hillside to the edge of the Wall, like a stilt walker at a fair. I build the columns higher and higher. I rise up the Wall of the Makers. It passes in front of my face, stone by stone, until I'm level with the crenellated top. A Maker soldier stands at guard a few feet away, staring out into the burnt wasteground moating the Wall. He doesn't see me, doesn't hear me step lightly off the air columns onto the skirting wall, then drop like a cat onto the path.

A lot of magic. I'm hungry now. I'll need to steal food soon. More urgently, I need to get away from here. If Pyramus is nearby he will have felt my magic. Did I make a mistake, choosing this place again? It was a gamble. But I know how to get to the Ministry from here.

I dodge through the Maker soldiers stationed atop the Wall. After five minutes, my fear of the assassin grows less, but I keep running. I'm in Elsewhere. As long as I don't use magic, Pyramus can't spot me. I must be safe now. But I keep running.

It's the second set of stairs down into the town that I want. When I come to them, I edge past the soldier guarding the stairwell and climb down into the city streets. Gengst is teeming with Makers: I've never seen the streets so crowded. What's going on? A carnival? Some celebration or festival? The air is full of excitement. Yes, must be a festival. I hardly pay attention to the chattering voices as I navigate a careful but swift route through the crowd. And then I hear the words:

Witch. Did you see? Never screamed. Like a suckling pig. Burn the lot. Skin busted wide open. Always the females. Eyeballs popped. Saw that? Foul little beggars. Took her sweet time to die. The demon in her. Smell put me off my dinner. Mage slaves. Witch. Burnt. Fire.

I stop moving and stand quite still in the middle of the street. The crowd passes by. Someone bumps into me, swears. The note of hysteria in his voice brings me to myself and I edge away and press into the wall of a building. I'm shaking. My mind seems to have gone into another, slow, confused place. All of Time has slowed for me. The Makers surge and babble around me at frightening speed.

Mistress Quint, with her round, smiling face. Her bobbing to and fro. Her kindness. Her skill. She is real. This is not. Real.

The shaking eases and I press harder into the building, wanting to melt into the safety of the dead stone. Could I become stone? Is that possible? Has any mage done that? I am mad: must be. Not rational. Not thinking. Not feeling. No, especially not that.

I look and see, rising up a few streets away, a thick, noxious black plume of smoke.

When I reach it, the square is half full of stragglers. It's a large open space surrounded by very old buildings. The raised platform of smoke-blackened granite dominating the centre of the square testifies that this square has long been a place of execution. Some of the audience have brought picnics, and are standing or leaning, finishing their meals. Drinking from flasks. Soldiers line all four sides of the square, but they stand at ease now, joking with their colleagues, sending the drunk and disorderly on their way with the slap of a scabbarded sword or a push of a metal-gloved hand.

The pyre is still burning. They used a great deal of wood. And tar to set it going, from the smell. The stake is charred nearly to charcoal, crumbing and falling slowly, like chunks of black snow. Drifting into the flames.

I turn and slowly, carefully, walk away from the place where Mistress Quint faced her enemy for the final time.

I stand, hidden in Elsewhere, outside the Ministry. I must make sure. I will destroy this place, but I must know the witchfinder is inside.

Snow, white feathers of ice, begins to drift slowly from the darkening sky. The black smoke of the city stains each crystal as it falls. Cold wet kisses melt on my cheeks. The falling snow outlines my invisible form. My boot soles leave their shape in the sooty-grey. I lurch to the safety of a doorway opposite the Ministry.

No one has seen. I look into the sky. Watch the snow spiral down, turning grey as it falls. It's evening. The working day is done. The queues of parents and children have melted away like the snow beneath my feet. Bureaucrats and a few guards begin to file out of the building. It must be now!

I detach a thin strand of consciousness from my mind, and send it seeking through the hallways and corridors of the Ministry. Ranging through rooms until I find him at last. The Minister is working late at his desk. Writing, scribbling, folding documents and melting sealing wax, pressing the shiny gold seal of his office into the red pools of wax with the concentrated pleasure of a child.

I gather my will. Rarely, for me – for it is my father's favourite element – I have chosen fire. Fires are a commonplace in any city. There is a chance I can do my work and no one will suspect magic. I do not want to endanger Philip or the rest of the Knowledge Seekers. I send the strand of thought to the basement, to dark, rat-scurrying places. I find timbers, doors, all the bits made of wood, and tell them to grow hot. To gather to themselves all the heat of the air and the stone. The wooden joists, doors and frames glow, smoke. And, finally, burst into flame.

Quick as a bird in flight, I send my thoughts from the bottom of the building to the top, and attack the roof timbers. Even more quickly – for they are drier – they ignite. Fire rages, above and below. The Ministry of Control is dying.

I return to Matthiu's office. He works on, undisturbed as yet. The sight of his grey head bent over his desk ices my heart. I send a burst of magic to rust the hinges of his door solid. I bang the shutters of his window closed and grow them into a single solid plank of wood. He looks up at that, stares, amazed. Stands . . . goes to the window. Tugs and pulls at the shutters. Runs to the door . . .

I wait. And watch. The screams and shouts begin. Those who can, flee the building. I feel no pity for those who are trapped. They earn their bread by the torturing of others, even if their hands do not hold the hot iron poker or pile the stones on the press. These bureaucrats warm their houses and clothe their backs by murdering children.

It seems to take forever, but is only a hundred heartbeats before the roof collapses into the heart of the stone building. I hear the cracking and hissing of the inferno; see the snow drift down, the flakes evaporating to steam long before they touch the flames.

I watch him to the last moment. Watch Matthiu tear the flesh of his hands as he pounds on the locked door. Watch him scream, cower, choke on smoke black as his heart. His death is too easy. Far too easy.

A freshening wind harries me down the streets. I lose my sense of direction in the maze of lanes several times, but finally I reach the northern edge of the city. Aidan said it was here: the workshops where Maker engineers, armourers and smiths make the weapons: the catapults, bolt throwers, the armour, swords and spears.

Somewhere, among these rectangles of buildings, on one of these uncannily straight streets, is where I will find Philip. He has my sword. And – if I manage to escape Gengst and survive the journey across the plains – I shall have need of it.

Pyramus will be searching for me near the Ministry. Or near the southern Wall where he would expect me to make my escape. I'll take the chance: it's the smallest, most discreet of magics. And I'm running out of time. Otter will be on my trail. Even a cage of stone won't slow the Guardian down for long.

I pause in a corner formed by two buildings and send a strand of consciousness to seek out the artist. It seems forever before I track him down in the maze of buildings. The sun is dipping towards the south-western horizon by the time I find the right building, squeeze past some fierce looking soldiers guarding the door, and push through a heavy oak door into a massive high-ceilinged room full of sawdust and tables. Men in leather aprons over their clothes sit at strange machines carving things out of wood, hammering or welding bits of metal together.

Light from three forges stains the room red, like a scene from the underworld. Windows cut into the high ceiling let in some light, but the day is dying. A small, grubby boy runs around lighting row after row of oil lamps, using a wick on a long pole.

I know Philip is here, but it isn't his presence that I sense as soon as I walk into the room: Aidan! The last person on this earth I want to see now. Now that I know the secret at the heart of his city. The secret he kept from me. Now that I am outlaw to all Makers.

Where are they? Time is ticking away. Pyramus . . . Otter. One or the other will be on my trail. Finally I spot them: they stand in the far corner, their backs to me. They're bent over a table strewn with papers.

I draw near, hidden in Elsewhere, and hear their voices. They are deep in conversation about gearing, ratios, tensile strength. I look at the plans: they're for some gigantic throwing machine. A foul thing, destined to kill hundreds of Tribute slaves, and yet they talk of it with such tenderness in their voices.

'You might at least have gone to see her die.'

Aidan stiffens and stands upright at the sound of my voice. Philip whirls around, eyes wide. But I'm in Elsewhere and invisible. Aidan turns more slowly. Fear and love battle in his face. He's heard something in my voice that has scared him. He knows me well now, this Maker boy. Do I still love him?

I have the memory of that love, and as long as I live, I will cherish it. But I am no longer that person. This is not that time.

'Zara?' Philip turns back around. Tugs Aidan around too. They make a show of studying the plans. 'It's too dangerous to talk out here,' the artist whispers. 'We will walk to my office now. Please follow. There are people there who will want to see you.' He straightens, gathers the scrolls. Aidan stumbles in his wake. Hurry, Aidan! No time. We've no time.

I follow them down a dim, smelly corridor. Philip opens a door and inside a small windowless room lit by lantern light, I see Hazel and Tabitha sitting at either end of a long table. They are drawing. They look up, startled, as Philip and Aidan enter. I slide in after them and close the door behind me.

Hazel stands up, her face pale. 'Who closed that door?'

'Only me,' I say.

Aidan looks towards the sound of my voice.

'Let us see you,' he says.

'I don't think so. Safer not.'

'Don't you trust me?' Hurt in the words, in his emotions.

'Trust,' I say. 'Trust has to be earned, Aidan. It can be lost so easily. Why didn't you go to the execution, Philip?'

'I wasn't allowed. None of us were.' His face is solemn, his voice deep with sorrow. 'I visited her last night. As did Tabitha and Hammeth. We were with her as long it was allowed. I gave her opium to take, Zara. Enough. If she took it, and I hope to the gods she did, then she'll have been dead or near death by the time they lit the fire. If she took it, she won't have suffered.'

'I see.' I don't know if I feel better at the words. Hate myself any less.

'We wanted to go, Zara.' Tabitha's voice is mournful. 'Don't be angry with us.'

'With you?' I ask, startled. 'You've done nothing. It's me. I should have known. Stopped her. I didn't notice her visits into the city because I was too busy with my own troubles!'

'The same could be said of all of us,' Tabitha says. 'It isn't your fault either.'

'Why are you here, Zara?' Hazel asks. Wary.

'I need my sword. Bruin's sword, Philip. Now.'

He blinks. 'Zara, you are upset. Obviously. We all cared for –'

'The sword. Quickly.'

'Zara!'

'Don't talk to me, Aidan of Gengst. It's over for us. It's been over since I learned the secret you didn't tell me. The secret Hazel hinted at. How can you live, any of you Makers? How can you bear it?'

'Oh gods.' Not Aidan. Philip.

'You knew? You as well?' I want to scream. To cry. I do neither. Too late. Far too late for anything but the sword. And Benedict.

'Hazel t-told me.' Philip's voice stumbles in his rush to explain. 'A few weeks ago. Zara, we can't do anything right now! We haven't got the power. It takes time to change attitudes. To make people understand. And to be honest, the rest of us, the rest of the Knowledge Seekers, aren't in a position to do anything. Half the city wants us to burn as well.'

'I know,' I say. 'I was in the crowd just now.'

'You didn't see . . .' Aidan's voice is horrified. 'Zara. My love!'

'I am not your love. I'm sorry, Aidan. I can't love someone who could live with that going on every day of their lives. And,

Philip, I know you can't do anything yet. I know your life is at risk. But you don't need to worry about the Ministry any longer. And I am going back to Asphodel to visit my father. That's why I need the sword. It was made for one job. I owe it to Bruin, to Twiss, to my sister. And to myself.'

'You are going to attack the Ministry, aren't you?' The Knowledge Seeker's face grows long and sorrowful. His eyes hold mine, imploring. 'Even if you survive . . . even if the Makers don't kill you, Zara, your father's assassin almost certainly will. You'll waste your life. You'll never live to reach Asphodel!'

'It's mine to waste. It's not worth much anyway.'

'I don't happen to agree. Nor does Aidan or Otter. Nor does Hazel.'

'Nor I,' says Tabitha. 'You mustn't do this, Zara. Even if you succeed, you won't be the same. There's a line we mustn't cross. You above all. It's hard, I know. But you mustn't use your power to kill in revenge. Leave Matthiu to the judgement of the gods!'

I sigh. 'The sword. Please.'

Aidan walks slowly to the desk, slumps into a chair. 'Give it to her.'

'Aren't you going to even try . . .' Hazel cries.

'No.' Aidan looks to where he thinks I'm standing. 'She's right. It's what I would do. What I should have done . . .' His eyes frown at the place where I was standing a moment before. Blue, beautiful. Sad. Still loving. 'Can I come with you, Zara? I can fight.'

'It isn't that sort of fight, Aidan. Not this time. If you really mean it, then carry on fighting here. But stop pretending child murder is not happening.'

Philip moves like an old man. Goes to one of the wooden chests lined against a wall, opens it and pulls out the scabbard. Bruin's blade of new-forged iron, and the hilt Tabitha wrought to hold the blade unlike any other. A blade which has tasted my father's blood once. And, if I am lucky, shall again.

The Seeker holds it out. I step forward, take it, and the sword comes into Elsewhere with all I wear or touch. Philip blinks. Aidan swears, softly.

'I haven't had time to analyse it properly.' The Seeker sighs.

'Sorry,' I say.

'Zara.' Tabitha stands up, her face twisted in pain. 'Don't do this. You aren't a killer. You can't set yourself up as judge and executioner. You don't have the right. Remember my trial. You stopped the Knowledge Seekers from killing me out of revenge.'

'You aren't Matthiu,' I say. 'The comparison isn't valid. And killing Matthiu would not have been enough. The death of one man would not have changed anything. They would have just put another bureaucrat in his place.'

'Innocent people will die,' Philip says.

'No one working there was innocent! No Maker alive is innocent!'

'So, will you kill us all? As complicit?' Hazel asks. 'Mages aren't exactly strangers to genocide.'

'That's why I'm taking the sword,' I say. 'Unfinished business.'

'If you do this, there will be no place left for you in this world,' Hazel says. 'You will be an outcaste.'

'I am already. Matthiu is dead. The Ministry is destroyed.'

I watch their faces change. Feel fear enter their hearts. There is nothing more to say. I turn away from those who were once my friends, and leave.

The night sky still vomits soot and ash as I trot towards the place in the Wall where I entered Gengst. I dodge the stream of townsfolk making their way towards the glow in the sky that marks the remains of the Ministry of Control.

The magic has taken its toll and my body complains: hunger, a slight chill. But I barely notice. I'm waiting for the arrow between the shoulder blades. For Pyramus's spike of ice. Which of them will kill me? Otter or the adept?

I see Pyramus in every plump Maker I pass. I'm in a muck-sweat of fear as I climb the stone stairs to the top of the Wall and creep along the top. It's dark now. Every crenellation could shelter my enemy. There's no way out of Gengst without magic. I gather my concentration. My palms sweat. Once I commit, it's final. If he's here I will be an easy target.

And then I'm lifting on columns of air. Swinging over the Wall and lowering down. I tumble too quickly to the ground, stumble and fall on hands and knees, my magic clumsy with fear. But I'm alive! Time's grace has granted me a while longer to live.

I'm nearly a league from Gengst when the Guardian finds me. I hear his horse before I see it. I don't try to hide. Just keep walking through the birch and pine forest. My only plan is to find the river and follow it towards Asphodel.

Otter reins up on the path ahead of me. I look up at the conjoined shadow of man and beast. The horse has travelled hard: I hear it panting.

'You'll founder it.'

'What have you done, Zara?'

'What needed doing. The building is destroyed. The man is dead.'

'How?'

'Fire.'

He's silent. The moon is out, but it's too dark for me beneath these trees to see his face. I still have one job to do but I know I can't kill the Guardian, not even to avenge my sister. So I wait. The decision is his.

He swings down from the horse. Instead of drawing his sword, he gathers the animal's reins. 'Climb up.'

'Why?' Always, he surprises me.

'I'm taking you back to the valley. You're a fool, Zara, but at least you had the sense to use fire. With any luck, no one will suspect magic.'

More than anything, I want to climb onto the horse, have Otter lead it on into the night until we reach Ash's valley. I want it so much! But there is one thing I want more. And there is no refuge, no place where I can be at peace in this world, until I have accomplished it.

'I'm going to Asphodel.' I put my hand on my sword hilt, and Otter grows suddenly still.

'Bruin's sword.'

'Yes.'

'We'll go together. When the time is right.'

'Your time is not my time, Otter. Your way is not my way. My whole life, since you came to my father's palazzo, you've treated me like an enemy, lied to me, not trusted me. I am neither a child nor your enemy, but I *am* my father's daughter. I have inherited power from my father, and I will use it to destroy him.'

'You can't defeat Benedict on your own!' Otter's voice is despairing.

The Guardian unshields his emotions, and I feel both his love and his despair. I accept the truth of his love for me. Sense its depth, its long growing and maturing. He knows me better than I know myself. And still loves me. And always will. Otter's love is real. Solid as stone. And I wish . . . but it's too late. And I know – Aidan has proved to me – love, perhaps even love like this, is not enough.

'Please, Zara. Come with me and let us start again. You're right: I've kept you at a distance, didn't confide in you, tried to control you. I was afraid . . . I didn't want to lose you. And I didn't believe that I could trust anyone, even you. I've always been alone. You know what that's like! I . . . haven't been as brave as you, been able to learn to trust. But I will change. Don't go to Asphodel! Your father will kill you. Or worse.'

'You should listen to the man, Zara.'

Otter is quicker than me. The Guardian yanks something from his saddle, slaps his horse and sends it charging into the forest in the direction of Pyramus's voice. Then Otter is rolling over the ground, leaping to his feet and dodging into the tree cover.

The stampeding horse gives me a space of time to recover. My shield is up a fraction of a tick before the net of air drops over my head. The capture net slides harmlessly to the ground and his burst of magic allows me to pinpoint Pyramus.

I need power. Something is happening to me. It's like the fight with the battle mages. I reach out, find the energy I need from my enemy, and take it to myself. And I feed my power with my hatred. I give myself over to intoxication. I want this power. I want more. I want to use it!

This! This is what I was born to do.

And once more I choose my father's weapon. The fireball I create is a blue churning hell. It's huge. I smash it towards Pyramus.

My father's assassin should be content to die. But he's a canny old mole. He goes to ground. Dives into the earth itself, tunnelling with his mind as he goes. It's a stunning bit of magic.

The earth clogs my sense of him. Pyramus could be anywhere, waiting to attack. Behind me. Beneath me! Fear crumples my control.

In that moment, I hear Otter shouting. Sense Pyramus's magic in the wood to my right. The Guardian is no match for an adept: not without a bow. I know fear such as I have never felt . . . not since that long-ago night when I was nine and I lost Swift. In a moment, I'm running towards the sounds, stumbling over roots and bumping into tree trunks.

Pyramus has set a circle of mage lights twisting overhead in the sky. Their cold red light illuminates a small clearing in the wood. Otter is crouched, at bay, in the scant shelter of a fallen tree. He has a crossbow in his hands – one of Philip's newfangled killing machines. Pyramus stands pressed against a tree, struggling, cursing. It takes a moment for me to realise that the adept has been pinned to the tree by a bolt through his hand.

My father's spy hisses in agony. He's using his magic to pull the bolt free, inch by inch. Why doesn't Otter finish him off before it's too late? And then I realise: the Guardian only had one bolt set in the bow. The rest will be in a quiver fastened to his saddle. Otter is backing away, preparing to run. He glances up. Sees me.

'Zara!' he screams. 'Get out! Take the horse. Get away!' And he's gone just as Pyramus pulls the bolt from his flesh and turns, grinning with pain and rage. And sends a fireball churning through the trees after the Guardian.

I don't wait. This time, I do what Otter tells me. I stagger back through the forest. I'll find the horse and the arrows. And then somehow I'll find Otter. If he isn't dead. If Pyramus hasn't just killed him.

28

I found the horse. But no Otter. I searched for nearly an hour before I gave up. I have to accept that the Guardian may be dead.

It's a good strong horse. It trots through the star-lit night for a long time before it finally slows, sides heaving. I let it walk on for a time. But the beast is slowing me down now. I'm better on my own.

Reluctantly, for the horse is a reminder of Otter, I rummage the saddle bag for rations and find a piece of flat bread and some dried meat. I stuff them into the pockets of my coat. Then I take the reins and saddle off the horse so it won't tangle itself in a bush and die of thirst or wolf. I point the beast's head westwards, towards the distant sea I'll never know, and slap it on the rump.

It squeals in outrage and plunges a dozen scrambling feet away, where it stops and turns to look at me. Shakes its head to make sure that the bridle is truly gone, gives me another hard look, and trots away into the dawn. The next moment I'm away myself, walking as quickly as my tired muscles will allow.

I need to find shelter. To sleep. To eat. To forget. My hand goes to the hilt of Bruin's sword. My stride lengthens. *I'm coming to find you, Father. I'm on my way at last.*

* * *

I wake to a ferocity of cold I've never felt before. Except once: in the cellars of my father's palazzo. With Twiss. I will never see the thief again. A cold, slow tear itches up and swells over my eyelid. Slow as a slug. Tries to creep down my cheek. And freezes to my skin.

Shades of all the demons!

Fear is a good antidote to exhaustion. I'm on my feet in a moment, pushing off the cedar branches I piled high in the hope of some shelter, shivering, beating my arms and legs to get feeling back. The morning pee is an excruciating exposure of already cold nether regions. As I tug my trousers back up, I swear with every word Twiss ever taught me, and some I invent myself. It warms me a bit. I warm more as I scatter the branches back over the forest floor; using the last to sweep away any trace of my burrow. Activity keeps the Guardian and his fate from my mind.

It's still early dawn. The sky greys above the bare tree branches. I tug out the packet of dried meat, bite off a mouthful and put the rest away. And I begin to walk among the tree giants, stumbling clumsy-footed over their heavy roots. Shuffling through the litter of long dead leaves.

The sky overhead whitens until the world shifts from black and grey to muted colour. Brown, stone, russet, grey. The colours of winter. The heavy forest thins, the trees shrink, turn to saplings scrabbling for a foothold. The ground beneath my feet climbs, descends, climbs again. Always, I follow the river that will lead me to Asphodel. The desire to reach my home, to avenge my sister, is the only thing that keeps me walking.

I leave the forest at last, walk out into an edge of a wooded hill and look down into a long, narrow valley. The river splashes down the hillside at my feet, a steep, slippery, stone-littered path. I see ice shining on the stones.

The valley stretches as long as I can see. Dark grey-purple shale lies on the shoulders of the hills. Once, this land was grazed. Enough sheep survive to keep the trees away. I spot a few woolly grey and brown backs wandering on the hillsides.

The spines of tumbled stone walls still mark the fields. Moss-covered spines. Here and there, I see the ruin of an ancient farmhouse. Sheep country. High, chill, beautiful. A lonely place, even when people lived here. The stream crashes down the stones below, dropping from ledge to ledge down to the valley floor and the journey southwards.

My journey down is slippery and unpleasant. A sprained ankle, or a broken one, would be fatal. I pick my way, scooting on my bottom when necessary. When my boots touch the valley floor, I'm starving again. I find a flattish large stone near the stream, and collapse onto it. I pull out the bread and cram it into my mouth. The first sharpness of hunger eases slightly. I'll save the last of the dried meat. The only food I can hope to find will be swimming in the river at my feet. And my chances of catching a fish without using magic are slender.

I stare at the surface of the water. The river runs shallow just here, racing over the huge grey-white slabs of the limestone bottom, slowing as it falls into the deeper pools that collect at the corners of wide meanders.

A beautiful, lonely, peaceful place.

I sigh. Stand and stretch. And hear the baying of a hound. Back beyond the head of the valley. Not a wolf. Certainly no fox out past its bedtime. That was a hound. And, as certainly as if I had set it on its trail, I know it hunts me.

Otter is almost certainly dead. Aidan won't want to find me now. There's one person only who would be tracking me down with hounds. As the Makers hunted him through the streets of Gengst. Pyramus.

Clever man. I had counted on Elsewhere saving me if the assassin found me. In Elsewhere I would be invisible. Even Pyramus couldn't track me down if I don't use magic. But Elsewhere doesn't stop a hound sniffing you out. And if I use magic to obliterate my scent, the adept will find me anyway. Pyramus didn't get to be my father's spymaster through stupidity.

I stare at the river. It will cover my scent. But it's such an obvious thing to do. He'll know. He'll follow. My only chance is to somehow slip by him. I'll have to use the river in the end. And Elsewhere. But not yet. Now I run. Run for my very life. South. Down the valley.

I run heavy-footed along the paths worn by deer and sheep. Jump over stones and fallen branches, tree roots that trip. After the first two tumbles, sprawling on bloody palms and bruised knees, I slow down. Stop letting fear drive me. And trot, like a tired mule. Like a panting dog. Like a fox chased by hounds.

The sky has turned an odd yellowish colour. The air has grown heavy, close. The clouds sit low and ominous, cutting off the tops of the hills.

The purple shale on the shoulders of the hills turns dark grey as the light dims. There's a storm coming. The back of my neck prickles with the energy loose in the air. And the hound howls in a frenzy of excitement as it picks up my trail. At the sound, I shift into Elsewhere and stop, panting, nearly foundered like the horse, and look back.

Pyramus is in the valley. He's on horseback. Travelling with the slouch-shouldered comfortableness of the seasoned horseman. The deadly calm of the hunter is in the set of his shoulders, the easy turn of his hatted head as he scans the valley.

And just as suddenly, I know that Pyramus, high adept, is in the dog as well. Sharing its mind. Tracking me. Smelling me. Hunting me on four feet as well as two.

Good that my stomach digested the bread so quickly. Or I would be sick where I stand.

I'm in the river in the space of a thought. Cold seeps at once through the leather of my boots, through the woollen socks. My feet burn with it. I begin to move, steadily, slowly, carefully. If I fall, if I get drenched in this icy water, then my father wins and I lose. Everything. All those deaths – Swift, my mother, Gerontius, Quint, the unnumbered Tributes – all those deaths will have no answer, no remembering . . . no vengeance. And the cycle will continue.

I keep my hand on the hilt of Bruin's sword. I keep my head down, eyes on the river bed. The sky grows darker. The first flakes of snow float down like a dove's soft white feathers. Gentle, beautiful. They brush my eyelids, my nose. Settle on my shoulders before slowly melting to drip into the water of the river.

The hound that is Pyramus is racing now. It's not bothering to sniff out my scent any longer. He knows where I am. I'm ahead of him. In the river. There's nowhere else.

I need to find a place to stop. To hide. Perhaps Pyramus will pass by and I can retreat, try to escape back the way I came. It's the slimmest of chances.

I plunge on, up to my shins now. My feet are gone: I can't feel them. A miracle I haven't fallen over: it feels like my legs are made of wood. I need a place. Please. Not here, in the open shingled bend. Exposed, and nothing to fight with. Nowhere to hide.

And then the river takes me round a gentle curve and narrows suddenly. And I see in the darkening light, ahead of me, the most extraordinary sight.

A bridge of stone. A curve made of enormous limestone slabs arcs across the river from bank to bank. It rests on a causeway made by giants. Chunks have been carried away, by fallen trees in the flood times no doubt. But most of its span remains intact. An old packhorse bridge. From a time before the war, before the Maker cities rose in rebellion.

Trees gather on either riverside. Bend thoughtful heads over the bridge. There might be something I can do here. In any case, I've no choice. My feet are frozen and the rest of me will follow soon. I must get out of the river.

A painful scrabble up onto the bridge. Slipping, sliding backwards. Grabbing with my fingernails as I nearly fall back into the river. I hang for a moment, then ease up one knee, then the other. Getting to my feet is the most dangerous thing yet. I can't even feel where they are. I have to look, place them with a hand, and remember how the muscles work. Push with ghostly calves and thighs. Pray for balance. I stand on two ice-dead legs, swaying. Reach up and grab the overhanging branch I've chosen. I pull myself along it, closer to the tree's trunk. It's an old willow, the weeping sort. Wide, soft, sad old tree. I pull myself up to sit on the branch, inch to the trunk. Hug it with hungry arms. Stand again. And begin to climb.

Without magic, it takes a long and slippery time before I reach the branch I spotted from the river. High enough. And now: it's up to the snow.

The gods are kind. The snow comes now quick and fast. A conspirator: it hides the signs of my struggle to get out of the river. Settles and smooths, and turns me invisible again with the magic of winter and wind.

The feeling is returning to my feet and legs, and the pain has me leaning over, pressing my face into the bark of branch I sit on to muffle my whimpering. I've never felt anything so painful in my life as the feeling of blood returning to the small vessels and flesh of my legs and feet. I hold on tight, fighting the pain. And suddenly, the dog is there. Below.

I hold my breath. Listen, eyes shut. It patters over the bridge. Stops. Circles. I hear it snuffling. Is the snow enough? Lord Time, grant me aid. Give me a chance.

Snuffling, snuffling. And then: the howl of discovery. I peer around the branch and see its muzzle pointed skywards. At me, though it can't see me. Gamble lost. It's now.

29

My knife is out and ready. The sword is too bulky. I have one chance. I slowly ease both my legs off the branch. Knife held high. One leap, and I strike as I fall. The knife glances off the hound's shoulder bone as I land – badly. Something in my right foot goes: I feel it snap, but there's no pain. Not yet. The hound screams. Lunges. Rears up, barking, teeth bared, snapping. But it can't see me in Elsewhere. It misses my neck and I grab its throat and plunge the blade deep into its chest. Tug it out and shove it in again. And the animal's eyes glaze and it collapses at my feet. Its body shudders and then stills.

Pyramus. Was he still inside the hound? Sweet thought, that he might lose his chance. Be slow to leave the dying body. Die too. Too easy, Zara. Far too easy.

I back away, panting. And now I feel the pain in my foot. Broken. A bone somewhere. I retreat off the slippery slab of the old bridge. To the eastern shore of the river. The sky lightens. Snow still falls steadily, but not fast enough to hide my trail.

A horse meanders into view. A man sits on its back. His left hand is bandaged. He shakes his head and clucks in disapproval at the sight of the dead dog.

'Really, Zara. I am extremely fond of animals. This is very distressing.'

His eyes lift. Scan the riverbank where I crouch. I step further back into Elsewhere. No chance of escape now. It will be a fight. Tired as I am, I fear I have only a slender chance against Pyramus. But he will know he's been in a fight. No preparation: he'd feel the elements shifting. A blast. An all or nothing. The most difficult magic to pull off.

'Zara? Come out now, and stop playing. You can't escape. Why prolong it?' Pyramus dismounts, casually ties the reins around a sapling branch. Strolls up and onto the bridge. Sticks out a booted foot and shoves the dog's corpse out of his path. It splashes into the river, bobs to the surface, floats, gently spinning, downstream. South.

'Unkind of you, you know. Just a bit vicious, killing the beast while I was in it. Unpleasant really. I shall have to forgive you, of course.'

He stands and looks up and down the river. Walks slowly to the end of the bridge, until he is standing only feet away from me. I think he must hear my heart thudding. Stare at him, at the familiar, so forgettable face of him: his slightly double chin, short nose, plump cheeks. Such an inoffensive, pleasant face. I wish him dead with all my heart. Pyramus turns and walks back to the centre of the bridge. Has he seen my trail in the drifting snow? I back up, bump into a tree.

'Amazing structure isn't it?' he says. 'I've no intention of killing you, Zara. You must realise that. Especially not now you've shown me how powerful you are becoming. Admirable, your destruction of the Maker ministry. And that fireball you unleashed in the forest! Simply beautiful! Your father will be very proud. And now that you know just how foul the kine are, how impossible it is to live in any peace with them, you will have revised your views and come to your senses. You will be forgiven youthful indiscretion. You've proved yourself your father's daughter.'

His words make my stomach turn. As they are meant to.

Concentrate. Ready yourself. For the attack, when it . . .

The tree behind me writhes. It flails its branches like a wooden octopus and I'm knocked flying, tumbling and sliding through the snow towards the river.

Frantically, I tell the rocky earth beside the river's edge to rise into a ledge. I crash into it but must leave my body to itself. It takes every bit of concentration in my frozen brain to fasten my will on Pyramus and force his power to flow into me. I devour the energy, like a flea sucking blood, and turn it back on my father's man. I make the willow tree lash out. Its huge trunk bends and it raises a heavy wooden arm and smashes it towards the bridge. Pyramus leaps into the air at the last moment, flying out of reach. The branch crashes into the stone with a boom that echoes through the valley. The bridge shudders, and the keystone in the middle of the span crumbles to rubble. The branch breaks from the tree and wedges into the bridge, the wood moaning as the river boils around and over it.

Where is Pyramus? I try to focus on his trail of magic, find a target to aim at, but the adept zig-zags through the air, never stopping. I can sense him tiring. He's using himself up. But so am I. I have to trick him. If he's telling the truth – if Pyramus intends to capture and not kill me, then it might work. Otherwise, the odds are not good.

Still in Elsewhere, I scrabble on my knees towards the broken bridge. It still stands – the broken branch wedged into its middle is holding the entire span in place. But it can't last long. I claw my way onto the snow encrusted stone of the bridge, drag myself to the middle and haul myself upright, holding to the branch. I can feel it shuddering with every surge of river water racing down the valley. Once I am balanced on my good foot, I leave Elsewhere. The snow has stopped now and my dark clothing must make me an easy target.

'Pyramus!' I shout. 'I give up! I agree! You're right: I hate the kine! I will go to my father and beg his forgiveness.'

And I wait. If the adept intends to take me alive, he can't attack me here for fear the bridge will collapse or I'll slip and fall into the water and perish. And if he does attack? Do I have enough strength left to fly in my turn?

Slowly, the adept approaches. He's shielding himself. I can see the shimmer of hardened air. I stay quite still, watching him as he floats to earth at the foot of the bridge, walks forward inside the glisten of his shield. I can see his face. He's not smiling now. He watches me like a cat watches a bird. Any moment he'll make the same coughing, chirruping cry.

Wait. Not yet.

'Are you hurt, Zara?'

'I've broken my foot.'

'Oh dear. We are a pair then, for the renegade slave skewered my hand. Before I killed him.'

I hold myself carefully still. My face doesn't shift a single muscle. Is it true? He wants a reaction. He wants information.

Given nothing, he smiles at me and steps one pace nearer, onto the bridge. Excellent. Keep still. Play birdie for the cat.

'I can't walk,' I say. The enemy is close enough for me to see the colour of his eyes. A rather beautiful green. I never noticed before. One didn't notice Pyramus. Eyes like green glass. Eyes that never leave mine. Another step closer. And I feel him, now. This close, I feel his emotions. Death. He wants me dead. He's jealous. He's afraid of me. That I will harness the wild power I'm learning to call forth. He will kill me, and lie to Benedict. Does he know I'm an empath?

'Then you must ride, child. Your father will be so pleased to see you.' Another step. He's two steps from me now. Nearly at the middle of the stone bridge. Nearly to the tree that keeps the whole from tumbling into the water. And now I feel the excitement building in his veins. He loves killing, this one. Loves to watch life leave the body, to marvel at the thinness of the line between life and death.

'Benedict,' I say. Preparing. Gathering my strength so smoothly, so naturally, that I am almost unaware of it myself. I gather the strength of my enemy too: his greed for power; his lust for destruction; I gather Pyramus into myself, and when I am ready, as he is ready, I say: 'My father will be very angry with you, Pyramus. When I tell him.'

'Tell him?' I've confused him. Just for a moment. And then he sees. And acts. Too late.

The tree shatters to splinters that rise into the air like a flight of dark birds. I fly up with them, high on twisting columns of air. And watch the bridge collapse, ancient stone groaning, cracking, crumbling. Destroyed, after ages of spanning the wild waters. I watch Pyramus fall without a cry, silent into the boiling water. Like one of the stones of the bridge. The river takes him, tumbles him. He follows his hound.

I land on the opposite bank. Panting. Shaking with excitement and reaction. I've won! I've beaten my father's assassin.

As I hug myself with glee, a column of ice bursts out of the river a hundred paces downstream. It rises into the air and forms a platform. A glowing, plump ball of warm air quivers on the top of the ice column. It vaporises, and I see Pyramus. Alive. Unhurt.

I've failed. I've lost. Death and defeat. I back away. Watch a fireball explode out of the sky towards me. Before I can even think, let alone act, the river raises a watery hand and bats the fireball away.

What?

I drop to my knees, stunned into stupidity. But even in coldest shock, I know her magic. Falu! The water hand grows fingers. Reaches. The river takes hold of Pyramus and drags him to its bosom like a child cuddling a doll. It carries him away on the journey to the far sea.

I try to stand. Fail. So I kneel, shivering, on the bank beside the now quiet river. And wait.

She never hurries. Her horse is a dappled grey, dark silver against the immaculate snow. It clips and clops at a leisurely horse's stroll. When it draws near enough, she gathers the reins into an elegant fist and sits, straight-backed and fur-clad. Her face is placid as she looks at me.

'So much power, Zara. And none of it well-directed. I must teach you to duel before we reach Asphodel.'

'You'll help me?' I ask. Shock is creeping over my mind like a film of ice, but I find the strength for the words: 'You'll help me kill Benedict?'

'No. You must do that yourself. You will come with me to his court, and offer challenge for the Archmagehood. You, Zara, are to be the next Archmage of Asphodel.'

30

'You're an empath, like Eleanor.'

It is a conversation we have many times during the journey to Asphodel. Late at night, listening to the horses tearing at the winter-killed grass, we sit wrapped in our blankets, staring into the dying embers of a fire lit and fed by magic.

I healed the bone in my foot – not my best work, but a fair job. Falu has taught me to hunt the birds in the air, the fish in the river, the winter hare. I am hungry, so I kill to eat. My old tutors never managed to make me kill the animals whose pain and fear I felt so keenly. But that Zara is dead and gone. There is no one left for me but this woman; no place left but Asphodel. And one last task.

'I think it is some strand of your empathic talent that allows you to borrow the power of others and use it for yourself.'

Falu sighs. I watch her profile in the flickering light of the fire, her face half-hidden by a wing of dark hair. 'A shame. I had hoped to learn the knack. But, like Elsewhere, it eludes me.'

I find the courage to ask, for the first time: 'Tell me about Otter.'

She turns her head to give me an appraising look. Tucks her hair behind her ear. 'I first met Otter when Benedict picked him to be his Guardian. And I sensed he was more than he appeared. An extraordinary boy who became an extraordinary man. He and I have been allies for many years. Working towards the same cause: the emancipation of the non-magic.'

'But why? Why would you, of all people, want to free the kine?'

'Because it is obvious to me that magekind must change or die.' She turns back to the fire, her voice suddenly strong with emotion she rarely shows. 'Benedict is a fool! He is afraid of dying. Remember that, Zara! And so he hopes to claim a form of immortality by being the archmage who wins the Maker war. But our race is dying out. The kine will outbreed us, and then what happened on the other side of the Wall will happen in the south. Genocide. Magekind will be wiped out. I will do anything – *anything* – to stop that happening!'

'They'll kill us all anyway. And the children.'

'The Ministry. Yes.' She looks at me again. 'The Makers are our blood enemies: the war with them cannot be lost or every mage will be hunted down and killed. And for the rest of time every unborn magic-user in this world – every child who might grow up to become mage or thief – will face death. The killing will be without end. We have one last chance for the survival of our race. If we allow our kine some freedoms. Govern with mercy and fairness. Allow them to learn, to prosper.'

'Most mages will never accept the humanity of the kine,' I say at last. 'And the non-magic will want to share power. They won't be ruled by us forever.'

'Those mages who can't change will die. We start with

Asphodel. I have already made sure of Thynis.' She smiles. 'No mage in Thynis will dare work against me. And the kine have not rebelled during my reign. You're wrong, Zara. Mages have to rule the non-magic – not by divine right, but because power itself insists on being used. But we must not deny the kine their humanity or the rights that entails. Oh, and we must make alliance with the thieves.'

'Thieves hate mages! They'll never work with us!'

'Thieves are magic-users. Your young friend, Twiss, will report what the Makers do to her tribe. The thieves will join us or face extermination. We have a common enemy now. That is another area where Otter will be invaluable.'

All the stages of my life, I have endured the loneliness of a love lost. My mother, murdered when I was barely out of babyhood. Then Swift, the sister who was the other half of myself. My old friend and teacher, Gerontius. I even miss Aidan and his troubled love. But nothing, nothing has felt so lonely as losing the Guardian. The words are so hard to say: 'Otter is dead.'

'Whatever makes you think that?' Falu laughs. 'I assure you, he's very much alive.' She smiles at the look on my face. 'Do you think I would let my most useful ally die? He's following us, with his army.'

'I thought Pyramus . . .' I stare at her, at the flames dancing on her smooth skin, shadowing her eyes, and for the first time in days I want to live. And for the first time in days, I am afraid, in case I don't.

And then: 'How far behind is he? I need to get to Asphodel before him. Otter will try to stop me challenging Benedict.'

'Yes . . .' Her eyes narrow. 'I told him that we will wait for him to arrive and enter Asphodel together. A tiny lie . . . What –' she studies my face – 'do you think of him?'

Gods! Is Falu jealous? Surely . . .

'Are you lovers?' I ask, pleased the firelight will disguise the warm blood rushing to my face. Why do I find the idea of Falu and Otter so shocking?

'Old history, child. I don't love the Guardian, never worry. I have only loved one person in my life, and that was your mother.'

'My . . .'

She reaches out, grasps my hand. And squeezes it until I have to bite my lip against the pain. 'You look so like her.' Her shadowed eyes stare at me hungrily. She loosens her grip at last and sighs.

'Eleanor was my greatest friend. Didn't you know she was born in Thynis? We studied together at the Academy. It was she who taught me, who argued long into nights spent over far too much wine . . . on our walks together in the hills . . .' Falu stares into the dark, into her memory. 'Having an empath for your best friend is not for the faint-hearted! She taught me to see kine differently. I didn't want to, I promise you!' A soft, remembering laugh. 'But she convinced me in the end. We decided we would change the world.' She laughs again, but this time without joy. 'We were heretics together. And then . . . she married Benedict.'

'Why?'

'Time knows!'

I feel a blast of pure hatred and Falu releases my hand.

'I begged him for her life,' Falu says after a long silence. I study her profile, outlined by firelight: marble-smooth, perfect.

'He knew I loved her. It gave him such pleasure: destroying us both. But I have great patience. It is my only virtue.'

She watches the flames, and I hear Death in her voice, and think of the other fire, and the man I killed.

By the time we see the tops of the Tournados Mountains tipping above the horizon, I have learned to duel. Falu is a patient but demanding tutor. She has trained me not only on the techniques of fighting, but honed my ability to borrow the energy of others.

'This strange talent of yours will give you victory, Zara. Benedict is the most powerful mage I have ever known. You will only win an official challenge by turning his power against him.'

I shift in my saddle. Nerves flutter my stomach. I put my hand on Bruin's sword, but this time, the touch of the bronze hilt doesn't give me comfort. We have entered the outskirts of Asphodel. Every rolling step of my horse, every creak of the leather saddle, takes me closer to the moment of my challenge. I am afraid.

'Swift, be with me,' I whisper.

Falu doesn't hear. Or politely ignores my prayer. She looks ahead, the faintest of smiles on her lips. I am a Time traveller: I have returned to my childhood. We plod through the outlying villages and towns that skirt Asphodel. I see the familiar fields. The olive groves. The southern air feels warm even though it's still late winter. The touch of the sun on my face – scrubbed free of cosmetic – reminds me of a flaw in my disguise: my mage marks. We are gambling that no one will examine the face of Falu's junior courtier too closely.

I look down at the robes I wear. Mage robes. I have not worn them for months. These are the gold and white of Falu's retainers. My hair is shorn and dyed to a muddy brown. It is too dangerous to attempt to disguise my mage marks with self-magic, but marks are only identifiable when face to face. I keep my head bent, and look like a thin and gawky boy terrified by his first visit to Asphodel. I am to be one of Falu's young relatives brought by his archmage to visit the great city.

'There is a council meeting at midday,' she says. 'We will attend as visitors. You will challenge Benedict there, in the council.'

'Today?' I twist in my saddle to stare at her, appalled.

'What point in waiting, child? And I urge you again to leave the sword behind. You risk discovery for reasons of sentiment. You will defeat your father with magic, not metal.'

'No.' I turn back to face forward, swallowing the dryness in my mouth. On this one point I have refused to follow her guidance. 'I'll keep it hidden in my robes. It comes.'

She sighs. But doesn't press the argument.

We clatter the last league on hard-packed roads that lead to the city gate. The walls of Asphodel loom above us, the white granite sparkling in the late-morning sun. As we near the ancient gate with its curved mouth and lancet-windowed gatehouse above, the duty guard comes out. And I see Tributes again. Not Otter's free young men and women, but the enslaved. The expression on their faces – the pitilessness of the unpitied – hits me in the stomach. I had forgotten that look. I turn away, look up, and see a fresh crop of heads on the spikes that protrude from the walls either side of the gate. Hair matted, eyes staring, bloodstained. The flies and birds are at them. I look away, nauseous. It has continued: all of it; all the time I have been away. We fled the evil: Twiss and I, and the Knowledge Seekers. But bad things don't stop just because you leave them behind. Did I think any of it would stop merely because I wasn't here to see it?

The Tributes bow low to the Archmage of Thynis and her companion, and we clatter onto the cobbled streets of Asphodel. And here, I do see change: the fire-charred ruins of houses still unrepaired from Otter's attack on the city. Frightened kine hurry about their duties, heads down, not daring to glance at passing mages. The stink of oppression fills the air, thicker than ever. I wonder if Mistress Floster, head of the Thieves' Guild, has survived these long months. If she and her tribe are still safely hidden in the catacombs, her archer-assassins harrying my father and the mages of Asphodel with deadly arrows from Elsewhere.

My heart beats double-time to the clop of our horses' hooves. All too quickly we are trotting up the tree-lined avenue towards my father's palazzo. The road of limestone flags is lined with half a dozen phalanges of guards, and I catch the nervous excitement of troops about to be sent into battle. With whom? I'm sweating inside my gold and white robes.

The great wooden gates of the palazzo creak wide at our approach. The guard have spotted us, and we slow to a walk and clatter into the courtyard. At once, my memory takes me to the moment I first saw Aidan in this very place. A prisoner tied on his horse, given by his own people as hostage to a false truce. So long ago . . .

Guards run, hold the horses' heads steady as we dismount. Guide us, with slavish servility, up the wide steps of the palazzo's main entrance, through the carved and painted doors, and into the cool marble interior of my home. The house where I was born; where my sister died. The house of my enemy.

My father's house.

And then I am scurrying after Falu, ducking my head and hoping I look like an embarrassed yokel newly come to court rather than a wanted criminal trying to avoid detection.

Falu glides through the corridors ahead of me; following our escort. She sweeps up the great marble stairs, robes billowing, and pauses outside the open doors of the council chamber.

I hear a herald announce: 'Her ladyship, Falu, Archmage of Thynis!' And I follow her into the room where my father sat in judgement as my mother was tried for heresy, where he condemned her to death.

The heels of my boots click over the marble floor. I keep my head down. I feel dozens of pairs of eyes upon us; hear the murmur of interest from the twenty-four councillors seated in the circular rows of the council dais; smell chill polish, old wood, perfumed bodies. And I am aware of the throne beneath the Great Clock, the throne where my father sits. Watching.

My heart is pounding against my ribs. But I am an old hand at deception. I became a spy for the Knowledge Seekers at the age of ten: that child learned to ignore her thumping heart, her sweaty hands; to slow her breathing, relax her muscles and smile at the enemy.

Falu chooses a seat, not in the visitors' gallery but in the middle of the front row of the councillors' dais, as is her right as an archmage. She gestures to me to sit beside her. I slide into my place. We are seated directly opposite the throne. I don't dare look up. Dyed and shorn hair and golden robes suddenly seem an impossibly flimsy disguise.

'The Archmage of Thynis honours us today.'

His voice! So familiar. Toxic. It floods through me like aural poison. And it takes all my long-studied powers of control not to shudder, not to look up, not to scream my hatred. My father's voice is chill and smooth and tinged with sarcasm. Even pleasantries to his allies warn: do not forget that I am the serpent.

'And to what, Falu, do we owe the delight of your presence?'

'A long-standing appointment brings me to Asphodel, Archmage.' Her voice is quietly amused. Gentle even. Still I dare not look up. 'And so I thought I would attend your illustrious council and find out the news of Asphodel myself, rather than trying to rinse facts from gossip.'

'Wise, as always.' Benedict's voice is complacent. His one weakness. 'And you have chosen an auspicious day for your visit.'

'You plan a campaign? I could hardly ignore the troops.'

'It is a great day.' He laughs. And now I do look up. Shocked. Fearful. For there is a note of hysteria – of madness – in Benedict's voice.

My father is changed.

I have been gone just half a year, and in that time Benedict of Asphodel has aged a decade. His black hair is filmed with grey, as though dipped in limewash. His lizard-brown eyes are dark-ringed; his skin pallid, pasty. His body beneath his black robes is stooped and shapeless. This man – who was always as lean as a greyhound.

Failure has done this. I have done this. Myself, Otter, Aidan, Twiss, Floster and her thieves. We have escaped, we have thwarted, we have destroyed his plans. And perhaps he waits for news of Pyramus. And none comes. And he fears . . .

As I stare at him, blanking the astonishment from my face lest it attract attention, my father is suddenly a mere man. No longer a demon. No longer omnipotent. Only a man, with no more control over the fates – over his destiny – than the rest of us enjoy. An evil man, but a man. Failure has given him back his humanity. For a fraction of a moment – a young child's heartbeat – I almost consider . . . am almost tempted . . . to feel pity. But then my gaze drops from his newly-lined face to the marble floor between the dais of the councillors and the throne of the archmage. And I see the prisoner hole. The circle of wood capping the human-shaped dry well where my mother stood as he tried her for the heresy of believing kine to be human, where she stood as her husband passed sentence of death.

But he is talking, and my attention is captured by a single word: '. . . thieves.'

What? What did he say? The end of the . . . *No!*

'So you have finally found their den?' Falu's voice is politely interested.

'At last!' Benedict laughs. Vicious. 'The catacombs! My troops have been ferreting through the city of the dead, catching vermin for a week now. It's slow and nasty work. They bite, like the rats they are. But now I control three quarters of the catacombs and today I order the final push. By dawn there won't be a thief left alive in Asphodel, above or below ground!'

I listen to the triumph in his voice, see the relish in his eyes, and feel sick with fear. Mistress Floster, Marcus! All Twiss's clan! How many are dead?

'It's just as well we arrived today, then, Benedict,' Falu says. 'You will have to put your plans on hold, I fear. The last thieves of Asphodel must be content to cower in their den for a while yet.'

Silence falls on the chamber. The whispers, the coughs, the rustling of robes cease.

My father frowns. The certainty in his eyes flickers. Anger replaces it. 'What foolishness is this, Thynis?' Threat in his voice. The tatters of all his old arrogance. 'I have waited too long for this day to let your whims delay me by a single minute.'

'Ah,' Falu says. I hear the smile in her voice. I am shaking. The moment comes. 'But even you, dear Benedict, cannot disobey the Challenge.'

'What?' My father's laugh echoes around the room, encircling us with his relief and contempt. 'You? Falu, you are a great adept. But you stand no chance against me. As you well know. Do you tire of life, woman? Be sensible. You have power enough, surely, as my ally and Archmage of the second city of the land. What is this joke?'

'An old appointment, as I said.' Falu stands, slowly rising to her full height, which is taller than my father. Taller than me. 'I have owed you this day since you killed Eleanor.'

A gasp. My mother's name is unmentionable. Voices rise in protest.

'Silence!' Falu's voice is cold as a frozen hell, and the room stills.

'You are a fool.' Benedict remains in his throne, but he has drawn himself to his feet. His eyes are deadly. 'To dare to mention her name. Do you challenge me, then, Falu of Thynis? If so, you will die today.'

'It is your day, Benedict,' she replies. 'Not mine. And it is not I who offers challenge. Speak now, child!'

Falu lowers herself in her seat and turns to look at me. Every face in the room turns towards me. I rise on legs surprisingly steady. Step forward into the middle of the room. I hold up my head and look at my father, and see his contempt turn first to puzzlement, then . . . slowly . . . to recognition. And fear.

'No!' he cries. But it is too late, for I have begun speaking the Challenge. My voice is slow and quiet at first. I make the words louder, stronger: send them ringing out like the chimes of a clock as it strikes the appointed hour.

None can stop me now. None can forestall this duel.

'I, Zara of Asphodel, daughter of Eleanor, daughter of Benedict, do challenge you, Benedict, Archmage of Asphodel, to a duel to the death. And the winner shall be newly made Archmage of Asphodel, and the loser shall travel to the halls of the dead and reside on this earth no more. And may Death be merciful to their soul!'

31

The room erupts in a volcano of noise. As suddenly, stillness falls.

My father rises to his feet. His face is purple with rage. He holds the arms of his throne and leans forward. Spit showers from his mouth as he shouts: 'She is a heretic! Guards, take hold of her! Throw her in the pit! I will condemn and execute her myself!'

Silence.

He stops shouting. Stares around the room. At the implacable faces.

'The Challenge has been given, Benedict,' Falu says. 'If you do not accept, every adept in this room will be forced to join with me and execute you for cowardice and despoliation of the office of archmage.'

My father looks long at her. Glances around the room once more. And straightens. He nods and gathers himself. Finds much of the old Benedict and clothes himself in arrogance and disdain. At last, he looks at me.

'Well, Daughter,' he says. 'I had hoped, even now, to avoid killing my own blood. But . . . like mother, like daughter.'

'Destroying your own has never worried you, Father,' I reply. I thought my voice would shake. Or I would scream and shout my hatred. But now the moment is here, I feel calm. Cold.

'You killed my sister, Ita, when she was nine years old. I trust you haven't forgotten. I gave you a scar that day. And your man, Pyramus, gave me one in return a few weeks ago.' I point to my cheek, to his mage mark. His eyes study my face with fascination. 'He didn't quite manage to kill me, Father. Not quite. He's dead, by the way.'

'You?' His face is greyer than ever.

'No. Falu killed him in the end. I've saved myself for you.'

Benedict laughs. Some colour returns to his face. 'You couldn't manage Pyramus on your own? Then you have no chance against me, Zara. I am sorry for it. I had hoped to re-educate you, for you have potential. But . . . Eleanor's blood is an ill strain. You are as mad as she was. You must share your mother's fate.'

'Enough!' Falu cries. 'Let the duel commence!'

She joins the councillors on the dais, and I feel them unite magic to form a protective air shield. I feel the excitement, the anticipation, from the official witnesses. There has not been a Challenge in any city-state for over a decade.

I know the form. We all do. Even those of us who have never witnessed a duel know the ritual from our school days. My father seats himself once more. Fingers the white lace ruff at his neck. Smooths his black robes. And waits. I feel him, even now, gathering his concentration. Feel his confidence growing, as mine diminishes. I try to remember Falu's teaching but my mind fuzzes white. Steady! Remember what Twiss taught you! And Otter and Aidan. Relax . . .

I step forward, into the centre of the chamber. I step over the prisoner pit, stand facing my father's throne, feet apart, head up. And I bow my best, my most elegant, courtier's bow.

'Archmage, I salute you. To the death, Benedict!'

'To the death, Zara.' His eyes are narrow, shadowed. Still he gathers his power. The room vibrates with it, like the high-pitched scream of a bat.

Benedict stares. Lizard-eyes holding mine.

No warning. Not even a blink. The magic comes: a single, crushing blow, as Falu forecast. To squeeze, to bind, to squash the very life from the muscles of my heart. The deepest, deadliest of magics: an attack on my body!

But I am not there. I am in Elsewhere. Magic pounds the place I stood a tick before, and I scoop up some of the energy before it scatters, soak it up like a dried sea-sponge, and bend it to my will. I'm alight. Flying up to the vaulted roof of the chamber, stone and wood, cobwebs and dead memories. Floating over my father, emptying the magic over his head like a bucket. A bucket of steam, a jet of boiling air and water, lashing down at his greying head.

Nearly! The force, the rapidity of my counterattack, has him reeling from his throne. Casting a curtain of fire arching over him. The jet of steam screams and hisses and is extinguished. And Benedict staggers to the middle of the room, bellowing with rage.

'Coward!' he rants. 'Filthy thief tricks will not save you!' Air daggers spit up into the sky, dozens, rattling against the stone vaulting, chipping, shattering, sending shards of stone flying. But I have already dropped to the ground, am crouched behind the throne.

My father stands upon the wooden cover of the prisoner hole. It is too tempting: I send a snaking thought, and the wood decays to dust and Benedict disappears into the hole with a shout of dismay.

Laughter. Jollity from the witnesses.

Benedict blasts out of the hole, rising, black robes flapping. Bat. Flying lizard. I feel his fury at the indignity. The laughter. I feel his control slip. Now. Now he will do something horrendous.

I sit in my father's place upon the throne. Falu's suggestion. He would hate to destroy it: all the centuries of duels held in this place, and no mage has dared damage the great throne of Asphodel. I cling to its safety as Benedict explodes with rage. A fireball builds, whirling black and yellow and fearsome orange, growing larger and larger until it is the size of a horse and cart. I can feel the heat, smell the singeing wool of my father's robes.

Head back, hair on end, eyes wild with the intoxication of magic, he shouts in a sort of delirium: 'A gift, Zara! My love for you burns me!' And he sets the fireball loose: a rampaging beast rolling around the room, bouncing off the air shield around the dais, scorching the white marble black, igniting curtains and paintings as it trundles, faster and faster, circling the room. Flying through the air. The fireball destroys the council chamber, but avoids my father . . . and the throne.

The air is thick with smoke. Benedict is coughing. My own chest is burning. It's the final act.

I gather all my power, all my concentration, and then I begin to gather my father's. Slowly at first, then faster and faster. Sucking up his magic until my blood tingles. My skin is tight-stretched with energy. I feel huge, limitless. The power is mine! I need it. I want it. I take it. The world slows while I quicken: I hear every breath, every heartbeat in the room. I see my father's eyes widen in alarm. Too slowly he frowns, steps back. And when I think I have stolen enough of his strength . . . I pray to the Lord Time I have enough . . . I grab the fireball with my mind and throw it with all the force of my hate and my love for Swift.

Our audience screams in delight at the quality of their entertainment. Benedict screams in fear. And the fireball strikes with volcanic force. The room shakes as though in an earthquake. Smoke, sparks. And silence. The fireball is extinguished.

But I know. I feel. And so I am ready when he rises again, soot-blackened but still alive, from inside the now watery pit in the floor. Clever, clever man. He's soaking. But the pit that killed my mother has saved his life.

Benedict staggers upright.

'Bitch!' he says. Quietly. No shouting now. Rage spent with the fireball. I have eaten up much of his power. I'm tiring too, but I still have strength for the last thing. The thing I have been planning. But he's doing it: trying to talk me into defeat.

'You're stronger than I thought, Daughter. Perhaps you are my child, after all. One last throw, I think, Zara. If I win, you will have no more worries. But should the Fates decree that you survive today, Daughter, do not think you have defeated me. I may die, but I will still win. If Death takes me and not you, Zara, remember the paperweight. If I die, you will never find its secret!'

The paperweight! Swift! Is this Benedict's admission that she *is* alive, a prisoner inside a glass disk? And if I kill him do I doom her to die in that prison?

His ploy works: I move. Or gasp. Something, enough.

And the arms of the throne detach from the seat and grab me around the waist. And squeeze. Hard. Harder. Pain such as I have never known.

Swift! Tell me what to do!

No answer. Only: I refuse to let him control me. To have his way. To win, as he has always done. Swift, if you live, forgive me. But I must fight.

Somewhere, I find the anger. And I take his power from him and feel its strength flow into my body, warming my blood like fire wine. Benedict's power is mine. It belongs to me. I am the stronger.

I hear my father's cry of despair as I steal his magic and use it to break the wooden arms squeezing the life from my body. I slide, still in pain, onto the floor, and use the last of his power to wrench the roots of the throne from the floor, to hurl it into the air and to bring it smashing down.

A blast of magic. His! The throne of Asphodel ignites, explodes in a shower of gold and bronze and red sparks that rain out of the sky. A billow of smoke wafts skywards. As it clears, I see my father. Kneeling on hands and knees. Exhausted. Head hanging. But still alive. I stare at him in disbelief. He should be dead! I thought I had taken all his power but he managed to find more.

I am near dead with magic. As is my father: he must finally be used up. I have enough strength for killing still, but with metal, not my mind. My hand finds the hilt of Bruin's sword. I gasp as I tug it forth. It comes clumsily, reluctantly, and I stagger as I hold it aloft.

A chorus of voices cries: 'No!' 'Metal!' 'Foul!' 'Stop the heretic!'

I totter forward two steps. Bruin's sword is heavy in my hand. My arm shakes with the effort of holding it.

My father does not lift his head. He waits, dragging one long breath after another into his lungs, for the blade.

Falu's voice: 'The Challenge will run to the end! Let no one interfere or I will kill them myself!'

Another step forward.

I look down on the sharp ridge of my father's backbone, rising from his black robe, bisecting his torso like the Wall of the Makers divides our world. There, where his spine joins his neck. That is the spot.

I grasp the hilt with both hands, fingers laced, raise the sword high over my head. And plunge it . . .

The blade strikes, bounds back, and I fall as a wall made of Benedict's will – of air turned hard as hardest oak – shoves me off my feet.

I land, flat on my back, spread eagled. The sword flies from my hands.

I try to roll away, to push up, but my father's air wall keeps me pinned, presses me into the cold marble floor. My head rests on the sharp lip of the prisoner pit, still flooded with water. The back of my shorn head lies in water. Wet creeps under my neck.

I have used everything. I have no strength left, no magic.

The room cries in one voice. Silences itself to watch – as do I – as Benedict struggles to his feet. He stands, unsteady, gasping with effort.

His eyes find mine. And he smiles. Slow: triumphant. His smile promises . . . the look in his eyes.

I am nine. And my sister lies, dead or dying. And my father turns to me. Readies his magic. And smiles . . .

I have lost.

Swift, forgive me! Twiss. Otter. Gerontius. Mother! Mother, please forgive me! Oh, Mother. Help me!

Benedict steps forward. Picks up Bruin's sword and holds it stretched in his two hands, examining it.

The chamber waits. Bodies shift, robes rustle, voices whisper. The witnesses. I feel their excitement growing, feeding on itself. They demand my death. They want my blood.

My father raises his head. And I see her waiting there: in his flat brown eyes. Death.

He holds the sword awkwardly, to one side. Not as the Maker holds a blade, nor yet Otter. Nor even me, who has learned a little. He holds it with hands clumsy with fear, shaking with eagerness.

I watch Benedict approach until he stands beside me, and his black robes puddle over my right leg stretched helpless.

I push against his magic. With my body. With my mind. But I have used all. I have nothing. Almost nothing.

My father's head tilts, enquiringly. 'You have a gift I have not met before, Zara. You use my power against me. I would love to take your head apart to find the secret before I kill you, but I see I cannot afford that pleasure. You are dangerous, child. Too dangerous to live.'

My father raises the sword in both hands, mirroring my own action only moments before. But this time. This . . . Time.

Down plunges the blade. Bruin's masterpiece of ironwork. The blade meant to kill the last Archmage of Asphodel. As it falls, the image of the paperweight comes into my mind.

The paperweight I threw at my father, the paperweight which scarred his face. The paperweight which witnessed my sister's murder. I see it clearly, as though it floats in front of my face. And I remember my nine-year-old rage of grief and loss. I remember the sister I loved more than myself. I return to that love, that loss, that sister, and I find a last wellspring of resistance.

The point of the sword plunges towards my chest. I cry out. And with my cry I focus the energy I have found. I seem to be in two places. I am in my body, and I am floating above my father, observing him in the act of killing me.

The front of my robes glows and a silver spiral, like a mage mark, forms a shield over my heart. Bruin's sword strikes this shimmering shield. As I watch – as my father watches – the tip of the blade vibrates. The metal screams with an almost human sound as the tip explodes, dividing into the dozens of metal rods that went into its forging. Bruin's sword is unmaking itself!

The shimmering mage mark fades and the many-fingered tip of the sword glows silver and unfolds like a flower opening. Rapid as silver-grey elven writhing through water, twisting and twining, the strands of metal splay outwards, bend backwards, travel back up the length of the blade as it unwraps.

Too late, Benedict sees the danger. Too late he tries to fling the sword from him. I crawl to one side and watch as the writhing strands of metal encircle my father's wrist, his arm. Quick as my thought, the transformed blade writhes its seeking tongues across his chest. They winnow past his black robes, through his white linen shirt, and plunge into his flesh. My father screams, beats with his hands at the metal flowing into his body. Falls onto the ground, writhing like the iron that burrows into his breast. Down and down, silver-sharp, the metal strands plunge, until they reach his heart and pierce the beating flesh. Benedict's body twitches violently, and then he lies still, dead eyes staring.

Our father is dead, Swift. Have I avenged you? Or . . .

Bruin's masterpiece is destroyed. Its unmade blade threads dozens of metal veins through Benedict's flesh. All that is left – the bronze and silver hilt so beautifully crafted by Tabitha – is pinned to my father's blood-riddled shirt like an ungainsome jewel.

The magic that transformed Bruin's sword flows away until no trace of it remains. Where did I find it? What was it? Desolate at its departure, numb, I collapse back upon the floor to stare at a smoke-smirched ceiling and wonder if I have killed my sister twice over.

32

I, Zara, am Archmage of Asphodel. I sit in my office. Not my father's library: not that hated room. But an office Falu has arranged. She arranges much. I am grateful. But wary. An archmage must always be distrustful.

The paperweight sits on the desk in front of me. I haven't had the courage to touch it yet – to see if I can feel life inside. I am terrified of finding a presence, and even more terrified of finding absence. So I put it off and remind myself that there is much to do. Much to discuss. The future of this city, perhaps of all the cities on both sides of the Wall.

Otter waits, with his army, outside the great gate of Asphodel. He demands an audience. Offers alliance. I will accept. I want to share power: with Otter; with the surviving thieves. I've had an emissary from Floster already: Marcus. It was good to see him. But not to see the mistrust in his eyes.

Still: an archmage is an unchancey friend. I must hope that he and Twiss – and Floster herself – will learn that their old companion hasn't changed. Not that much. I hope to learn it too.

Philip and Tabitha, to my sorrow, have stayed in Gengst. I have had no word from them, nor from Aidan. I greatly fear the Maker is my enemy now. And I his. Time himself knows, and the god keeps his discretion. But the rest of the Knowledge Seekers: Hammeth, and Fredda and all the rest, have come home. I want to share power with them too. If they can trust me. If I can trust myself.

I am Zara, last Archmage of Asphodel. The times are changing. Our lives, those of us who live in this city, will never be the same again. There is no easy path, but I have to believe that a way can be found.

I stare down at the paperweight. And gather sufficient hope. And reach out a finger . . .

GLOSSARY

adept: The most powerful mages (magic users). Mage children are tested from infancy to determine the level of their telekinetic ability (the facility to mentally manipulate the atoms and molecules of the physical world). Those with exceptional talent are chosen to train at the city's Academy, and upon graduating become adepts. Adepts are the political and social elite of mage society.

Asphodel: The most powerful of the mage city-states and geographically closest to the northern plains and the Wall of the Makers.

archmage: The ruler of a mage city-state. Historically chosen through mortal combat, an archmage holds near supreme political power in their city. At any time, a pretender may challenge the incumbent archmage to a magical battle to the death. The winner retains power until defeated in his or her turn.

city-state: The main political unit of both mage and Maker societies. Each city-state is equivalent to an independent country.

counters: The accountants of the mage world, counters are the non-magic guild in charge of counting and measuring restricted materials or resources, such as precious metals, paper, iron ore or coal. Counters report directly to their mage overlords in mage Council. In return, counters are given special privileges and held in suspicion and dislike by other guilds and the general non-magic populace.

Elsewhere: Going to 'Elsewhere' is a mental ability possessed by members of the Thieves' Guild. It makes them 'mentally invisible' and therefore invulnerable to mind-control by mages. Depending on how far into Elsewhere a thief goes, they can enter a form of deep hibernation, used for self-healing. If a thief goes too deeply into Elsewhere they may not come out again and will eventually die.

the first precept: A mage must never mind-control another mage, on pain of death.

Gengst-on-the-Wall: The largest and most powerful Maker city. Its city wall is part of the great Wall of the Makers itself. Gengst is Aidan's home town and the cultural and industrial centre of Maker culture.

guard: A Tribute child chosen at the age of five to be trained to be a mage guard. Guards undergo severe physical training and regular brainwashing to ensure loyalty. They serve as prison and city guards or as officers in the Tribute army.

Guardian: A former guard who has been chosen by one of the seven archmages to be her or his personal servant, bodyguard and assassin. Chosen for their physical and mental abilities, Guardians, like guards, are brainwashed from the age of five and totally loyal to the archmage they serve.

guild: The main unit of social structure in the non-magic society on both sides of the Maker Wall. Girls and boys are apprenticed to guilds around the age of eight. They learn their trade and live with the family of a 'master' of the guild. By the age of sixteen, most young people will have 'graduated' to become a journeyman or woman and continue to work with their master until they attain sufficient knowledge, skills and experience to be declared a master themselves. They may then set up their own business. Guilds in the mage world are strictly overseen and taxed by the mages through the Counters' Guild. Literacy is forbidden in the mage world, so all learning is practical. Technology is strictly controlled and anything which might challenge mage supremacy is forbidden.

kine: The mage word for non-magic people – the approximately eighty per cent of the population without telekinetic powers. The word itself means 'cattle'.

the Kine Rebellion: Several centuries prior to Zara's birth, the non-magic population in the north of the continent rose up in a mass rebellion. The rebellion was bloody and prolonged. Many thousands died but, in the end, the sheer numbers of the non-magic majority overwhelmed their mage masters and every last mage in the north was hunted down and killed.

Knowledge Seekers: A rebel group of guild leaders in Asphodel who are working for the overthrow of the mages in order to end their feudal state of slavery and gain the freedom to learn in a society where literacy is a capital crime.

mage: Approximately twenty per cent of people in Zara's world are born with an ability to perform telekinesis. Because the ability is genetic, strict legal and social taboos exist that outlaw sexual relations between the magic and non-magic (the fourth precept), although mage-on-commoner rape is a frequent occurrence. The crime is neither socially nor legally acknowledged by mage society and therefore never punished.

mage marks: Three abstract designs magically carved in the face of a mage in a ritual naming ceremony performed upon the child's third birthday. The marks are formed by inserting fine strands of silver into the skin of the child's face. The mother's mark goes on the right cheek; the father's on the left, and the child's own personal mark – the soul sign – on the forehead. It is a dangerous and painful ritual performed by up to six adepts working in unison. Rarely, a child will die.

Maker: The people who live on the technologically-oriented non-magic side of the Maker Wall.

middlings: Thief children below the age of puberty.

mind-magic: Although ordinary mages have almost no ability to read or control the minds of others, most adepts have some degree of telepathic abilities. Mind-control of animals is used for intelligence gathering and sport. Mind-control of non-magic commoners is lawful, although even among mages it is considered unsavoury and is seldom used except for the gathering of official intelligence.

not-seen-not-heard: The ability of thieves to become, to all extents and purposes, invisible and soundless. This is achieved through two means: 1) retreating partly into Elsewhere; and 2) great skill in the physical art of smooth, controlled movement.

safe-sworn: The leader of the Thieves' Guild may declare an individual under his or her personal protection. That person is then 'safe-sworn' and any thief who harms them will be cast out of the guild. A pendant (the safe-sworn) belonging to the guild leader is worn around the neck of the protected person.

the second precept: Any child born as a result of sexual union between a mage and commoner is considered a religious abomination by mage society and must be killed at birth. Of course, since rape is so prevalent, half-mage children are sometimes born and escape detection. More often, the commoner mother will expose or kill the child herself, such is the loathing and hatred felt towards mages.

Thieves' Guild: Although the thieving community call themselves a 'guild', they are more accurately described as a tribe. Unlike the other guilds, there is no intermarriage between thieves and other commoners. Thieves prey on the magic and non-magic alike and their community is close-knit and secretive. They are considered the lowest social order in both Maker and mage worlds, and are mistrusted and feared by all. The greatest achievement and honour for a thief is to kill a mage, and their folklore centres on recounting tales of the great mage-killers of the past, both historical and allegorical.

Time: One of the seven gods of Zara's world, and the mages' primary god. Mages both worship and resent

Time. Although they possess near god-like powers, mages are not immortal and Time will kill even the greatest adept in the end.

the third precept: A mage must never physically assault another magic user. All combat must be mental, on pain of dishonour. A mage so assaulted may challenge their assailant to magical combat.

Tribute army: An army of children sent to patrol the Maker Wall and keep the Maker threat under control. The greatest fear of any mage is that the Kine Rebellion will spread to the remaining mage city-states.

Tribute child: Non-magic children given to the mages at the age of five. Tribute children are both slaves and a guarantee against rebellion, as every family must give their firstborn. The children serve as domestic servants when young; at the age of twelve, they are sent to serve in the Tribute army, to fight and die in the war against the Makers.

Tribute tax: A child tax levied by the mages of the seven city-states on their commoner populations.

Wall of the Makers: An enormous wall that spans the continent from ocean to ocean. Built by the Makers in the aftermath of the Kine Rebellion (called the

Great Rebellion in the Maker world), it is patrolled by Maker soldiers and armed with war machines such as catapults and giant crossbows. Much of the Maker economy is given over to arming a defensive force and the creation of machines of war to protect their borders.

wards: A magical alarm system that adepts can use to guard certain rooms or buildings. If disturbed, the alarm will alert the adept who set it. Usually, animal mind-control is the preferred method: a mouse, rat or cat (more rarely, a bee or wasp) will be set to watch for intruders.

Acknowledgements

With grateful thanks to the many people who helped with the birthing of Outcaste:

Sharon Jones, for her advice and unwavering support

The editorial and design team of Hot Key Books, and especially my editor, Sara O'Connor

My agent, Jenny Savill of Andrew Nurnberg Associates

And both last and first: my family, for enduring yet again the phases of the writing process, which are as predictable as the phases of the moon, if somewhat less beguiling

Ellen Renner

Ellen Renner was born in the USA, but came to England in her twenties, married here, and now lives in an old house in Devon with her husband and son. Ellen originally trained as a painter and surrounds herself with sketches of her characters as she writes. She spins wool as well as stories, knitting and weaving when time allows. She plays the violin, fences (badly!) and collects teapots and motorcycles.

Her first book, *Castle of Shadows*, won the Cornerstones Wow Factor Competition, the 2010 North East Book Award and was chosen for both the *Independent* and the *Times* summer reading lists and, along with the sequel *City of Thieves*, was included on the *Times* list of best children's books of 2010. *Tribute* was Ellen's first YA book, and you can follow her at www.ellenrenner.com or on Twitter: @Ellen_Renner